JOIN A FAMILY OF MEN AND WOMEN WHOSE COURAGE AND LOVE OF CHALLENGE SEND THEM TO THE SCENE OF AMERICA'S MOST EXCITING MOMENTS: THE HOLTS, YOUNG SECOND-GENERATION PIONEERS WHO KEEP ALIVE A CHERISHED FRONTIER SPIRIT AS THEY EMBRACE THE FUTURE. NOTHING CAN STOP THEIR PASSIONS, NO ONE CAN HALT THEIR AMBITIONS, AND NONE CAN MATCH THEIR FIGHTING PROWESS AS THEY MOVE FULL SPEED AHEAD TOWARD A HORIZON FILLED WITH PROMISES . . . AND BREATH-TAKING SUSPENSE.

THE HOLTS: AN AMERICAN DYNASTY

CALIFORNIA GLORY

THE HOLTS: THEY FIGHT ON THE SIDE OF RIGHT. WHEREVER THE INNOCENT ARE OPPRESSED, THEY LEND THEIR STRONG ARMS AND STALWART HEARTS . . . AS NOW THEY HEAD FOR THE BLOODY STRIKES THAT TEAR APART A NATION AND WAGER ON PROGRESS . . . AS AMERICA HURLS TOWARD THE 1900s.

TIM HOLT—

Headstrong and as smart as a whip—like his legendary wagonmaster ancestor Whip Holt—this rough-and-ready newspaperman goes after the stories of Pennsylvania's great mining strikes and Illinois's railway strikes, to land in a blazing storm of anger and fear . . . and discovers his own heart is aflame for a woman he is forbidden to love.

ROSEBAY BASHAM WARE—

A country gal gone to the big city, she is as lovely as a wildflower, as sweet as honeysuckle, and as intoxicating as moonshine. She is Tim Holt's only love, his destiny or his downfall . . . for she is another man's wife.

EULALIA HOLT—

No woman has more pride or a finer heritage than the strong, wise matriarch of the Holt clan . . . until a secret enemy begins to erode her confidence, rob her of her dignity, and put into action an insidious plan to steal her sanity and the Holts' good name.

DAN SCHUMANN—

A viper's heart hides behind the charming smile of this handsome Chicagoan come west to the Holts' Madrona Ranch. Ruthless under his veneer of friendliness, he has a trap ready now to be sprung on an unsuspecting old woman.

EUGENE DEBS—

A man dedicated to America's workers, his backbone of steel may not be enough to stop the iron prison door from swinging open to claim him. This leader of the great Pullman strike must look to one last hope— Tim Holt.

PAUL KIRCHNER—

A knockabout lad who has disappointed his Midwestern beer-brewing family, he wanders into the Madrona Ranch and a budding tragedy. But this vagabond has a heart of pure gold and the wits to spot a snake in the grass . . . if only he can convince someone of the danger to Eulalia's life.

LADY TEDDY MONTAGUE—

Eccentric English explorer, she holds the key to saving Eulalia's life and fortune. But will she return from her adventures in South America before it is too late?

MIKE HOLT—

A youngster on the threshold of manhood, he struggles against the smothering love of his concerned parents, Toby and Alexandra Holt. His frail health is at war with his Holt determination, and no matter what the consequences he will become a runaway . . . seeking adventure and love.

PETER BLAKE—

A financial genius, the eccentric son of Henry Blake and a German baroness, he is about to take possession of millions of deutsch marks . . . and wager them all on a crazy American dream called the automobile.

RUFUS GOOCH AND CALVIN ROGERS—

One is certifiably crazy, one is just plain nuts, but both are brilliant engineers who have an invention that will either catapult a family to new fortunes . . . or crash their future on a raceway of dreams.

TOBY HOLT—

Head of a family, leader of a nation, he has wielded his Washington power for justice—but angered rich and powerful men who will now topple him from office if he doesn't support their interests. But trying to tell a Holt what to do amounts to a fighting challenge—and Toby Holt will pull no punches in the battle for his ideals!

THE HOLTS: AN AMERICAN DYNASTY
VOLMUE FOUR

CALIFORNIA GLORY

DANA FULLER ROSS

 Created by the producers of
Inheritors of the Storm, The
Heiress, and the Wagons West series.

Executive Producer: Lyle Kenyon Engel

BANTAM BOOKS
NEW YORK · TORONTO · LONDON · SYDNEY · AUCKLAND

CALIFORNIA GLORY

*A Bantam Domain Book / published by arrangement with
Book Creations, Inc.
Bantam edition / May 1991*

*Produced by Book Creations, Inc.
Lyle Kenyon Engel, Founder*

*DOMAIN and the portrayal of a boxed "d" are trademarks of
Bantam Books, a division of Bantam Doubleday Dell Publishing
Group, Inc.*

ISBN 0-553-28970-5

Published simultaneously in the United States and Canada

PRINTED IN THE UNITED STATES OF AMERICA

OPM   0 9 8 7 6 5 4 3 2 1

THE HOLTS: *An American Dynasty*

THE HOLTS

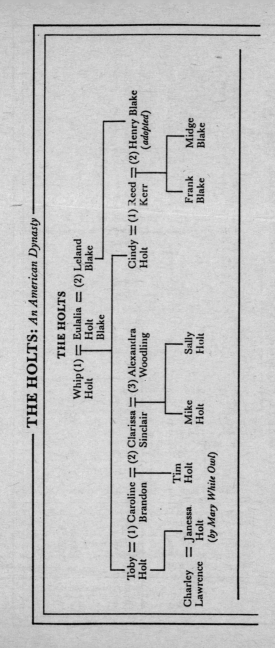

Whip(1) = Eulalia = (2) Leland
Holt   Holt   Blake
          Blake

Toby = (1) Caroline = (2) Clarissa = (3) Alexandra   Cindy = (1) Reed = (2) Henry Blake
Holt   Brandon   Sinclair   Woodling   Holt   Kerr   *(adopted)*

              Tim   Mike   Sally   Frank   Midge
              Holt   Holt   Holt   Blake   Blake

Charley = Janessa
Lawrence Holt
          (by Mary White Owl)

THE BLAKES, THE MARTINS AND THE BRENTWOODS

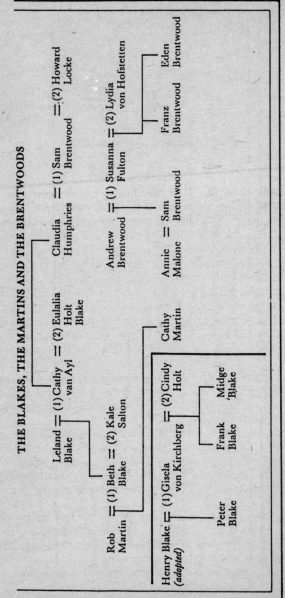

I

San Francisco, August 1893

"Well, now, Mr. Holt, my health hasn't been good."
Horace Woolwine, the owner of the *San Francisco Clarion*,
looked mournfully at his visitors from red-rimmed eyes.
His gray mustache seemed to sag in sympathy with the
droop of his watery eyes. The mahogany desk at which he
sat was covered with layers of papers, which he picked up
and laid down again, apparently at random.

"So I understand from Mr. Howard." Tim Holt nodded
at the man who had accompanied him to this meeting.
Waldo Howard was an employee of the rival *Chronicle* but
an old friend of Tim's. When Tim had indicated that he was
in the market for a paper larger than the one he now
operated in Oklahoma, Waldo had suggested that the
Clarion might be had for a song. Looking at its owner, Tim
thought the man seemed too dispirited to pick up a copy
pencil, much less inspire a staff of reporters to anything
livelier than lethargy.

"Not good at all," Mr. Woolwine said. "So many . . .
things . . . to attend to. Things all over the place." He
picked up a sheaf of accounts and let them drop again.

Tim decided that if Mr. Woolwine finished out the day
it would be a miracle. "Why don't you show me the plant,
sir?"

Mr. Woolwine shuffled to his feet. Tim followed,
restraining his urge to herd the old man along. So far, the
Clarion looked perfect. It was housed in a six-story building
on Kearny Street, with bay windows and elaborate cast-iron
decorations upon its cornices and above the main door, a

1

gargoyle with a pencil behind its ear. Tim had fallen in love with the gargoyle and was prepared to love the rest of the *Clarion*.

Within the newsroom, the staff attended to its work on a fleet of serviceable Remington typewriters. A system of pneumatic tubes connected the newsroom with the composing room below, leaving the copyboys to deliver material for reporters to their respective editors and to fetch coffee. The pace of the newsroom seemed to Tim just a shade too slow for the time of day, but with Mr. Woolwine setting the metronome, that was not too surprising.

The news staff looked up at their entrance, and a murmur of interest followed them across the room.

"Who's that?"

"I heard he's some galoot from Oklahoma, wants to buy the place."

"He's got a paper in Oklahoma. He must know—"

"He doesn't know enough to save this rag. What's Waldo Howard doing with him?"

"Probably cadging a free drink."

The city editor, a rumpled man in shirt-sleeves, smacked a coffee cup down on his desk and glared at them. "He buys it or he doesn't. In the meantime, it might help if we could get it out on the street this afternoon." He took a bottle out of the bottom drawer of his desk and poured some whiskey into his coffee cup. He picked up a folded length of copy, pages glued together end to end, and gulped down the contents of the cup, apparently to give him the fortitude to read his reporter's efforts.

As he followed Mr. Woolwine down the stairs, Tim dutifully admired the brass railings and the ornate brass doors of the elevator, which, Mr. Woolwine explained, they could not ride because it was stuck.

"Anybody in it?" Waldo asked.

"God knows," Mr. Woolwine replied apathetically.

Tim followed him into the composing room, where a dozen typographers, perched like frock-coated storks on high stools, were setting copy from long banks of type.

Mr. Woolwine sighed. "I'd like to have a Linotype machine, of course. The *Los Angeles Times* just got Linotype."

Tim's blue eyes gleamed. Ottmar Mergenthaler's type-setting invention was rapidly becoming an obsession with him. The machine cast slugs of type, one column wide, from molten lead, automatically justifying the right-hand margins. One man at a Linotype keyboard could do the work of half a dozen typesetters hand spiking type.

"Has the *Chronicle* got Linotype?" Tim asked Waldo.

"Wants it," Waldo answered. "Who doesn't? It's a big investment, though, and the public never sees it. Take it from me, kid, and put your dough in reporters' salaries. Linotype just processes what you give it. It won't write you brilliant copy."

"Neither will half the reporters I've got," Tim told him. He narrowed his eyes at the composing room, mentally replacing the type racks with machines of his imagining.

Mr. Woolwine seemed to find the subject of Linotype depressing. With Tim and Waldo behind him, he shambled through the far door and down another set of stairs to the pressroom. When they were halfway down, the press roared to life, and they could feel its vibrations through the stairs. Woolwine pushed the door open, and the roar enveloped them.

Inside a room two stories tall was a huge, steam-driven, web-fed cylinder press. An iron catwalk ran around its upper level. The noise was deafening. Tim walked around the press and craned his neck to look up into its works. The inside of the pressroom was as hot as a Turkish bath, and the steaming air was heavy with clouds of ink.

"You're in the way, buddy." A pressman wearing a newsprint cap elbowed past Tim, and Tim got out of the way. He spotted the ladder to the catwalk and climbed it, while the pressman shook his head and looked up dubiously, as if expecting Tim to fall into the press and get killed. But Tim had reached the catwalk with no trouble and was prowling along it. Mr. Woolwine squinted up with an expression that said if a prospective buyer fell to his death and ruined the press's workings, it would be in accord with Mr. Woolwine's general view of the way of the world. Tim thought he had never seen such a depressed-looking man.

After he had peered down at the press from all angles,

he climbed back to the floor and nodded at Woolwine. "Let's talk."

They went to the washroom to remove the faint overlay of ink that had settled on their hands and faces in the pressroom and then adjourned to Woolwine's office again. Tim looked around, mentally removing the flotsam and jetsam that spilled from Woolwine's desk to the floor and putting himself behind the mahogany desk, which would be quite a lovely piece of furniture once it was excavated.

"You definitely want to sell?" Tim asked.

"Oh, yes." A long drawn-out sigh drifted through the room on the heels of Woolwine's affirmative response.

"Then let's discuss business." Tim cocked his head at Waldo. "And you go home to the *Chronicle*. I'll buy you dinner later at the Press Club, but what you don't know about the *Clarion's* finances, you can't be asked." Not that Waldo would spill the beans on purpose, but he was known to have a loose tongue after a few drinks.

The negotiations took the rest of the afternoon, partly due to Mr. Woolwine's being prepared to wring every possible penny from the deal and partly due to a general lethargy that caused Mr. Woolwine to produce each new file and record with tortoiselike slowness. It drove Tim to distraction, and by the time the transaction was concluded, he was jiggling on the edge of his chair, one foot tapping the threadbare carpet.

Eventually they settled on a price consistent with the sale of the *Prairie Recorder* in Guthrie, which Tim had already negotiated, and affected by the substantial amount of the *Clarion's* outstanding debts. Tim signed a check for the down payment and a promissory note for the balance as soon as the sale of the *Recorder* was concluded. Mr. Woolwine signed a bill of sale and a deed to the property and agreed to remain in charge for one month. When they shook hands, Tim thought he detected enough pulse to keep Mr. Woolwine upright for thirty days.

The bill of sale felt almost warm in his pocket, as if it were a living thing. On the front steps, Tim stopped and looked up at the gargoyle with the pencil behind its ear.

Had the morose Mr. Woolwine conceived the gargoyle? Impossible. At some point the *Clarion* had had a man with spirit behind it. Tim grinned. He thought the newspaper would take to him just fine.

Tim took a deep breath and looked around him in the lamplit dusk. San Francisco had always struck him as a magical place, where ordinary laws of the universe did not apply. The hills, for instance—nobody had bothered to grade the ragged hills that appeared to be pegged to the flatter earth by the houses at their tops. The inhabitants had simply invented cable cars to run straight up and down them. The little cars flowed with apparent effortlessness up each sheer climb and down the other side on gradients that would destroy a buggy brake in a week.

And the air! Even in midcity it smelled of raw lumber and fish, much the way his hometown of Portland, Oregon, did, but with the sharp tang of salt overlaying it—the briny scent of the great bay. San Francisco was a seaport, given birth by gold, and its spirit showed in its nightlife. Now at dusk, Market, Kearny, and Montgomery streets were long, gaudily illuminated bazaars, populated by Italian balloon sellers, street-corner drummers hawking stomach bitters and electrical belts, a sidewalk organist with a monkey in a red gypsy vest, ad carriers passing out saloon handbills, and barkers shouting the services of phrenology and palmistry booths. On a corner, a Salvation Army band valiantly attempted to stem the disreputable tide that flowed around it.

Tim hailed a hack and told the driver he wanted to go to the Press Club on Ellis Street. It occurred to him that he had told Waldo to meet him there and that since this dinner was to be on Tim, Waldo might be running up a considerable bar bill. He sat back and noted the illuminated signs as they passed: *Prof. Holmes, Astral Seer . . . Prof. Diamond, Courses in Hypnotism . . . Dr. Ball's Indestructible Teeth. . . .*

San Franciscans were prepared to believe in nearly anything, he decided. It was evident that they still believed in romance. The available ladies who strolled down Market Street in the evening possessed a demure assurance that was a reminder of the West's woman-starved past. Females of any type were still at a premium, and they were treated with respect. A girl from a Barbary Coast brothel, Waldo had told Tim, could walk in the shopping district, and hats would be tipped to her. And one Kearny Street madam, so Waldo said, had married off six of her girls to millionaires and then retired. Waldo seemed to know a good deal about it.

At the Press Club Waldo was awaiting him in the company of a cartoonist who was introduced as Jimmy Warrington. Warrington sported a stiffly waxed mustache and a pair of plaid trousers that a carnival barker might have thought about twice before wearing. He was, Waldo explained, between jobs at the moment.

"Bring some of your work around next month," Tim told him, "when I settle in. I'll take a look." He wondered if Waldo was going to supply him with an endless parade of down-and-out journalists. Tim had no idea whether or not he needed a cartoonist.

"I could show you some tonight," Warrington said hopefully. When the waiter paused by their table, the cartoonist looked at his empty shot glass with further hope.

Tim knew perfectly well that if he fell in with these two for the night, he would have the great-grandmother of all hangovers in the morning. "Not tonight," he said firmly. "My little brother is coming in on the steamer from Hawaii at eight tomorrow morning, and I have to meet him." He bought Warrington another drink, though.

After the cartoonist had downed it and gone on his way, seeking hospitality among the other tables, Tim cocked an eyebrow at Waldo. "He any good?"

"Course he is," Waldo said. "Why would I introduce him to you if he wasn't?"

"You owe him money?" Tim suggested. "You're in love with his sister? You lost a bet? Never mind, I'll look at his stuff."

"What's your baby brother doing in Hawaii?" Waldo asked, interested.

"Not a baby," Tim said, chuckling. "Mike's seventeen and feeling his age with great seriousness. He went with my uncle Henry and aunt Cindy to see the islands and visit my disreputable courtesy cousin Sam, who's become a gentleman sugar planter, Lord help us." Tim gave a hoot of amusement.

Waldo grinned as the waiter brought their steaks and a bottle of champagne in a silver bucket—Tim was feeling expansive. "Annie hasn't given him the gate yet?" Waldo inquired. Tim, Waldo, and Sam and Annie Brentwood went back to the wild Virginia City silver days together.

"She did for a while," Tim said, cutting into his steak. "But Sam's father drowned at sea, and Sam ended up with his half sister, Eden, to raise. Annie came back to keep Eden from growing up as wild as a range colt. My brother Mike's in love with Eden—at their age!—and he doesn't want to come home."

Waldo shook his head. "Puppy love. Very painful."

"It's more complicated," Tim said. "Mike had rheumatic fever as a kid. He's got an iffy heart. Our parents have been inclined to wrap him in cotton wool, and he's starting to kick at it. I'm delegated to meet the boat and to get him to confide in me on the way home to Portland."

"Fine thing to saddle you with," said Waldo. "I have no living relatives, but when I did, they sapped my energy—energy that could have been better spent chasing a story."

"I don't mind helping them out," said Tim. He liked his family and had an itch to spend a few days loafing in Portland and letting his stepmother's servants do his laundry and fuss over him. As the waiter poured more champagne, Tim sat up, alert, ears tuned in the direction of an alcove on the far side of the dining room.

The Press Club was a noisy hubbub of newspapermen, and the cacophony was made louder by a private party in the alcove, where a few adventurous souls were entertaining the cast of a musical comedy revue from the Columbia Theater. They had begun to sing songs from the show, accompanied by a sportswriter with a banjo. He played poorly but with enthusiasm. Tim's line of sight was clear, and he was startled to see Mr. Woolwine among the revelers. No longer morose, Mr. Woolwine's thin arms waved like semaphores in time to the music, and his gray handlebar mustache twitched up and down. Bright spots of color burned on his cheeks, and his sunken eyes fairly shot sparks of intensity.

Waldo followed Tim's eyes. "Someone sure stoked his fire."

"I don't like a man who just sold a paper being that happy about it," Tim said uneasily. "I thought he was an invalid."

"Oh, he is," Waldo said. "He just gets off the leash every so often. You made a good deal."

"You don't know whether I did or not," Tim retorted. "And you haven't got any business sense anyway."

"Can't deny that," Waldo said, unnettled. "But I know a paper with possibilities when I see one." He took another bite of steak and studied Tim's dubious expression. "Relax. You did all right with the last deal I put you on to."

Tim pointed his fork at Waldo. "You got me drunk and sold me a debt-ridden rag that nearly got me shot."

"You got yourself drunk," Waldo protested. "And I didn't sell it to you; I lost it at poker. Just in the nick of time, too," he added. "I'm not cut out for management."

Tim put his fork down. "If there's something funny about the *Clarion*, Waldo, I'm going to tear you limb from limb."

Waldo crinkled up his face in earnest, champagne-soaked denial, and Tim's expression softened. Waldo was a hopeless businessman, but he knew the news game inside out. Just now he reminded Tim of the gargoyle over the *Clarion*'s door. He found it impossible to mistrust Waldo.

Waldo downed his champagne, hiccuped, then reached for the bottle in its snowy napkin. "Tell you what," he offered, "I'll come with you to meet your kid brother. We'll show him the town."

Tim shuddered. "No, you won't. My aunt Cindy wouldn't take to you at all." He watched Waldo pour the last of the champagne. "You won't wake up early enough anyway."

After an evening with Waldo, even one determinedly cut short at midnight, Tim almost overslept the next morning. He dragged himself out of bed, dressed quickly, then left his room at the Palace Hotel—too expensive a place for journalists or for newspaper owners, but he was celebrating—and ran down a few flights of mahogany stairs to the patio of the Palm Court. The court was encircled by seven tiers of balconies lined with statuary and palms, rising to a glass roof. Hacks and silver-mounted carriages were already sweeping in through the Montgomery Street driveway, and Tim hailed an empty hack. As the hack raced down the Embarcadero Tim put on a pious face of Sunday morning rectitude, which, he feared, would not impress his aunt one bit.

It didn't. Cindy Blake, his father's sister, ran an art gallery in Washington, D.C., and was a formidable force in that sophisticated world. Despite her own slightly Bohemian air, she expected nephews to be dutiful and sober. Cindy looked him over carefully, kissed his cheek, and informed him that his cravat was crooked.

Tim shook hands with his equally formidable uncle, Henry Blake. He was a colonel in the army but generally fulfilled his duties—and hardly anyone ever knew quite what they were until afterward, if at all—in civilian clothes.

"How were the islands?" Tim asked him casually in the tone of the merely curious.

"Very pleasant," Henry Blake replied in the tone of one who was merely a tourist. Hawaii was undergoing a revolution in which the United States government was still undecided about how much to intervene. "I met your man Hugo Ware out there. He tells me that Peter is doing well."

"Peter's fine," Tim said, referring to his business manager, Henry's son. "He has an amazing aptitude for finances. Much of my success is due to Peter's efforts."

Henry smiled as passengers streamed past down the gangplank. Cindy looked around and collected her offspring with a blue-eyed glance that could pretty well be translated as "Front and center!"

Frank Blake was fifteen, gangly in short pants but beginning to fill out across the shoulders and show the promise of his father's muscular build. Midge was nine, with more of Cindy about her, but she had the same square-jawed Holt face, waves of sandy blond hair, and the look of determination that Tim possessed. Both Frank and Midge were freckled from a season in the islands.

Tim hugged them, then held out his arms to Mike, who was coming down the gangplank after them. Seeing

Mike was a jolt to Tim. At first glance he always looked less like a Holt than anyone else because he was so thin and had his mother Alexandra's red hair. But something else set Mike apart from the other two children now: At seventeen he was hovering on the edge of adulthood. Mike's face had taken on definition since Tim last saw the boy and had begun to settle into its adult mold. His body was no longer thin but sinewy, as elastic as one of the tough little range ponies that had run loose on the West Coast since Spanish days. And there was something about his eyes—gray-green eyes, the color of the water at the foot of the wharf where the harbor seals dove in and out. Tim lowered his arms and held out his hand instead.

Mike shook it. "You look good," he said, studying his older brother. "Respectable."

"Of course I'm respectable," Tim said. "Pillar of the community back in Guthrie. Any day now I'm going to get fat and take up side-whiskers. You look good yourself."

"I am good," Mike replied. "There hasn't been a jump out of my heart. Not a peep. Not that Dad will believe it." He scowled down at the harbor seals barking for fish heads from the ships' cooks cleaning out their galleys. "I suppose you're the officer in charge. You can put away the handcuffs. I'll go along quietly."

"Don't be an ass," Tim said.

"Don't tell me you aren't here to make sure I go straight to the Madrona." The Madrona was the Holt family ranch in Portland.

"I'm just going for a visit," Tim said airily. "I'm planning to tell the country cousins all about San Francisco. I just bought a newspaper here. So put that in your pipe and smoke it."

"Hmmph," Mike said.

Mike knew what was what, Tim decided as they waited for a drayman to load the passengers' trunks. If Mike did not choose to go to the Madrona, he could easily give his older brother the slip. And if Mike did not care to confide in Tim, nothing could be done about that, either.

On board the train for Oregon, Tim relaxed a little. Henry and Cindy and their children, who were bound home for a family visit as well, were in the seats in front of him, and Mike was by his side, not exactly handcuffed but without anyplace to go as long as the train was moving.

"Suppose you tell me why Dad thinks you might slip the leash," Tim ventured.

"We just don't see eye to eye," Mike muttered.

"On what?"

"On anything."

"Oh, that's informative." *Was I this rebellious when I was seventeen? Probably.* "Can you be a little more specific? Is it politics? Religion? Philosophy of life?"

"Put it in your ear," Mike growled. "Don't patronize me."

"Aha," Tim said. "It's love."

Mike glowered. "I am," he said quite distinctly, "going to marry Eden as soon as we are both legally old enough. I'm not willing to wait, because no one thinks we ought to do it at all, and the longer we wait, the longer we'll have to put up with people telling us that. I am not going to have Eden bullyragged about it, and I am not going to put up with much of it myself."

"Well, why on earth shouldn't you marry her?" Tim demanded. "When you're older, I mean. I know Sam's a jackass, but Dad can't object to him that much."

"The doctor's advised me not to marry," Mike said grimly. "He feels that I stand too good a chance of leaving a young widow."

"Oh." Tim digested that. He looked at Mike carefully. "That's rough. How does Eden feel about it?"

Mike let his breath out in a long sigh. "She says she'd rather have the time we can get than none at all. I tried to talk her out of it—I'm not a selfish bastard. But that's not what *she* wants. She loves me. God knows why, I don't, I'm just grateful for it. We're serious about this. Do you honestly think she'd be happier apart from me?"

This is puppy love? Tim thought. *Somebody's sized this up all wrong. This is serious.* "I don't know," he said helplessly. "Probably not. Maybe if you settle in at the Madrona and learn to run it—you know Dad means you to inherit it, Mike; don't think any of us mind that—then Dad will feel easier about the idea of your marrying in a few years."

"I don't want to *wait* a few years," Mike said stubbornly.

"You're seventeen, for God's sake!"·

"And what's my life expectancy?" Mike snapped. "Nineteen? Thirty? Fifty? Who knows? But what if it's nineteen?"

Tim scratched his head. What had seemed a straightforward question was developing a disturbing complexity. Mike might not *have* any more time to grow up.

"There's more, too," Mike said. "I wish Dad would pick on one of you because I don't *want* the Madrona."

Tim groaned. He had seen that coming for years. Mike was no rancher.

"I love the place," Mike said. "It's home. But I don't want to run it. When I think about spending my whole life worrying about the price of hay, I want to scream."

"Well, that's awkward," Tim commented. "I feel the same way. Now what are we going to tell Dad?"

"Maybe Sally will grow up and marry a farmer," Mike said gloomily. "I suppose Janessa's out of the question."

"Janessa would rather be up to her elbows in somebody's diseased liver," Tim said. Their older sister was a doctor. "We'll just have to find some country boys to court Sally. Would I be prying if I asked you what you *do* intend to do?"

"I'm going to make moving pictures," Mike said. He glared at Tim, waiting for him to protest.

"Kinetoscope pictures? There's a living in that? Why don't you build miniature cities out of toothpicks or something practical?"

"Not kinetoscope pictures," Mike said scornfully. "Those are just a novelty. You have to stick your eye up to the viewer and turn a crank, and only one person at a time can look at them. I'm talking about moving pictures shown on a big screen."

"I haven't heard of that. Can you do that?"

"One of Thomas Edison's men has done it," Mike replied. "But Edison isn't doing anything with it; he's just fooling around with kinetoscopes. He thinks it's all just a fad. Think's he's got more important fish to fry. Man's an idiot."

"Edison's an idiot," Tim said solemnly. "The man who invented the automatic telegraph and the incandescent lamp."

"He can't see what he's got with the moving picture camera," Mike insisted. "But I can, and I want to get at it before he figures it out. I plan to get a job at his laboratory and learn everything I can—"

"And then one-up the boss," Tim said. "Ambitious."

"You think I can't do it?" Mike challenged.

"After this conversation, I think you're capable of anything," Tim said frankly. "Just don't go off half-cocked. You think Edison pays enough to support a wife?"

"No," Mike said glumly. "I'm working on that."

"Just out of curiosity, what are you planning to tell Dad?"

"Nothing," Mike said, suddenly alarmed. "And don't you rat on me! This was a confidence."

"I wouldn't have the nerve to rat on you," Tim said. "Dad would have apoplexy. I don't want to be around for it."

Mike nodded. "Sort of like the time you ran off to Virginia City with Sam Brentwood to get rich on mining silver. Dad took that real well, too."

Tim looked embarrassed. "Well, I was pretty young, and—"

"You were older than I am," Mike said, "and I've got more brains than *that*."

"All right, all right, I won't say anything. Just give it a lot of thought, will you, before you do anything crazy?"

"I'll ponder it until my eighteenth birthday," Mike offered. "I can't wait till I'm twenty-one. I may not see my twenty-first birthday."

"Oh, wonderful. Serious thought. Look, do you think you could stick it out a little longer than that if I could convince Dad to loosen up some—not be so determined to keep you under his nose for college, for instance? Let you go somewhere and be on your own?"

"I'm not going to play 'what if,'" Mike said. "It's a losing game. And I don't want to go to college; they can't teach me the stuff that Edison's working with. Greek philosophy and outdated engineering aren't what I need."

"Dad feels that college makes a man well-rounded, whatever he does," Tim pronounced, his voice sober, but Mike caught his eye, and Tim couldn't hold the expression. He gave a snort of laughter and pulled his hat down over his eyes. Tim had gone to college, to Harvard, but he had left in the middle of his sophomore year to mine silver in Virginia City, and any rounding out he had acquired had been done by life.

"Okay, I'll work on Dad for you, but don't get your hopes up if you're stuck on moving pictures." Tim doubted seriously that their father was going to be interested in any ideas about substituting life for education when it came to his brother Mike's case. Mike wasn't supposed to do anything that was interesting, for fear of his heart.

The subject of their speculation was also homeward bound, on another train. At fifty-two, the role of patriarch was one Toby Holt accepted uneasily. He was used to being the one in the midst of action. The staid pace of a senatorial career, coupled with the annoyances of raising children who seemed destined to create crises wherever they went, occasionally galled him. He had decided it was time he went home and got out of the shark pool of Washington for a while.

Looking out the window, Toby watched the jutting heads of the Rockies slide past. The vastness of the country never ceased to amaze him, nor did its infinite variety. Even with its burden of clinkers and soot, the air that streamed past the Pullman car window smelled crisp and cool in contrast to the hot, humid air of Washington, D.C. Toby set his chin in his hand and watched the Rockies float above and below them as the engine neared the Continental Divide. He smiled, aware that his mother, wife, and daughter, seated next to and opposite him, were less impressed.

Toby's mother, Eulalia, widowed for the second time, was going home to Oregon to pack up all that remained of her married life and to settle in her son's house for her last years. Her late husband Lee Blake had been a military man, and there was no way that Eulalia could have kept her house on the grounds of Fort Vancouver had she wished to, and she was resigned to the change. The army had bent its rules by allowing Eulalia as much time as she needed to return to the fort and get herself moved out. Moving from Fort Vancouver would be a sad chore; Lee's belongings would be all about the house on the base, just as she had left them before their last trip to Washington.

Toby's youngest child, Sally, sat beside her grandmother, booted feet stuck out in front of her and an expression of willful annoyance on her ten-year-old face. She looked like an ill-tempered Botticelli cherub. Sally was outraged to be snatched from the bosom of her best friend, Alice Roosevelt, Civil Service Commissioner Theodore Roosevelt's daughter, and taken home to the wasteland of Oregon where there was "no one to play with." Toby thought it would not take Sally long to fall in love with the ranch again and would certainly do her no harm to take a vacation from Alice. Sally was strong willed enough (*pigheaded* was a better term, Toby thought) without Alice Roosevelt to egg her on. Toby was aware that Alice utterly unnerved her stepmother and even her father, and Toby had no intention of allowing Sally to get to that point.

He glanced at Alexandra beside him. She had her eyes closed and her traveling veil pulled over her face to keep the soot away. She would not, he was certain, wish to be awakened to view the Rockies. Two days on a train with Sally would try the patience of a saint, and Alexandra had never claimed to be a saint. Toby tucked the pillow a little more firmly behind his wife's head and caught the handbag that was about to spill its contents onto the floor. He ducked his face around the stuffed bird that peered at him from the top of her hat and kissed her forehead through the veil.

They had been married eighteen years. *Through thick and thin,* Toby thought. He wondered which the next couple of years would prove to be. In a little over a year, his first term as a U.S. senator would end, and he knew his reelection was far from certain: He had annoyed too many of his backers by voting his conscience and not their pocketbooks. He had warned them of that probablity when

they first persuaded him to run for office—a fact that carried
no weight now with Portland's irate Democratic Party
leaders. Alexandra enjoyed Washington, Toby knew. She
liked the social whirl, the parties at the embassies, and she
enjoyed being a noted hostess. How much would she miss
it? he wondered. Toby sighed and stared at the mountains
again, enjoying the crisp feel of the air. Was he running for
reelection because he wanted another term as senator or
because Alexandra wanted it for him?

Dusk fell, and a porter came down the aisle to make up
the berths, bracing himself expertly against the sway of the
cars. Toby thought how much the railroads had improved
since the days when the seats consisted of hard wooden
benches, on which people both sat and slept. *We're spoiled*,
he thought sleepily. *Everything's gotten much too comfortable*.

Sally climbed into her upper berth and peered at him
balefully through the curtains. "It's too lumpy," she announced.

To everyone's relief, the train shrieked into Portland
the next day. Escaping steam hissed out in great clouds
around the engine's monstrous drive wheels, and Toby saw
White Elk, the Madrona Ranch foreman, coming toward
them through it, a grin on his dark Shoshone face. He
snatched up Sally and hugged her before she could try to be
dignified.

"You've grown, Puddin'." He smiled at Toby. "Good to
have you back, Boss. And ladies." He bowed elaborately. "I
brought the surrey. The boys can put your trunks in the
wagon."

A sense of homecoming began to wrap itself around all
of them while the surrey rattled through Portland. As they
left the rambling Italian Renaissance shadow of the Union
Depot, Sally hung over the side of the carriage, interested
in spite of herself. They passed the Skidmore Fountain with
its bronze maidens supporting a basin and lions' heads
spouting water. The fountain was the central rendezvous
point in Portland for old men with chess sets and gossip,
young men with nothing to do, and young ladies with new
costumes to show off to the young men with nothing to do.

White Elk swept the surrey around it once, and Toby realized they were taking the scenic route. The horses trotted through Chinatown, and Sally hung farther over the edge. Sally loved Chinatown, the more so since White Elk's wife, Mai, had come from there. Dried turtles hung in the shop windows, and strange sea creatures were displayed on mats in the sun. Flame-colored notices in black calligraphy were tacked on the bulletin board that covered a whole wall of Pine Street.

Alexandra and Eulalia began to lose some of their weariness, and even the overpowering scent of salmon that came from the canneries along the river seemed welcoming. Once outside Portland, Eulalia and Alexandra leaned forward for the first sight of the Madrona. A long winding avenue of the trees that had given the ranch its name led to the house, a rambling red and white structure of brick and clapboard with a round tower on the east end and a pavilion on the west. Curlicues of gingerbread decorated the porches, on which nearly every employee and resident of the ranch had gathered to welcome them.

With intense pleasure, Toby saw a thin, red-haired figure—taller than he remembered—detach himself from the crowd. Mike. And Toby's sister, Cindy, was waving to him from the porch swing. Then a cloud of dust erupted from around the corner of the house, with a thrashing steel-gray horse in the middle of it. Toby grinned. Tim was home, too, and he had that worthless animal Trout out, trying to knock some manners into him. It was always the first thing Tim did on a visit.

Contentedly, Toby got down from the surrey, his uneasiness fading, then helped his mother and wife down. With almost all the family at home, he felt that little could go wrong. He watched affectionately as Alexandra pulled Mike into her arms and hugged him.

Toby ruffled Mike's hair. "We've missed you, Son," he said. "But now we can settle down for a nice long while."

II

Fort Vancouver

Toby couldn't know, Eulalia thought sadly, looking around her dust-sheeted parlor. He was so full of talk about how good it would be for her to come and live on the Madrona. He could not know what it cost her to part with this house, where she had lived for so many years with Lee. One's children didn't ever understand things like that.

"Where do you want to start, Mrs. Blake?" White Elk's Chinese wife, Mai, a kerchief tied over her thick black hair, surveyed the room. Dust motes danced in the sunlight that slanted from the tall mullioned windows. From outside came the sounds of an army post at its daily business: the faint call of a bugle, the faraway bark of an officer's command, the dim drum of hoofbeats. Inside, the holland covers on the furniture were streaked with several years' dust—the Blakes had been a long time in Washington with Toby. Lee had taken sick on their first visit and never felt well enough after that to come home. He was buried there, at Arlington National Cemetery, where he had wanted to lie. Now, in Portland, Eulalia did not have even his grave to grieve over—only this house . . . empty, its furnishings waiting to be dispersed.

Eulalia straightened her shoulders to the task of the inevitable. "I'll start upstairs, I think, where Lee's things are. I want to go through them myself. This is just bric-a-brac." She waved a hand at the lamps, vases, and decorative objects that cluttered the tables, making little hills and valleys under the dust sheets. "Maybe you would pack those for me, dear. I'll sort them later. The furniture

18

is to go to the Madrona. What there isn't space for there in my rooms, I'll store in case some of the grandchildren want it."

Upstairs, Eulalia tied a kerchief over her hair, which was as white as the scarf now, and gathered in her apron the belongings from the bureau drawers. All of Lee's familiar brushes and razors had been with him in Washington, but things were always left over and left behind in a house one had lived in for as long as they had lived in this one.

Eulalia laid the odds and ends on the bed and sorted them with thin fingers: a watch that had long ago ceased to run but had been kept for its inscription from Lee's long-dead first wife, who had been Eulalia's friend; a small leather case of military insignia—tarnished now; a handful of shirt studs; a portrait of herself on ivory, young, spoiled, pouting Southern belle with hair nearly as black as Mai's. A souvenir of long-gone years, the portrait was cracked and could not be mended, but Lee had treasured it from the day he had first come upon it in a box in the attic.

Eulalia had been middle-aged when she married Lee, but she thought that he had always looked beyond that aging face to the girl in the frame and had known and sympathized with that spoiled child as few others could. *I was impossible then,* Eulalia thought with a faint smile. And how like Lee to have loved her in spite of that, as well as adored the woman she had become. Eulalia wiped her eyes and packed the things into the box with Lee's lieutenant's insignia.

Her own bureau yielded more memories: First she found a pincushion laboriously stitched for her birthday by Cindy at the age of eight. The embroidery was dirty, and the spot on the edge where Cindy had pricked her finger and bled over it had faded to rust. Eulalia pulled out a bent pin and put the pincushion in her pocket. In the back of the drawer were handkerchiefs monogrammed with similar ineptness by Janessa, and a leather box with the wedding band that Whip Holt, Cindy and Toby's father, had given to her. Another box, flat and quilted and made to hold the handkerchiefs that she had removed from it, held Lee's letters to her, written once a week every time they had been separated. Eulalia started to draw one from its envelope and then put it back and slammed the lid down on the box. Later, she thought, when she could bear it. . . .

Within the hour the memories were packed away, and Eulalia was bent on the practical task of listing the furnishings she wanted in her new rooms in her son's house. It had been her house once, but it wasn't anymore. Eulalia stroked the quilted satin box with its letters.

"That's what comes with age, darling," she whispered to it.

Tim, who in a couple of brisk outings had ridden Trout's homicidal bent into temporary submission, drew rein and watched his grandmother and Mai returning from this first expedition. As the buggy clip-clopped up through the madrona trees, he thought that his grandmother looked weary. It was always a fresh shock to him to see how old she was. People had taken to saying that about him lately, too, but at twenty-six he took it as a compliment if people thought he had finally stopped looking like a kid.

He swung down from his saddle and smacked Trout on the nose when the blue-steel head swiveled out at him, teeth bared. "Watch it. If it wasn't for me, you'd be glue." Trout flattened its ears and snorted.

"That animal hasn't gotten a bit better," Eulalia remarked as Tim helped her down from the buggy. "He looks demonic."

"He needs to be ridden," Mai explained. "No one else but White Elk will touch him, and White Elk hasn't the time."

"Maybe I'll have him sent to San Francisco for me," Tim said.

Eulalia closed her eyes. "He'll kill someone, and you'll get sued."

"You look done in, Gran. Come inside and rest before dinner." He led her in a wide path around Trout, while Mai drove the buggy to the barn.

"That girl's a good child," Eulalia said as Mai expertly swung the vehicle through the gate. "What you need in San Francisco is a good wife, not a crazy horse."

Tim didn't rise to the bait. Everyone seemed to think he needed a wife. He was used to it. He patted her hand.

"Take a nap, Gran. Maybe you'll think of someone who'd have me."

Eulalia rallied a little. "I will rest better when I have my own bed again. You tell your father I want a wagon sent out to the barracks tomorrow. If I am going to make this tiresome move, I want my own things immediately." She gave him a smile that still had a trace of its old spunk. "And I don't *know* anyone who'd have you, more's the pity."

Watching his family at dinner, Tim decided that it was good timing that his parents were returning to Washington in two months. Eulalia and Alexandra were each used to being mistress in her own house. They were very fond of each other and had lived together very amicably in Washington, but here, on home turf so to speak, there might be a bit of a strain. Eulalia and Whip had built the original cabin that the Victorian house now enclosed, and under the circumstances, it might be difficult to determine who was in charge.

We're a strong-willed lot, Tim thought, eyeing his collected relatives. So far Mike had made no rash statements to his father, but his expression had some of the ears-back rebelliousness of Tim's pet horse. Tim had taken it upon himself to suggest to Toby that Mike be given a longer leash.

Toby had raised his eyebrows with the stubborn look that was practically the Holt family expression. "Mike needs to learn the limitations imposed by his health."

Tim had taken a sip of the whiskey and water that Amy Givens, the Holts' maid, had brought them on the porch before dinner and tried to be tactful. "That's pretty hard for a boy his age. What were you doing when you were seventeen, Dad? You weren't sitting around with a blanket on your knees."

"I was itching to enlist in the army," Toby replied. "But there wasn't anything wrong with my heart. My mother didn't like it anyway," he added thoughtfully. "But it's not the same thing."

Tim thought there might be elements in common. "Mother's scared to death of losing him, isn't she? He's her pet."

"Now you know she loves you all just the same."

"I didn't say she didn't." Alexandra was Tim's step-mother, but he had ceased long ago to make that distinction. "But we're all pretty tough, even Miss Priss over there." He nodded at Sally, who was stalking about the lawn, wavering between sulking over being in the boon-docks in Oregon and climbing one of the madrona trees—if she could do it without her mother catching her. Sally's citified veneer was already slipping. "Mother just can't believe Mike's tough, too," Tim went on.

"He's not tough," Toby said. "He's *got* to resign himself to it."

"For whose sake?" Tim prodded. "For his? I'm not sure you're doing him a favor."

Toby put down his empty glass. "You aren't required to be. You aren't his father. When you settle down somewhere and have a brood of your own, I'll be more inclined to listen to your opinions on child rearing."

"I am settled," Tim said. "San Francisco newspaper tycoon, that's me." He hooked his thumbs in the armholes of his vest, tycoon fashion, but his father didn't crack a smile.

"Dinner's ready," Toby said. "Don't be late. You aren't a robber baron yet."

"Captain of industry," Tim had said.

But now as he ate his dinner, he felt a certain relief that he was catching the morning train for Oklahoma. Being coddled in the bosom of his family had proved not to be such a relaxing experience after all. The dilemma with Mike would shake out by his next visit to Madrona, Tim ex-pected. He just didn't want to be around while they shook it.

The Henry Blakes accompanied Tim on the train east to Guthrie, Oklahoma, in order to see Peter on their way to Washington. The colonel spent the journey writing an interminable report. Since he warily guarded the contents of it from his journalist nephew, Tim whiled away the trip teaching Frank to play poker. By the time the train steamed into Guthrie, Tim had instilled in Frank (rather expen-sively) the folly of drawing to a three-card straight.

"One more hand," Frank said plaintively. "My luck's bound to change."

"Not if you go on counting on luck," Tim said. He put on his hat and picked up his carpetbag. "Poker's skill and skulduggery."

The conductor let down the iron steps, and Tim hopped down, feeling bouncy from being released from three days' confinement on a Pullman car. He was also cockily exuberant over the *Clarion*'s bill of sale in his breast pocket.

Peter Blake, as usual looking more like a banker than a newspaperman, was on the platform to meet them. His chestnut hair was slicked down under a bowler hat, and he had a general air of knowing things about money that made him look older than his age, which was nineteen. His expression was more solemn than Tim would have expected just then, though.

"You look like an undertaker," Tim remarked.

"I've got reason."

Tim's eyes narrowed. "What now? Can't I leave for a couple of weeks without something unraveling?"

"The deal's gone sour," Peter said. "I'll explain later." His father and Cindy were coming down the steps onto the platform.

Tim didn't even ask which deal—there wasn't but one. A horrible knot tightened in his stomach, and he had the queasy sensation of having drawn to a three-card straight himself. The sale of the *Prairie Recorder* had been sealed with a handshake. That should have been enough, too, since the hand was attached to Jeb Morrison, although Peter, predictably, had said it wasn't enough. Tim had not wanted to wait for paperwork, terrified that the *San Francisco Clarion* might be sold in the interim to someone else. It had only been a matter of Jeb's dealing with his bank—Jeb had the money, there was no question of that—and he was probably the most honest man alive.

Tim's stomach knotted and unknotted, then tied itself up again even tighter. He tried to figure out what could have gone wrong as he climbed with the Blakes into the waiting carriage. The vehicle rolled down Oklahoma Avenue, and the answer presented itself with horrible clarity as they passed Jeb Morrison's elaborate brick house: There was a black wreath on the front door.

"Heart attack," Peter said over his shoulder. "Yesterday."

Tim thought he might have one himself. His chest felt tight, and the *Clarion's* bill of sale now gave him more the sensation of a lump of lead than a warm embrace.

Peter drew the buggy up in front of the Cherokee Hotel's imposing stone front. Shading his eyes with his hand, Henry looked up at it. "Boomtown architecture," he commented. "Imposing."

"We're very up and coming," Peter agreed. As if to corroborate that statement, a doorman appeared, stately in his scarlet jacket and gold braid, to hand the ladies down from the vehicle. An imperious gesture produced a pair of bellboys to deal with the baggage.

"The carriage is Sid's," Peter said. "Why don't you go to the office, and I'll be around after my folks are settled. I sent flowers to Jeb's family," he added.

"Wonderful," Tim growled. He turned the buggy in the street, mentally berating Jeb Morrison for being so inconsiderate as to be dead. He dropped the vehicle at Sid Hallam's livery stable, then stalked next door to the *Prairie Recorder* offices.

"When's the funeral?" he shouted at no one in particular, and slung his carpetbag into the corner behind his desk in the editor/publisher's office.

Hugo Ware stuck his head around the office door. He was a tall, fair Englishman with a deceptively layabout expression that had fooled more men than one into confiding to him what they ought not to. He was also a very fine writer, and Tim had already made him an irresistible offer to work on the San Francisco paper if the deal there came to fruition.

"Funeral's this afternoon," Hugo said. "Not much ice in August. Poor Jeb. They say he didn't know what hit him."

Tim groaned. "I feel the same way. I liked Jeb, but this is a hell of a thing to happen to me."

Hugo lounged in the doorway. His blue eyes were faintly amused despite the macabre conversation. "I don't imagine Jeb was awfully enthusiastic about it, either. Of course, he was probably less worried than some of us about where he was going to land in the afterlife. But still. . . . You might court the widow some," he suggested.

"I feel like a ghoul," Tim said. "I'm going to change my clothes. You go court my uncle Henry, who's holed up at the Cherokee. See if you can't get a parting shot out of him about the situation in Hawaii. If I have to sell this rag all over again, it had better look good."

"Yes, my captain." Hugo gave him a mock salute and retreated.

Tim, in black frock coat and silk hat, felt horribly hypocritical attending Jeb Morrison's funeral. He watched Jeb's widow sniffling in the front pew of the Methodist church, with her son beside her. Pauline Morrison's first husband had died, also. She and Jeb had been married only two years, after Jeb had finally given up on Rosebay Ware. Half the men in Guthrie had been courting Rosebay before she settled on Hugo. Now Pauline had had Jeb snatched away from her, and Tim was feeling worse about the deal that had fallen through than he was about Pauline's sorrow. He felt as if he ought to say he was sorry for that, and since he couldn't very well apologize to Pauline, he muttered a disjointed prayer, trying to explain it all to God.

Rosebay, seated between Tim and Hugo, who had slid in at the last minute, shook her head in disapproval. "She shouldn't have all this hoopla," Rosebay whispered to Tim. "Jeb was raised a Quaker. He liked things quiet."

Hugo bent over her. "Methodists aren't exactly high church as these things go," he whispered. "I'll take you to a Catholic church in San Francisco if you want to see hoopla."

"Will you two be quiet?" Tim hissed. "Or you won't *see* San Francisco, unless you ride in a boxcar."

Rosebay put a hand to her mouth and stifled a giggle, but she bent her head repentantly. She had liked Jeb. Everybody had liked Jeb.

When the service was over, Tim made sure that Pauline Morrison saw him among the mourners. She clasped his hand gratefully, and Rosebay's delicate black-gloved one with somewhat less enthusiasm. Tim went home to wait out the few days until he could decently call upon Pauline.

"I've had a letter from Germany, Peter," Henry Blake informed his elder son. "From your mother's trustees. It chased me around the Pacific for a while and finally caught up with me at the Madrona, so I need to answer it quickly. They're probably in a swivet already."

Peter chuckled. "They've been in a swivet since Mother died. They never did like you much, did they?"

"That is beside the point," Henry said. His first wife, the baroness Gisela von Kirchberg, had been possessed of an enormous fortune, with trustees and accountants hanging from it like limpets. These gentlemen had been thoroughly horrified when the baroness married an upstart American army officer. They had set about tying up her fortune so that it could only be gotten at, as Henry remarked, by seven silver keys and a magic incantation—certainly not by true love's kiss. They had gone to an unnecessary lot of bother because Henry didn't want Gisela's fortune in the first place, but that concept was not within the trustees' grasp.

Peter had been the sole offspring of that union, and his chestnut hair and slightly hooded eyes were the genetic legacy of his mother. Gisela, a conservative sort fiscally if not romantically, had allowed the trustees and accountants to arrange his inheritance so that he came into control of one-third of the principal at the age of twenty-one and the rest when he was thirty.

"They're a little early, aren't they?" Peter inquired. "I won't be twenty-one for eighteen months."

"They don't move very fast," Henry said. "You could race them with snails. They need to begin the process early." He adopted a mock Prussian accent and stuck his nose in the air. "They hope you will realize the wisdom of allowing them to continue to guide you in these uncertain financial times."

"They're in for a shock," Peter remarked.

His father narrowed his eyes at Peter. "Are you sure you want to take these old boys on? They're pretty formidable. Also, they *may* know what they're doing. Your mother thought highly of them."

Peter had gathered from all accounts that his mother had been pretty formidable, too, but he shook his head decisively. "I want to manage my own money. That means taking my own risks. You'll have to admit I've done pretty well here. The *Prairie Recorder*'s been in the black from the beginning." Peter rolled his eyes. "Up until now, that is. I *told* Tim to get that deal signed—"

"Could we put Tim to one side for the moment?" Henry asked. "We let you come out here with Tim because you were having a certain amount of difficulty with the military school—"

Peter gave a whoop of laughter and suddenly looked his true age. He had attempted valiantly to follow in his father's and grandfather's footsteps, but his approach had been so unorthodox that the commandant of his military school had said flatly that Cadet Blake should consider some other career for the sanity of all concerned. "You could put it that way," he said, chuckling. "Now look, Dad, the fact is that I've been able to build a very respectable bank account from my own investments as well as keeping Tim in the black. But I haven't got enough saved for my purposes. You can tell my trustees that I'll come to Germany in February to discuss the matter with them. If you wish to hint that I may decide to let the reins stay in their hands, go ahead. I wouldn't want them to worry too early."

Henry took note of the gleam in his son's eyes. "You mean you don't want them forewarned. All right, I'll write to them. I don't suppose you'd like to tell *me* what you have in mind?"

Peter considered. "No, I don't think so," he said finally. "You might start trying to talk me out of it. Or those fossils in Grevenburg might get wind of it."

Henry looked affronted. "Not from me."

"Not unless you thought I was nuts," Peter said.

"Might I?" his father demanded. "Peter, what are you up to?"

The devilish light in Peter's eyes flared a little brighter.

"Come to Grevenburg with me and see. I may need the moral support."

Henry crossed his arms on his chest. "If you thought I had any intention of letting you gad about Germany without me, you *are* crazy." Then a faint light in his own eyes mirrored Peter's. "And I don't think I want to miss this."

Tim, his top hat on his knees, sat in the widow's red plush parlor and wondered what on earth had possessed Jeb Morrison to give Pauline such a free hand with the redecorating. The walls were lined with paintings of bowls of fruit and dead game and black-clad women mourning over tombstones. All the heavy oak furniture was uphol-stered in deep red horsehair. Maroon draperies kept out the sunlight. All in all, the parlor looked completely suitable for a funeral.

"So kind of you to call on me," Pauline Morrison was saying. "It is very difficult to bear up in these sad days."

Tim nodded gravely. "Of course, Mrs. Morrison."

Pauline sighed. "Exceedingly miserable for a woman alone. There is the carriage works to be thought of, and my Donny is simply not old enough to run it. I find business quite impossible to understand."

Tim leaned forward. "Actually, I hoped to discuss business with you. I know it must be very confusing—"

"You are very *kind*!" She misconstrued what he had said with evident delight. "To offer to help me in my hour of need."

"Well, uh, actually, Mrs. Morrison—"

"Pauline," she breathed. "Do call me Pauline. I can't tell you what a comfort it will be to me."

Tim felt his shirt collar growing tighter. He didn't want to court the blasted woman, he just wanted to sell her a newspaper. Now what had he done? And Jeb hadn't been dead but a week. "Well, Pauline . . ." His voice sounded strangled, even to himself.

"Let me offer you some sherry." As she rang a bell for the maid she smiled at him wistfully. Her hair was done up with a black ribbon in a suitably mournful coiffure, and her gown was of unrelieved black. Even her handkerchief was black bordered. She dabbed delicately at her eyes with it.

"I don't usually touch spirits, of course, but the doctor has prescribed sherry for me. I find it so hard to rest, what with all my troubles to haunt me."

"Of course."

The maid came in and handed Tim a tiny, sticky glass. He held it in one hand, afraid to set it down on anything. "I'll be glad to give you any advice I can, of course, Pauline, but—"

"I *knew* you would help me! I married for the first time *quite* young, you know, and have led a sheltered life."

She leaned toward him, and he juggled the sticky sherry glass from one hand to the other as a sort of shield. She leaned farther forward and detached it, setting it down on a table with no apparent concern for the finish.

"You are so kind, Tim," she whispered.

"Well, actually, I'm going to be leaving town," he blurted.

Pauline froze, her hand on her own glass, which she had been in the act of setting down beside Tim's. She picked it up again.

"It was a deal I'd made with Jeb that brings me here," Tim said. "And to pay my condolences, of course." Pauline had begun to look annoyed. *Oh Lord, I'm going to snarl this whole thing up,* he thought. "The thing is, Jeb was going to buy the *Recorder*."

Pauline blinked at him. "The newspaper? Whatever for?"

Tim spread his hands. "Jeb believed we were a voice of reason in Guthrie—more evenhanded than the *Oklahoman*. When I told him I had my eye on a paper on the West Coast, he thought he'd like to try his hand at this one. Jeb's been successful—was successful—so I guess he figured he'd earned the chance to try to guide the town a little."

Pauline folded her arms and glared at Tim. "He never mentioned it to me," she informed him.

Tim had a feeling that she might be the kind of woman that you didn't mention things like that to, not until after you'd done them. "I'm sure he was getting ready to discuss it with you," he said feebly.

"I don't want a newspaper," Pauline announced. "I do not feel that it is a suitable atmosphere for Donny. Some of your men, Mr. Holt, are not well behaved at all." The look she gave him indicated that she didn't think he was, either.

Tim wondered if she was embarrassed to have misconstrued the reason for his visit or just annoyed. It served her right for making sheep's eyes at him in the middle of a condolence call, he thought, ignoring the fact that it had not been strictly a condolence call from his point of view.

Pauline Morrison dabbed her eyes with the black-bordered handkerchief, but there was steel in them. "Did Jeb sign any papers, Mr. Holt?" she inquired.

"Well . . . no," Tim conceded.

Pauline smiled—or at least her mouth did. The rest of her expression looked very much like someone watching a hanging. "Then I am afraid you will have to find another buyer. I simply could not bring myself to become involved in . . . journalism." She made it sound as if she were saying "matricide." "I cannot believe that Jeb would have chosen to expose us to that."

"The *Prairie Recorder* tells the truth to the city of Guthrie," Tim said indignantly. "No more, no less. Truth is the one thing God intended to go naked."

That went too far. Pauline looked at him, outraged. "I have my good name in Guthrie to think of. And Donny's." She smiled thinly. "I daresay standards may be different in San Francisco."

"How did it go?" Hugo inquired as Tim stalked into the office.

Tim took off his top hat and studied it morosely. "I gummed it up, Hugo. She thought I was laying the groundwork to court her when she comes out of mourning. When she found out I wasn't, she was steamed."

"Pauline Morrison would have wrecked the paper anyway," Hugo consoled. "Look at it that way. She'd have introduced social columns and guest editorials by temperance lecturers and kowtowed to the men with money. The boys in the back shop would have been ashamed."

"The boys in the back shop would still have had jobs," Tim pointed out. "Hugo, I don't think you've quite grasped the fact that I have to sell this paper to make the payment on the *Clarion*. If I don't, the court will auction it to make the payment, and it will go for two cents, and I'll be poorer than a church mouse and still in debt. And you will have to get an honest job."

"Have you consulted Peter? He's the one who knows money."

"Peter's working on it," Tim said. "There are buyers. That's not the problem. The problem is we need a buyer *now*. And if word gets around that I've already bought the *Clarion*, they'll know they've got us over a barrel." He prodded glumly at his top hat with a pica ruler and swore when it fell off the edge of his desk.

"If you don't want word getting around," Peter Blake said, coming in and pulling the door closed behind him, "will you for God's sake close your door? I've got Nate Hurley out there, and he's got ears like a coyote."

"Hurley?" Tim glowered. "What does that weasel want?" Hurley owned the opposition, the *Oklahoman*.

"He wants to convince you to sell out," Peter said and grinned. "I told him you couldn't possibly consider it, not to him. But that you did want to move on, and if the offer was sweet enough. . . . He gave me five dollars for the tip."

"I wouldn't sell to him! The *Oklahoman*'s a lying, slanted disgrace to journalism, and all he wants to do with the *Recorder* is fold it! I wouldn't sell to Hurley—"

"A little louder," Peter suggested. "I want him to hear this."

Tim stopped in midtirade. "Damn it, Peter, I won't do it. That's selling my soul."

"Horse apples," Peter scoffed. "It's business. If the court takes the *Recorder* to pay your debts, Hurley will get it anyway. I *told* you to get that contract signed before you left."

Tim flopped down in his desk chair, looked mule headed but at bay. "All right," he snarled. "I'm just going to say this once, so listen: You were right. I was wrong. Now how the hell are you going to get me out of it?"

"He's out there," Peter said.

Hugo edged the office door open a crack. "He's reading the morning's edition," he said.

"Of course he is," Tim grumbled. "I read his, too."

"He asked me a lot of stuff about the cash flow and the staff size," Peter said. "I don't think he wants to fold it."

"Well, what else would he do with it?" Tim demanded.

"Shift the *Recorder* or the *Oklahoman* to the afternoon and run it as a sister paper," Peter replied. "That's my guess. It would pretty much make Hurly top dog in Guthrie. None of the other papers could compete with the combined circulation."

Tim snorted. "Just what Guthrie needs. A sensationalist rag morning *and* night."

"Will you quit being so self-righteous?" Peter snapped. "You can't afford it. If that's what he wants, he's going to want to be quiet about it, before any of the other papers get wind—which means he's in a hurry. Which we are, too. And if you don't ask him in here and talk to him, I'm going to quit."

Tim pointed a finger at him. "You are a nineteen-year-old whippersnapper," he said. "Will someone tell me why I'm listening to an accountant who's not old enough to vote?"

"Because I know what I'm doing," Peter said, and went to escort Mr. Hurley in.

"I don't like your politics," Tim said.

"I don't like yours, either." Hurley extracted his pen from his vest pocket. The pen was an expensive onyx one with gold fittings. "Your staff is excellent, however, and your plant is up to date. Politics are easily changed."

"With the wind," Tim agreed.

"Really, Holt, you can't expect to sell a newspaper and still control it."

"I want it in writing that you aren't going to fold it," Tim said.

"I'll specify a year," Hurley agreed. "If the experiment doesn't work, I'm not going to lose my back teeth for the sake of your principles."

Tim found it irritating that he was now forced to wish good fortune on Nate Hurley, who had been on the opposite side of the fence from Tim Holt on every civic issue for the last four years. *I'm going to mend my ways*, he thought. *I'm going to start listening to Peter and get sensible about money.* "All right," he said, feeling as if his own teeth were being pulled.

Hurley uncapped his fountain pen and started to write. It wasn't as much as Jeb Morrison had been going to pay, but it was enough to squeak by.

III

San Francisco

"There you are, Mr. Woolwine. It's been a pleasure to do business with you." Tim signed the check with a flourish.

Mr. Woolwine nodded morosely, and Tim wondered once again what had come over him that night of gaiety in the Press Club. Today his eyes had all the sparkle of a couple of lumps of lead shot.

"Good luck to you," Mr. Woolwine said. He put on his hat and picked up a soft-sided attaché case, out of which protruded various personal files and a half-full bottle of stomach bitters. As Woolwine shuffled down the hallway, Tim looked at the wasteland left behind him. No telling what all this stuff was, he thought. He began to gather it into an unwieldy stack in the middle of the desk. He had told Stu Abrams, the city editor, that he wanted an editorial staff meeting later in the day. Maybe Abrams could sift it out.

Tim sat down behind the desk and began to make notes. There didn't seem to be a managing editor. Woolwine had done the job himself, which was ridiculous for a paper this size. And Tim would have to think about a new financial manager before February; Peter would stay on until then. Mr. Woolwine hadn't seemed to have had one of these, either. And Tim needed to look over the editorial staff to make sure he wasn't overloading it by adding Hugo Ware. If there was a good candidate, he might move someone up to assistant city editor.

He worked for several hours and was casting about for another fresh sheet of paper when the door burst open.

Mr. Woolwine, eyes aflame, stood on the threshold.

"Ha!" Woolwine lunged at the desk, extracted a sheaf of handwritten scrawl slanting down a page of yellowed copy paper, and jammed it into his coat pocket. "Ha!" Another page, this one with unintelligible diagrams in red ink, which looked to Tim as if they might vaguely represent the solar systems or the mechanism of a clock, went into the attaché case.

Woolwine bounced on the balls of his feet while Tim goggled at him. The man's mustache stuck out stiffly to either side, apparently of its own accord, and his bushy eyebrows waggled up and down. "I thought I'd lost these," he said with feeling. "Very important. Vital." He made another grab at the papers on the desk.

"Certainly, Mr. Woolwine, anything you need." Tim stared.

"Not *Clarion* business at all," Woolwine said, sweeping the stack into the case. "Abrams has all that. I'm tired of that." His feet, in polished shoes and spats, danced across the office floor as he pulled books from the shelves, flipped them open, and stuck them back again. One volume went into the case. Tim saw the title as it disappeared: *Congressional Record. Washington, D.C., 1854.* "Ha!" Mr. Woolwine erupted.

Tim managed to find his voice. "Are you all right, sir?"

Woolwine fixed him with beady eyes. "Perfectly. Couldn't be better." He hopped from one foot to the other. "Important work to do." He spotted an abalone shell and a pair of pliers and added them to his trove. He executed another dance step and smacked his top hat down more firmly on his head. "I've ordered your Linotype for you," he announced, and departed.

"You *what*?" Tim was out of his chair and at the door in a lunge, but Woolwine was already rocketing down the hall.

"Knew you'd want it," Woolwine called over his shoulder. He swerved around Stu Abrams like a giant bat and was gone.

"Jesus Christ," Abrams said. "He's got his cluckers on."

Tim stared at the empty hall. "Was he drunk?"

"Naw," Abrams said. "He doesn't drink. He's just crazy."

"He sure acted like it," Tim said. "What got into him?"

Abrams gave Tim an interested stare. "He's crazy," he said simply. "You mean you didn't know?"

"You mean literally?" Tim demanded.

"Hell, yes. I'd say he's certifiable. There's some fancy brain doctor's name for it. You could ask Raphael Murray; he's our police reporter, sees all the nut cases. It causes mood swings. Half the time he's down in the doldrums so far you can't be sure he's breathing. When he comes out of that, he's as high as a kite and goes off on some wild tear. Once he was down here at three in the morning painting astrological symbols on the office walls. Said he was going to focus the planets. His sister came and took him away."

Tim groaned. "He said he'd ordered a Linotype. You don't suppose he really did?"

"Probably ordered three," Abrams answered. "Maybe you can stop 'em if they haven't been shipped."

Tim put his hand to his forehead. He was going to kill Waldo Howard when he found him.

"You want to meet the staff?" Abrams asked. "Might as well see what else you got yourself into."

Tim followed the city editor down the hall and into the newsroom. The reporters were gathered around Abrams's desk, sitting on chairs and adjacent desktops. There were only five of them.

"Where are the rest?" Tim asked.

"We're it," one of them said. He was a thin man in his late twenties with wavy, dark hair and paper cuffs protecting a shirt that was almost too far gone to be worth the trouble. "Except for Philburn. He's probably asleep. I'm Rafe Murray. Police beat."

Tim felt a sense of nightmare beginning to enfold him. "This is the entire staff? What happened to the men who were here a month ago?"

"Quit," said a beefy blond man. "Well, Woolwine fired two, but the rest quit. I'm Chet Sheppard—sportswriter. I haven't been paid, either," he added.

"You don't do any work," Raphael Murray said.

"None of them do," Abrams grunted. "But they're what you got to go on with. I'm starting to think you bought a pig in a poke, Mr. Holt."

"Why didn't anyone see fit to warn me?" Tim snapped. "Exactly how much of Mr. Woolwine's condition was common knowledge?"

"Well, his sister doesn't like it to get out," Murray said with a grin. "She's had to bail him out once or twice, but she managed to keep it hushed up."

"Hell, *we* hushed it up," Sheppard admitted belligerently. "Doesn't do any good for people to know you work for a loony. Not if you're looking for another job."

"You'll be looking for another job unless you tell me everything else that nobody saw fit to mention," Tim snarled. "Now!"

They looked at him speculatively, obviously trying to decide whether to cut their losses and resign or hang around to see if Tim Holt could get the paper on its feet.

"The place owes me five weeks' pay," one of them ventured.

"You have a problem with advertisers," another one said. "A lot of the big stores won't let our salesmen inside since Woolwine called one of the store managers a cannibal. Woolwine ran a line under his ad, saying that the man ate babies. Stu didn't see it in time to stop it," he added apologetically. "A whole press run got out on the street."

"You may need to butter up City Hall some," Raphael Murray offered. "Woolwine took a cooch dancer to the mayor's daughter's coming-out party last week. He got it in his head that the poor little thing was the mayor's long-lost child. The dancer was working a scam, of course, hoping someone would buy her off—I don't expect she'd seen too many hot dinners. To her, going with Woolwine must have been like finding gold in the street. His sis was there and got them out before any of the other papers got hold of it, but the *Clarion*'s corpora non grata, so to speak. Woolwine tried to take her home with him after that. I think he was gonna reform her."

"Hot damn," Sheppard said gleefully. "I hadn't heard that. He still got her?"

"What do you think?" Murray said scornfully. "His sis took him home by the ear and left little hoochy-cooch to reform her own self, back in the Tenderloin where he got her. He'd have forgotten about her by now anyway."

Tim massaged his temples again. He had a fearsome headache. The five reporters and the city editor watched him.

"You want a drink?" Stu Abrams offered. He pulled a bottle out of his desk drawer, found an empty coffee cup, blew out the dust, and poured in a generous slug.

Tim accepted the cup, took a swallow, and grimaced. It tasted as if it had been brewed in old football shoes.

Abrams shrugged. "I haven't been paid, either."

"You drink rotgut when you're flush," Murray said. He took the bottle and poured himself some.

Tim decided he had better deal with them while they—and he—were still sober. "I'll have my man go over the books," he said. "If they don't blow up in his hands, I'll see you get paid in a couple of days at least half of what's owed. Will that keep the wolf from the door?"

"It'll back him up some," Abrams said. "You got a plan?"

Yeah, he had a plan, he thought. He was going to strangle Waldo Howard. Tim sighed. Waldo hadn't known. The staff had taken some pains to hide Woolwine's aberrations, and it sounded to Tim as if the old coot had gotten worse in the last month. He'd bet Waldo knew now, though. No wonder Waldo hadn't met his train.

Tim picked up the coffee cup and drank the last of Abrams's rotgut. "Just get a paper out," he said wearily. "And don't let Woolwine through the door again. I don't know whether you'd be interested in telling me why none of you warned me?"

"We wanted somebody to buy it," Sheppard replied. "Stands to reason nobody in this town would."

Tim snorted. "Well, since I do happen to have hopped off the turnip truck here in the big city, you bastards owe me. Don't expect a raise in the foreseeable future."

Murray got off the desktop on which he had been perched. "We shall slave for you, Sire." He picked up his battered hat and salaamed. "Provided that you yourself do not become unhinged. Now if you other wage slaves will excuse me, I have a hanging to go to."

"That ought to cheer you up," Abrams grunted. "Skip

the poetics this time and just give me five inches on justice done, if you think you can manage it."

Tim waited while the other reporters moved away. He looked at Stu Abrams. "Mind telling me why you're still here?" he asked him.

"This used to be a good paper," Abrams answered. He looked at Tim, considering. "Might be again."

"Might fall through a hole in the ground, too," Tim said. He felt oddly philosophical on half a cup of Abrams's whiskey. He supposed that would wear off later. "We'll see. You give it what you've got, and we'll see." He headed back toward his office.

"I need at least four more reporters!" Abrams called after him.

Tim looked over his shoulder. "You'll get them—if I haven't bought a Linotype instead."

The Linotype arrived three days later, already paid for with a rubber check that Woolwine had written on the *Clarion*'s almost nonexistent account. Tim would now have to make good on it. He spoke with the bank manager in placatory statements and assurances that Mr. Woolwine no longer had the power to sign anything. Tim was thereby allowed to avoid disgrace.

He had the machine installed in the composing room. It nearly caused a riot among the union typographers.

"Just shut up and listen to me, damn it!" Tim yelled as they surged around him. "Nobody's going to lose his job, but mechanization's the coming thing, and neither you nor I can stop it if we want to stay solvent and competitive. So you can learn to use it"—he gestured at the corner where the Linotype sat smoking over its caldron of molten lead— "or you can be a bunch of old ladies picking out type with tweezers while the rest of the world is heading for the twentieth century."

"The *Chronicle* hasn't got Linotype!"

The *Chronicle* hadn't had Woolwine, either. The *Chronicle* wasn't in hock to its elbows and a laughingstock at the Press Club. "That's right!" Tim said. "We're the first. Now that's something to be proud of. We're the only paper in California besides the *Los Angeles Times* that has this amazing invention!"

The Linotype was monstrous, a diabolical-looking engine on a cast-iron frame, as black as coal and as hot as a griddle. At the touch of a key, small brass matrices would fly down the channel to their proper places in line and cast an entire line of type in one lead slug.

One of the typographers peered at the keyboard. "Etaoin shrdlu," he said. "What the hell does that mean?"

"It's French," Tim seethed sarcastically. "How do I know what it means? It doesn't mean anything. It's just a keyboard."

"I don't like its looks."

"It's not alive, for God's sake," Tim said. The lead in the caldron burbled ominously.

The shop foreman glared at him. Typesetters were the elite of the back shop and came to work in frock coats and tall hats. "And how many men does it take to run this—contraption?" he demanded.

"One," Tim said patiently. An obvious answer. "Therefore we will be able to do far more job printing, with the assistance of typographers who are not setting the daily edition. Therefore we will make money, a novelty for this paper. Therefore you will keep your jobs—which will not be the case if I have to eat this Linotype, which is already paid for."

"The union isn't going to like this."

Tim poked a finger at the man's natty vest front. "I've been a union man since before I got my first paper. So don't teach your grandmother to suck eggs."

They stood in a semicircle around the Linotype, staring at progress, black and ugly.

The foreman touched an index finger to the keyboard. With a heave and a rattle, the Linotype dropped a matrix out of the front. "Blow us all to kingdom come, I shouldn't wonder," the foreman said gloomily.

One of the younger men came forward. "Aw hell, Harry, that's what my old man said about the steam press." He shot his cuffs back and wiggled his fingers. "Let me take her for a spin. Let's see what old Etaoin Shrdlu can do."

Tim, departing, chuckled as he heard the machine

rattle into life. Even with the door shut behind him, the Linotype, up and running, was incredibly noisy. It had been his experience that progress usually was.

He went upstairs and found Peter Blake in Peter's newly established office. The young man wore a green eyeshade and clenched a pencil in his teeth. He was rummaging with both hands through stacks of account books.

"You've got trouble," Peter said around the pencil.

"Lord, why don't I just have that phrase typeset, and we'll make it our motto."

"Might as well," Peter said. "Unless you want to learn to look before you leap."

"Well, I didn't know the old man was one jump ahead of the loony catchers."

Peter sighed. "You never do. I never saw a man who could take more things on faith that ought to be looked at with a good lamp instead. And that reminds me, Waldo Howard is in your office. Hugo's got him in there, and he's standing in the door like a sheepdog so Howard can't get out."

Tim grinned. He had sent Hugo after Waldo since Waldo didn't know Hugo and wouldn't run away when he saw the Englishman. Tim had tried twice to scare up Waldo, but Waldo had made a narrow escape out the back door of the *Chronicle*'s newsroom both times.

"Good. I want him."

Peter took the pencil from his mouth. "What about this?" He gestured at the stacks of record books and stuck the pencil back in again.

"You've got till February to get us in the black," Tim said. "You can't go to Germany and leave me with this."

"I don't suppose you'd like me to find the Holy Grail while I'm at it," Peter said around the pencil. "It might be easier."

"Just find some money so the bank doesn't close me down. I'll do anything you say—the finances are your department. But if I don't spend time doing my job, which is editing the paper, there won't be any point."

"To begin with, then, don't hire Waldo Howard," Peter said. "I've been listening to the scuttlebutt. Howard lets money run through his fingers like water. He's got a tab at all the saloons on Market, and he owes half the bookies in town."

"I want a managing editor. Waldo's a good newspaperman. One of the best."

"Then he won't jump ship from the *Chronicle* for what you can afford to pay."

"He will for the managing editor's slot."

"Don't pay him more than he's making now" was Peter's parting shot.

Tim found Waldo at bay in his office. "I didn't know!" Waldo yelped when he saw Tim. "Honest, Tim, I didn't know."

"I was going to yank your ears off," Tim said, "but I've thought of something better. I see you've met Hugo."

Hugo stretched and stood away from the door. "We played a hand or two of poker for the wages I don't have yet," he said.

"Don't play poker with Waldo!"

"He won," Waldo said gloomily.

"Murray's going to take me around to City Hall," Hugo told Tim, picking up his hat. "I'm to trot out my pedigree and disarm the mayor. I hope I don't mean that in a literal sense," he added thoughtfully.

"If the mayor didn't shoot Woolwine, he won't shoot you," Waldo said. "Probably."

"Comforting." Hugo looked at Tim. "Don't forget to show up tonight. Rosebay's expecting you."

"Tell her we'll do the town," Tim said. "If you haven't been shot."

"Is his old man really a baron?" Waldo asked when Hugo had closed the door behind him.

"The genuine article. Hugo was a blot on the family escutcheon, so they shipped him over here. He's a heck of a good reporter, though."

"He is if Rafe Murray took to him." Waldo sighed. "I always say it takes deep tragedy to get a man into this game."

"Stow it," Tim said. "You got in because your heart pumps ink instead of blood. I think that's what's wrong with your brain." Waldo was at Tim's desk, so Tim pulled up a chair, turned it around, and straddled it. "You've been dodging me."

"You wanted to yank my ears off," Waldo protested. They stuck out handily under his thinning hair. "I swear to God I didn't know about Woolwine."

"That's because you're as crazy as he is. I've got a proposition for you."

Waldo looked at him warily. But soon Tim was proved right. After some howls of protest over the salary—and an offer, declined, to play a hand of poker for the difference— Waldo Howard signed on as the *Clarion*'s managing editor.

They shook hands on it, satisfied. Waldo went to make a list of who else he thought might be raided from the *Chronicle*'s staff. Tim washed his face and hands and put on a clean collar in the washroom, then went to keep his engagement with Hugo and Rosebay Ware. Whistling cheerfully, he trotted out under the saturnine eye of the *Clarion*'s gargoyle. Showing San Francisco to Rosebay would be fun. Tim had been saving up sights for her. . . .

Hugo had returned to the house the Wares had rented at the foot of Telegraph Hill, two blocks from Tim's residence. They all had plans to come up in the world, "up" in San Francisco being a literal as well as figurative move, to the heights of Rincon Hill and Nob Hill. But for now the lower slopes, with neat clapboard houses crammed side by side, were economical.

Rosebay had held out for a house far larger than two people needed on the grounds that she could supplement Hugo's reporter's salary by taking in boarders. Hugo knew enough not to argue with her. She had cooked for pay in Guthrie, setting a better and cheaper table than the hotels, and would, Hugo admitted, be a whiz at a boardinghouse. Already Raphael Murray, lured over by Hugo for dinner, had packed his bags and moved in.

As Tim walked the two blocks from his house to the Wares', he appreciatively sniffed the cool salt air and let it blow from his mind the vision of a Linotype chewing up money and spitting out red ink. He had had Trout shipped from Portland so that he could, as Hugo put it, court death in Golden Gate Park in the mornings, but he didn't really need the horse for transportation. Nearly everything in the city was accessible by the red cable cars that slid up and down the hills on their humming wires.

Rosebay had fed her single boarder, who was now preparing to go out and prowl the darkening city—anything interesting that happened on the police beat occurred at night—and she was putting on her hat in front of the hall mirror when Tim came in the door.

"Do I look all right?" she asked him.

"You always look all right," Tim said. Rosebay would be beautiful dressed in an old feed sack. She had a cloud of blond hair, so pale it was like moonbeams, which escaped from its chignon in little tendrils about her face; pale, translucent skin; and bright cornflower blue eyes. Nobody had ever looked at her mouth and not thought about kissing it.

"I don't know. . . ." Rosebay peered dubiously into the mirror. She had on a walking dress of teal faille, and a tiny hat with pheasant feathers sat jauntily on her head. The outfit was her best, but she wasn't sure it was up to San Francisco's standards. Rosebay had never had nice clothes before she married Hugo, and she was still unsure of herself in them.

"Quit primping," Tim said. "You look fine."

"Better than fine," Hugo added.

"Seems to me this hat's too pert for an old married lady," Rosebay said. "But you picked it." She linked one arm through Hugo's and the other through Tim's and let out an excited breath. "I want to see *everything*."

"As much as we can stuff into one evening," Tim promised. Rosebay was an Appalachian mountain girl who had made the Oklahoman land-run in an old buckboard with a horse and mule for a team. Her husband had been shot in a drunken brawl the night before, and she had claimed her land alone, with her man's body in the back of the wagon, then dug him a grave with her own hands before nightfall. Under that beautiful package, Rosebay was steel clear to the core. She was endlessly fascinated by the world she had found since she had left Mossy Creek Hollow. Guthrie, Oklahoma, was the most cosmopolitan place she had ever been. Like a pair of conjurers wanting to strut their stuff, Tim and Hugo had been eagerly waiting to show her San Francisco.

They set out, occasionally dodging goats that wandered down the steep paths from the top of the hill. A dark-eyed girl ran in hot pursuit, her mother shouting in Spanish from the balconied shanties above.

In a block, they caught the cable car, and Rosebay settled herself excitedly on the bench as the car swooped downward into the business district. Dinner first, Tim and Hugo had decided. They were going to do their sightseeing properly, on full stomachs. San Francisco's French restaurants were famous, but none as much as the venerable Poodle Dog on Bush and Dupont, just on the edge of exotic Chinatown. The Poodle Dog had existed under various managements since the gold days and in its present incarnation served "the best dollar dinner on earth." It was famed for its frogs' legs à la poulette and its terrapin à la Maryland, and for the assignations that took place on the third floor. In the public dining rooms on the first floor, respectable wives and daughters might dine. In the private dining rooms on the second, they might venture with husband or father. Third floors in San Francisco were not mentioned by ladies.

Rosebay, having been informed of these interesting gradations by Hugo, looked enthralled at the massive plush-carpeted staircase. The waiter appeared to take their order, and while Hugo thought Rosebay wasn't paying attention, he ordered escargots for her.

"That's snails," Rosebay said indignantly. "You aren't going to make me eat them. Nor frogs' legs, either."

Smiling blandly, the waiter crossed out the order.

"Bring the lady a lobster," Tim suggested.

Rosebay had never had a lobster, but she decided she was game for that. "What do snails taste like?" she whispered to Tim while Hugo ordered them for himself.

"Like rubber, with garlic butter," Tim replied. "Hugo's showing off." He thought maybe he was, too—he had only had escargots once in his life. But it was such fun to watch Rosebay wide-eyed over the sights and the strangeness. *Poor kid*, he thought. *She hasn't ever had much fun before, just a lot of hard work*. Tim liked Rosebay. In fact, now that he thought about it, he would probably have walked through fire for her.

He ordered champagne, two bottles, and they drank it and laughed and told one another stories the way the three of them always did when they were together. Rosebay was a born storyteller, in the tradition of mountain dwellers, and Hugo was an amateur historian who knew things about wars and princes and royal dynasties. Tim's contributions were more down to earth, born of his varied experiences and the adventures of his father and grandfather.

The lobster appeared, and Rosebay regarded it with comic dismay. "Now look what you've gotten me into," she admonished. Tim showed her the right way to get the meat out without shooting the shell off the plate. Hugo ate his escargots and offered advice.

All three were a little silly and tipsy when they left the Poodle Dog and headed for the Orpheum Theater on O'Farrell Street. More intellectual entertainment could be had at the Alcazar and a higher-toned program at the Tivoli, but Tim insisted on the Orpheum. It suited his mood. The Orpheum was a vaudeville house that advertised every week "a show of amazing magnitude" and made good on it. Prices ranged from ten cents in the balcony to twenty-five cents in the reserved section and fifty cents in the boxes, and everyone in San Francisco went there. Tim had bought tickets for a box and happily escorted Rosebay and Hugo into it.

Rosebay settled in with a little shiver of delight and admired the painted curtain and then the painted ladies making their stately way down the aisle to seats in the front row, each on the arm of an admirer.

"Oh, look at their dresses," she whispered.

"You aren't supposed to look at them at all," Hugo whispered back, amused.

"Well, I know a tart when I see one," Rosebay said. "But, oh, what pretty clothes."

The queens of the gaslit demiworld, dressed in creations from France, were the fashion plates of the city. Their bills topped even those of Nob Hill matrons, who paid up to a thousand dollars for a gown from Worth in Paris, and their diamonds were larger than any a respect-

able woman would have worn. They displayed their ornaments with the gaudy, blissful certainty that the only gazes
worth attracting were male, and they knew that their
clothes set the fashion pace for the upright ladies who sat
with burning cheeks and gazes fixed firmly on the stage.
What the demimondaines wore this month would be copied
in subtler colors and with less lace by the respectable ladies
next month. And no one would ever admit it.

The curtain rose on a new soubrette, and then on a
comic. Hugo had brought a sketchbook and was doing
quick, telling caricatures of the audience: a portly gentleman who had the guilty look of a fellow out without his wife,
then a debutante wearing a pearl dog collar.

Tim watched Rosebay as much as he watched the
show. Her childlike delight was endearing, and he was
fascinated with her endless curiosity. When Rosebay
wanted to know something, she asked and didn't worry over
whether she seemed ignorant. So far she had demanded to
know what made the cable cars run, why it didn't snow
here, what the Turkish baths were like, and whether a lady
could bathe in them. Tim had answered everything he
could: The cars were attached to a cable underground, the
ocean kept the air too warm (he felt a little vague about
that), and yes, a lady could bathe in the proper ones. But he
could see that she was storing up more. She would probably
keep Hugo awake all night with her questions.

Tim didn't let his mind dwell on the thought of Hugo
and Rosebay at night. It was a subject that ate at Tim's
guilty conscience until the only way he could deal with it
was to pretend, as he thought Rosebay had done, that their
brief affair had never happened.

Unfortunately, every time he looked at her shining
eyes, translucent skin, and the flowerlike curve of her lips,
it came back to him. They hadn't meant to make love; but
Guthrie was a boomtown, and it had bred a lot of bad, wild
times, and they had been going through one of them.
Rosebay and he had both been feeling lost and miserable
and had taken comfort, at least for the moment, in bed with
each other. Afterward, Tim had felt like a skunk, but
Rosebay had said that it had been her fault, too, and never
reproached him. Hugo didn't know, hadn't known when he

had married her, and still didn't know. Tim was not foolish enough to ease his conscience by telling his friend. Unfortunately, every time Tim looked at Rosebay lately, he remembered that night in far too much detail.

I've got to quit this, Tim thought. *I need a girl*. The only trouble was that the waitresses in the saloons on the Barbary Coast didn't appeal to him, and neither did the more expensive ladies in the front row of the Orpheum. He was interested in something more than sex. What exactly, he was not sure, but it wasn't anything he ought to have in mind while looking at his friend's wife.

The Orpheum curtain dropped on the final act, and the Hungarian Orchestra struck up "Captain Jinks of the Horse Marines." Rosebay gave Tim a smile that turned his insides to water. He was sure that she had given Hugo a similar one, but Hugo was entitled.

"Where now?" Rosebay asked as they left the theater.

They strolled down the wooden sidewalk, and Hugo bought Rosebay a balloon while they pondered. The Englishman looked wistfully at the saloons that comprised San Francisco's famed Cocktail Route, but they couldn't take Rosebay there; the Cocktail Route was a gentleman's progression that began at five in the afternoon and might last, for the hardy, well past midnight.

"Haquette's!" Tim said, seized with inspiration.

"Certainly!"

Rosebay tied the balloon to her wrist, and the men swept her along breathlessly. Haquette's Palace of Art Saloon on Post near Kearny was noted for its oil paintings and crystal chandeliers. Women were allowed there, as they might be admitted to a museum.

Tim and Hugo bought Rosebay a champagne cocktail and ordered themselves each a Stone Wall of Jamaica rum and cider. Glasses in hand, they moved toward the free lunch, a specialty of Cocktail Route saloons. Haquette's included a huge Virginia ham cooked in champagne. Surrounding it were an immense wheel of French cheese, salami, smoked salmon, green onions, radishes, and loaves of crusty rye bread. It was entirely possible to take one's meals solely from the free-lunch counters of San Francisco's saloons.

Hugo spread a slice of rye with liver paté and handed it to Rosebay. "You'd better eat something." She giggled and bit into it, the balloon bobbing above her head. The bartender smiled at her indulgently. It was plain that she was a nice lady, out with her husband, and not too stuffy to have a good time. And she sure did dress up the place.

Hugo decreed that one cocktail was enough for a nice lady, so the friends went on down the street, letting Rosebay peer through the windows of the forbidden males-only saloons. The sound of a violin playing ragtime spilled out of the Peerless as they passed. Steve Douglas, who played in all the saloons along the route, was said to know more than eight hundred verses of "Frankie and Johnny." Rosebay's foot tapped as they guided her along.

On Market Street was the patent-medicine peddlers' field, a Gypsy encampment of wagons and tents, torchlit and loud. Banjo pickers, Japanese tumblers, jugglers, barkers, and shills extolled their wares. Beyond were the Eden Wax Museum and Dr. Jordan's Museum, where one might view, preserved in a jar, the head of Joaquín Murieta.

They ended up on a cable car going the wrong way. Laughing, they rode it to the end of the line and back again, the balloon flying out behind on its string in the dark salty air.

> "I'm Captain Jinks of the Horse Marines,
> I feed my horse on corn and beans—"

Hugo, hanging on to the railing at the back of the car, caroled happily as they flew downhill again. Except for an Italian housewife with a string bag in her lap, they were the only people on the car.

Rosebay leaned out and watched the gaslit city swoop by. When Hugo had finished his song, Rosebay began the melody they had heard coming from the Peerless Saloon.

> "Frankie and Johnny were lovers,
> O Lordy how they could love—"

And she had shot him dead with a forty-four, Tim thought, *for fooling around.* What would Hugo do if he found out about the love affair? Not shoot them, certainly, but their relationship would change forever.

They passed a huge building that hummed in the night. It contained the mechanism that endlessly reeled in the underground cable. Tim felt as if that one night with Rosebay had somehow become looped like the cable, so it passed over and over through his mind. He looked at Rosebay apprehensively, caught her looking at him, and wondered with sudden uneasiness how strongly the memory might come along the next time.

IV

Portland, Oregon

"Holt, you're a lying, conniving, coolie-loving—! Ach, the hell with you!" Ephraim Bender puffed furiously on his cigar and shot smoke at Toby Holt.

"Now, Ephraim—" Willis Larken attempted to get the meeting back on track. It was ostensibly a friendly conclave between Oregon's junior senator and his possibly erstwhile political supporters. In reality everyone else who happened to be hanging around the Jefferson Democratic Club of Portland today knew that Larken, Bender, and their cronies were in the private conference room calling Toby Holt on the carpet.

"I warned you," Toby said mildly. He lit a cigar and puffed smoke back at Bender. "When you wanted me to stand for election, I warned you that I wouldn't vote your pocketbook. And, as I recall, you were hot to make sure the coolies didn't all get shipped back to China."

"We didn't want them going around with the same voting privileges as white men," Bender complained. "This federal elections bill you've been supporting will have the Chinamen running the whole city. They breed like rabbits, curse it."

Toby chuckled. "At the rate you've been selling shoddy housing to unsuspecting easterners, Bender, I figure you can keep them outnumbered."

Bender glanced at him. His Portland Land and Auction Company prided itself on a reputation for Oregon boosterism. If its houses tended to fall down after five years, Bender didn't like it mentioned.

51

"Maybe you just didn't think it out," Willis Larken said hopefully. Larken was a banker and used to diplomacy. "This election bill is designed to keep the southern states in line, prevent them from denying freedmen their vote. We're all for that. But you didn't think out what it would do to the coolie situation here in Portland."

"I see," Toby murmured. "It's all right for Negroes to vote in the South as long as Chinese can't vote in Portland."

"Well, we haven't got that many Negroes in Portland," Donald McCallum said practically. "But the coolies now, we need them, you understand, but they have to be controlled."

"Once a railroad man, always a railroad man." Toby chuckled. McCallum was the Portland chairman for the Union Pacific. "Your folks brought the Chinese in. If you created a six-headed monster, I don't have much sympathy."

"Oh, for Pete's sake!" Willis Larken threw up his hands. "Have another drink, Toby, and don't be so stiff-necked. We put you up for election because we needed a man who could walk some kind of line between these blasted unions and the businessmen." Larken meant between the factions that wanted to expel the Chinese and those that didn't—primarily because the Chinese would work for lower wages than white men would stand for. Neither faction wanted them to vote, however.

Toby poured himself another drink, but he did not look conciliating. "I got the union vote," he pointed out. "And the coolies are still here. I didn't sign on to take further orders."

They glared at him as if the coolies might not be the only six-headed monster of their construction.

"That's not all," Bender growled. "Now you've let that Roosevelt loose on the city like a-a—"

"Wolf in a sheep pen?" Toby inquired. As civil service commissioner, Theodore Roosevelt was just beginning to sink his fangs into Portland's time-honored political-spoils system. "I may as well tell you, gentlemen, that the force hasn't been discovered that can stop Theodore Roosevelt. Presidents have tried it." He laughed. "Postmasters have tried it, and they have even more clout than presidents. If

Roosevelt thinks Portland needs investigating, it's not part of my job to lie down on the rails in front of his engine."

"Nor do ye want to!" McCallum snapped. "Ye're a do-gooder bloody anarchist out to upset the way of things. To my mind, ye're dangerous!"

"You ought to be grateful," Toby said. Now that they had started in on him, he was almost perversely enjoying himself. "It's in the railroad's interest"—he eyed Ephraim Bender—"and the land developers' not to have it said that Portland's a den of iniquity and corruption."

Willis Larken intervened again as he noted McCallum beginning to steam like one of his own engines. "Now let's try to be reasonable here. We know you have to vote your conscience, Toby. And we remember that you warned us at the outset. But if your conscience gets too many people riled up, the state legislature is going to vote you out next election. And then how much good are you going to be able to do? We'll get a Republican shoved down our throats, as like as not," he added gloomily.

Toby folded his arms and shook his head. "I won't back down on the elections bill, and short of shooting Roosevelt, I can't stop him. Is there anything else you want to complain about? I'm late for lunch, and my wife and my mother are expecting me." When this trio had been courting him to run for senator six years before, they had fed him an enormously expensive lunch at the Esmond Hotel. A whiskey bottle was all they had provided for chewing him out.

No one seemed to be able to think of anything else to say that wasn't incendiary. Willis Larken looked like someone trying to get a peace pipe lit in the middle of a war dance. Bender's and McCallum's expressions indicated that if Toby Holt was determined to be a one-term senator, that was all right by them. They would find someone else, someone more malleable.

Toby described the meeting to Alexandra and Eulalia when he slid into his place at the luncheon table. Sally was just finishing grace over a platter of Columbia River salmon. Alexandra and Eulalia sighed in unison.

"Just like Ephraim Bender," Alexandra said distaste-fully.

Eulalia nodded. "Absolutely like him. Your father wouldn't have liked that man at all."

"Who's Ephraim Bender?" Sally demanded.

"He builds cheap houses," Mike said. "They fall down if you breathe on them. He calls himself a developer, but slum landlord is a better description."

Sally waved all that away with a flick of her hand. "I mean, why doesn't he want Dad to get reelected?" That was the question that concerned her. "I'll *die* if he doesn't get reelected," she announced.

"Don't be so dramatic," Mike said. "You're too young to languish and have the vapors."

Sally shot him a haughty glance. "At least I don't moon around all the time writing poetry and talking to a photo-graph. 'Oooh, *Eden.*' It's terrible poetry, too."

"You're a brat," Mike said. "Eat your salmon before someone spanks you. I'll do it if you go in my notebooks again."

"Have they been like this all morning?" Toby inquired. "They're worse than McCallum and Bender."

Alexandra rolled her eyes heavenward, and Sally followed suit. Alexandra's personal maid, Juanita, had been left behind in Washington to watch over their house, and her assistance with Sally was dearly missed.

"Shouldn't Sally be stitching a sampler or something?" Toby asked.

"Would that she could," Alexandra said. It was doubt-ful that the domestic arts were going to be Sally's strong point.

"When women have equality with men," Sally said, "they won't need to sew samplers."

"Fine," Toby agreed. "You can go out with the crew and learn to bale hay." He was prepared for Sally to sniff and say that was boring—her word of choice at the moment—but she brightened.

"May I really?"

"It would pall on you pretty fast," Toby warned. He had baled more hay in his younger days than he liked to think about. "But you can put on a riding skirt and come out with me. I'm going to go over the place with White Elk."

Sally shot from the table before anyone could say "Finish your lunch."

Alexandra sighed. "I'm never sure whether we're raising a cowboy or a prima donna."

"Maybe we can blend them," Toby suggested. "Knock off some of those Washington airs and graces."

"Good," Mike commented. "She's getting to be an awful pill."

"She's not alone," Toby said pointedly. "Would you like to come, too?"

Mike shook his head, and Toby didn't press it. After he had finished eating, Toby changed into work pants and an old cotton shirt, then went out to the barn to find White Elk. Sally was there ahead of him, sitting on an overturned feed bucket, watching White Elk saddle the horses. She had on a divided denim skirt and a plain shirtwaist. A battered felt hat that looked as if she had filched it from one of the ranch hands crowned her rose-gold curls. They still hung down her back, but she had tied them out of the way with a piece of ribbon.

"When women are equal with men, they'll saddle their own horses," Toby teased.

Sally made a face at him. "I already did," she said.

"I got Sundance out for you," White Elk said, swinging a work saddle onto a palomino gelding. "He needs the exercise."

"Did you hear if that devil of Tim's made it to San Francisco without kicking the boxcar to pieces?" Toby asked.

White Elk grinned. "Trout was fine, but the wrangler came back and asked for double pay."

They led the horses out into the stable yard and mounted. Sally rode astride, which was just beginning to be respectable. Alexandra had determinedly set a fashion for it in Portland because she loathed sidesaddles, although Alexandra could have ridden sidesaddle without the saddle and not fallen off. Sally was nearly as good. All the Holts were accomplished riders.

"There's a fence down in the lower paddock," White

Elk said as they trotted out under the bright August sun. "That new stallion went courting on his own accord and took three rails with him. I've put Howie Janks and Coot Simmons on it. We ought to take on a couple more hands, though, if we're going to put in enough hay to increase the herd."

Toby nodded. "You pick them. Try to get a couple who'll stay long enough to learn the place." Oregon was still young country, and there was too much opportunity for work. The Madrona raised cavalry remounts, with Alexandra's show beasts as a sideline. Ranch hands had a tendency to tire of haying and would often decide to try being orchardmen, or sheep farmers in the high mountains. When that proved to be equally strenuous and boring— apricots and sheep had about the same general level of intelligence—the men would drift again. Toby thought that there was probably a single rotating stock of ranch hands that made a slow circle of all the spreads in Oregon, maddening foremen to distraction and high blood pressure.

"I'll see what turns up," White Elk said. "Somebody always does. I'll hire the next couple that come through if I don't think a posse's after them."

They rode out to the lower pasture and stopped to watch this year's crop of colts, born in the spring, chase one another through the field. They swerved in a wide spiral, tails up like flags, while the mares grazed.

"We got a good batch this year," White Elk said. The shadow of his hat made a sharp line across his cheeks, and beneath it the sun glinted on copper-colored skin. He wore a drooping handlebar mustache, as nearly every man did, and it gave him a roguish look, but he had settled into the foreman's job with the easy authority of having been bred to it. Stalking Horse, the Madrona's first foreman, who had died a few years before, had been his foster father. Only the new hands grumbled about "taking orders from an Indian," and they didn't grumble long. White Elk chivied them along, swore at them, cajoled them, and did more work than any two put together, and they knew it. And despite the prevalent anti-Chinese sentiment, White Elk's wife, Mai, had rapidly become their darling. Even though she was pregnant and had a three-year-old to raise, she cared for the ranch hands when they were sick, consoled them when they were crossed by love, and made them clean out the bunkhouse when the mess piled up hip deep. They adored her.

Thank God for the pair of them, Toby thought. In his and Alexandra's absence, Eulalia would now theoretically be in charge, but she was too old and frail to sit up at night with a sick man or a sick horse. She could make financial decisions and leave the physical demands of the Madrona to White Elk and Mai.

White Elk pushed his hat back on his head and pointed down the field. "There's one horse out of this crop it would be a shame to geld," he said. "That bay colt, there. I'd like to keep him if you don't think it would be too much inbreeding. Or you could sell him for a stud and get a good price."

"Keep him if you think so," Toby said. "Breed him to the new stallion's get."

"Why?" Sally looked interested.

"Oh Lord, I clean forgot you were here," White Elk said.

"I know where foals come from," Sally said regally. "I am not a baby."

"All right then, since you know so much. Because too much inbreeding spoils the bloodline and makes the foals unhealthy. It's why men aren't allowed to marry their sisters."

"Oh." Sally appeared to be mulling that over.

Toby wasn't sure how his mother would take to this conversation, but he believed that farm girls had a better grip on the realities of life than other, more sheltered members of their sex. It saved them no end of shock when they married. Alexandra had told him that she had known girls who were absolutely ignorant until the moment that their newly wedded husbands climbed into bed with them.

People were idiots, Toby thought musingly, and from there it wasn't a very long step to reflecting for the fortieth time that Ephraim Bender and Donald McCallum were idiots, too, with no more grip on the nature of man than those poor befuddled schoolgirls. He had *told* them. He had warned them when they asked him to run that he wouldn't dance to their tune. Now they were acting like outraged virgins.

Toby took a deep breath of air, heavy with the scent of horses and grass, and looked over the rolling gold swell of the hay fields and the emerald carpet of the pasture. The new colts were kicking in the sun. Behind them rose the green mountains. There had been a mist, and now a shred of rainbow hung in the air, dissipating as he watched.

Why the hell do I want to go back to Washington anyway? he asked himself. Muggy Washington, thick with the vaporous air of politicians. *Partly because I am needed.*

Oregon did need him to counteract the Benders and McCallums so the state might grow up with some kind of responsibility and compassion for all its citizens. Toby grinned to himself, aware of his motivations. He liked being among those who made events happen.

Well, we'll see, he thought. If he didn't get reelected, he could very happily spend a lot of time on the Madrona in this clean, green peace. But he was going to give reelection his best shot. And he would do it his own way. Ephraim Bender could stick that in his pipe and smoke it.

Toby put his heels to the palomino's flanks and followed White Elk down to the brood-mares' pasture, where a ranch hand was pouring oats into a feeder. In the distance he saw a slender figure in work pants and a slouch hat stalking along the fence line opposite, coming from the house toward the lower hay field. Toby thought at first that it was Alexandra, who occasionally wore trousers when she was reasonably certain that no genteel acquaintance from Portland might come calling that day. Then he realized that it was Mike, who was taller than his mother now and had a more loose-limbed stride. When he took off his hat, his red hair flamed in the sunlight. Mike wiped his forehead and put the hat back on without breaking step. He was, Toby saw with a kind of exasperated irritation, using the fence as a guide to keep him from walking into trees because he wasn't looking where he was going. He was reading from a sheaf of papers in his left hand, while the fingers of the right trailed along the fence rail.

Toby knew exactly what the papers were: Eden Brentwood's letters. When Mike wasn't writing to Eden, he was rereading the letters she had sent to him. Toby would have given a lot to know what was in those missives. How serious could the children be, really, at sixteen and seventeen? Tim thought it was the real thing, worth being careful with. But what did Tim know? *What do I know, for that matter?* he wondered.

Neither he nor Tim had had any sense at seventeen, and for both of them, first love had been an unmitigated disaster. The mere mention of the names of the respective young ladies was still enough to make them both flinch. Mike seemed to be in another situation entirely. But this obsession with her letters . . . with reading and rereading them and writing to her for hours. Toby had thought of putting a stop to that, of limiting Mike to one letter a month, of trying to defuse the situation, but he was fairly sure that Mike would simply write to Eden on the sly. No, forcing him into subterfuge wouldn't solve much.

Toby gazed at Mike again. He was standing perfectly still beside the fence. He was reading, but he looked poised for flight, one palm against the post as if to push off from it.

I can't leave him here, Toby thought. *If I go back to Washington, he goes, too. I can't turn my back on him.*

Mike looked down the gentle slope that swelled from the far side of the field to the flat creek bottom in the brood-mares' pasture and thought he could see his father watching him. Toby was too far away for Mike to be absolutely certain he was being watched, but he was pretty sure he could feel his father's eyes on him.

Someone was always watching him. It made him restless and edgy to be so hemmed in. Maybe they watched him because he was restless and edgy—he didn't really know.

He had hung a calendar on his bedroom wall and marked off each day as it came. Plenty of people did that all their lives, but Mike had a specific place to *stop* marking: 4 July 1894, his eighteenth birthday. After that, he had promised himself, he would never be in a hurry for a day to end again. He knew very well that because of his tricky heart, he might not have too many days. . . .

*   *   *

Toby saw Mike stick the letters back in his pocket and start walking again, not toward the house but down to the creek bed, angling away from where Toby, Sally, and White Elk were riding. A deliberate change of direction, the pace of someone who didn't want company.

Sally saw him, too. "He gets so surly," she complained. "I risk my life just to talk to him."

"Mike's having a tough time," Toby said. "Try not to rile him."

"He riles *me*," Sally protested. "And he locks his door all the time, even when he's in there."

"Stay out of his room," Toby said. "That's Mike's territory. When you're older, you'll feel the same way."

"When I am older," Sally said loftily, "I will not moon around kissing boys' pictures and writing them silly poems. *They* will have to write them to me."

Toby blanched. The thought occurred to him with horrible inevitability that once he had Mike raised, Sally would be next in line. She was going to be neither dutiful nor docile, although she was most certainly going to be beautiful. Sally was going to test her parents' sanity.

Toby spent the next month going over the ranch with White Elk, riding every square inch of it, inspecting every hay bale and saddle leather. He wrote an amused letter to the quartermaster at Fort Vancouver, who wanted to buy remounts from Madrona stock and seemed to expect Toby to lower the price as a tribute to the late general Blake. Raising the price would be more appropriate, Toby informed him, so as to support the general's widow in better style.

He wrote less genial letters to his political supporters, real and theoretical, announcing both his intention to stand for reelection and his refusal to change his spots in order to do so. He went over the herd books—the pedigrees as carefully kept as those of Mayflower descendants—and pored over the account books, preparatory to giving his mother the financial reins of the Madrona. The latter would simplify his life greatly, Toby thought, and Eulalia most certainly could run the ranch—she and his father had begun it.

By October they were ready to go back to Washington. Sally was gleeful. She had a store of tales to tell Alice: She had grown half an inch over the summer. She was taller than her cousin and archrival Midge Blake and might be taller than Alice, too.

Mike was not ecstatic, but neither was he disturbed. If he wasn't with Eden, it didn't matter much to him where he was. He packed his trunk when told to and went back to reading Eden's letters.

"What are we going to *do* with him?" Alexandra asked. She looked distracted by more than Mike.

Amy Givens, the housemaid who was helping with the packing, wore an expression that said that Mrs. Holt had been in a tear all day.

"Watch him like a hawk," Toby suggested.

"Oh, Toby, do you mean that? I can't bear to think that Mike would do something . . . well—"

"Impetuous?" Toby suggested dryly. "Ill considered? Flat-out stupid? All I know is, I'm not giving him the opportunity while he's in this mood. He's too much for my mother to handle, so he'll just have to go back to school in Washington. It's his own blasted fault."

"I'm just so worried about him I can't concentrate," Alexandra said. "He doesn't like that school. And everything seems to be happening at once." She ran her hands through her hair, making it stand out wildly. "White Elk says the roan mare is going to foal tonight—you know, the one who always nearly dies?—and you know what *that's* like. We'll be lucky to get through dinner."

"There is no reason for you to help a mare foal," Toby said. "White Elk is perfectly capable of—"

"And Howie Janks is sick, and of course he won't go to the doctor unless White Elk practically ties him up—"

"Which White Elk is also capable of doing. Alex, why are you getting all wrought up about this stuff? The horses and the hands both get taken care of just fine when you aren't here. I know you're worried about Mike, but you seem to be compounding that into a feeling that the whole world will fall apart without your personal attention."

"Maybe I am," Alexandra admitted distractedly. "I can't seem to think straight about it. And now this boy's coming to dinner. And don't tell me to leave *him* to White Elk, because—"

"What boy?"

"The Schumann boy. I told you this morning. No, maybe I didn't. Maybe I told Abby."

"You told Abby," Amy confirmed from the depths of the trunk. Abby Givens, Amy's sister, was the cook. "She's going to bake a nice fish. And a cobbler."

"I don't need the menu, thank you," Toby said. "Alex, will you please calm down? And, Amy, will you keep out of it? Now, who is the Schumann boy? Not Dieter's son?"

"One of them," Alexandra said. "Yes. He telephoned this morning from the Esmond Hotel. He's in Portland on business. He sounded quite nice."

"Fine. We'll be glad to see him. But you don't have to do anything more than just feed him. It's not a visit of state. His father probably told him to look us up." Dieter Schumann was an old friend and business partner. "It'll be interesting to see how he's turned out. It's been years since I last saw the boys. Which one is he? What's his name?"

Alexandra looked blank, then panic-stricken. "Oh, no! I can't remember!"

"Walter or Daniel?" Toby said. "You have a fifty-percent chance of being right."

"Daniel," Alexandra breathed. "Thank God."

"You know," Toby observed, "if you go completely crazy, I will have to lock you in the attic and feed you gruel and toast."

A piercing shriek erupted from the hallway outside the door. "Let me go! Oooh, you beast, let me go!" Sally's voice rose in an infuriated howl.

"Stay out of my things, or I'll put you across my knee," Mike threatened.

"I didn't want to read your dumb letters anyway!"

"The attic would be quite restful," Alexandra remarked to Toby. "See if you can arrange it."

The Holts entertained Daniel Schumann at dinner with Abby's "nice fish." Toby had collared Sally and Mike beforehand and threatened them with banishment to the kitchen if they squabbled during dinner. Instead, Sally made faces at Mike across the table and Mike ignored her with aloof disdain. Dan Schumann seemed to be entertained by them, and when they noticed it, they were annoyed.

Schumann was a personable young man in his twenties. He was solidly built like his father but with a more dapper air. His mahogany-colored hair had a slight and well-subdued wave across his forehead, and his evening clothes and his manners were impeccable. He greeted Alexandra with the utmost propriety, but custom dictated that more flattering liberties might be taken with old ladies, and he bowed over Eulalia's hand and kissed it. When they went in to dinner, he took charge of her fan and cane and settled her into her chair. Eulalia beamed at him.

Mother's eating this up, Toby thought, amused. "I'm afraid we're leaving for Washington tomorrow," he said, "but you're welcome to stay here for a few days. I know Mother would be delighted."

"Of course I would," Eulalia said.

"That's very kind. The Madrona's a wonderful place. You must be extremely proud of it."

"Your father's well, I hope?"

"Oh, Father's thriving." Dan smiled. "He sends his regards."

"You're in Portland on business for the firm?"

Dan waved his hand in a gesture of gentlemanly embarrassment. "Well, not exactly. That is to say, I am, but it's been concluded. Actually, I'm in search of employment. Father feels I ought to have experience outside the firm. I've been kicked out of the nest, to tell you the truth."

Toby laughed. "Not permanently, I trust."

"Good Lord, no. But Father is firm about my having outside experience. He thinks it will make me a better manager."

"I think that is entirely sensible," Eulalia said. "What sort of position are you looking for?"

"Dear Mrs. Blake, anything at all," Dan replied. He looked penitent. "You see, I'm partly to blame. Father and I had a mild disagreement on how to handle a deal, and I made the mistake of saying that I could get another job in a week if I felt like it. He gave me two weeks. I'm going to be mortified if I can't put my money where my mouth was."

"I expect my mother can introduce you to some likely prospects," Toby said. "I'll be glad to give any son of Dieter's my personal recommendation."

"That's awfully kind of you. I'm charmed with Portland. It seems very . . . well, clean and promising, after Chicago. It would be pleasant to live here for a time."

"It's still new country," Toby said. "My father led the first wagon train to come to Oregon, you know. My mother was on it."

Dan gave Eulalia an admiring look. "Before I leave I hope you will tell me all about your adventures. What experiences you must have had!"

"I did indeed," Eulalia agreed, "although at the time they seemed extremely unpleasant and vexatious. Only in hindsight does one realize that one has made history." But she smiled at him, and when he smiled back, she relented. "Very well, if you want the whole—and, I assure you, quite interminable—story, you shall have it. Tomorrow, when I am feeling fresher."

"That young man has made a conquest," Alexandra said, laughing, to her husband the next morning as they watched Eulalia and Daniel Schumann return from a prebreakfast ride. The grass and the madrona trees still sparkled with dew, and from their window Toby and Alexandra could hear the quiet clip of the horses' hooves and Eulalia's silvery laughter. "He rides very well, doesn't he? Quite a beau."

"He's pleasant enough," Toby allowed. "And kind to pay attention to Mother. I like that, even if he is just being polite for his father's sake."

"Well, it's good for your mother. If he settles in Portland, maybe he'll call on her while we're gone."

They went down to breakfast to find Eulalia and Daniel already at the table.

"Did you have a good ride?" Alexandra asked. "And where are Mike and Sally?"

"They already ate," Eulalia answered. "They were

grazing in the pantry when we set out. And yes, we had a lovely ride—although I'm glad Daniel was with me, or I would have landed in the creek."

"Mrs. Blake's horse took exception to a large frog on a rock," Dan explained with a grin. "Froggy shot into the water right under the poor horse's nose and completely unnerved it."

"The beast bolted with me." Eulalia looked at her hands and sighed. "I'm simply not strong enough anymore. Dan rode up beside me and reined us in."

"I'm relieved you were there, young man," Toby said. "Thank you." He turned to Eulalia. "Maybe you shouldn't ride by yourself, Mother."

"I shan't in the future," Eulalia assured him.

She seemed unhurt, but Toby thought she was shaken. When breakfast was over and they were waiting for White Elk to bring the wagon and buggy around, Eulalia cornered Toby in his study.

"Toby dear, didn't you tell White Elk to hire two more hands?"

"I did, but nobody suitable has come along yet."

"I know, dear. That's why I wanted to talk to you. You're in charge, of course, but I think Daniel would be perfect. I'd like to offer one of those jobs to him."

"He couldn't want to hire out for a ranch hand," Toby said. "I imagine he was quite high up in Dieter's firm. I know you'd like to have him stay, but—"

"That's where you're wrong," Eulalia said briskly. "Daniel says he's looking for a change—'since I painted myself into a corner' was the way he phrased it—and a chance to work in the fresh air instead of sitting behind a desk. He can't stay forever, of course. He's bound to go back to his father once he's proved his point. But if he wants to take a vacation from business by working as a ranch hand, I don't see why we shouldn't help him."

Toby kissed her cheek. "All right, Mother. Whatever you wish." He could see Alexandra pacing in the hall and hear the crunch of wagon wheels in the carriage drive outside. "In any case, you're in charge now. Hire him with my blessing. I'm always glad to do Dieter's family a favor."

V

Dan Schumann watched as the departing buggy rolled down the drive, followed by the loaded wagon. Beside him, Eulalia waved a handkerchief at the buggy. Dan put a hand gently on her arm. "You're going to miss them."

"Oh, I am." Eulalia sighed. "You'd think by now I'd be used to it. Toby's father and my second husband, General Blake, rarely stayed in one place for more than a month at a time. I feel very bereft when my loved ones leave. Maybe I'm just getting old."

Dan smiled affectionately. "Not you!"

Eulalia gave him an amused glance. "You are an accomplished flirt. I have no idea where you get it. Your father was never that way."

"He often used to flirt with danger, I've heard, but now he never flirts with anything. My father is much too solemn."

"Shame on you," Eulalia scolded. "Dieter Schumann is a good man. One of the best. And you know it."

Dan chuckled. "Of course I do. But a fellow can't hop along in his dad's footsteps all his life; he's got to cut a trail of his own if he's going to be any kind of a man."

"So he does," Eulalia agreed. "And when you've cut yours, you and Dieter will both be better for it."

"I'm sure we will," Dan said. "Now if I'm going to earn my board and keep, I had better send to town for my things and present myself to your foreman. I'm planning to write to Father tonight, too. Shall I give him your regards?"

"Please do."

And that, Dan thought, satisfied, *ought to keep the old lady from writing to him herself.*

Dan had shaded his description of his parting with his father. According to Dan's viewpoint, it was the old man who had been at fault.

Dan had never been able to understand how a knock-down businessman like Dieter Schumann could have gotten so pious, just on account of Toby Holt's influence. Dan had heard the stories of what his father had been like: Every competitor in the lumber business had been scared to death of Dieter Schumann. What Schumann wanted, Schumann took, and he was as slippery as mercury and as ruthless as a shark. Then Toby Holt had come into his life like some damned preacher, and Dieter had just rolled over and licked Toby's boots.

Eulalia had gone in the house, and Dan stopped by the stable yard and looked around contentedly. He'd show his father that it paid to deal smart and leave the praying to the preachers and old maids. His mouth twisted as he remembered his parting interview with Dieter Schumann. . . .

"I won't have it!" Dieter's fist had come down hard on his big mahogany desk, rattling the inkwell and slopping water out of the bowl of flowers that his wife put there every morning. "No son of mine is going to give this firm a name for sharp dealing. Do you hear me, damn it?"

"I hear you," Dan snapped.

Father and son glared at each another. They were both big men, muscular and competent looking. Dieter was heavier than his son, and he looked on the verge of testing if he was still stronger. His eyes blazed under bristling red brows, and he thrust his chin out.

Dan shrugged, knowing that that particular gesture infuriated his father. "I haven't done anything illegal, and I've made a nice profit for the company. If the city of Chicago accepts the work as done, then why the hell should I run around trying to give away money?"

"You've allowed this firm to do substandard construction," Dieter retorted. "If some city official is willing to take a payoff for allowing that, then he's as dishonest as you are. If that building crashes down someday and kills innocent people because the reinforcing's no good, you'll answer to God for it."

Dan's anger flared. "Where do you get off preaching at me? You used to be the toughest customer in town. Just because you've gone soft doesn't mean anything except you've lost your nerve. Well, I haven't lost mine."

"I've stopped construction on the job," Dieter said flatly. "The building will be pulled down and rebuilt. That's going to be expensive, and I'm stopping your salary until I've recouped what you've cost me."

Dan yelped in outrage. "What am I going to live on?"

"You live at home with your mother and brother and me," Dieter pointed out. "The only reasons you need money are for helling around in saloons and whorehouses and playing cards. It might do you good to give up all three for a while."

Dan glared at him. "You're trying to humiliate me publicly. This company would be twice the size it is now if you'd listen to me."

"I built this company," Dieter fumed. "From nothing, after the market crashed and we lost it all. We could lose it all again, too—that's how life is. Life doesn't owe Daniel Schumann a living, and you aren't special. The only thing that gives life some meaning is people watching out for the good of other people. Society has to connect with itself, has to care for its own. If you put yourself outside that system, then you aren't a man."

"I've turned a profit, haven't I?" Dan asked belligerently. "What the hell else do you want?"

Dieter Schumann smacked both fists on the desk. "You still don't get it, do you?" He half rose in his seat, hands resting on the desktop, still balled into fists. "I was the toughest kid on the block, tougher than you ever dreamed of. I grew up poor. Nobody ever handed me an allowance."

"I know, I know." Dan waved his hands wearily.

"Listen to me," Dieter said. "I sold produce out of a cart. I always claimed the busiest street corner. If anybody sold produce for less, I wrecked his cart and smashed his melons. When I had enough money, I started in with lumber mills. And when someone underpriced me, I hired a few men to cause accidents at his mill."

"You got rich that way, you hypocrite," Dan pointed out. "Principles were an afterthought."

"Rich and then poor," Dieter said. "Poor taught me a sight more than rich. The only decent thing I had in life back then was your mother. God alone knows why she married me. If I hadn't changed, she might have worked up the strength to leave me. Abigail nearly died of loneliness. We were invited everywhere—everyone was too scared of me not to—but no one was a friend. I had no idea what I was doing to her and to you boys. You and Walter hardly knew me, and when you did see me you used to flinch. I must have stomped around looking as if I was about to hit somebody. After I turned my life around, I never knew things could be so good. Even when we lost all our money, Abigail stuck with me, and we had good times. I had come down to working as a day laborer, doing odd jobs for farmers to keep you boys fed, so don't you yowl about having your salary cut. I slogged my way through until Toby Holt gave me his lumber business to manage."

Dan snorted. "Oh, yes, the sainted Toby Holt. Why don't you just build a shrine to him in the living room?"

"Why can't I make you understand?" Dieter said, frustrated. "Toby Holt turned my life around, and I owe him for it, and I'm going to go on owing him. When I first met him, I thought he was the most stupid, naive bastard I'd ever met. He believed that a man could get ahead by playing fair. But I knew that people who played it straight got their backsides kicked by people like me. Then he asked me a question I couldn't answer."

Dan took a cigar out of the humidor on his father's desk and lit it. He blew smoke out impatiently.

"He asked me what my life was worth," Dieter continued quietly, "in terms of what point and purpose my life had. I couldn't answer. My life didn't have any point. All the money I was so hot to lay my hands on wasn't making me happy, and a lot of people already looked forward to dancing on my grave. Nobody but Abigail would mourn me—assuming that she stuck around."

"Most women will stick around as long as the money holds out," Dan said lazily.

Dieter stood up now, kicking his chair back. His eyes nearly shot sparks, and Dan realized he had gone too far.

"We are speaking of your mother!" Dieter shouted. "You haven't listened to one word! Maybe it's all my fault; maybe it's in your blood. You're just like I was at your age. But I overcame it, and you will, too. I am suspending you without pay for six months, effective immediately. Spend the time thinking about your life, and if you come back a better man, I'll allow you to work for this company again."

Dan stood up, too, and flung the cigar into a brass bowl on the floor by his father's desk. "How can you kick me out? I'm your son!"

"Since your philosophy is every man for himself," Dieter said, "that shouldn't matter to me; however, I am trying to do you a favor. Somebody has to wake you up, Dan, or you'll be a worse animal than I ever was."

Dan turned and stalked out, and that was the last interview he had with his father. He went home and flung clothes in a trunk while planning how to exact his revenge on Toby Holt. Then he told his mother good-bye and left for Oregon.

He had stayed a few days in Portland's Esmond Hotel, to give the impression of having conducted some business, before he telephoned the Madrona and introduced himself. It had required all his self-control to cross Toby Holt's path and be pleasant. But he had a burning desire to create problems in this man's life and to prove that his father's idol had feet of clay. That would fix Dieter Schumann! And he had already come up with a very good idea.

"Daniel, you must be exhausted." Eulalia gave him a concerned look as he sank onto the parlor settee with a sigh of relief. She had assigned him a bedroom in the big house so he wouldn't have to live with the ranch hands.

Dan gave her a quick smile. "I'm just out of shape. I've been working behind a desk for the last seven years. A few weeks, and I'll toughen up."

"Well, you mustn't overdo."

Dan chuckled. "Tell that to White Elk, Mrs. Blake."

"Yes, he does work the ranch hands rather hard. But you said that was what you wanted." Eulalia sat beside him and patted his hand. She looked around her at the twin tables at either end of the settee and the round, marble-topped one in the center of the parlor. All were cluttered with framed photographs, wax flowers, seashells under bell jars, and all the other accumulated bric-a-brac it was fashionable to display. "Now what have I done with it?" she murmured.

"What have you done with what?" Dan got up. "Allow me to fetch it for you."

"My knitting, dear," Eulalia replied. "I was certain I brought it in with me. In a straw basket. You know the kind—like a picnic hamper?"

Dan scanned the room. "There it is!" He pounced.

"How curious." Eulalia stared as he retrieved the knitting basket from the window seat on the other side of the room. "I never sit there. It is much too hard on my back."

Dan presented the knitting to her with a flourish. "Perhaps it migrated on its own. Certain items have a tendency to do that, I find."

"Only when there are children about," Eulalia said. "I must have put it there myself, but I can't think why."

"Then don't bother to try," Dan said. "Are you cold? It's really fall tonight, isn't it?" He unfolded a lap robe from the armchair opposite and spread it over her knees. "Now all you need is a cat to hold it down." Five or six cats had the run of the Madrona, but after dinner they generally congregated in the kitchen for leftovers.

"No, cats get tangled in the knitting." Eulalia chuckled. "But thank you for the thought."

"How about a cup of tea, then?"

"Thank you. I should like that very much. Just ring for Abby."

"I'll fetch it," Dan offered. "Abby has plenty to do."

Eulalia smiled after him and snuggled comfortably beneath the lap robe. She got out her knitting, and the needles began to click. In a few minutes Dan was back with the tea. A cat was slung under his other arm.

"Tea for you, cat for me," he said, settling himself at the other end of the settee. The cat purred in his lap.

"You'll get hair all over your trousers," Eulalia protested.

"I'll brush it off. I like cats. I expect I take after my aunt Min."

"Was she a cat lover?"

"She's the one I told you about who—" He cocked his head at her thoughtfully. "You don't remember my telling you about Aunt Min?" Then he said briskly, "Well! I must not have. I just thought I had. I'm *sure* you'd remember Aunt Min. . . ." His voice trailed off.

Eulalia looked at him, puzzled. "Usually I don't forget things. First my knitting and now—"

"I probably never mentioned her in the first place," Dan said heartily. "So now I shall. Aunt Min had forty cats. She never did get along with her husband, Uncle Bob. He hated felines, so to spite him, she kept getting more cats. Every time Aunt Min and Uncle Bob would have a fight, she would get another cat. Whenever he sat down, a cat would jump on his lap, and he'd start to puff and wheeze. After Uncle Bob died, Aunt Min used to wear black serge mourning costumes so covered with cat hair that she looked like a woman in an odd fur coat."

Eulalia laughed appreciatively. "Of what did your uncle die?"

"Well, theoretically he had a heart attack, but Mother suspected he died as a reaction to all those cats. Aunt Min had a cat carved on his tombstone, so I expect he's still upset."

"Turning in his grave, I should think," Eulalia said.

"No doubt. You are certain I didn't tell you about Aunt Min before?"

"I-I don't know," she said. "I didn't think you did, but . . ." Her face was troubled in the glow of the gaslight, and her hands stilled the clicking needles.

"Then I didn't," Dan said. "My memory is dreadful, truly it is." He patted the cat, and it yawned at him. "I think maybe this beast has the right idea. It must be bedtime."

Eulalia nodded and put the knitting away. She tucked the basket into the corner of the settee and gazed at it as if to assure herself of where it was. Dan gave her his arm, and they mounted the stairs. He patted her shoulder at her bedroom door, saw her safely inside, then went back downstairs to turn off the lights. The parlor lamp's glow faded. Dan waited until his eyes had adjusted, then he picked up the knitting basket and made his way back upstairs.

In the morning the sun streamed in the bedroom windows, warming Eulalia with its light. She washed her face in the basin in the bathroom—Toby had a most up-to-date house—and dressed quickly. She was always up early. Abby would just now be starting the fire in the stove. The air was chilly but invigorating. *There's nothing wrong with my memory,* she thought, her doubts of the night before beginning to fade.

Dan, dressed for work in boots, denim pants, and a flannel shirt, was waiting for her at the breakfast table. He still looked starched and pressed somehow, and Eulalia wondered how he did it. His natural urbane polish appealed to her, and his take-charge air, so like her husbands' and son's, accorded with her ideas of how a man should behave. He passed her the biscuits and poured her a cup of coffee, and Eulalia basked in his attention. She was honest enough to acknowledge that and enjoy it anyway.

"Thank you, dear." She sipped her coffee. "You are very comforting to an old woman."

"Now, you stop thinking of yourself as old," Dan chided. "The only thing that makes people act old is if they think about themselves in that way. It's all in the mind."

That last sentence caused Eulalia to experience a little ripple of apprehension. And in the evening she couldn't find her knitting basket again.

"Fine whiskey, Mr. Bender. Mighty fine whiskey." Dan Schumann downed the last swallow and nodded approvingly. "Always glad to do business with a man who knows his whiskey."

Ephraim Bender poured them both another drink from the bottle he kept in his office. Bender's business suite in Portland's financial district was solid and prosperous looking, with heavy oak furniture and thick rugs. Everything in it was heavy, as if to reassure prospective clients that Ephraim Bender was no fly-by-night; this was a man with the weight of responsibility on his shoulders, a man on the up and up.

It was Bender's not so up-and-up enterprises that Dan Schumann was interested in, however, and they both knew it. Dan had informed Ephraim upon their first meeting in the parlor of Maisie's, Portland's most elegant brothel, that he could smell a crook a mile away. Ephraim had laughed appreciatively and said the same.

"I'll be glad to invest some money for you in a few good ventures," Bender said now. "Maisie has a girl who wants to open her own whorehouse, given the right backer. Maisie gets a cut, so she's amenable. Just don't let old Mrs. Blake get wind of it. She's pious enough to shame a preacher, and she could make real trouble."

"I wasn't born yesterday," Dan informed him. "Or even in Portland. In Chicago we got the hang of these things long ago."

"Then you know I'm not running a charity house," Bender said. "I'm going to want something in return."

"I expected as much," Dan said dryly. "I have a better proposition for you than a cut of my profits, though."

"Everybody thinks he has," Bender said wearily.

"This is a first: Local rumor has it that you've been itching for years to get your fingers on a piece of the Madrona."

"I bought a piece of it a few years back. Holt didn't want to sell to me, but after a brutal winter of nonstop blizzards, he got in a financial jam. A lot of farmers and ranchers lost their shirts or their lives. Toby was forced to sell a few acres to raise cash, and he let the land go to some eastern investors. I got it off of them a couple months later and put up some nice little houses on it. Mrs. Holt was in such a fury you'd think I'd put whorehouses there."

"You'd like more acreage from the Madrona, wouldn't you?"

"Of course I would," Bender growled. "Portland's growing so fast, developers can hardly keep up with the demand. All those folks need houses, and I'm the man who builds them the fastest. That's prime land over there on the Madrona, going to waste as pasture."

"Well, I may be in a position to help you, if you'll just keep your mouth shut and leave it to me."

Bender studied Dan for a long moment. "All right," he said finally. "I'll take a flyer on that. What kind of timetable are we talking about?"

"This isn't a railroad," Dan said. "We're not talking about any timetable. There's some delicate maneuvering involved, and if you push it, it'll blow up in our faces."

"What are you up to? Holt's in Washington. Bad cess to him," Bender added. "He'll be lucky if he can get elected to rubbish disposal commissioner in the next election."

"That's of very little concern to me," Dan said, "as long as he stays in Washington for the time being."

Bender looked as if understanding was dawning. "The old lady, eh? Eulalia's a tough old bird. What makes you think you can get around her?"

Dan grinned. "I happen to know what ladies like, Mr. Bender."

Eulalia stood staring at the heavy cut-glass bowl laden with fresh chrysanthemums and ivy on the hall table. She touched the flowers tentatively, as if to make sure they were real.

"Amy?"

Amy Givens appeared from the parlor, dust rag in hand. "Yes, ma'am, Mrs. Blake?"

"Amy, where did these flowers come from?"

Amy gave her a puzzled look. "I guess you fixed them, Mrs. Blake, like you always do."

"I did nothing of the sort!" Eulalia reached out to touch the flowers again, then drew back.

"Well, you must have," Amy said, shrugging. "They're just like you do them. And I asked Mr. Schumann where you was this morning, and he said he saw you in here fixing flowers."

Eulalia turned abruptly and went into the kitchen to speak with the cook. "We'll have a chicken for dinner tonight, Abby," she said. "And peas." *I am not going to think about those flowers.*

At dinner she looked nervously at Dan. White Elk and Mai ate with the ranch hands, so it was just the two of them at the table. "Dan, dear, do you remember what time it was when I arranged the flowers? I, er, put some pastry in the oven when I started, and it was overcooked when I took it out. I'm wondering if I read my watch wrong."

"Pretty early, I should think," Dan said, buttering a biscuit and giving the matter some thought. "I was just on my way to the barn. Seven o'clock, maybe."

"Then I did do them," Eulalia whispered.

"Well, of course you did. And very pretty they are, too. I like flowers in the house."

"I don't remember arranging those flowers," Eulalia said. Her mouth quivered as if she were frightened and about to cry. "And my knitting was lost again this afternoon. I found it upstairs, but I don't *ever* take it upstairs."

Dan put down his knife, reached for her hand, and patted it. "You mustn't read too much into a little absent-mindedness, Mrs. Blake. I'd forget my own head if it wasn't attached."

"My grandmother forgot things," Eulalia said. "Toward the end of her life she was . . . well, she couldn't be left alone. Since I have gotten this far with a clear mind, I had hoped that I had escaped impairment."

"And I am sure you have," Dan said heartily. There was just the faintest forced note in his voice. "You mustn't worry so much about a few flowers."

Eulalia looked at her dinner and smiled shakily. "I'm not sure I'm really hungry, dear. Please excuse me."

It would all seem better in the morning, she told herself, undressing for bed. She simply needed more rest than she had been getting, trying to run the Madrona at her age. At her age. . . . What if she was losing her memory? losing her mind, like her grandmother? No! Eulalia pushed the thought away. She felt quite clear in her mind; she was certain that she did. She could see a doctor, of course. . . .

And what would Dr. Bright say? That she was fine. There really wasn't any reason to make an appointment. She was far too busy, and it would be a waste of the doctor's time, too. Doctors hated old ladies with imaginary complaints. But what if it wasn't imaginary? She could talk to Toby about it, but he already had enough to trouble him.

Eulalia prided herself on her ability to bear up, no matter what the adversity. But her mind fading? She didn't know how she could cope with that. She counted the instances that troubled her: losing the knitting, twice; not remembering the floral arrangement. . . . It really didn't amount to much, looked at that way. Silly, really.

Eulalia climbed into the four-poster bed that she had shared for so many years with Lee. She focused her eyes on the window opposite, tracing every line and angle, and the pattern of the madrona tree outside it, holding to that clarity of vision.

Downstairs, Dan finished his dinner at a leisurely pace and poured himself a glass of port from the decanter that Abby had set before him. Dan was a favorite with the Givens sisters. They were plain to the point of nonentity, and Dan was certain that very few men even noticed their existence. He, however, treated them with a gallantry that never crossed over into the vulgar or the overly familiar but that nonetheless acknowledged them as women. They loved it.

After Dan had drunk his port, he lit a cigar, stepped out onto the front porch, and stretched. His muscles were finally accustomed to physical labor, although he disliked it intensely. He was thankful that it was merely a means to an end.

Lights were on in the bunkhouse, meaning that the hands had finished their meal and were settling in for the evening. Another pool of light spilled down the porch steps of the foreman's cottage across the road from the bunkhouse. Dan walked in that direction.

He found White Elk sitting with his chair tipped back, booted feet on the porch rail, while his little son played on the floor. Mai sat in a rocker, stitching a baby garment. They were a hell of a pair to be running the place, Dan thought irritably. He didn't like Indians or Chinese. By the time he was through, they'd be long gone.

Just now, however, he settled himself politely among the hands who were sitting on the porch steps. Bill Eddings had brought his guitar, and the hands were arguing over what he should play.

"You slumming, Schumann?" Howie Janks inquired. He moved over to give Dan a place to sit, but the remark was only half-joking. Dan generally spent as little time as possible among the other workers.

"Mrs. Blake's gone to bed," Dan said with a grin. "So I'm off the hook for family duty one night. My father is a friend of Toby's. He'd skin me alive if I wasn't nice to the old lady."

"Is she feeling all right?" Mai asked. "It's very early to go to bed."

"Not if you're seventy-six," Dan said. "She was upset because she couldn't remember tonight what she'd been doing this morning."

"That doesn't sound like Mrs. Blake," White Elk commented.

"We all get old, friend," Dan said. "Mental faculties break down along with the rest of our body."

"Mrs. Blake is perfectly clear in her mind," Mai said firmly.

"I hope you're right," Dan said. "I'm awfully fond of her."

Bill Eddings began to play, and Dan decided he had taken it far enough for one night. He wasn't about to rush his fences, no matter what Ephraim Bender might want. His machinations were complicated, and a power of attorney wasn't something Mrs. Blake was going to sign over to him unless she was desperate. The trick was to make her desperate before Toby Holt showed up again. Dan figured he had plenty of time for that.

VI

The smell of salmon permeated the air. It was tangible, like the grease on the walls. Paul Kirchner thought he could reach out a hand, grab a lump of the stench, and mold it into a live fish. He had never smelled anything so over-powering, or by this point so nauseating—not even in his family's Wisconsin brewery, to which he had shown the back of his heels five years before.

He inhaled deeply, trying to breathe past the fish, as the open cans rattled past him on the conveyer belt, to be stuffed with fish before proceeding to the next station, where the air would be extracted, lids slapped down, and the whole mess heated to the proper temperature to prevent spoilage.

"I'll tell you, Paul my boy, it's getting to me." McCarty Brewster, the next man on the factory line, shook his head dolefully at the never-ending belt of open-mawed cans. "I never thought I'd get tired of salmon, mind you, but a man can't take but so much. It's time for me to move on."

Paul wiped his hands on his black rubber apron, which served only to smear the fish oil already there. "Where to?" With loathing he eyed the bin of salmon fillets before plunging his hand into it once again. "Not too many jobs open for a man with vast experience at stuffing fish in a can."

McCarty considered that. "Well, I don't know, but there's bound to be something. Clerk in a store, maybe. I got a girl—her daddy's a policeman. I might get on the force."

79

Paul gave a hoot of laughter. "Sure. They'll just fall all over themselves trying to hire you, being the prize you are."

"Well, I don't have to tell them about that trouble I had in Utah now, do I? I always say a man ought to pride himself on his discretion."

"Yep," Paul agreed, "especially if he's got a criminal record."

"Well, I've got to get out of here," McCarty said. "I don't care what I have to do. Me and salmon canning have just flat come to the end of the line."

"Let me know if the police department wants two new men," Paul said. He was beginning to feel much the same way. He'd had the cannery job for six months, and that was about all the human nose could stand. The men who had been here stuffing salmon into cans for years had probably destroyed their sense of smell completely, he thought.

"Oh, no," McCarty said. "Give people a choice between us, and they'll take you, you being so clean-cut and all."

Paul chuckled. He was slender and not particularly muscular, with straight fair hair and the wandering eye of a dreamer. He had neither a bar-brawl scar nor a tattoo, whereas McCarty had both. "That's just because I have extensive experience at a number of vocations," Paul said. "Unfortunately, I wouldn't want to do any of them again."

"Such as?"

"Baker. Blacksmith. Cowboy. I was an artist's model once. You'll find me hanging over the judge's bench in the circuit court of Laramie, Wyoming, in the person of Perseus rescuing Andromeda. Classical themes are thought to soothe the overwrought during their day in court."

"Perseus who?" McCarty asked.

"Perseus and Andromeda. Figures from Greek mythology."

"You got any clothes on in this picture? Seems to me them Greeks were naked all the time."

"Not in court in Laramie," Paul replied. "I was a brewer once, too."

"And you *quit*?" McCarty looked at him in bafflement that anyone would leave a job with such opportunities.

"It was my mother's brewery," Paul explained. "I was supposed to be the next master brewer, carrying on the tradition of the Obergs. The minute I could, I took off as if the hounds of hell were after me."

"Lord God a-mercy," McCarty groaned. "When you could have settled in to live in a brewery?"

"People who work in breweries don't drink the beer, you ignorant soak," Paul said. "My mother eats, sleeps, and lives beer, but she doesn't drink it."

"How come?"

"Spoils the palate. She tastes it and spits it out. Never seasons her food, never drinks anything but buttermilk and water."

"And she wanted you to do the same? No wonder you left."

"Well, it wasn't entirely her doing. I had other reasons. But she was among them."

"If your family's rich enough to own a brewery, what are you doing here stuffing fish?" McCarty asked. "Must have been better jobs you could get."

"Only if I had stayed home and could have fended off Mother. But I wanted to see the world. Very exciting, seeing the world—at least I thought so just last year."

The factory whistle shrieked, and Paul and McCarty gratefully filled a last can each as the belt rumbled to a stop. Then they shuffled down the slatted walkway, which was slick with water and smelled pungently of the scraps of fish that fell through the slats to the yard below. They stuck their time cards through the glass window, where a disinterested clerk stamped them and shoved them back.

"Checks will be ready in an hour," the clerk said in a bored voice. "Or you can pick them up on Monday."

"I'll wait," Paul said. He stuck his face against the glass and made a fish face at the clerk. "Fish will no longer rule my life. I'm quitting."

McCarty brightened at this announcement. "Me, too," he declared. "Me and Mr. Kirchner here plan to seek a better class of employment."

"Good luck," the clerk said, stamping the next man's card. "Next?"

The two young men moved out of the way to wait.

McCarty sat down next to Paul on an upended crate. "Where you gonna look?"

"I think I'll try cowboying again," Paul replied. "I know a place where I might have an in." He shook his head at McCarty's hopeful look. "That's providing I don't bring you along. These are nice folks."

"And I ain't?" McCarty asked indignantly.

Paul contemplated the white scar on McCarty's chin, which had been inflicted by the broken end of a long-neck beer bottle. "You 'ain't' indeed. You go court your policeman's daughter, butter up her old man." He grinned down at the tattoo of the bare-breasted lady who writhed sinuously along McCarty's forearm. "Keep your sleeves rolled down."

"Hard to court a girl on cannery pay," McCarty said glumly. "My next check's kind of spoken for."

"Is Louie Weasel still after you?"

Louis Wessell, who ran most of the gambling joints in Portland, had been christened Louie Weasel by unfortunates like McCarty, who found themselves caught in his snare.

"I'm into him for another fifty, but it'll bump to sixty by next week if I can't pay."

"Louie's just a small-time little hood, isn't he?" Paul asked.

"Not if you can't pay him," McCarty answered. "Then he's real big-time."

Paul dug into his pocket and pulled out a ten-dollar bill. "Look, just pay him off with your check, all right? This ought to feed you till you can get a new job."

McCarty accepted the money that had been pressed into his palm. "You're a sport, Paul, I swear you are. I'll pay you back as soon as I get work, word of honor."

"Just stay away from Louie Weasel, okay?" Paul knew McCarty wasn't going to pay him. He never had yet.

Lady Theodora Montague drew her buggy to a stop in the circular drive that swung past the Madrona's rose garden. She stuck the buggy whip into its socket, pulled off her pigskin driving gloves, and climbed down easily. She inspected her crumpled tweed skirt, apparently deciding that it would do, straightened a sensible felt hat on her graying pompadour, then marched up the porch steps. A couple of brisk thunks with the door knocker summoned a response.

"Good afternoon," Teddy said to the plain-looking housekeeper facing her. "I am here to see Senator Holt on a matter of business." The voice was brisk, strong, and of the British aristocracy. "My card." She produced a square of pasteboard and eyed the housekeeper expectantly.

"He's not here," the young woman said. "But you come in. I'll get Mrs. Blake." Unspoken but obvious was the thought, *Maybe she'll know what to do with you.*

The guest sat on a hall chair to wait, balancing a walking stick across her knees. In a moment she could hear a woman's voice say "Good heavens" in the next room, and then a regal, elderly woman appeared, with a dapper young man behind her.

The woman held out her hand. "Lady Theodora, I'm so delighted to meet you. I am Eulalia Blake, Senator Holt's mother. We've heard of you, of course, from Edward Blackstone."

"Call me Teddy. Everyone does. I don't stand much on ceremony. I'm the family disgrace."

"Lady—Lady Teddy is an explorer," Eulalia said to the young man. "Allow me to present Daniel Schumann, who is the son of another old family friend."

Teddy and Dan shook hands and sized each other up.

"I'm here to buy horses, Mrs. Blake," Teddy explained. "Edward Blackstone tells me you sell cavalry remounts. Just the thing, I said to myself."

"Of course," Eulalia said. "My son is in Washington, but I have no doubt we can accommodate you. Our foreman is very experienced. I'm sure he can help select what you need. And if I am to call you Teddy, you must call me Eulalia and stay with us for Christmas. It isn't but a few days away."

Dan coughed gently. "Well, perhaps slightly longer than that. Just a few weeks."

"Weeks then," Eulalia said. "I haven't completely lost track." She gave Dan an uneasy glance, and he smiled and patted her hand. "It's just that time seems to move so quickly now at my age."

"Thank you, I should love to stay," Teddy said. "Weeks or days—it is immaterial to me. I should like a family Christmas. No fixed abode, you know. Don't get many holidays properly celebrated. I don't suppose there will be children?" she added hopefully.

Eulalia smiled. "I'm afraid Toby's brood won't be home this time. But there is little Tommy White Elk, our foreman's son. He's three and a half."

"Well, I don't know what better offer you could make me," Teddy remarked, "than Christmas with a three-year-old."

"Are you fond of children, Lady Teddy?" Dan asked.

Teddy found something a trifle patronizing in his smile, the sympathetic look of a handsome young man conversing with a tall, stocky old maid. "Yes," she answered thoughtfully. "They are very unspoiled at that age and haven't learned to put on airs." She didn't know when she had ever taken such a thorough dislike to a man at first sight. She wondered why and wondered if maybe she had more vanity than she had thought. If so, it was her problem, not Dan's.

With that thought in mind, she managed to stay much more in charity with him during dinner and even to consider him quite personable when she found he knew horseflesh.

"You can help me pick them out," she said cheerfully, offering that as a high treat to make amends. "I want the toughest little beasts, the scraggly ones that can live on thistle if that's what's handy. And I don't much care what they look like. No budget for beauty, you know. I pried some money out of my brother when I realized I have to have pack animals, but he was shirty about it."

"Your brother doesn't approve of your explorations?" Eulalia asked.

"If he could prove I was insane, he'd lock me up," Teddy said frankly. "As it is, he shuffles his feet and looks sheepish when my name comes up, and he tells everyone I'm eccentric. When I need money I threaten to come home and lecture to the local geographic society on tribal ornamentation among the Zulus or some such."

"That hardly sounds objectionable," Eulalia said.

"What the Zulu ornament is is their bodies." Teddy chuckled. "They hardly wear any clothes, whereas I think Vincent, who's the earl of Banbridge, wears a cravat to bed. The maddening part of it is that if I were his brother instead of his sister, he would be quite proud of me. Nonplussed— Vincent can't see any point in knowing about anything beyond the borders of the empire—but still proud."

"It is certainly an unusual profession for a female," Dan remarked.

"Any profession is unusual for a female," Teddy retorted. "That is precisely what needs to be changed."

"Are you a suffragist, Lady Teddy?"

"And proud of it," Teddy said flatly.

Because Dan wisely declined to pursue the incendiary topic further, dinner continued genially, with a discussion of Teddy's numerous jaunts about the world.

"I've just been to Palestine and the Sahara—amazing place—and ventured a bit into the Gobi, although you want to go very carefully there and pack good rifles and hire plenty of men to shoot them. Been to Tibet."

"Have you traveled in the Western Hemisphere before, Teddy?" Eulalia asked. "It all sounds very exotic and extremely troublesome, but I can tell from your enthusiasm that you couldn't have borne any other life."

"Right you are. Edward Blackstone and I took a jaunt to the Amazon," Teddy said, grinning. "Nearly ended up with our heads on poles. We came home with rubber-tree seeds—*most* illegal and very secretive, but the East India Company was tickled. I was paid a very fancy price for those seeds, which kept me in travel money for years. That was almost twenty years ago, though. I've had the urge to go back to South America ever since."

"What is your destination?" Eulalia asked.

"Tierra del Fuego. It's never been properly mapped, and I've a fancy to be the one who does it. Very bleak country, a fine place to sort out your soul if you've a need to." Teddy raised both eyebrows in a characteristic expression that meant that she was about to state what everyone knew—although possibly declined to admit. "We've all got a thing or two to unload from our souls. I find that the bleak places are the best for shedding that sort of baggage."

"I suppose they are if one is carrying any," Dan said in the manner of a man who considered his soul to be without blemish.

"Pooh," Teddy scoffed. "Everyone's carrying something." She narrowed her eyes at him. "It may be that some people just don't know their baggage when they see it—or would just as soon hang on to it. It could be that."

If she had hoped for acknowledgment of fallibility from Dan Schumann, she was mistaken. Dessert was served and eaten amicably, with no further discussion of anyone's soul.

But Teddy watched thoughtfully as Dan helped Eulalia up the stairs. It would drive her crazy, Teddy thought, to have someone hover over her in that fashion. But Eulalia Blake looked to be in her midseventies, Teddy was fifty-five, and those twenty years made a world of difference. Furthermore, Eulalia obviously liked men, especially as suitors and gallants, whereas Teddy perceived them as obstacles or hunting companions. It took all kinds to make a world, and Teddy Montague knew that she was in the minority and therefore in no position to be scornful of feminine women.

All the same, something indefinable about the relationship between Eulalia and Dan bothered her.

When Teddy Montague came down to breakfast in the morning, Dan was in the kitchen, arranging a vase of flowers. He jumped at her footstep and put the vase down with a quick, fluid gesture as if to hide it. *Maybe he's embarrassed to be caught doing women's chores,* Teddy thought disgustedly. He struck her as a very masculine man in all the most annoying senses of the word. *Well, I won't let on that I caught him.*

"I'm going out to view the stock after breakfast," Teddy said. "Would you like to come with me?"

"I'll be there involuntarily," Dan said affably. "I'm a working guest. I answer to White Elk for my pay. Mrs. Blake kindly supplies the room and board, and I try to pay her back as best I can with my moral support. It's a great burden to run this place by herself, and she's beginning to feel it."

"Well, I'm sure she's glad to have you," Teddy said absently, scanning the morning newspaper, which was picked up in Portland every day by one of the ranch hands and left on the kitchen table.

Abby Givens bustled in. "You two are early birds, and me with my biscuits not even started. I declare, we've had more traffic through this place! There's a young man at the back door now, looking for work. I tell him I don't need anyone to help me pluck chickens, but he just laughs and says he'll wait for the boss. I say the boss is in Washington along with the rest of the politicians, sending the country to hell in a hand basket, and he can wait for Mrs. Blake, who isn't up yet, or White Elk, who's up and gone. So he has the nerve to ask for breakfast and says he'll chop firewood for it."

"Will you give it to him?" Teddy asked.

"Course I will. We don't ever turn anyone hungry away from this place—boss's orders. And I could use a stack of wood. Every time I try to collar one of those cowboys, they come up with an excuse that they've got to see a doctor or mend a hole in the fence or some such silliness. Cowboys are useless. That's all there is to it."

"Abby, you have nearly shamed me into volunteering to chop wood," Dan said, "so I am vastly relieved that this drifter outside needs breakfast."

"You need breakfast, too," Abby said, "and if you don't git, I won't have room to fix it." She was shaking flour into a sifter as she spoke, and Teddy and Dan beat a retreat into the backyard.

"Might as well look at some horseflesh now," Teddy said. She strode off toward the barn, with Dan behind her. She had the oddest feeling that he was dogging her footsteps to keep an eye on her and not just because she had invited him.

In the yard they found Abby's drifter splitting wood. He took off his battered felt hat when he saw Teddy and said, "Good morning, ma'am. Are you Mrs. Blake?"

"Mrs. Blake is not up yet," Dan said. "What's your name, fellow?"

The man with the ax started to reply, but then he took his hat off again, scratched his head, and surveyed Dan.

"Puddin' Tame," he said. "I'm here to see Mrs. Blake."

"Mrs. Blake will see you when she's had breakfast," Dan said. His voice held an edge. "I asked you your name."

"Puddin' Tame. Ask me again, and I'll tell you the same." Paul went back to splitting wood.

Teddy grabbed Dan's arm before he could push it any farther, which he looked about to do. "We were just headed for the barns," she said firmly. "It was nice to meet you, Mr. Tame. Perhaps we'll see you at breakfast."

She heard a chuckle from the man as the ax sheared through an upended log and buried itself in the chopping block. "My manners are better at breakfast," he said over his shoulder.

As Teddy walked toward the barns, she saw Dan shoot a look back, suggesting that hell would freeze over before he would let Mrs. Blake hire the newcomer. Teddy decided that she might just put in her own two cents' worth.

After inspecting the horses, Teddy and Dan returned through the kitchen, wiping muddy boots on the doormat, beside a neat stack of freshly chopped wood. They found the interloper inside, with his arms in a tub of bread dough.

"A man of numerous skills," Teddy approved.

"I always earn my breakfast, ma'am."

Dan gave him a look of loathing. "Don't plan on eating it with Mrs. Blake. She will give you an appointment when she is ready to see you."

The man bent his head toward Teddy as Dan went into the breakfast room. "I've already been invited. Mrs. Blake is quite nice."

"And did you get around to introducing yourself, or are you still Mr. Tame? My name, by the by, is Teddy Montague."

"Mine's Paul Kirchner," said the man. "You're quite nice, too. How did you come to be in the company of yon surly lout?"

"I am a fellow guest. And you, if you want a job, will not aggravate him. He's a pet here."

"You got that bread dough punched down yet?" Abby

appeared and stared appraisingly at the tub. "That'll do. Put the cloth on it and leave it rise again. Get washed up for breakfast."

"Yes, ma'am." Paul went to the sink and began to scrub the dough from his hands.

Curious, Teddy went into the breakfast room and, finding nobody there, continued on into the parlor. Eulalia was there, warming her hands at the fire. In heavy black mourning clothes that seemed to weigh her down, she looked very frail to Teddy. Dan sat on the loveseat nearby.

"Good morning, Eulalia. Inundated with guests, eh?"

There was a light in the old woman's eyes, half exasperation and half amusement. "That curious young man belongs to Maida and Frederick Kirchner. We knew his parents when Toby had a lumber business in Wisconsin. They brew Oberg Beer."

Teddy raised her eyebrows. "I've tasted that. Fine stuff."

"Toby thought them an interesting family. Maida is German, the last of the Oberg brewers. She's an odd woman. Maybe that accounts for young Paul."

"He seems personable enough," Teddy said. "I liked him."

Eulalia waved a hand in resignation. "I'm glad to hear you say that because I had to give him a job. He's the son of friends, and we need another hand. I hope White Elk takes to him. I've usurped his prerogative."

Dan smiled at her. "You're the boss lady. If you want to hire orangutans, White Elk will have to put up with it." He chuckled. "I expect he might prefer the monkeys to young Kirchner, though. He's a shiftless drifter by my estimation, and I'm a pretty fair judge of men."

"He's split a load of wood and prepared bread so far this morning," Teddy defended. "More than any of us claim to have done."

Dan looked irritated, but he didn't say anything. Abby stuck her head into the empty breakfast room from the kitchen and yelled, "It's ready!"

They filed in and sat down. Eulalia and Teddy settled at either end of the table, and the young men took seats between them. The sunny yellow breakfast room opened to the kitchen at one end and the dining room at the other. Outside the window nearest the kitchen was a sill where Abby had spread toast crumbs for the birds and corn for the squirrels and chipmunks. It was crowded with finches at the moment, jostling one another and snapping up crumbs or fighting their own reflections in the glass.

"Human, aren't they?" Teddy observed. "Battering away at their own image."

Paul laughed gently, but Dan, buttering toast, said, "Humans generally aren't so foolish as to waste time fighting phantoms instead of the real enemy."

"One's fellowman?" Paul suggested.

"Those who make it necessary," Dan replied.

"Satan," Eulalia said. "There is the adversary."

"And so often found in one's mirror," Paul said.

"Only if he's looking into it," Dan said smoothly.

Teddy wondered what else Paul saw in his mirror and what Dan Schumann would find in his if he looked at it squarely. It would be an interesting Christmas, she thought. Any minute now the two young men would begin to bark and snarl at each other like rival dogs.

Eulalia seemed to sense that, too. She laid a hand on Dan's arm to convey affection, agreement, and the wish that he should be quiet. He patted her hand and remained silent for the rest of the meal. Paul Kirchner finished his breakfast, carried his plate into the kitchen, and headed for the barn without waiting for Dan.

White Elk had returned, and Paul planted himself in front of the foreman. "Mrs. Blake sent me," he explained. "She's sorry for hiring me without consulting you, but my parents were friends of the senator's."

"What can you do?" White Elk asked.

"Ride fence. Green-break horses. Blacksmith."

"Can you bale hay?"

"Reluctantly."

White Elk looked amused. "Well, if you can really blacksmith, maybe you won't have to bale hay. You can start by shoeing that one."

He jerked his thumb at a sorrel stallion pacing in a

loose box. The horse rolled its eyes at Paul, snorted, and gave the slats of the box a good kick for effect.

"Sure," Paul said. "Get me someone to put a twitch on him."

"I like a man who isn't foolhardy," White Elk approved.

When Dan, after his second cup of coffee, passed by the blacksmith shed on his way to join the hay-baling crew, he saw Paul heating a shoe at the forge and whistling "Red River Valley" with many grace notes and flourishes. He put the shoe on the anvil and shaped it while the sorrel stallion waited.

A rope noose was twisted around the stallion's upper lip, and a ranch hand held it tightly. Dan had a strong desire to rip the twitch off the horse and hope the beast kicked Paul Kirchner into next week. That that layabout should have been given a job by a warm forge while Dan was about to go out and bale the last of the hay in near-freezing weather seemed a gross injustice. Paul Kirchner would be thrown off the ranch as soon as Dan got his hands on that power of attorney. He had laid a little more groundwork this morning: He had quickly poured Eulalia's tea while she was in the kitchen with that horsey old maid, then sat back and watched her start to pour more. She had flinched when she realized that her cup was already full. He'd thought the old lady was going to cry.

Paul watched Dan stare at him angrily and then veer off toward the hay fields. *He's up to some game,* Paul decided. Paul had been on the road too long not to recognize a man with an angle. Exactly what he was plotting was less certain. Since Paul had very little certainty about his own motives, he sometimes found it difficult to fathom others'. His mother's, for instance. Paul held the shoe against the sorrel stallion's off rear hoof and thought about his mother. The shoe was a near fit. He put it back on the anvil and gave it another lick, thankful that he had never gotten to the point of striking out at his mother. He had wanted to often enough.

Maida Oberg had come from Germany specifically to brew beer in Wisconsin. She was the last of a long line of master brewers as single-minded, humorless, and unstoppable as railway engines. In Maida's case, her one-track personality had been clothed in an eye-pleasing package, and Paul's father, Frederick, had married her out of sheer adoration. That love had continued unabated and left Frederick singularly ill-equipped to mediate between his wife and his son.

Frederick Kirchner had been shy and unassuming and a severe disappointment to his own robust, hearty father. Frederick's idea of reparation for that was that Paul should be the son that Maida wanted. She grew her own hops and was as monomaniacal about their cultivation as she was about everything else connected with beer.

If young Paul had been a tun of stout, he would have received far more attention than he had as a child. From babyhood, he had been trained to follow in his mother's footsteps. Only his maternal grandmother had seen and understood how he hated it. When he was nine, in desperation, he had blurted out to his mother that he didn't want to make beer. They had not stopped fighting with each other since.

Maida had tried everything: shouting, whippings until he was too old to put up with them, and accusations of unfilial behavior until he felt that his mother thought the world would end if no Obergs brewed beer. "You have a responsibility to your ancestors!" she would shout. "You are last of a line! You cannot let it die! You are a *disgrace*! You are not fit to brew my beer!"

"I don't want to brew your beer!" he would shout back, and they would scream at each other until his teeth were on edge.

Frederick would never venture out while these cyclones were raging. He would hide in his office with a bottle of his wife's beer until the shouting ceased. Dinner would be eaten in silence. After dinner Paul would retreat to a book, and his mother would immerse herself in minute calculations on her brewing calendar. If there was work to be done in the brewery or the cellar, she would prod him until he either came with her or refused, and the cycle would begin again.

Paul had felt a certain kinship with the silly finches

outside the breakfast-room window. Whether he was his mother's reflection or she was his, they had both been pounding their heads against each other's for years.

Probably he wasn't ever going to understand his mother, but she wasn't going to understand him, either. It was all part of the orbit around which they rotated, opposite each other. It wasn't ever going to change. It was why Paul had left. He could stand being tied to that orbit only if he could keep a few hundred miles between his mother and himself. It made the circle so big that most of the time he didn't notice the curve.

VII

"Of course I'm not too tired. If a man is in top condition, then physical exercise is merely invigorating." Dan smiled and patted Eulalia's shoulder. "You're the one who's tired. If I thought I could take all this responsibility off your hands, I would, but I don't quite have the hang of running the ranch yet."

"You will," Eulalia said. "You really are a comfort to me, Dan. There are times when I feel so exhausted. If Teddy takes those ten horses, will the lower pasture have enough feed to see the rest through?"

Dan looked at his calculations and nodded. "Yes, I think so. Although you might want to check my math."

"All right, if it will make you happy." Eulalia took the notebook and ran the figures over in her head. "They look accurate to me." She wondered if she would know if they weren't. The last time she had reviewed Dan's figures, she had gotten different answers each time, while he always came up with the same one. She was feeling frightened that her mental capabilities were faltering. She made a joke of it to mask that. "I trust your mathematical abilities. Didn't you tell me you took a prize in it?"

"The Senior Mathematicians' Prize in college," Dan said. "But the truth is, there wasn't much competition. Now, about these patent feed racks that White Elk recommends . . ."

"Yes, tell White Elk to go ahead. Toby installed those in half the stalls a few years ago. I'm sure he would approve of adding the rest."

Dan gave her an odd look. "I hope so," he said, "because you told us to order them two weeks ago. I was trying to tell you that they've arrived."

Eulalia, wide-eyed, stared at him. Her hand crept up to her lips, and her fingers shook. "Dan, I don't remember that."

"I'm sure it just slipped your mind," Dan said. The false assurance in his voice would have fooled no one. "Now then, let's not worry about anything. I'll try to take all the burden I can for you."

"I hate to lean on you like this," Eulalia said wearily. "You have your own work to do. Maybe White Elk could hire a part-time hand and free you for half the day to assist me. Would you mind?"

"Why, Mrs. Blake, of course I wouldn't mind! It might be beneficial for me. I want to learn all I can about managing livestock. I feel very strongly that my father should diversify as protection against another depression, and ranching would be a perfect choice. If he had someone with experience to manage the venture, I think he would agree. There are also some experimental farming ideas that I'm interested in. Agriculture has to modernize to stay profitable. But I don't know enough yet to be certain of my ground."

"Very well," Eulalia said. "I'll tell White Elk."

"If he could get a little more work out of Paul Kirchner," Dan said, chuckling, "he might not need the part-time hand."

"I'm afraid Paul isn't exactly a ball of fire," Eulalia agreed. "Be grateful that you were born with more ambition."

"Some men naturally lack ambition," Dan said. "Or possibly they fear success. Success involves responsibility, and men like Paul Kirchner shy away from that. It's why he left his family business, I imagine, and he's probably led a disreputable life since then. It's very charitable of you to keep him on these last few weeks." Dan picked up Eulalia's hand and kissed it gently. "You have a very kind heart."

"Maybe if he stays on, he'll learn to be more like you," Eulalia said. "Through example. I'm sure his mother hopes so."

*   *   *

The subject of their discussion was shoeing a restive horse. Paul spoke to it in soothing tones as he worked. He was so engrossed in caressing it with words that he didn't notice Teddy Montague, who had strolled over from the barns to join him.

"You'll know a dragon pony by its whiskers," he informed the roan horse while it cocked its ears at him. "Disguised dragons all have dragon whiskers—they can't hide them. So if you meet a mare with droopy whiskers, just like an old Chinaman, well, I'd look out if I were you." Paul took the roan's front hoof between his knees and pounded the first nail in. "You don't want to get mixed up with a girl like that."

"Gypsies talk to their animals," Teddy said. She sat down on an overturned feed bucket. "They whisper in their horses' ears and blow up their nostrils and such nonsense to calm them, but what really does the trick is the talking. Horses don't seem to care what is said."

"Not so far as I can tell," Paul said, amused. "Although I've always found them fond of Hänsel and Gretel."

Teddy laughed. "And of dragon ponies. You'll give them ideas. Have you traveled much in China?"

"Not at all," Paul said. "I've just been talking to Mai. She's fascinating—very American and very Chinese, and the two cultures seem to be wrestling within her. We're all finches at the window, I expect."

"Most certainly," Teddy said, picking up his allusion immediately. "Are you coming to dinner tonight to watch us do it formally?" It was Christmas Eve, and although Paul had a standing invitation to the big house, he chose as often as not to eat with the ranch hands and to sleep in the bunkhouse.

"I've been informed that I'm expected," he said gravely. Despite the fact that Eulalia and Paul seemed to have nothing in common, she determinedly treated him as the son of old friends, and as such, he would certainly spend Christmas Eve with the family. "I'll put on a cravat and the shirt with no soup stains." His eyes smiled at Teddy over the roan's hoof.

The Englishwoman gave a bark of laughter, and the

roan swung its head around, startled. It jerked at the foot between Paul's knees, and the horseshoe nail he had been about to drive home slipped and ran itself into the roan's fetlock. The roan lunged and sent Paul flying. It lashed out with its back hooves and stamped the smithy floor with its front ones. The nail was jarred loose, but the horse had already worked itself into a panic. The front hooves came down again hard as Paul rolled frantically out of the way, trying to draw a breath of air. The roan jerked its head back again and snapped its halter rope. Teddy tried to grab the flying end, but the animal shot past her into the stable yard.

"Oh, hell and damnation," Teddy said. She looked at Paul, who had climbed to his feet and was dusting himself off beside her. "I'm sorry. That was my fault."

The roan had cleared the fence and was galloping, head up and tail high, across the front lawn of the ranch house. The creature looked as if it was having a good time.

"Apology accepted." Paul forced a grin. The roan's hoof had caught him in the spine, and the welt burned like fire under the shoulder blades. "Life is like that."

He crawled under the fence and then nearly toppled over at the stabbing pain in his back. He found Teddy in his wake. The roan stopped in the middle of the lawn and watched them. As they neared, it flung up its head again, snorted, and began to race in circles.

"Do you think it's amusing itself?" Teddy asked, panting.

"I'm certain of it."

"Let's see if it's above the lure of oats," the woman suggested. "You stay here."

Paul put his hands on his hips and stared at the horse. The roan stared back. Paul eased forward. "You're going to be awfully embarrassed if someone has to get a lariat and rope you," he told it softly. The roan nodded its head. "That's right. Think how humiliating." He took two more cautious steps. "If you were a dragon pony, you could just turn back into your natural form and swallow me whole. But you're not, are you? You're just an old cow pony, about as dumb as a box of rocks, and you're going to come along nice—"

He eased forward again. He was only about five feet

from the roan when he saw a flash of movement beneath the madrona trees that lined the drive behind the horse. The roan reared with a shriek and came down nearly on top of Paul. Someone had thrown something, a rock most likely, at the roan—Paul had seen a shirt cuff in the shadow of the trees, as white as a crescent moon against the dark red trunks of the evergreens.

There wasn't time to worry about who it might have been now, though; the maddened beast seemed to associate him with the newly experienced pain, and, teeth bared, it lunged at him again and knocked him flat. Paul rolled, realizing that the horse was deliberately trying to trample him. The roan came after him, and he made a desperate dive for its halter rope, using the trailing end to pull himself up and the roan's head down. The horse snapped at him, and its teeth sank like pliers into Paul's forearm. Paul swore, punching the soft flesh of the horse's nose with his fist until it let go, leaving his arm smeared with blood and foam.

The roan reared and lashed out again with its front hooves, one of them dangling a half-nailed iron shoe. Paul yanked on the broken halter rope, cursing whoever had thrown that rock. The roan was seriously trying to kill him. The half-nailed shoe had twisted, so that with every step the roan's foot was wrenched sideways. This seemed to madden the creature further. It reared, shaking the hoof. Paul ducked, terrified. If that shoe came off at the right angle and with enough force behind it, it could go clean through his skull.

The roan came down on its hoof again, screamed furiously, and snapped its teeth at Paul as he tried to bring his grip on the rope up to the roan's headstall.

"Great Scot!" Teddy shouted, climbing the fence without bothering with the latched gate. She ran toward Paul. The oat bucket was gripped in her right hand and left a trail of feed along the ground.

"We're going to need more than oats for this baby," Paul grunted.

Teddy nodded and dropped the bucket. She pulled at the scarf around her neck as she tried to position herself to help.

While Paul hauled on the rope, Teddy made a tackle at the roan's head that would have done credit to a football player and got the scarf around its eyes. "Hold him!" she cried out.

"I've been trying to," Paul managed from between gritted teeth. But the roan was already beginning to stop heaving.

"Remarkable how dumb horses are," Teddy said, knotting the scarf. "If they can't see, they often settle right down."

Paul stroked the roan's bony nose. "Well, you're a fine, dumb beast," he said softly. The roan's ears twitched toward the sound. After a moment the horse whickered softly. Paul leaned painfully against the roan's shoulder.

"You'll have to put this lawn to rights." Dan Schumann's command snapped Paul's head around. Dan was strolling toward them across the churned-up grass. He bowed in Teddy's direction. "You're a masterful horsewoman, Lady Teddy. I was about to come to offer aid, but you seemed to have the situation well in hand."

He paid no further attention to Paul, other than to inspect the torn turf and hand him a clod chewed out of it by the roan's flashing hooves. Paul handed it back. Dan's fingers closed around it automatically, and then he angrily dropped it. Paul's eyes followed Dan's wrist and not the clod of turf.

"All dressed and ready for dinner?" Paul asked. "Perhaps I'll go and change, too." He took the roan's lead and started back toward the smithy.

In a moment Teddy caught up to him. "You'd better clean your arm. And I'll hold the beast while you finish his shoes," she offered. "It's the least I can do."

"You didn't set him off the second time," Paul said. "Someone shied a rock at him. A pretty sharp one, I would imagine, with some muscle behind it."

"Who?" Teddy demanded. She did not argue that it had happened.

"Someone with a nice white shirt on," Paul replied. The cowboys all wore work shirts. It was doubtful that any of them even owned a white one. Teddy did not ask anything further. The answer was obvious.

*   *   *

With a feeling of frustration Eulalia surveyed the guests around her Christmas Eve dinner table. Used to a gathering of the whole Holt clan at the holidays, Eulalia was trying now to make a kind of substitute family of Teddy, Dan, and Paul, but she was finding them unwieldy. Paul looked uneasy and very much as if his cravat were choking him. Dan was attentive and solicitous, but something was on his mind. Twice Eulalia caught him looking thoughtfully at Paul, who was staring back at him in a manner that Eulalia could only describe as rude. *Really*, she thought, *Paul is a very trying boy*.

Teddy seemed to be enjoying herself, but no one could have called her a sentimental person. Teddy had a disinclination, as she said, to "wallow in treacle." Eulalia doubted that Teddy would be interested in singing Christmas carols around the tree.

Only White Elk and Mai, with their little son, Tommy, seemed to have the proper spirit. Mai looked very like a Chinese Madonna—their next baby was due in another month—and White Elk hovered over her. His dark copper features, which were capable of scaring the daylights out of recalcitrant ranch hands, appeared softened, and his expression was doting.

As dinner ended and they stood, Eulalia felt a sudden stab of longing to be Mai's age again, with one child by the hand and another in her body and a young, strong husband beside her. She was ashamed to be feeling so sorry for herself, but the anguish wouldn't go away. Every day she felt less capable of coping. Her dependence on Dan grew stronger, and she was terrified that she would have trouble managing things when he was gone. *I must tell Toby*, she thought, and then, panic-stricken, decided, *I can't!*

"Mrs. Blake, are you all right?" Mai's soft, musical voice broke her reverie.

"Yes, child, I'm fine. I just get to thinking about the past."

Mai nodded. "I, also," she said solemnly. "I wish my babies could know their grandparents." She put a hand on Tommy's head and another across her belly.

Eulalia's eyes followed the hand on Mai's stomach.

That child has dropped, she thought. *Are we going to have a Christmas baby?*

There was a knock at the door, and her thoughts flew away again as if they ricocheted off the walls in this almost empty room. A babble of voices drew her into the parlor. Amy and Abby's nieces and nephews stood in the doorway, bundled against the cold, with songbooks in their hands. Their mouths made little puffs of steam above their woolen mufflers as they sang.

"Carolers!" Eulalia cried joyfully. "Now it's Christmas! Abby, get some hot cider for these children."

"I got it cooking," Abby said. "But you kids are early. I haven't done my dishes." The sisters always spent Christmas at their father's farm a mile up the road.

"You go ahead," Paul said in Abby's ear. "Your dishes will get done."

They sang "The Holly and the Ivy" and, eyes shining, slurped down hot cider. Then Paul pushed Abby and Amy out the door. It wasn't until the rest of the gathering had returned to hold their hands to the parlor fire that Eulalia saw that Paul was missing.

"Where is that boy?" she asked, vexed. "We're going to open presents."

"He's in the kitchen," Teddy said quietly. "I'll fetch him."

"*I'll* fetch him," Eulalia said. Her eyes snapped. "For goodness sake!" Paul persisted in behaving like no man she had ever encountered, at least not within the family or its far-flung connections. Paul had a kind heart, but he also possessed the unfocused gaze of a dreamer and so far as Eulalia could tell, not an ounce of ambition. He spent all his spare time, Teddy Montague had mentioned, discussing the Shoshone and Chinese cultures with White Elk and Mai, but he didn't seem to be planning to do anything with the information. He was just curious. Even a ne'er-do-well like Sam Brentwood had had more get-up-and-go.

She found him with his hands in a dishpan of soapy water.

"Paul dear, whatever are you doing?"

"The dishes," Paul said unnecessarily. He whistled a

few snatches of "The Holly and the Ivy" and lifted a plate carefully out of the suds.

Eulalia tried to get a grip on the conversation. Talking to Paul always made her feel exasperated. "That is Abby's job."

"Abby went on with her carolers," Paul said. "I told her I'd do these. I sort of like it."

"Well, I would sort of like it," Eulalia said, her temper rising, "if you would come and open presents with us. You can wash these later, if you insist."

Seeing no escape, Paul dried his hands. He was just hanging up the towel when the swinging door from the breakfast room banged open, and Teddy, eyes wide, stopped abruptly in the doorway.

"Mai says the baby is coming," she announced in tones of utter horror. "Now, she says."

"Merciful heavens!" Eulalia said. "We must send for the doctor. But if it really is coming now, he's not going to be in time."

"White Elk already sent one of the hands," Teddy said, "but he said the same thing. He said she had Tommy in no time flat."

"I thought that baby had dropped," Eulalia remarked. "Well, let's get Mai home and into bed. Fast." She bustled through the kitchen door, calling into the parlor as she went. "White Elk, get your wife home as quickly as you can."

"They've already left," Dan told her. "I don't think I'm likely to be much help, so I thought I'd stay out of the way." He was sipping a glass of port.

"No, indeed," Eulalia agreed. "I'll go over there. Everything's going to be fine."

Dan got up. "I'll escort you," he offered. "Where's your coat?"

"On the hall tree. Bless you."

"Thank goodness," Teddy said to Paul when they were alone. "I have dealt successfully with murderous Sherpas and Amazon pythons, but human babies are beyond me— much too fragile. Scare the daylights out of me."

"I delivered a baby once," Paul said. "A little boy. I've always wanted to know what happened to him."

Teddy raised her eyebrows in patent interrogation.

"The mother was a whore in a border town," Paul explained. "The doctor didn't have the time or inclination to bother with her." He looked sheepish. "Pardon me. She was a lady of the evening."

"I believe in calling a whore a whore," Teddy said. "You don't solve a problem by giving it a prettier name."

"Mama?" a small voice piped plaintively at their feet, and Teddy bent over to look under the settee on which they were sitting.

"Well, goodness," Paul said, bending likewise. He reached and gently pulled Tommy White Elk from under the settee and into his lap. "They forgot you, didn't they?"

Tommy nodded. He had his thumb in his mouth, and his almond eyes brimmed with tears.

"Are you scared?"

The child nodded again.

"Well, guess what?" Paul said cheerily. He stood with the child in his arms. "Your mama's having a baby, so you're going to have a little brother or sister any minute now."

"Don't want one," Tommy protested.

"You aren't allowed to send them back," Paul explained. "But you'll be glad you've got it when it's big enough to play with. Why didn't you tell Mr. Schumann you were here before Mrs. Blake and he went bustling off?"

"I don't like him," Tommy said.

"Astute child. Where's your coat? Would you like me to take you home and play with you until you can see your mama?"

The thumb went back in his mouth, but Tommy nodded. Teddy produced the child's coat, a sheepskin-lined leather jacket like White Elk's. It made Tommy look nearly circular when it was on. Paul hoisted him up on his shoulders. "Duck your head."

They went out into the yard and around the house toward the foreman's cottage. The night was crisp and cold, and the ground shimmered with frost. They passed Dan Schumann coming back. No words were exchanged. Paul began to trot and felt Tommy's hands dig into his shoulders for balance. Paul slowed and turned his head. "Is that too fast for you?"

"No," Tommy said firmly. "Giddyap."

White Elk's cabin was a plastered log house with a sloping roof that protected a wide porch. Inside were a main room that ran the width of the cabin and two smaller rooms behind it. A murmur of voices came down the narrow hall that connected them. "Let's just sit in here by the fire," Paul suggested. "They'll come tell us when you can see your mama."

Tommy sat down on the hearth and put his thumb in his mouth again while Paul tried to decide what on earth to do with him. "Would you like to hear a story?"

Tommy nodded.

"How about 'Jack and the Beanstalk'?"

"I heard that."

Paul grinned. "Your daddy had a classical education, huh? Well, how about the sand goblins? I bet you haven't heard that one."

Tommy shook his head.

"You better not have," Paul said with relief. "I haven't made it up yet." Paul arranged himself cross-legged on the rag rug by the fire and pulled Tommy into the space between his knees. "Once there were three sand goblins who lived in a tunnel underneath the Gobi Desert. . . ."

When White Elk and Eulalia emerged from Mai's room half an hour later, Tommy was asleep on Paul's lap. Both Paul's legs were asleep, too.

White Elk, grinning sloppily, bent down and shook Tommy's shoulder. "You have a sister," he said. "Do you want to see Mama?"

Dr. Bright arrived at nearly the same time, pronounced mother and child healthy, and suggested they name the baby Christmas Present.

"I had thought of Christina," White Elk admitted. "That's as far as I'm willing to go."

"So I should hope," Eulalia approved. She turned to the doctor. "What a thing to do to a child."

"I had an aunt named Easter Sunday," the physician said. "Nobody ever mixed her up with anyone else, but suit yourself."

Christmas Present, Paul thought as he walked back across the rime-encrusted grass. He thought contentedly of

Tommy drifting to sleep in his lap and of the way Mai had looked, her hair dark against a lace-edged pillow, with the tiny newborn snug in the crook of her arm. The grass in the yard crackled underfoot, and the blades gleamed like diamond slivers. There was a full moon, and when he looked back over his shoulder he could see his footprints in the crystalline grass. The foreman's cottage was still aglow with yellow light, and Eulalia, having found a length of pink calico, was draping it across the porch railing so in the morning the ranch hands would know what had happened. Paul pulled out his pocket watch and looked at it by moonlight. It was almost midnight. He tilted his head back and turned in a slow circle, taking in the starry wheel of the sky, then continued to the big house.

He found Dan in the parlor again, still drinking port. *I've had a better Christmas than you have, pal*, Paul thought, and went to bed.

Christmas dawned sunny and sparkling cold, the kind of morning when all things were possible. Paul awoke feeling as if he could go downstairs, join the others, and open the presents forgotten the previous night without feeling uneasy and inadequate. Christmases at home had always been unpleasant enough to make him shy away from holidays like a magnet turned the wrong way around. It had never mattered what he had given his mother; it had never been what she wanted, and certainly she had never given him anything for which he had felt the remotest desire.

Mai had helped him pick out presents for Teddy and Eulalia. He had bought them each an ivory comb in Portland's Chinatown. He would have to give them eventually and open whatever they had found for him, so it might as well be now. This morning Paul was fortified with hope and reasonableness from the miracle of little Christina, asleep in her mother's arms across the yard.

He went downstairs whistling, with the intention of making biscuits and omelets because Abby wasn't there. Eulalia shouldn't have to cook on Christmas morning, and Paul, having tasted Teddy's efforts on a previous cook's day off, had no desire to do so again.

He found Dan in the kitchen and raised his eyebrows

in surprise. Dan's hands jerked when he saw Paul from the corner of his eye. Paul looked at him, interested. Dan had been doing something that he wanted to keep a secret. *What?* Paul wondered.

He located one of Abby's white canvas aprons and tied it on, not particularly bothered by Dan's snicker. He pulled the flour bin open and stuck a scoop in the contents, raising as much dust as he could manage. Dan and his black frock coat beat a retreat. Paul dumped the flour into a bowl and looked around. For the life of him he couldn't tell what Dan had been doing. Nothing was on the kitchen counter except a few flakes of candle wax. Whatever Dan had been up to, Paul decided that he had just finished with it and that it had been worth Dan's getting up early for.

When Eulalia came downstairs Paul was just putting biscuits on the dining room table. She blinked at him as if he were an alien creature from a Jules Verne adventure. "Why, Paul dear. Thank you. That, uh, really wasn't necessary. None of the men in my family ever learned to bake, so I'm quite used to doing it myself on Abby's day off."

Teddy walked in, prepared to set the table. "You're not to lift a finger today, Eulalia. This is Christmas. It was necessary for Paul to bake—if you didn't want me to do it," she said.

"I'm sure your biscuits are— Oh, dear . . ." All color drained from Eulalia's face.

"What is it?" Teddy set down her stack of napkins and hurried over.

Eulalia was staring at the ornate silver candelabra that still decorated the table. They sat in pools of wax, their candles having burned down completely. Long waxen stalactites drooped to the mahogany tabletop. "Oh, no! I was supposed to blow those out last night. I was so sure I had." A tear ran down her cheek. "Now the table's been ruined, and worse, the house might have caught fire."

Paul thought of the candle wax in the kitchen and Dan Schumann's furtive look. How long would it have taken for those candles to burn down if someone got up early and relit them? Paul wondered. And added some extra wax for

effect. Eulalia looked so distressed that he blurted out:
"Don't be so sure that you were at fault."

"Who, then?" Eulalia asked, distressed. "I was supposed to blow them out." She wiped the back of her hand across her eyes, irritated by her own tears. "I believe in taking responsibility."

"I think Dan relit them." Paul knew he had made a mistake as soon as the words were out of his mouth. He sounded like an idiot.

Eulalia stared at him. "That makes no sense. Nobody lights candles in the morning. Paul, you must learn to think things through. That could be why you've had so many different jobs, you know. A man needs to look ahead and plan if he wants to make something of himself, the way Dan has done. Do you know what quality Dan has?"

"An eye to the main chance?" Paul suggested.

"Paul, I will not have that kind of talk! It is very unbecoming to criticize a young man who has used his birth, breeding, and education to advance himself in the world, while you have squandered your advantages. If you would emulate Dan, it would be to your benefit."

"Yes, ma'am." Paul fervently wished that he had kept his mouth shut. He retreated to the kitchen, feeling Teddy's sympathetic eyes and Eulalia's critical ones boring into his back. He began to whip eggs in a bowl, glad that the swinging kitchen door muffled their conversation.

"Of all the aggravating—" he heard Eulalia say before the door swung to.

The morning's meal was not as convivial as Paul had hoped for upon waking. The omelets were complimented, enthusiastically by Teddy and with a certain smirk in his voice by Dan, which gave Paul to understand that real men couldn't cook and real women—a glance at Teddy—ought to.

"Dan is a particularly annoying young man," Teddy remarked to Paul as the Madrona's light buggy turned through the front gates toward Portland, bound for Christmas morning services. Ahead of them, White Elk was driving Dan, Eulalia, and Tommy in the surrey.

"He's up to something," Paul muttered. "He was

mucking around in the kitchen with candle wax this morning. I wasn't just talking through my hat."

"I knew you weren't," Teddy said sympathetically. "You don't quite think before you speak. It isn't a matter of not knowing what you want to say, it's a matter of not thinking out how you want to phrase it—or whether you ought to say it at all."

"I don't like him," Paul said. "There's something . . . manufactured about him."

"That," Teddy said dryly, "is a characteristic of most of our species. It's why I couldn't ever settle down to live in society over the long term. I kept wanting to pick people's artificiality off. That upsets my brother to no end."

"I envy you," Paul said wistfully. "It must be wonderful to go, to see things, to find things out."

"But that's exactly what you've been doing for the last five years," Teddy pointed out.

Paul chuckled. "Not on the scale you have. I could have done without a lot of what I've seen."

"You yearn for foreign climes, I suppose. No one's ever satisfied with his own backyard. Well, I can't say I blame you. Would you like to come along on this next expedition to Tierra del Fuego? I always hire on some crew besides whatever natives I pick up. I can't afford to pay much— well, nothing, actually—but it ought to be exciting."

Paul's eyes momentarily glowed at the idea of a beckoning adventure. He could almost see Tierra del Fuego shimmering in the road ahead of them. But then he returned to the problem at hand.

"But what if I leave and I'm right about that skunk?"

Teddy didn't ask which skunk. "You think he's really up to something?"

"He is or he's trying to be," Paul said. "Mrs. Blake won't listen to my warnings, and I doubt she'd listen to yours, either—not about Dan."

"I can guarantee she wouldn't," Teddy said. "She'd think it was only because I'm fond of you. I tried to tell her you're not such a layabout as she thinks—might as well call a spade a spade, my boy—but she couldn't see it."

"Neither could my mother," Paul said ruefully. "I *am* a layabout by a lot of people's standards, I suppose. There are so many interesting things to do, I get fed up with conversations that don't really matter. I'm not interested in planning my life and being the pillar of the community."

"You get bored too easily; that's your problem. Then you want to move on. I sympathize."

"To tell you the truth, I'm bored right now," Paul confided. "I'd give my eyeteeth to go with you. But Mrs. Blake's been nice to me. I can't square it with my conscience to waltz off and leave her when I don't know what Dan's got hidden under his hat. I never saw a fellow who was more obviously getting ready to work some scam."

Teddy chuckled. "You're awfully cynical."

"I've been on the road awhile," Paul said. "By and large I've found people to be pretty decent. But I do know a bad apple when I see one."

"I expect you do," Teddy said. "So do I. Well, I won't try to change your mind. You stick around for a while, and you'll have an untroubled conscience. There'll be more expeditions—and a place for you on any of them when you want it."

Paul nodded. A misty vision of Tierra del Fuego appeared in the road ahead of him and then faded to a cold December landscape in Oregon and the back of Dan Schumann's head, self-righteously erect under his Sunday hat.

While Paul had been keeping an eye on Dan, Dan had been watching Paul, and in January he was incensed to discover that Teddy Montague had offered to take Paul with her but that he hadn't gone.

"No ambition," Dan said to Eulalia, shaking his head. "No ambition at all." Dan's hands twitched in fury, and he consciously stilled them. By this time, if he could have arranged Paul's departure at pistol point, he would have done it. Dan was tired of feeling Paul's eyes on him and a little worried by their speculative look. Somehow Paul had to be pried loose from the Madrona and sent on his way. "He's completely lacking in prudence, throwing away an offer like Lady Teddy's."

"I fear so," Eulalia responded. "I've given up expecting Paul to possess your desire for accomplishment."

"I'd be happy if he just displayed average competence," Dan said. "He let a horse get away from him Christmas Eve and made the most awful mess of the lawn trying to catch it. It was like the clown act at a carnival."

Eulalia sighed. "I wish you two got along better. Paul has many deficiencies, but you can afford to be generous, Dan. Try to be charitable toward him even if he isn't particularly charitable toward you."

"I'm not surprised that he doesn't like me. I don't know what he's told you behind my back"—he kept the amused note in his voice—"but he's probably afraid I'll report how often I've found him leaning on a hayfork when he's supposed to be working."

"Oh, Dan." Eulalia sighed again. "I just can't think about it right now. I'm exhausted." She pulled herself up from her chair and went slowly toward the stairs.

Dan noticed that she kept her head turned so she wouldn't see the vase on the hall table. She obviously couldn't remember arranging the flowers that morning because he had surreptitiously done it for her—just as he'd done three times since Christmas and convinced her that she had taken care of them but forgotten. One day he made her believe that she had done them twice. This afternoon she just couldn't bear to look, he thought, in case it had slipped her mind again. He wanted to laugh.

In her bedroom Eulalia took Lee's photograph from the bureau and stared at it, tracing the ridges of its brown leather frame. Through the window she could see White Elk and Paul in the yard with one of the young horses. White Elk said that Paul wasn't lazy and that he spent a lot less time whittling than most hands.

Throughout her life Eulalia had been strong-minded and capable, and she had always had a man she could depend on. Now, at her advanced age and a widow, it all seemed too much to do alone.

As she stood in the cold sunlight, her thoughts drifted from Paul to Dan to Lee. She fought the fear at the back of her mind, the terror that she might wake up one day and not remember anything at all.

Eulalia traced Lee's eyes and mouth with her fingertip.

"I don't know what to do, my darling." A tear slid down her cheek. "Can't you come and tell me?"

Dan Schumann blew out a thick cloud of cigar smoke and crossed his arms across his waistcoat to show that he could not be intimidated by the likes of Louis Wessell.

"The money is there, Mr. Wessell. My request for a loan is purely due to a matter of timing. It's more convenient for me to make the investment in the whorehouse now, rather than wait the few weeks until my funds become available."

"So you want me to front it," Louie Weasel said. "What you got for collateral?"

"I wish to avail myself of a short-term loan," Dan said. "And I have prospects that, I am sure, Mr. Bender has already outlined to you."

"Bender don't get seen talking to me. You better not, either, iffen you don't want Miz Blake to get wise. All right, all right—" He waved his own cigar as Dan began to respond indignantly. "You got Miz Blake on a string, Bender vouched for that, so we'll call that collateral. Just let me draw up some papers. . . ."

Wessell rummaged in an overflowing desk drawer and produced an account book. He dipped a splayed pen in an inkwell while Dan looked around the room with distaste.

Louie Weasel's digs were a disreputable set of rooms above a bakery, and not even the aroma of fresh bread could mask the odor of Louie and Louie's cigars, which were of a much less notable brand than Dan's. Dan wrinkled his nose.

Louie grinned, showing two gold canine teeth. "You're wondering why I operate out of a rattrap like this. I'll tell you, buddy boy. I like to keep a low profile. And my clients better remember it. Nobody talks about me, you got that?"

"Frankly, I wouldn't admit to knowing you," Dan said.

"Fine. Lots of my clients feel like that. I don't get my feelings hurt." He shoved a paper at Dan. "Now this contract here is just for my records. If you welsh on me I won't take you to court; I got better ways of collecting. You got that, too?"

"That won't be necessary," Dan said with dignity,

trying to convey that he wasn't scared of small-time oper-
ators like Mr. Wessell. "Hey!" He stared at the interest
rate. "That's extortion! That's not what Bender said you
charged!"

"It's what I'm charging you," Wessell said. "Take it or
leave it." He offered Dan the pen. "You got somebody else
you feel like explaining your collateral to?"

VIII

San Francisco, February, 1894

Peter Blake looked at Tim Holt from under the green eyeshade that Peter invariably affected when dealing with the *Clarion's* ledger books. It made him look prudent and sagacious, Peter had decided, and impressed upon Tim the seriousness of the situation. Tim said it turned Peter's skin the same color as money.

"Just quit stewing," Peter said. "Starting Monday Barlow will take over as financial manager. You'll be in good shape as long as you restrain your unholy passion for new equipment."

"I didn't order those Linotypes," Tim protested indignantly.

"You wanted to," Peter said.

"Well, what the hell has that got to do with it? If you could jail a man for what he wanted to do, there wouldn't be anyone running around loose. And why am I standing here in front of your desk like a copyboy? I'm the boss." Tim sat down. "Why aren't we in my office?"

"Because the books are in here," Peter replied. "And because you never have the patience to wait long enough for anyone to get to your office."

"What do you expect?" Tim ran his hands through his hair. It stood up on end above his forehead. "Lighting out for Germany a year before you need to—just when I thought I could start to relax."

"You wouldn't have relaxed anyway," Peter said. "I don't know what's eating you, but the paper's solvent . . . sort of. If you're feeling jumpy, it's over something else, so

113

don't blame me. Besides, I warned you last fall that I was going."

"Why are you so hot to tackle these old boys now?"

"Because I'm going to turn twenty-one in a year, and I want a check waiting for me, so to speak. I want control of that money as of my birthday. The trustees are going to put up a fight, so I thought I'd get it over with."

"If they find out you're planning to build automobiles," Tim said, "they'll bust a gut."

Peter grinned. When he got that light in his eyes the accountant face vanished, and he looked his age. "They sure will. They may have some company, too—Dad doesn't exactly approve. The last opinion *he* ventured on automobiles was that they would scare all the horses and nobody in his right mind would want one or need one."

"What's good enough for the cavalry is good enough for the man in the street," Tim said with mock solemnity.

"That's going to be the popular opinion in Grevenburg," Peter told him.

"I can't agree," Tim said, serious now. "I think the internal-combustion engine is going to revolutionize transportation to an even greater extent than the steam engine did. It's going to change the face of this country within fifty years."

"Thirty years," Peter corrected. "Maybe twenty."

"I want a piece of it," Tim said. "When the paper's in the black and I feel secure, I want to buy in. You need someone to hire your engineers. You know money, but you don't know mechanics."

Peter nodded. "True. That's why I don't fool with them. See if you can't treat money the same way while I'm gone."

"I'll put my complete faith in Barlow," Tim grumbled. "I want to make sure I leave myself time to worry about everything else." Tim stood up and ran his hands through his hair again, leaving it looking like a cockatoo's crest. He stalked down the hall.

Peter, watching him go, noted that halfway down the corridor Tim threw his hands in the air, as if gesticulating to someone who couldn't be seen.

*   *   *

Peter dutifully devoted several hours over the next few days to wondering what was eating Tim, but by the time his train reached Washington and he was met by his father and introduced to his father's bankers, the question of his cousin's unknown difficulties was losing importance. Since it wasn't over money, Peter knew he couldn't do anything to help. He was going to have plenty to do about solving his own problems.

During the weeks spent steaming across the Atlantic, Peter formulated exactly the proper things to say to his trustees and the proper German in which to say them.

"If you think you're going to butter them up, you're mistaken," Henry said, watching Peter practice a courtly Viennese bow in front of the mirror in their stateroom. "Trustees don't butter."

"You mean they wouldn't butter for you," Peter retorted. "An American of highly suspicious origins, seducing respectable German ladies." *He's probably a spy*. He didn't say that aloud. Even in the family, that didn't get said aloud. "*I*, however, am the son of the baroness Gisela von Kirchberg. She unwisely chose to marry the American but is still 'our' baroness. For me, they will be buttered." He clicked his heels together and bowed again in his father's direction.

"Don't get cocky," Henry warned. "You haven't met them. They're so old it's a wonder they're still aboveground, and they haven't approved of anything that's been invented since Napoleon's day. And you're going to try to interest them in motorcars!" Henry gave a hoot of laughter.

"I don't care whether they're interested or not," Peter informed him. "They ought to be, mind you. Benz has built an automobile right under their noses."

"They wouldn't notice it if it was tangled up in their mustaches," Henry said. "I'm tired. I'm going to turn in, but if you want to stay up all night practicing your court manners, go right ahead."

Peter waited until his father had climbed into his bed, and then he went up on the promenade deck to think. The moonlight made a white bar across the water, and it was as cold as ice on the North Atlantic in winter. Why had he been in such a swivet to make this trip? It would have kept until summer, he knew. Maybe it wasn't the inheritance he was after so much as it was learning about his mother, Peter thought, crossing his arms on the railing. When he was twenty-one, part of her money would become his, and for some reason that legal transfer made Peter feel as if he would lose all vestige of Gisela von Kirchberg from his life.

Hardly anyone talked about the baroness, who had died when Peter was two. The murder, planned by Henry's enemies, was intended to cause him mental anguish. Henry had been expected to marry his childhood sweetheart, but instead he had fallen into bed and then love, Peter thought, with Gisela in Germany. Since the childhood sweetheart was Toby Holt's sister, Cindy, a family uproar had ensued. Cindy's mother, Eulalia, and her husband Lee were Henry's stepparents. Infuriated, Eulalia had stopped speaking to Henry and hadn't resumed again until Gisela was dead. Peter, a serious and irresistible tyke, had, without his knowledge, played an important role as peacemaker. Both Eulalia and Cindy lost their hearts to him, paving the way to a reconciliation with Henry. Ultimately Henry and Cindy, who had married someone else and been widowed, too, had married.

Cindy had never treated Peter any differently from her own children; but he *was* different, and there was no getting around it. For one thing, he stood to inherit more money than anyone else in the family had ever seen in a lifetime, and the Holts were not poor.

Thank God I won't be inheriting the title, too, Peter thought. Through some convoluted and Germanically incomprehensible document of entailment, the title of baron von Kirchberg and the castle at Grevenhof that went with it had fallen on the shoulders of a distant fourth cousin because Gisela had married into the von Kirchberg family and was not herself of noble ancestry.

According to Cindy, who had visited the castle before accepting Henry's proposal, the residence was large enough to form the seat of government of some Balkan principality and ugly enough to be a local landmark even in a country given to massive architectural overstatement. Henry had once remarked that the only suitable mode of travel about

the place was roller skates. Fortunately for the current
baron, a considerable fortune went with it, although not as
substantial as the late baroness's private funds, which were
Peter's inheritance.

Henry and Peter would have to call on the current
baron for form's sake and probably even spend their stay
with him at Grevenhof. Peter would be an outsider there,
just as he seemed to be everywhere he went, he thought—
not quite family, with his American father and his birthdate
inscribed on the Grevenburg village records a little too
close to the date of his parents' marriage.

No matter how people looked at him, he didn't quite
match anybody else, Peter thought moodily. Even his name
was an oddity: Peter Heinrich von Kirchberg Blake. *Heinrich* because his mother had called his father by that name.
Peter for his paternal grandfather. Henry had been an
adolescent on the loose and probably headed for no good
when Lee and Eulalia Blake adopted him. Henry's real
father, Pete Purcell, had been a gunslinger of some reputation, although many years retired at the time of his death.
Death by gunshot, young Peter had been given to understand, although no one had ever been very specific. What
information he had on all this had been pieced together
over the years from various family members. It was all very
interesting, and Peter thought that there was probably a lot
more to it than he knew. Discretion prevented him from
asking his father outright.

It was getting colder on the promenade deck, so he
walked faster, jamming his hands in the pockets of his
greatcoat. The hum of the ship's engines was a steady throb
as the North Atlantic sea slapped against her sides. No one
else was on deck. The debutantes who thronged the
promenade in the early evening, traveling in flocks like
bright birds, were all inside in the grand saloon, dancing
with suitable young men or dutifully playing whist with
their grandmothers. Peter felt mildly scornful of them even
as he yearned for the warmth of the saloon. But just now it
suited his mood to feel the outsider, preparatory to flaunt-
ing his gunslinger's blood before the old men in Grevenburg. In the same way, his mother's foreign blood had

prevented him from feeling totally integrated with the
Holts and Blakes.

He did not feel rejected for his disparate heritage. It
was because of the differences that each side of his family
seemed to try to swallow him whole and make him all
theirs. The Holts and the Blakes never mentioned Gisela,
and the trustees wanted Peter to consider himself a German.

The young man exhaled a puff of warm breath into the
cold salt air. It hung in a cloud before him, as amorphous as
a ghost. He reached out a hand as if he could somehow
coalesce this emanation from himself into something solid,
his true form and identity.

"Naturally, nothing can be decided so swiftly." The
first trustee looked down at Peter. He was tall, as elongated
as a stork. His long nose resembled an opossum's but
twitched like a rabbit's. Beneath it he sported a mustache of
a most Prussian military appearance, and on his chest he
wore a lovingly polished medal on a scarlet and black
ribbon.

The second trustee was round, nearly spherical, with a
gold watch chain that ran across a vast expanse of stomach.
The third had a face narrow above the nose and broad
below, the proportions repeated in thin chest and substantial backside. Peter thought of them as straight line, a
circle, and a triangle.

"Naturally not, given the seriousness of the situation."

"Naturally."

"Very grave indeed."

They spoke either in unison or in quick succession, like
a choir singing a round, doubling and redoubling one
another's words.

"Utmost importance. A full year, at least, to reach a
conclusion."

"Indubitably."

The air in the bank library at Grevenburg was nearly as
dusty as the trustees, and Peter sneezed. Out of the corner
of his eye, he could see his father sitting by the door. A
certain tautness to Henry's expression informed Peter that
he was stifling laughter. Peter decided that it was time to

fish or cut bait. If one of them had a heart attack, then there would only be two left.

"I trust it won't take you gentlemen as long as a year," he said, "because on the day of my twenty-first birthday, I am going to expect a check for one-third of my inheritance. I am investing in an automobile company, and by then I will require all the ready cash I can come by to begin production."

The triangular trustee made a noise as if he had choked on something. The round one's eyes widened to match the rest of him, but only a faint burble emanated from the back of his throat. For once, two out of the three had been rendered speechless.

The thin one, however, had more to say, and he spoke for them all: "Impossible!"

"It's perfectly possible," Peter protested.

"We won't permit it." The straight line bent forward, his mustache twitching faster than his nose. "Irresponsible. Malfeasance. Colonel Blake, have you put him up to this?"

"Certainly not," Henry denied.

"Then where has he come by the idea? Eh?" The trustee glared at Henry.

"Please talk to me and not to my father," Peter demanded. "You have no choice. If I want the money, you have to give it to me."

"I never heard of such a thing."

The other two found their breath.

"No, indeed."

"Certainly not."

"Won't entertain the notion for a moment."

"Young man, your mother did not tend her fortune with careful concern every day of her adult life in order for you to squander it on motorcars."

"I'm not going to squander it," Peter said, irritated. "I'm going to invest it. You ought to be able to comprehend the difference." *You impervious old fossil*. He crossed his arms on his chest and stared back at the trustee.

"Investment in anything so foolish as a self-propelled carriage is tantamount to squandering," the trustee said stubbornly.

"Haven't you been paying any attention to what's been going on?" Peter demanded. "Karl Benz has already built a motorcar that's being sold in Paris."

"The French will buy anything!" the third trustee snapped.

"Still, if our young man were to invest in a German company . . ." the second mused.

"With proper supervision, of course. After all, Benz is a German, but his company would be entirely unsuitable."

"It would be what the baroness would have wished for—to keep her fortune in her own country."

"I plan to invest in an American company," Peter said.

"Never!"

"Out of the question!"

"I never heard of an American motorcar company. What is the name of it?"

"The Blake Company," Peter responded with satisfaction.

"You are planning to begin your own company?" They stared at him in horror.

"You will lose it all!"

"Every penny!"

"And the baroness will turn in her grave."

"I don't care if she haunts you," Peter said vindictively.

They all swung around to stare at Henry.

"Colonel Blake, I refuse to believe that this is not your doing. It is a ploy to transfer German funds to America for your own ends."

"Peter happens to be an American," Henry said. "And I haven't got any ends. Furthermore, gentlemen, I've read the will; if Peter demands this money in a year, you legally will have to give it to him. If you don't, he could take you to court for malfeasance."

"Do you mean to tell us that you approve of this scheme, this lunatic scenario to take our beloved baroness's money and throw it down a well? to the wolves? to the wind?"

"Make up your mind. No, I don't approve of it. I think automobiles are a passing fad. They are noisy and unreliable, and no city will permit them on its streets because they will cause havoc among the horses. As far as I can see, motorcars will have only limited recreational use."

The trustees breathed a collective sigh of relief. The father was going to be reasonable.

"Very well then. Now we will discuss more rational options, eh? We have put together for you, young Mr. Blake, a list of prudent investments—German firms, of course—where my colleagues and I can continue to keep an eye on the funds for you. You may, of course, make your own selections from the list. After all, it will be your money."

Peter stared at them. "Are you under the impression that my father is in charge of my decisions?" he shouted. "I respect his opinions, but I do not necessarily live by them."

The trustees jumped and stared back.

"You will turn that money over to me," Peter continued heatedly, "or I will take you to court!"

"You're a little loud, Peter," Henry observed. "All the same, gentlemen, I think you'd better listen to him."

The trustees' hearts sank collectively. It had been too much to hope for that the American would be reasonable, too much to hope for that the American was even sane. The trustees had known it all along, of course. Americans were flighty and unrooted. It was what came of having no history to speak of.

"We will, of course, give your wishes every consideration." It was necessary to be polite, even when facing chaos.

"Naturally the baron is eager to make your acquaintance. He is planning a small soiree in your honor and looking forward most happily to your visit with him." The first trustee brightened. "He has invited all the eligible young ladies of his acquaintance, and they are eager to meet Baroness Gisela's heir."

Peter was getting bored. "That's very kind. I'm sure I'll see you there." He bowed the graceful court bow he had been practicing, but there was no subservience in it. He expected he would see the trustees everywhere for the next month, popping up like trolls out of the ground with new arguments as to why he should leave his fortune in their keeping.

*   *   *

"They won't give in without a fight, you know," the baron said dolefully. "Personally I just never had the strength to argue against them."

The baron looked very much to Peter as if he hadn't the strength to do anything. He was lanky, with watery blue eyes and a disappointed air. He was wearing several layers of clothing, ending with a leather shooting jacket, because Grevenhof was cold.

"This is the gallery," the baron pointed out.

Peter peered down a wide hall lined with enormous portraits in oil paint. He stared into the hooded eyes of a sixteenth-century lady in a green velvet gown.

"That's by Holbein," the baron remarked. "Everyone's frightfully proud of it. She was Anna von Augsburg, a holy terror by all accounts. And that's Freidrich von Kirchberg. He married her and spent the next twenty years trying to convince the pope to unmarry them. He looks depressed about it, don't you think?"

Peter took another look at Anna von Augsburg. He thought she would have depressed him, too.

"And there's your mother, Baroness Gisela." The current baron paused in front of the frame and contemplated it.

Peter stared into his mother's eyes. He had seen portraits of her before, of course. His father had several, as well as photographs. But this one was life size and minutely detailed. He could almost believe it was the breathing woman. She had chestnut hair and a beautiful and imperious face.

No wonder Father fell in love with her, Peter thought. To do otherwise would be like trying to resist a steamroller—a very beautiful and loving one, but a steamroller all the same.

"The trustees are hoping you're going to marry one of my cousins, you know," the baron was saying. "I have hundreds," he added gloomily.

"I don't want a wife," Peter said. "No offense intended. I'm sure they're charming girls."

"They'll try," the baron said. "The trustees, I mean.

My aunt Magda, too. They want to keep that money in the country."

"Let them try," Peter said dryly.

There was no shortage of young ladies willing to do so, he discovered as soon as the guests arrived for the baron's "soiree." The event bore far more resemblance to a state ball than to the informal evening that its name had led Peter to expect. There was a ten-piece orchestra, a full dinner served at midnight, and a profusion of hothouse flowers and silk draperies decorating the "small ballroom" of Grevenhof. Because it was a soiree, the young female guests were to show off their accomplishments in an informal program before supper.

The baron's aunt Magda took up her stand by Peter. An evening gown of royal blue encased her buxom form, and her graying fair hair was relentlessly pulled and twisted into a chignon. She was approximately two ax handles wide.

A demure young woman in a white muslin dress took her place at the end of the room, songbook in hand. Magda clucked her tongue. "Poor thing has no talent. Her mother will keep sending her to a voice teacher, but it is hopeless. It would be far kinder to let her stay out of the public eye."

The girl began to sing a popular German air, no worse and no better than dozens Peter had heard at home. He was grateful, not for the first time, that young men were not put through this idiotic display. A polite spattering of applause greeted the end of the song.

Another girl took her place and recited poetry, and a third attempted a Wagnerian aria. Peter ran his finger around the inside of his evening shirt collar and wished for another glass of champagne. Across the room he could see his father, elegant in a stiff-fronted shirt and black tailcoat, sliding easily into acquaintanceships formed twenty years before. Peter was aware that the number of eyes resting on him was equaled by those observing his father. Two decades earlier Henry Blake had been very interesting to Grevenhof's neighbors as the man who had gotten the Iron Baroness into bed with him. They didn't seem to have lost interest, not with all the money that was tangled up in the story.

Another girl took her place at the end of the room and adopted a pose of demure patience while two liveried manservants wrestled something through the door behind her. Peter saw with foreboding that it was a harp case. He thought even more longingly of champagne and perhaps a stroll on the balcony outside.

Magda's hand tightened on his arm. "That is my Lisette," she announced.

Peter abandoned himself to his fate.

IX

San Francisco, April 1894

Tim Holt lounged in the doorway of the *Clarion*'s city room and surveyed the chaos within. At any rate, it looked like chaos, although Tim knew that it was not. The noise level was substantial, nearly as loud as in the Linotype room downstairs. Ten typewriters clacked and rattled, and everyone was talking at once—into the telephone, across the room to Stu Abrams, or just to himself. Deke Merwin always recited his stories out loud as he wrote them, and Rafe Murray sang. Every so often someone would throw something at him.

The Associated Press wire sputtered and started to click. A copyboy dashed over to it, then unreeled the lengths of punched tape as they came out the machine's mouth. He frowned at the tape. He was just learning to decipher it.

"Gimme that." Sid Appleton, the national-news editor, yanked the tape away and read it, chewing on his cigar.

"Aw, c'mon, Mr. Appleton. I was just getting the hang of it."

"Go practice on old tape," Sid growled. "The whole country could have been overrun with anarchists and socialist revolutionaries before you got through reading the lead."

"Are we in imminent danger, Sid?" Rafe Murray called. He made as if to pick up imaginary skirts and flee.

"Just of a fat lip," Appleton muttered. "They're rioting in Pennsylvania over this coal-mine business. Place called Connellsville. Eleven men dead."

125

"Innocent bystanders?"

"Hell, no. Bunch of unionists. I don't know what the country's coming to."

"The country's shaking off despair," Rafe Murray declared. "Its people are sitting up and seeing they don't have to be slaves anymore. You ever work in a coal mine?"

"No, and I never been a butcher nor a baker nor a candlestick maker, either. What's that got to do with it?"

Murray dropped his bantering tone, and his voice grew impassioned. "Try it, Sid, just once, before you slam the unions. Try working in a hole in the ground, where the sun never comes in and the air's so stifling with black dust you can hardly breathe. The mine's passageways are so short you have to walk bent over or crawl. And all that earth is hanging over you, and you never know when it's going to come down and bury you alive—or worse, leave you with just enough air to last you a little while but not long enough to be rescued. There's poison gas that you can't see or smell. You've got no dignity, no pride, as a miner. You get paid in scrip that must be spent in the company store, which robs you. You live in a company town in a company house, and you can't ever get loose. You know your kids are going to follow you into the mines, too, down into that black hole in the ground that sucks the soul right out of your breast. You try it, Sid, and if you're still human in six months, then you can slam the unions." Murray's voice quivered at the end, and he slammed his fist on his desk.

"Jesus Christ, Murray," Sid said. "You ought to go join the unions yourself. You're a rabble rouser."

"And you're a flunky for any man that's got money," Murray shot back.

"Industry is the lifeblood of a healthy economy," Sid defended. "You all want to go back to picking nuts and berries in the woods."

"They're at it again, boys," someone said.

"One, two, three," another reporter called out, and a barrage of wadded-up copy paper assailed Sid and Murray.

"Shut up or we'll start throwing glue pots."

"Murray, where's my piece on the Seaside Strangler case?" Stu Abrams's voice cut through the demands for silence. "You guys get into it every time. I just made a new rule: Nobody argues politics in this newsroom. Now shut up or I'll make one of you go work in Doaks's office."

Maxedon Doaks was the religion writer. He had a small private office next to Waldo Howard's on the grounds that no one could cover church affairs with the proper attitude while subjected to the atmosphere that prevailed in the city room.

"Send Appleton," Murray said, unrepentant. "He likes a pious environment as long as it doesn't inconvenience him any."

"Just get me that strangler piece," Abrams growled. He looked up and saw Tim leaning in the doorway. "I got an idea," he said. "Send one of these clowns to Pennsylvania and let 'em put their money where their mouth is. Get 'em out of my newsroom."

"I'm sending Hugo Ware," Tim said. "I came to tell him."

It had been obvious for several days that the miners' strike in Connellsville was going to heat up. Tim had heard Sid read the AP tape and was mentally cursing because he hadn't gotten Hugo there already. Waldo was going to be in a similar snit. Waldo had been ready to charge out to Pennsylvania himself, what with a good riot promising to erupt, but Tim had squelched that notion. Covering riots was a young man's game. When state troopers and company guards lost their tempers, they often didn't discriminate between newspapermen and striking miners, and Waldo wasn't as fleet of foot as Hugo.

"You'll break Ware's heart," Rafe Murray said, grinning. "If I had a wife like his, I'd take up a line of work that didn't require travel. She was just in here looking for him, and half these poor bastards haven't recovered yet. Poor Doaks took one look at her and nearly had cardiac arrest. I expect he's praying or confessing it now."

Tim chuckled. Rosebay's mere presence could cause work to stop in any business. The *Clarion*'s bachelor reporters were notoriously susceptible to feminine charms, although their track record was dismal. Rafe Murray had a list of old flames as long as his arm, all of whom had sworn for varying reasons to shoot him on sight. He still owed money to some of them and would bemoan that fact while trying to correct it at the poker table.

"Mrs. Ware's not your type," Tim informed Rafe. "She's much too intelligent. I don't suppose she mentioned to any of you besotted mooncalves where she was going? If I'm shipping Hugo to Pennsylvania, I'd better break it tactfully to the missus."

"She was looking for you," Rafe said enviously. "Seeing that she couldn't find Ware."

There was a general chuckle at this, and Tim glared at them. "That's a little too close to disrespectful. You watch how you talk about Mrs. Ware. She's a respectable woman."

"A thing that crosses our path but seldom," Murray said mournfully.

"Too good to have her name bandied by you louts."

"We know. We yearn for the unattainable," Murray said.

"That's fine. You just yearn respectfully." Tim went out and down the hall toward his office.

Rosebay was too beautiful, he acknowledged. When men started talking about her looks, they usually got to equating that much beauty with flightiness. Someone had to stick up for her character. Tim had been Rosebay's self-appointed defender since he'd met her the night her first husband was shot in a brawl.

Back then she had provided him with an object lesson in human nature that marked a turning point in his path to adulthood and his understanding of his species. People, he had discovered, based their assumptions on visual clues that were entirely unreliable—on another's physical beauty or lack of it, for instance—and they clung stubbornly to those assumptions in the face of specific evidence to the contrary.

Tim turned the handle of his office door and discovered afresh that he wasn't immune to lusting after Rosebay, either. She was sitting in his visitor's chair, lips pursed over a notebook in which she was figuring something with a pencil from his desk. She looked so appealing that any man passing by would probably want to stop and sweep her into his arms. Tim certainly did.

"The boys told me you were here," he managed in a

strangled voice that he hoped did not convey to her everything he was thinking. What was the matter with him?

"I came looking for Hugo," Rosebay said cheerfully. "But since he wasn't here, I thought I'd visit with you." There was still a trace of the Appalachians in her voice. "It's been a right long time since we've seen you. I came to beg another roll end for pattern paper. I'm planning to reupholster that awful old red settee. I was going to have Hugo ask the boys in the pressroom for one. I'd have gone myself, but it's dirty in there. I'm not prissy, but this is a good dress. Is it too coming of me to ask the boss instead?"

"Not when it's you asking," Tim said gallantly. "I'll have someone bring it around for you. Would you like a cup of tea before you go?" *Don't ask her to stay, you fool. Haven't you got any sense?*

Rosebay looked delighted. Her blue eyes glowed as bright as little gas lamps at him. "I surely would. I was just thinking how much I wanted tea."

"I'll put the kettle on." Tim turned the flame up on the gas ring he kept in his office to brew coffee when he slept too late in the morning to have any at home, which was often. He set out a pair of coffee cups—heavy, chipped restaurant china, probably stolen by Woolwine—that had been in the office. "Not elegant, but serviceable."

"Anything will do," Rosebay said. "I'm flat tired. Just now I'd drink tea out of my boots."

Tim sat on the chair arm while he waited for the kettle. *Don't do that. Go sit at your desk,* said the voice in his head that had grown more insistent the more he ignored it.

Tim continued to ignore it. What could be a safer environment than his own office in broad daylight? The time Rosebay and he got into trouble had been at night, way out in the country in Rosebay's isolated cabin, when they'd both had a little whiskey under their skin.

Now, while Tim waited for the kettle to boil, he let himself look at Rosebay just a little too long and realized that she was gazing at him. Their eyes locked, and Tim found himself falling into those two blue flames. The next thing he knew, he was kneeling on the floor beside her with his arms around her, and she was kissing him back as if she meant it.

Good intentions, not to mention good sense, flew out the window. She turned in his arms with a little moan, and his hands slipped up over the front of her tight-fitting bodice to stroke her breasts. She moved sensuously under his caress. Tim couldn't see anything or hear anything until Rosebay whispered his name. He pressed his face against her breasts, and her lips brushed his hair.

His own blood was pounding in his ears, and he never even stopped to think that his office door had a glass panel. Only the fortuitous screaming of the tea kettle dragged him back to sanity.

Tim jerked upright, rocking back on his heels, and stared horrified at Rosebay. His face felt flushed, and he could see two bright crimson patches on Rosebay's cheeks, too. Her eyes were heavy lidded.

"Oh, God, Rosebay," Tim stammered. "I'm sorry."

"I wasn't trying to stop you," she whispered. "Go turn off that kettle. It sounds like a fire alarm."

Tim stood shakily and turned the gas ring off. The kettle rattled against the teapot as he poured the water, and a few drops splattered and scalded his hand. He set the kettle down with a thud and picked up the cups and the teapot, wondering if he could carry them without dropping everything.

When he turned, Rosebay, her skin still flushed, had smoothed the creases from her dress where he had lain his head. He watched in horror as a tear slid down her cheek.

"Rosebay—" He set the tea things on his desk, and the teapot slopped over.

She shook her head. "I won't have you reproach yourself. This time it was my fault. I reckon I just got to keep a better rein on myself and quit acting like a floozy."

Tim stared at her with growing horror and an overwhelming epiphany: He was in love with Rosebay. Under the circumstances, that was worse than feeling lust because it couldn't be satisfied for him by some other woman. It was all horribly more complicated than he had thought.

"You're no floozy, and I wouldn't hurt you for the world. I've got to stay away from you. I love you," he added flatly.

A faint trace of anger flashed in her eyes. "You're late," she said.

"I'm what?" Tim looked back at her, bewildered.

"Just what I said. You're late. I've been in love with you since I met you, you moron. Now you go and fall for me when I'm married to somebody else. I think you got rocks in your head."

"I think so, too." Tim looked at her helplessly. "Do you still want some tea?"

Rosebay nodded.

"I guess my timing's not so good, is it?"

The anger faded, and Rosebay shook her head sadly. After a moment she managed a half smile. "Your timing's terrible. I don't know anybody with worse timing."

"I guess not."

Rosebay sighed. "Except maybe for having this happen here in your office, where we couldn't do anything worse about it. Maybe that was good timing."

Tim poured the tea into the heavy cups. He clenched the china so hard that had it been a delicate teacup he would have broken it. He handed Rosebay her tea. "What are we going to do?" he asked hoarsely.

She gave him a look of determination and misery. "You let me marry Hugo, Tim. We're both going to have to live with that."

After Rosebay had gone, Tim sneaked out the side door into the dusk. As he came around to Kearny Street, the *Clarion* building's gargoyle glared down with what Tim thought was scorn.

I know what you've been up to, the little demon seemed to say. *You skulked out the side exit so the night crew wouldn't see your shifty face, but you can't fool me*.

Tim was in no mood to go home. He cut across Sutter Street to Dupont, turned up Dupont, the conduit to all the places he wasted his breath telling his reporters to stay away from—except, of course, if there was news there. Tim wasn't looking for news tonight. He wasn't sure quite what he was looking for, except maybe trouble.

He passed Morton Street, a dingy alley that San Francisco natives liked to point out to tourists with a kind of reverse pride as "the wickedest street in the world's wickedest city." Its notoriety rested solely on the sale of sex, and from its window ledges leaned women of every race, naked or nearly so. Their faces appeared blank beneath their long tousled hair, but their hands were quick to grasp any man who passed beneath and entice him up the stairs. Their voices cried like cats in the darkness of the alley. Grimacing, Tim hurried by.

Farther up Dupont, the streets narrowed into a maze scented with fish, incense, and opium. Tim liked being in Chinatown. Above him were gilt and red lacquer balconies. Below him, or so it was rumored, a maze of tunnels existed, through which slave dealers and tong members moved on their secret society's furtive errands. Around him traveled men with long queues and women in embroidered robes and trousers. Jade ornaments adorned their oiled black hair.

Tim found the Chinese no better and no worse than his own race. They were prideful, set in their ways, and highly suspicious of foreigners and change—all attitudes that could also be considered quite American, in fact. The Chinese had adapted easily to American politics; the Chinese boss Little Pete protected the profitable illegal operations and was, in turn, under the wing of the white boss Blind Chris Buckley. Wheels within wheels. They all spun efficiently.

Beyond Chinatown was the red-light district known as the Barbary Coast, which had its heart along Pacific Street where it crossed Dupont. As Tim sauntered down Pacific he was lost in thought, but the outer edges of his mind remained alert to the shapes of shadows in the alleyways and the possible intentions of the pair of loungers on the wooden sidewalk outside the Red Rooster. More than one unfortunate had been shanghaied on the Coast and waked to find himself at sea. Mostly the crimps drugged their victims in the waterfront dives, but when business was slow they had been known to knock them on the head on the street.

Tim turned into the smoky doorway of the Lorelei, a dance hall that, like all Coast establishments, also provided anything else its patrons might desire. He sat down at a rickety table and ordered a glass of steam beer from a

waitress whose face was weary beyond her years. Had Tim
been interested, he could have purchased her along with
the liquor she served. She wore a hip-length pleated skirt
and a shirtwaist unbuttoned to reveal bare breasts.

Jimmy Warrington the cartoonist had remarked that a
salesman of ladies' undergarments would starve along the
Coast, and he was probably correct. But to Tim the girls
seemed more repellent than seductive. Their overtures
were joyless, their eyes haunted. He turned away from the
waitress and drained the mug moodily. It was bitter, not
worth the nickel he had paid for it. He still wasn't sure why
he'd come to the Coast. He had some serious thinking to
do, and the dangers and despair of this neighborhood
seemed somehow to heighten his perceptions and delineate
what was important.

There was no sending Hugo to Pennsylvania now. Tim
knew that he wanted Hugo out of the way, and that fact left
him disgusted with himself. Sid Appleton had the experience to cover the coal strike and could be replaced on the
national desk, but Sid was prejudiced against the miners.
And similarly Rafe Murray was too much in favor of them.
Neither man was capable of filing objective dispatches.

Tim drank a second beer. *Well, what the hell*. He stood
up, his decision made, and he felt defiant about it. Waldo
would throw a fit. So would Hugo, who had certainly heard
by now that Tim had been intending to send him. Rosebay
would know what was going on, and she would understand
that he wanted her kept safe.

Tim put another nickel on the table for the waitress,
wondering if she would actually get to keep it. The Lorelei's
bouncer glowered at Tim as he came toward the door. The
Barbary Coast was the turf of the city's roughest sailors and
crimps, the toughest trollops, and the legions of life's
hopeless and luckless. Its denizens thought little of uptown
swells who went slumming, except to roll them if they
could. The Coast took care of its own; outsiders were the
ones who made trouble. Occasionally some society boy was
drugged and shanghaied, or a soldier from the Presidio,
rolled of his month's pay, came back with his whole
regiment to turn the place upside down. Then there was
trouble for everyone, and the Coast's bouncers, in an

uneasy alliance with the policemen who patrolled the wooden sidewalks, would have to sort it out.

Tim stepped warily through the doorway with a nod at the Lorelei's bouncer.

"Keep your eyes open," the tough advised.

"Always do," Tim replied.

The bouncer nodded, and his expression shifted from annoyance to a measuring look. "Two big ones sailing in the morning," he murmured.

Tim lifted a hand in acknowledgment and stepped off the wooden sidewalk and into the street, a little farther from the darkness of two culs-de-sac, Bullrun and Bartlett alleys. With two ships going out on the morning tide, the crimps would have a ready market with any captain who had berths to fill—and there were always berths to fill. Nearly half of some crews jumped ship when they could, often to drink themselves into a stupor along the Coast and be shanghaied once more.

He thought of Rosebay and decided that he had been shanghaied already. The suspicion crossed his mind that he had fallen for her because she was unattainable, but he knew better—she was too attainable. She loved him. *I can't take advantage of that,* he thought.

Tim saw a flicker of movement in a doorway just ahead, and suddenly a raging fury came over him. He had been wanting to fight with something all evening because it was impossible to fight with himself. Well, if these bastards wanted to take him on, let them try. . . . He was too consumed by his own anger to consider that they might get the better of him. Crimps were tough and muscular and as ruthless as barracudas. But Tim was tough and muscular, too.

He angled a little closer to the shadowed doorway, tempting whatever was in there to come out and jump him. As he came abreast of it, a hand shot out and caught at his shoulder, and a blackjack whistled past his ear. He ducked, caught the hand with the blackjack, and bent it backward until he heard the bone crack. He took an intense satisfaction in the sound.

The man gave a shriek of pain, and Tim staggered under a fury of lashing fists. There were two crimps. He caught one man around the waist and hurled him so hard into the adobe wall behind him that the man slumped and didn't get up. The one with the broken wrist tried to flee, but Tim grabbed him by the collar, sent a booted foot between his legs, and dumped him on the sidewalk. The man came down hard on his injured hand and howled.

Others were in the streets, but no one came to the crimps' defense. A couple of drunken sailors hooted, and an unseen woman laughed softly in the night, but no one else took notice. Tim lifted the man with the broken wrist and punched him with a solid precision in the jaw. The man slumped. Tim propped him against the wall beside his friend, then waved at another doorway across the filthy street, where he had noticed a faint movement and the reflection of light in dark eyes.

Tim walked down the street, not looking back, although behind him he heard a furtive scuttle. He nursed the scraped knuckles of his right fist and smiled in a particularly unpleasant manner. He felt better now. The crimps he had left on the sidewalk would wake in the morning and find themselves at sea. The Barbary Coast ate its weaklings.

"You look like you been in an alley fight," Waldo Howard said, trailing Tim up the stairs of Tim's house. Waldo had followed his friend from the office and was not going to give up until Tim threw him out. "What in the hell have you been doing?"

"None of your business." Tim got out a suitcase and began to throw shirts into it.

"And this is just about the most damn fool thing I ever heard of." Waldo glared at the suitcase.

"Go away, Waldo," Tim said.

"You're crazy. You know that? You just got the paper straightened out."

"That's why I hired a managing editor—so I could go off when I needed to."

"You're the publisher. Why the hell do you want to go off chasing fires?"

"This is a national story. I want to get back in the field. I'm rusty."

"You're *supposed* to be rusty! You're the boss!"

Tim slammed the suitcase shut and sat on it. A shirt-sleeve protruded like a stuck-out tongue, and he got up and stuffed it back in. "As long as you followed me home, you might as well drive me to the station."

Waldo narrowed his eyes speculatively. "You're up to something. Yesterday you were going to send Hugo Ware."

"Waldo," Tim said clearly, "if you bring that up one more time, I am going to lay you out." He latched the suitcase.

Waldo stared at him. He scratched his head, baffled. "You in trouble with the law?"

Tim began to laugh, but the laugh faded as quickly as it had come. "No," he said bleakly. "I just have to go away for a while. Don't ask me why."

Connellsville, Pennsylvania, was a city on the edge of hell. If Tim had wanted a place to mirror his own despair, he had found it. Company houses, their paint peeling, clung to the hillsides in the shadow of mine tipples. The main street had a hotel, a post office, and the company store. A white-steepled church tried vainly to claw its way through the coal dust that settled over everything and to lift some scrap of glory toward heaven. The dirt in the main street and the glass in the windowpanes were as black as the cinders of the rail bed, and the miners whose faces slid past the windows of the train looked as if their very skin was permeated with the coal, never to be scrubbed clean again.

The streets seemed ominously quiet. Men stood in tense, silent knots on the corners, staring at the coal company's offices. A woman in a calico dress hurried down the street, dragging a little girl by the hand, tugging the child into a trot, while the men on the street corners watched.

Two company guards came out of the office and blocked the sidewalk so that the woman and girl had to step into the street to go around them. The woman looked nearly ready to cry as she lifted the child into a protective embrace. The guards grinned as she ducked quickly past them and scurried up the hill toward the rows of weathered houses. Tim guessed from the line of the woman's back that she was forcing herself not to run. The men on the street corners could have been striking miners or scabs. It didn't matter. In this menacing dusk, she appeared to be afraid of them all.

The coal companies, Tim knew, paid their miners in scrip, which was only good in the company stores. Prices were high in those stores, and the miners who had trouble making ends meet were encouraged to charge. By payday a man might owe the company more than he had coming to him in wages, ensuring that he could never quit. It was an effective form of legal slavery. Combined with a growing number of mine cave-ins, it had produced a riot a week earlier that left eleven men dead and Connellsville in a state bordering on war.

The train slowed to a stop in a cloud of steam, and the conductor shouted, "Connellsville!"

Tim heaved his bag from the overhead rack and followed three other passengers to the car door. One—a broad-faced Russian in heavy boots and a threadbare shirt—looked as if he might be a miner. Another was obviously a Pinkerton man, a hired security guard. His bowler hat and slightly too tight blue serge suit were nearly a uniform. The third had wire-rimmed glasses and slicked-down hair and might have been a bank clerk—might have been but wasn't. Tim blinked the shock of unexpected recognition, then gave the man a bland look. For an instant apprehension flashed in the other's eyes, and then he turned back to the car door.

Tim hopped down onto the platform to find the Pinkerton man waiting for him.

"What you getting off in Connellsville for, bud?"

"Because this is where my ticket goes," Tim answered. "And my name isn't Bud."

"Let's see some identification."

Tim crossed his arms on his chest. "Why? You get hired by the police, or are you just a free-lance goon?"

The man's hand shot out and grabbed Tim's right arm. It took the hired security guard a moment to realize that his stomach was being prodded by a small pistol, which had appeared in Tim's right hand.

"Back off," Tim said conversationally.

The Pinkerton man let go of Tim's arm. "If you're a union organizer, you ain't going to live long enough to shoot that more than once."

"Once might be plenty. I hate to disappoint you, but I own the *San Francisco Clarion*. Timothy Holt's my name. You got any particular reason to be so jumpy?"

"No union man comes in here," the Pinkerton man growled. "And you can put that in your paper—that we don't allow outside agitators to stir up our people."

"Sounds to me as if they got pretty stirred up on their own," Tim observed. "Or maybe it was having eleven men killed by company thugs."

"Those men were rioting. Company property was destroyed. We enforce the law."

"I didn't realize you had been elected to the police force."

"H. C. Frick Coal Company elected us. That's all it takes."

"I'll let my readers know," Tim murmured.

"We're expecting the union to send in a big gun," the Pinkerton man explained. "We're gonna give him a surprise. If I find out you're lying, you'll leave town in a box. If you talk to any union agitators, you better tell me about it. You got that?"

"It's engraved on my brain," Tim said with sarcasm. "If I meet a union organizer, you expect me to set him up for you."

"Just watch what you print," the Pinkerton man threatened.

Tim sauntered on down the street toward the hotel, which was really a glorified boardinghouse. Dusk was coming fast now, and the loiterers in the street were drifting away, to accomplish who knew what under the curtain of darkness. Tim was not surprised to find the man in the wire-rimmed spectacles falling into step beside him.

"Let me guess," Tim said. "You're visiting your sick mother."

"You tell that Pinkerton thug who I was?"

"If I had, he'd be ramming your head into a wall right now," Tim said. "I run a newspaper. I don't take sides. You never could understand that, Pitts."

"You took sides in Virginia City," Billy Pitts retorted.

"I was a union man till you threw me out," Tim replied. "My personal opinion is still that the union's right; otherwise, I'd have fingered you to that goon. You tossed me out for what Sam Brentwood did, not for anything you could hang on me. So don't expect any special favors. I'm here to report the truth."

"What do you want?"

"I want the story," Tim said. "Fix it up for me to talk with the strikers. I don't seem to be having any trouble making contact with the owners' boys."

"I have to get the lay of the land first," Pitts said. "And there's someone else coming in."

"If you stall me, I can go around you, Pitts. I can tell that Pinkerton in the derby back there where to look for his union organizer, too."

Pitts shrugged. "All I had to do was get off the train safely. If he wants to roust me out of the coal camp, he can try. He'll get a surprise."

Tim grinned. "Then you owe me one, for looking more like a thug than you do. I want to go down into the mine."

Amusement flickered over Pitts's face. "Tomorrow. I'll let you know."

He slipped into the dusk, and Tim went up the steps of the hotel. It was Billy Pitts's stock-in-trade to look like an accountant, but he was a strike organizer with a well-deserved reputation as a tough. If the union had sent Billy Pitts, the union meant business.

Tim tipped his hat to the woman who opened the door. "I'm looking for a room, ma'am."

"You with the Pinkertons?" she asked him suspiciously.

"No, ma'am. I'm a journalist."

She snorted. "I got a parlor full of them. You can stay if you ain't with the Pinkertons or the union. I won't have neither one here. I got kids, and it ain't safe. There's been enough men laid out in this town."

Tim followed her through the house. The furniture was old and massive, cracked with age and the indignities of taking in boarders.

"Here's another one," she said, and the four men in the parlor looked up with interest.

"That makes enough for a game of stud," one of them commented. He was a few years older than Tim, with crinkly brown hair that was beginning to recede from his temples, and a nose that looked as if someone had broken it. He held out his hand. "Felix Runyon, AP."

The others introduced themselves. One was from the *New York Herald*, another from the Philadelphia paper. The fourth Tim recognized from the *San Francisco Chronicle*, and they gave each other a mock salute, thumbs cocked, fingers pointed like pistols.

"What's the good word?" Tim asked, grinning.

"Thievery and corruption. What's yours?"

"That'll do. Many more of us in town?"

"More than the miners, nearly."

"It's been quiet since the recent unpleasantness, but something's coming," the AP man predicted. "The owner's brought in scabs in case of a general strike. The union doesn't ever take to that."

"They'll blow the tipple, likely."

"Or march on the Pinkertons' camp and try to chase them out."

Tim nodded sagely. It was all part of the game. If they really knew something, they wouldn't be sharing the information.

"You hear anything about some hotshot organizer?" the AP man asked.

Tim shook his head. "Not a word. You fellas got a deck of cards?"

A small boy carrying a tin bucket of beer stopped on the sidewalk and looked up at Tim. "You Mr. Holt?"

"I am."

"Pa said if I saw you whilst I was fetchin' his beer to tell you to take a walk about eight o'clock tonight, down past the church."

"I see." The boy scurried on, and Tim turned into the coal-company store. It was empty except for a man chewing tobacco behind the counter. When Tim got out his notebook and began to write down prices, the man leaned forward heavily.

"What you doing?" he demanded.

"Making notes," Tim said. "Seems to me you charge a lot more than most stores around here. How do you get by?"

"Get out," the man ordered. "You can't buy here except with company scrip. You don't need to be in here."

"I surely don't," Tim agreed. "If I were a miner making two dollars a day, I reckon I'd be even worse off."

The man began to come from behind the counter, and Tim beat a strategic retreat.

That evening Tim discovered how much like a war zone Connellsville had become when he took his walk as ordered and found a pistol pressed into the small of his back as he reached the shadow of the church.

"Keep quiet and continue walking."

He was led up the slope above the town and into the tattered woods that still clothed the scarred hillside. Then they went down the slope by a route that couldn't be seen from below and through the rows of company houses.

"You might put that gun away," Tim complained, "seeing that I *want* to come with you."

"I reckon we might, by this time."

When Tim heard the hammer being let down gently, he let out his own breath along with it. He was marched into a house that, behind drawn shades, turned blind eyes to the street. Tim blinked. The room was full of men in miners' hats. They held lanterns in their hands. A white-haired old lady with a sweet, motherly face sat in a cane-backed rocker in their midst. Someone's grandmother, Tim assumed. Billy Pitts stood behind her.

"We've got a message for the company," Pitts told the gathering. "Now's the time to deliver it."

The men lit their lanterns, then surged toward the door, carrying Tim out with them. They flowed down the hillside and along the streets, pounding on the doors of the company houses, shouting for men to join them in the night. Tim knew there was no point in asking questions. Whatever was going to happen would be plain soon enough. Pitts had arranged some form of show and taken pains to see that the press recorded it.

The growing crowd swelled out across the street and

surged down the mountain toward the company offices. Tim was startled to see the old lady at their forefront, side by side with Billy Pitts. Lights were beginning to come on in the town below, and there were shouting and the sound of running feet.

The miners flooded down the last block and jammed the street in front of the company office. Pinkerton men with shotguns stood blocking the doorway.

"You're trespassing!" a security guard shouted. "Get on home before we open fire. Any man still in the street in five minutes has lost his job!"

"No man in this street is going down in that mine at all!" a clear feminine voice shouted, and Toby saw the old lady stand eyeball-to-eyeball with the Pinkerton man.

The guard snorted with derision.

"Go home, Granny."

"My name is Mary Jones, and I won't go home," she said, then turned to the crowd of miners. "These men have had you buffaloed, but the time has come to raise hell and stand up for yourselves like the men the Lord God Almighty made you! Join the union, boys!"

X

Tim had never seen anything like it. Little Mrs. Jones had a round, sweet face and wore a little black bonnet atop a mound of white curls. She resembled his third-grade Sunday school teacher. She looked as if she ought to be sitting in a rocker, knitting socks.

But she let those men have it, miners and Pinkerton men alike. She scolded the hard-faced miners as if they had been errant children, told them they needn't be content with their lot in life and shouldn't allow the mine owners to beat them down, then exhorted them to stand on their hind legs, trust in God, and join the union. When the Pinkerton men tried to drag her off the street, she dared them to shoot an old woman. She told them their mothers hadn't raised them right and one day they were going to stand in front of Saint Peter and answer for their sins.

"All right, that's enough of that," one of the Pinkerton men growled.

The hard-faced miners were snickering, and the miners' wives were yelling, "Shame! Shame!"

"You run along, Grandma, or I'll throw you in jail."

Mrs. Jones laughed. "I've been in jail before. Can't say I liked it, but the company was better than in some places I could name."

"If you don't want to cool your heels in a cell, you'd better get on a train tomorrow."

She glared up at the guard. "I stand by my boys. They don't call me Mother Jones because I get on a train and leave them. This is a union rally. *You* don't belong here."

"I belong here when you hold your damn rally in front of company offices on company property. I can arrest the lot of you for trespassing." The Pinkerton man looked ready to explode. He had clearly been about to open fire on the crowd, but if he hit the old woman, the union would use it against the company.

"Go ahead and arrest us," Mother Jones taunted. "This whole town is company property. That's what's wrong here. But you can't stop justice."

"This is private property! Get off!"

They knew it was an impasse. For now. Tim stood to one side, taking notes furiously. He saw that the rest of the reporters from the boardinghouse had arrived. Noting his being there ahead of them, they glared at him suspiciously. Tim grinned back. Pitts had promised to have a union man take him down in the mine. The reporters didn't know that, either.

In the morning Tim was beginning to wish he hadn't been such a wise guy. The company bosses were never going to permit a reporter into the mine, so Pitts had given Tim a miner's hat, dinner bucket, and a disreputable set of clothing and sent him off as a helper to a man named Kane Powell, whose loyalty to the union was still a secret from the company. Powell introduced Tim as his cousin from Idaho.

It wasn't the first time Tim had been down into a black, airless hole in the ground to dig wealth out of it for somebody else. He had been a silver miner in the drifts that catacombed the earth beneath Virginia City, Nevada, and he had nearly died in a cave-in. It made him profoundly reluctant to climb onto the mule-drawn cart that rattled down the gangway into the heart of the Connellsville coal seam. For one thing, his Virginia City experience had left him with claustrophobia, and the gangway and the headings that opened off the seam were as black and narrow as the inside of a cannon barrel and charged with as ominous an atmosphere. It was perpetually hot underground, and the ventilating fans rendered the air no more than barely breathable. The gases that the miners called damps were a constant terror. Firedamp—marsh gas—constantly seeped into the mine and, mixed with a sufficient quantity of oxygen, could blow the whole mine to kingdom come. White damp followed an explosion of firedamp or occurred with the blasting of the coal face. It burned with a beautiful blue flame, smelled sweetly of violets, and killed any man who breathed it. Black damp was more common and produced numbness, headaches, and drumming in the ears.

The ventilating system relied on trapdoors to control the air flow, and trapper boys swung the big doors open to let the mule-drawn carts through, then shut the doors behind them. It was the first job a young boy might have in the mines, progressing from there to mule driver, to helper, to miner, and finally to be assigned his own "room" to work, paid by the ton of coal.

"That's my son, Jerem," Kane Powell, the union man with Tim said proudly as a small boy with skinny arms and legs dragged the door open ahead of the cart. "He's only seven. Don't hardly know what the sun looks like, but then neither do I. His ma don't like it, but Jerem's got to learn the trade. We can't get by elsewise."

When the trip driver paused for a moment to fiddle with a loose harness strap, young Jerem paused by the big door that dwarfed him and grinned at his father. "Hi, Paw."

"Son." Kane winked. "You're doing a fine job, boy. You remember your dinner pail?"

The child nodded.

Tim found himself listening. . . . Gone were all the familiar noises of the outside world—no birds, no wind, no carriage wheels, no barking dogs. Only an intense silence broken by the faraway *tick-tick* of a miner's pick, the faint creaking of the roof, and the soft rustling of mine rats in the gob, the edge on either side of the track where mine waste was thrown. The mules were stabled underground, and their spilled oats, as well as leavings from the miners' dinner pails, fed the rats.

The roof began to pound and rumble, and Powell cocked his head at it in frozen motion. Tim could just see his tense face under the flickering light on his hat peak.

"Roof's starting to work," Powell explained after a

minute. "The timbers splinter, and then the slate starts to break. She'll come down in a day or two."

"How can you tell she won't come down now?" Tim demanded, trying to keep a rein on his terror. He wondered just how undignified it would be to beat a hasty retreat to the surface.

"By the sound," Powell replied. "You either learn to know a roof working, or you don't come up one day. Then there's the rats. As long as you're knocking rats out of your dinner pail, you can keep shoveling."

Tim listened to the rodents' rustle as the cart began to move again. Many of the miners put such faith in rats that they hand-fed them from their dinner pails. Then their population grew beyond control, and they started eating the soap and drinking the lamp oil. Dinner pails had to be left buried under piles of slate against rodent scavengers. When a rat might be all that stood between you and death, you got funny about rats.

The cart turned to the side into a heading, and the lamps glimmered on the shiny outcrops of the coal and on the low overhanging roof beams. Fungus thrived in the hot, damp atmosphere and drifted from the beams in ethereal cottony filaments. The rotting wood gave off an odor like creosote, and pale insects—moths and flies and gnats—whirled about the white strands.

The mules stopped, and Powell beckoned to Tim. They climbed from the cart and went into a room separated from the next by solid pillars of coal left to brace the roof. A miner and two helpers were already at work in the next room, their faces and the shadows of their picks in sharp relief in the rings of lamplight, moving in some intricate pattern.

After the rooms in one section of the mine were worked out, the last task would consist of "robbing the pillars," taking down the coal columns supporting the roof.

"Dead work," Powell muttered, and Tim wondered if Powell was echoing his own thoughts: that mining the pillars—and betting your life on when and how the roof would come down behind you—was work for only the most skilled. The pay was the highest in the mine, but the death rate was, too.

But Powell was glowering at a tumble of rock at the face. It would have to be moved before any more coal could be brought down, and nobody paid for rock. The Frick Company paid only for tonnage loaded. *Dead work* meant unpaid work—laying track, moving rock, timbering the roof, anything but loading coal. Payment for dead work was one of the union's demands. Miners, desperate to make a living wage, would stint on dead work when they could, risking an unpropped roof in order to load more coal.

Powell looked at Tim, his eyes already ringed raccoon-like with coal dust. "You know which end of a shovel?"

Tim sighed. "I've mucked ore." He picked up the shovel.

Powell nodded. "You'll have a tale to tell then."

Tim began to shovel rock out of the way, to be dragged out and dumped in the gob. Only clean coal could go up in the car tagged with Powell's number. Beyond them, in the next room, and in the next, he could hear voices, and Powell clucked his tongue.

"That damfool's at it again,"

Tim caught a glimpse of a strangely dapper man in a miner's cap and elegant business suit. He was clambering among the coal with a sheaf of papers in his hand and scribbling furiously as he talked.

"He sells life insurance," Powell explained. "Comes round three or four times a year to take sign-ups."

Tim stared. "And the foreman permits him down here?"

"No skin off the foreman's nose." Powell grinned. "Fine industry for life insurance, the coal business. He does a right brisk trade."

Tim lifted a shovelful of rock and tossed it. His back and shoulders ached already. Powell was lying on his side, holding up his head, and using his pick to make a cut into the base of the coal seam. The undercut would go three or four feet into the coal, and Powell with it, until he was lying under an overhanging block of coal that might weigh a ton or more.

"How old are you, Powell?" Tim asked.

"Thirty this year. Been a miner for twenty-two."

Thirty. Tim looked at Powell's arms, muscular and as

black as the coal dust, at the gnarled hands and the deep creases in his face, and at the way the cords of his neck stood out when he lifted his head to hack at the coal that was only inches from his face. Powell was only three years older than Tim, and he looked older than Tim's father.

"How long does it take you to make that cut?" Tim asked, taking mental notes for the background piece he intended to write.

"Two, three hours," Powell responded. "Then I have to drill a hole down from the top to shoot it. You can go with what I dropped yesterday." He nodded at the fall of coal that lay beyond the rock. "Had to brush the roof to make some headroom. That's what brought down all the rock."

Tim was stoically digging his shovel blade into the rock fall again—after all, he had asked for this—when there was a thunderclap of sound. The whole mine was lit as if by lightning, illuminating for one white, frozen second the deep black sheen of the walls, the pale, drained faces of the miners in the next room, even the motionless figure of a mine rat, its claws splayed in terror.

Then came a roar of air, followed by blackness and searing flame. Tim felt himself lifted and thrown as if by some rough hand larger than his body. He crashed against the sidewall and gasped for air as a river of fire passed over his head.

The Day of Judgment, when tombs would stand open, could not have been more fearful. By the hellish light of the fiery blast that had miraculously passed him by, Tim saw the charred form of a miner from the next room twisting and writhing on the floor. The singed, terrified figure of the insurance agent clawed blindly at the unyielding face of the coal seam, as if he might somehow open some way of escape. The half undercut coal face that Powell had been working on shuddered, creaked, and collapsed with a crash, creating another flash of blue fire around it.

Kane! A hand grasped Tim's arm as the room sank into blackness. "Get up," Powell's voice urged hoarsely. "Get out while there's a chance."

Tim grabbed Powell's arm. He had thought Kane was buried under the coal.

"Move, damn it!" Powell said. "This whole mine's going to burn. I got to find Jerem."

Tim staggered to his feet, and Powell and he began to make their way up the heading toward the gangway. Tim stumbled behind the miner through the blackness that had engulfed their lamps. They were too afraid of another explosion to light them again. They could hear voices calling to one another behind and before them, and the moans of the dying, burned beyond recognition or pinned in falling shale where a weakened roof had crashed down. A mule was shrieking ahead of them.

The volatile coal dust had fed the fire of the gas explosion. The mine was burning in its depths now. The air was thick with smoke and dust, and the trapdoors, opened or blown clear off their hinges by the explosion, fed the fires with oxygen. Jerem wasn't in the gangway when they passed his post.

"She'll blow again! Get out!" Panic-stricken voices echoed through the gangway and the headings. And then there was an ominous rumble.

As Powell grabbed Tim and shoved him against the sidewall, the rumble accelerated to a deep boom, and then a laden coal car, driverless and with an unset break, hurtled past them and plunged down into the mine. There was a scream just behind them, and Tim turned back trying to see what had happened. But Powell yanked at him again.

"Get on! Get up there!" Powell shoved him, and Tim staggered on. At the end of the gangway, the hoist room was filled with dazed and injured men. The hoist rattled down, and the men fought one another to clamber into it.

"Get back! Line up!" the mine foreman and a grim-faced superintendent were shouting.

"Jerem!" Powell cried out. "*Jerem!*" There was no answer. "I'm going back to find my boy," Powell told Tim. "You get in the hoist as soon as there's room."

"I'm coming with you," Tim said.

Powell didn't wait to tell him he was a fool. He ran back down the passage. A cart with a frightened adolescent driver came up the track, with injured men in the front car.

"Jerem!" Powell shouted at the driver. "Have you seen my Jerem?"

"Back there," the driver said, pointing. "He's gone, Kane. We couldn't get him loose."

Powell began to run. Tim, his heart pounding, lurched after him. The last time he had been this afraid that he was going to die had been in another mine, but the danger there had been suffocation. Would it be worse to burn, he wondered, to be caught in that mouth of hell, seared until he was unrecognizable? It wasn't so much the notion of fire that he feared, as the trapped feeling—of being caught like a thing in a snare, to wait for whatever horror would come to kill him.

Powell was scrabbling in the gob near Jerem's door and crying his child's name. Tim realized from the sounds that the boy was pinned under his own door, which had been blown off its hinges. Tim put his hands out and felt a small, still face beyond the boards that Powell was frantically trying to lift. No wonder Jerem hadn't answered their cries.

Tim wedged his hands under the edges of the iron-bound door and heaved with Powell. Frightened men were falling over them, and they could hear the distant boom and roar of further explosions. Once again the whole passage was lit in white lightning. They seemed to stand forever, bent, struggling against the weight of the door. Slowly it came up, toppled over, and crashed down, and Powell bent to scoop up his small, limp child. The blackness of the gangway was beginning to fill with a red glow that seeped upward from below.

"Run!" Powell rasped.

They fled up the gangway and shoved themselves into the hoist as it lifted with the final load. It rattled toward the surface, and as it broke into the light, a last spew of flaming air erupted from the earth's depths, and a roar devoured all other sound.

Aboveground a frightened, weeping crowd had already gathered. The sunlight shone harshly on the black ground and the weathered boards of the coal tipple. A doctor was moving among the men laid out on the earth, and women clung to the arms of the mine foreman and sobbed the names of their missing loved ones.

"We don't know yet. We don't know. We'll call out the names as we find them."

But Tim and the others knew that a coal-mine fire might burn for years and that some bodies might never come out. The unreachable ones would be locked forever in the mountain, with the sealed-off burning seam.

Tim looked around for Powell and found him kneeling over his son, with the doctor beside them. The child's eyes fluttered open, and Tim nearly sobbed with relief. Beside them, the insurance agent lay perfectly still. He had found his way out of the mine only to die of scorched lungs. As Tim stroked his boy's forehead, Powell gathered Jerem in his arms. Then the child's eyes rolled back, and with a shuddering breath he died.

"Got more tale to tell than you bargained for, I reckon," was all Powell could say.

Tim told his tale and sent it to San Francisco by cable that night. The other reporters slapped him on the back to congratulate him for not being killed. They gave him a drink and dealt him into their perpetual poker game.

"Hell of a way to get a story," Runyon of the AP said.

"That's me," Tim said wearily. "Close to the source."

"Think the rest of the miners'll go out with the union now?" the *Herald*'s man asked.

"That Jones woman's bound to be at them, too," the Philadelphia man remarked. "That woman's a flat-out anarchist."

"She's good copy," Runyon told him. "Deal the cards and don't argue politics."

Slowly Tim relaxed into the easy camaraderie of the other reporters. It was a professional necessity for the men to distance themselves from the reality of what they reported on; otherwise, their emotions would be too raw to bear. It was not that they didn't sympathize with the maimed and the burned and the widowed. It was just that the horrors of the world stacked up too high to be affected by them year after year.

Tim took another drink and discovered that he ached all over. He shifted in his chair so that the pain in his right leg, where the empty runaway cart had slammed into it, eased just a little.

In spite of his discomfort, he went out again the next

day with the rest of the journalists and moved in unspoken anguish among the women still waiting by the tipple for some word from below. When it was possible, he went into the mine, dropped in the hoist. His heart was in his mouth as he watched the eerie reddish glow flickering up the gangway. Fire-fighting crews moved down to it.

The mine boss chased him out, so he followed the small, furious figure of Mother Jones as she stomped from one group to another, comforting the bereaved and telling them that they knew what they had to do about it.

"No miner is afraid of the sheriff or a jail!" she said. "No miner fears anything but his God! Nothing, not even thugs with guns, is more dangerous than what a coal miner does for his living every day of his life! And until that changes, until the Frick Company cares for human life beyond its profits, no miner will fear them. Join the union!" She noticed Tim, limping behind her. "Write that down."

The image of the bleak-faced women who, like their men, were old beyond their years, standing motionless by the tipple as the sun began to set again, stayed with Tim all through the night. He scrubbed himself clean in a galvanized tub for the second evening in a row. His landlady informed him that she didn't have time to fill tubs and clean up after dirty miners; that was why she didn't allow them in the house. There were boardinghouses for miners—hers was a higher-class place.

Tim mumbled something conciliating as he looked longingly at the hot water. It was all he could do not to strip and fling himself into the tub before she left. Coal was oily and left a black smudge that didn't brush or blow away but ground itself into the skin and clothes. It was so hard to keep a house clean in a coal camp that miners' daughters were notorious for staying single rather than doing what their mothers had done. Few of the company houses had running water. A miner had to bathe every night, so his wife hauled the water for it, in addition to doing the cooking, cleaning, laundry, and childrearing. She made ends meet with chickens and a garden and taking in washing for the supervisor and mine bosses.

Clean and dried and in bed, Tim reached out to blow

out the lamp but changed his mind. Instead, he took up his notebook and a pencil and wrote:

> Few men who think they have done a good day's work have experienced the backbreaking labor that belongs to the miners of coal or to the women who marry them. Their children begin work at the age of seven—in the darkness of the earth if they are boys, and in the lint-filled air of the textile mills if they are girls. The textile mills are located in coal towns because the owners know that these miners' daughters are a ready work force. This is not just a camp of working men but of despairing women and weary, sad-eyed, dying children. . . .

By the next day, most of the Connellsville miners were on strike. Pitts and Mother Jones took a train to Columbus, Ohio, and in a few more days the press corps got word that the miners there were getting ready to strike. Connellsville was not alone in its despair, and the labor movement was determined to show the world its strength.

"Wrong year for it," Runyon of the AP said sagely as he and Tim settled into the train to Columbus. "Things aren't bad enough yet to get the general populace behind them."

"Aren't bad enough?" Tim echoed. "How much worse do they have to get than seven-year-old babies working and dying underground?"

"I thought you said you came out here because you couldn't trust anyone on your staff to be unbiased," Runyon said with a chuckle.

Tim sighed. "I did. But it's getting pretty plain to me this is one of these issues where a paper has to take a side. That's the boss's decision to make, not a reporter's. I happen to be the boss."

"Elegant logic," Runyon said. He pulled his hat over his eyes and leaned back in his seat as the train swayed down the mountain. From the stories he had told, Runyon, Tim knew, had put in a lot of time on the road and had seen nearly everything. Over the years he had learned not to break his heart over it.

Tim and Runyon arrived in Columbus the very day that one hundred thirty-six thousand miners struck. Their complaint was wages, but at the bottom of that issue were slavery to the company and the terror with which they worked daily. Their terror included not only the working conditions but extended to a fear of the company itself and the violence sanctioned by the owners. Miners who organized or talked of organizing were arrested by the deputy sheriffs of the coal camps. Known union sympathizers were ambushed in the night and shot. The workers who went down into the ground and wrestled with the earth for a living were not tame men, however, and they fought back. Scabs and mine bosses were shot, too, and the strikes and riots escalated into a war. Four days after the miners of Columbus struck, an accident at Franklin, Washington, killed thirty-seven miners, and civil war between the United States and its workers seemed possible.

"The Pullman workers are next," Runyon predicted as he and Tim sat at a bar after a long, disheartening day. "You mark me. They're making a mistake, but they'll be next."

"Coxey's moving," Tim said. "Have you heard?" There wasn't any point in trying to keep anything that big from the AP.

"Coxey's been moving," Runyon replied.

The phenomenon of Coxey's Army had kept the reporters who were covering the coal strikes enthralled. Jacob Sechler Coxey, a wealthy quarry owner from Massillon, Ohio, possessed a social conscience that could only be termed visionary. Coxey's Army was a ragtag band of some four hundred marchers taking their protests to Washington, D.C., to put their plight of unemployment and poverty under President Cleveland's nose and see if he could ignore them—or so was their stated mission. Originally named the Commonweal of Christ, the movement had swollen to epic proportions and taken the name the press had given it: Coxey's Army.

Other armies of like-minded laborers were gathering, moving, surging, toward the capital from all over the country, a "petition in boots," in this depression year. They were driven by their belief that the government would never legislate for working people but only for the corpo-

rations, coal companies, railroads, and the industries that
Toby Holt had spoken of, not without truth, as robber
barons.

The press loved Jacob Coxey. Nothing so interesting had come the journalists' way in a long time. Not the
least interesting was Coxey's partner in the venture, Carl
Browne, who dressed like Buffalo Bill, believed in reincarnation, and knew publicity when he saw it. No bizarre
moment of the march—and there were many—went unre-
ported by the gleeful press. Occasionally they went too far,
and Carl Browne lost his temper. A few weeks before,
when the difficulties of plodding through the mud and snow
of northern Ohio had been duly reported and some reference made to internal arguments, Browne had character-
ized the journalists as "Argus-eyed demons from hell."

The press liked that description so well, they formed a
fraternity, the AEDH, and when Coxey's Army reached the
Chesapeake and Ohio Canal for the last leg of its journey to
Washington, the press chartered their own boat and christened it the *Flying Demon*.

The *Flying Demon* was Tim's destination. It was color,
the personal side of a story, that he was after. Regretfully he
did not have enough staff to send for another reporter to
stay with the strikers, but a time would come when the
Clarion would have the staff to cover everything. Anyway,
Runyon would stay with the strikers, and the *Clarion* had
an AP franchise. For now Tim would have to impress his
readers with footwork and human-interest stories.

"Hah," said Runyon, downing a second whiskey as Tim
explained this theory. "You just want to put your nose in
everything you can. You weren't a reporter long enough to
get it out of your system—that's your problem. Either that
or you're crossed in love and feeling restless." He blinked
at the expression that flashed across Tim's face. "Did I step
on a sore spot, Holt? I didn't mean to."

"Not at all," Tim said lightly. "You're right. I've got
things to get out of my system." *And never mind what*.

He took a train for Cumberland, Maryland, where the
Commonweal of Christ was encamped, waiting for its
flotilla of dubious boats to be ready. The Chesapeake and

Ohio Canal had seen better days. It was thick with abandoned and deteriorating canal boats, in many of which
out-of-work families had taken up squatters' rights. To the
son of a privileged family, it was one more piece of evidence
of "there but for the grace of God . . ." Tim's odyssey
began to be very educational.

He found the press corps leaning over the bow of the
Flying Demon to watch as a beaming Carl Browne, in a
striped linen shirt with a sailor collar, oversaw the disman-
tling of the wagons. Twenty fractious horses were being
coaxed up the gangplank of a boat that looked as if it might
sink at any moment.

Thousands of townspeople from Columbus had turned
out to watch the flotilla set out and to cheer for hours under
the broiling sun. At noon, when the factory whistles blew,
Browne moved to the prow of the flagship *Benjamin
Vaughn*, where he struck a nautical pose beneath a portrait
of Christ, which he always carried with him, and gave
orders to shove off. The reporters finished cleaning their
own craft—it had previously carried coal—and followed.

The flotilla passed beneath the South Cumberland
Glassworks and a steel and tin-plate factory. The workers
came out and cheered. On the poop deck of the *Benjamin
Vaughn*, Browne was giving orders in a firm voice to the
inattentive mules on the towpath. Tim wondered what
Mother Jones would make of Carl Browne.

At each lock, curious West Virginians and Marylanders
turned out to watch the army glide by. Train engineers
shrieked their whistles in greeting while their passengers
waved handkerchiefs out the windows.

"Your old man's in Washington, isn't he, Holt?" a
reporter from the *Washington Post* asked Tim. "You think
this hullabaloo is going to get anywhere?"

"Hell, no," another man interrupted. "It's just a big
circus—lots of clowns and no direction."

"Clowns capture the public's attention," Tim mused.
"Maybe you have to get people's attention before anything
gets done."

"I think Coxey knows what he's doing," another man
commented.

"*I* think he's under Browne's influence. Crazy man thinks he's Christ reincarnated."

"Coxey?" Tim asked.

"No, Browne. Coxey thinks he's Andrew Jackson."

At nightfall they entered the locks across the Potomac from Green Spring, West Virginia. A whippoorwill called insistently from a sycamore, and a chorus of frogs peeped from the silvered waters of the river. It was a strange, almost magical night as the flotilla glided down the canal under a scattering of stars in the velvet sky. *Romantic,* Tim thought, *if only I had a woman with me. One woman in particular . . . Quit that!*

At midnight the boats slid into a tunnel that had been bored through rock. The passengers called to one another to hear their echoes. A mule on the towpath brayed, and the sound ricocheted inside the tunnel like a tin drum. So much for romance. . . .

The passengers on the *Flying Demon,* looking for something productive to do, interviewed the *Demon*'s skipper, Captain Barger. He had been on the canal for a long time and refused to be impressed by anything. But as the boats slid past the memory-laden Civil War country west of Harper's Ferry, Captain Barger grew uneasy.

"I used to hear about John Brown before the war and how he stirred up the people," the captain remarked. "I 'low that Coxey is doing just the same. Everything is going wrong—Congress, the President, and the millionaires—and there has got to be a war and lots of bloodshed before any change will come."

Is change always bloody? Tim wondered. *Don't we ever learn anything?* He thought he saw a certain uneasiness on the faces of the other reporters as well. A man who had covered Harper's Ferry all those years before, during the war, turned away suddenly and shouted that it was time for a drink.

Someone slapped Tim on the back. "You arrived at the perfect time, Holt. We damn near died going over the Alleghenies with those loonies. Trust a newspaper publisher to hook on just when it gets easy."

"That's right," Tim agreed. "We got no principles."

There was general laughter at that, and the mood of premonition faded. Fourteen reporters, four telegraphers, and one lineman were on the *Flying Demon*, and they had brought with them on the old barge six cases of bottled beer, two kegs of beer, and four gallons of whiskey in stone jars. When they went ashore to file their stories, they replenished the supply. They had rented two extra mules for the trip so they could catch up with the army again.

The demons had proclaimed one of their number the rank of admiral and given him a paper hat and tin horn. Every quarter hour he blew his horn and ordered all hands below for a drink. By nightfall the demons were singing, dancing, and drunk. W. P. Babcock of the *New York World* wrote them an anthem:

> Demons come from all the states,
> Brought together by the fates,
> Yet they are the best of mates
> For all are blooming reprobates!
>
> Ta Ra Ra Boom De Ay
> The demon's life is gay
> Until the first of May.
> Ta Ra Ra Boom De Ay.

Not very good poetry, as Tim said, but it captured the spirit of the voyage.

When the demons finally settled down well after midnight, one wakeful soul sneaked up again and yelled suddenly, "Fire! Murder! Help! Save the mules! Run for your lives! The hoboes are upon us!"

The other journalists grabbed him and threw him in the canal, but after that they were all awake again, so they painted themselves a flag by lantern light: "Demons of Hell" in blue letters on a red ground. They hoisted it proudly the next day, but Coxey said it looked too much like the red banner of socialism and told them to take it down.

The reporters, not wanting to comply, gleefully threatened to file stories that assured their readers that rumors were false and Coxey was *not* a socialist—guaranteed to make every reader believe otherwise—but Coxey was adamant. The demons hauled down the offending banner when they stopped that night to file their stories.

The telegraph corps was under the management of E. P. Bishop, an experienced hand who had gotten the Johnstown Flood and the Homestead Strike on the wires in past years. To send copy, a lineman scrambled up a pole, cut the telegraph wire, and hooked in a portable telegraph key. Four telegraphers, sometimes working on bare ground, transmitted the reporters' copy. As often as not, the reporter would be sprawled on the ground beside the telegrapher, scribbling further news as fast as it could be sent. Some stories ran to several thousand words, and the operator of one local telegraph station locked up his shack and went home when he heard the demons were coming.

"What the hell did he do that for?" Bishop demanded of the ferryman at the canal bank.

"He went to bed, Cap'n, and told me to tell youse all he was dyin'."

As much as the demons could send on Coxey, their papers printed. Times were dull, to the journalist's eye. All other news was depressing, but Coxey was good for color and gossip and the personal hard-luck stories gleaned from his followers. Coxey needed publicity, and the press obliged with alacrity. By May Day, the only people in the country who hadn't heard of their demonstration were those too young to read a newspaper.

The other workers' armies were converging, too. Coxey's idea and Browne's recruiting had spread. Leaders ranged from the itinerant labor reformer Lewis C. Fry of Los Angeles to the wild-eyed "General" Stephen Maybell of San Francisco's Heaven at Hand Army.

Hugo Ware had already sent Tim a report on General Maybell: "It is part of our religion to seize the government of the United States and reform it," Maybell had told his listeners on Market Street. "It is my intention to march straight to Washington and demand a government for the people and by the people. If we don't get it we will eject Congress and behead Cleveland."

"He foams finely at the mouth," Hugo had written to

Tim, "but I don't think the President needs to worry just yet."

All the same, the government was getting a little nervous. The number of armies of the unemployed beginning to converge on Washington was growing. The Treasury Department ordered sixty-five carbines and one hundred rifles for use by their personnel, who were feeling distinctly jumpy about the idea of thousands of hungry, out-of-work men marching quite so close to all that money.

Coxey's men marched out of Frederick, Maryland, for the last leg of their journey with a sheriff's posse of ten men behind the column. In their wake also trailed a growing crowd of souvenir sellers with pictures of Coxey and with badges, poems, and books. Swindlers with shell games tagged along to fleece the rustics. The sheriff's posse proved useful in dispersing the former at the request of a wrathful Coxey. But secret-service agents also shadowed Coxey, and two joined the ranks of the marchers.

Rumors flew: There had been bloodshed along other armies' routes. . . . Troops from Fort Myer in Maryland had been sent to kill a few marchers and deter the rest. . . . Coxey was meeting with anarchists, and the march was the first step toward revolution. . . .

Toby Holt watched all these preparations with interest. He read his son's stories in the *Clarion* and the other demons' work in various other newspapers. He pushed his glasses up on his nose and looked from the latest piece in the *Post* to the window, where he could see marines parading in the street. At the Arlington Barracks, the Navy Yard, and the Marine Barracks, an unusual amount of parading and weapons drill was occurring, and the saber rattling was beginning to make people skittish.

Toby pushed the button for his secretary, and when the man stuck his head in the door, Toby grinned and said, "You're going to get a chance to see Coxey up close, Watson. My son's out there somewhere with the rest of the gentlemen of the press—probably drunk on a flatboat. Go round him up for me and tell him to come and have dinner."

XI

Watson located the senator's son encamped with the other demons outside Rockville, Maryland, the last stop before entering Washington. It was beginning to rain, and a high wind was howling. Tim looked despairingly at Watson.

"You want me to come out in this? I'm beat to death already."

"I can tell your father it's not convenient," Watson said sarcastically. He looked around him at the Coxey encampment. Not far from the demons' tent was Browne's "panorama wagon," which sported a giant canvas of Christ and fourteen smaller panels depicting Browne's economic theories. These dealt largely with unemployment, reincarnation, and non-interest-bearing bonds. "Damnedest thing I ever saw," Watson muttered, shaking his head.

"You haven't heard him preach," Tim said, pulling on his coat. "The last time, he started out with a poem."

"'The Mystery of the Whence'" several reporters intoned solemnly in chorus.

"Then, to explain reincarnation, he drew a lot of diagrams that looked like spiders. And he wouldn't let any of the fellows eat until he was through. They nearly rioted." Tim wrapped a muffler around his neck and jammed a felt hat down over his eyes. "If Dad wants to go to a fancy restaurant, he can lend me some clothes."

The ride into Washington got wetter by the minute, and Tim was soaked by the time he presented himself at the Senate offices. Toby gave him a hot drink and some spare clothes of his own—which, on Tim, were a little too tight in the shoulders and too large in the waist—and took him off to Hancock's Restaurant on Pennsylvania Avenue. Hancock's, practically a government institution, was reputed to have the best fried chicken and cocktails in Washington. Toby waited until Tim had been served both before he led the conversation away from the trivial.

"Best meal I've had in weeks," Tim said, wolfing down the chicken. "I didn't want to come out in the rain, but now I'll bless you for it."

Toby contemplated the framed souvenirs along Hancock's wall. The place had been the haunt of Clay and Calhoun and all the other famous men of antebellum politics. Its trophies included a beaver hat belonging to Zachary Taylor as well as other oddities, the strangest of which was a piece of the blanket in which John Wilkes Booth's body had been carried from the burning barn. It had been framed and hung beside Stanton's offer of a hundred thousand dollars for the arrest of the Lincoln conspirators.

"This place convinces me that everybody's a little bit crazy," Toby said. "Is Jacob Coxey crazy?"

"Not strictly speaking," Tim answered.

"He named his baby Legal Tender," Toby pointed out.

"He feels strongly about economic issues," Tim said. He grinned. "Lord, I don't know whether he's crazy or not. I do know he's started a truly amazing movement, and it hasn't been just the press that's kept it rolling."

"You haven't done it any harm," Toby said.

"I know that. But nobody else has given us such good material in years. Being colorful isn't all it takes to inspire thousands of jobless men to walk across the continent."

"They aren't all walking," Toby grumbled. "They stole a train in Montana."

"There is that. But Coxey's not responsible for those western troops."

"Somebody had better be," Toby said. "Look, you've been traveling with them, and you've been hanging around with the United Mine Workers. I want to know what you've seen out there—not just what you can put in the newspaper, but how it feels to you: the unsubstantiated stuff, rumor and innuendo."

"That's our specialty," Tim said. "Sniffing the wind, I mean. What you sniff in the wind this year may not make it into the paper until next year, but that doesn't mean it isn't out there. It's just . . . solidifying."

Toby beckoned the waiter for another whiskey rickey and a second plate of fried chicken. He had no idea where Tim was putting either, but they were steadily disappearing.

Tim chewed and swallowed. "I'll tell you what I think is happening: This country's industrializing. We're creating a whole new category of worker, someone who doesn't have either a piece of land or a little business of his own but who depends on another man to hire him and pay him a living wage. It's getting so that's how most men earn their bread. And they all, hundreds of thousands of them, depend on a very few men who own the industry. So a tiny minority controls the entire existence of all these hundreds of thousands of others. And when you feel as though someone controls your life and he's not doing right by you, you feel helpless and not quite a man. Otherwise, you could *make* them do you right. Eventually the impotence turns to anger."

"Angry enough to strike."

Tim nodded. "Striking is the only weapon they've got—that or make some big show like Coxey's folks and embarrass the government into helping. In my opinion, it's a wonder there hasn't been worse violence. When someone makes a fool of you—puts you on a leash, takes away your rights, and makes you work for slave wages—then you get angry, a deep kind of fury that makes you want to hit back."

"Finding another job is always an alternative," Toby suggested.

"You aren't being realistic, Dad. Most of these miners *can't* quit. They owe money to the company store, and the corporation sees to it that it stays that way. There aren't any other jobs anyway. What do you suppose Coxey's people are trying to tell you?"

"Then you think they represent a valid movement under all the carnival hullabaloo?"

"I do. I think they represent a movement that Washington better pay some attention to. As I recall, King George started out thinking American Revolutionaries were just a bunch of sideshow rabble rousers, too. *They'd* been pushed about as far as they'd stand for."

"I'm not ready to compare Thomas Jefferson with Carl Browne. Jefferson was a literate man who had the advantage of making sense."

"Browne's merely a symptom," Tim said. "The people you need to worry about aren't Coxey and Browne; concern yourself with their followers, who don't have any work or any dinner. And I think you can probably compare Mother Jones to Jefferson or anybody else you want to. I never met such a terrifying old lady in my life."

The next day, the Coxey cavalcade reached Brightwood Riding Park, their Washington encampment, and gratefully halted. Tim discovered that in his absence the wind had brought the reporters' tent down about their ears, and he felt more grateful than ever for the dinner at Hancock's and the dry bed at his family's house on Connecticut Avenue.

The Commonweal of Christ set up its tents inside the half-mile oval riding track. Browne positioned his panorama wagon and portrait of Christ at the gates and stationed a marcher to collect contributions from the Sunday sightseers.

Tim took Toby, Alexandra, Mike, and Sally to join the eight thousand other Washingtonians who turned out to see the show. Senators' carriages jostled with farm wagons filled with black families; bicyclers zigzagged in and out of the crowd, and foreign dignitaries turned out for the spectacle. The monocled British ambassador was seen on a thoroughbred horse, and two members of the Chinese legation appeared, splendid in embroidered robes and long braids. The entire Mexican legation turned out, as did the Japanese ambassador and representatives of France and Italy.

Browne preached his Sunday reincarnation service, shedding his buckskin jacket for a black cutaway and leading the army's choir in its rendition of "Hold the Fort." He interwove prophecy and finance, Saint John and the sugar trust, while Toby's eyebrows rose steadily higher under his hat.

Browne was followed by Jacob Coxey, who took the opportunity to apprise Congress further of his dual plans for better roads and better money. "This revolutionary spirit of seventy-six is making the moneylenders tremble now. Congress takes two years to vote on anything if left to itself. Twenty million people are hungry and cannot wait two years to eat!"

The spectators were less interested in rhetoric than they were in Coxey's followers, who looked like tramps one and all. Fashionably dressed congressmen's wives, munching gingerbread cookies bought at the front gates, interviewed them as if they were sideshow freaks or curiosities in a museum: Had the walk from Ohio been pleasant, or had they preferred the final part of the journey, on the canal boats? What sort of man was Mr. Coxey? Was it true that Mr. Browne thought he was possessed of his dead wife's spirit? They gaped at the ragged wagons and battered tin plates that hung from them, and with no apparent concern for the fact that they were discussing fellow human beings who could hear every word they said, the wives exchanged critical comments on the appearance of the weary marchers who were stretched on the ground with their coats rolled up and used as pillows under their heads.

The next day, after considerable annoyed discussion between Coxey and Major W. C. Moore, the District of Columbia commissioner of police, over the legality of making a speech from either the steps of the Capitol or the street outside it, an infuriated Coxey stormed around the Capitol in search of either the vice-president or the speaker of the house, both of whom were lying low. He did, however, sign two hundred autographs.

The following morning was May Day, International Workers' Day, and the Commonweal of Christ's day of glory. With or without permission, the army was going to march, and Coxey and Browne intended to speak— nothing had stopped either of them yet. Coxey rode in his black carriage, with Mrs. Coxey and little Legal Tender beside him. Before them on a white stallion rode Coxey's seventeen-year-old daughter, Mamie, in her role as the goddess of peace. Her willowy figure was encased in a snow-white riding habit, and her auburn hair crowned with a liberty cap of red, white, and blue. She was beautiful enough to start a riot on her own.

The Commonweal turned onto the dusty road that led downtown, with the great white dome of the Capitol in the distance. Spectators spilled from the sidewalks, and on Fourteenth Street the Chinese legation leaned from the windows to wave their parasols and fans.

Carl Browne's panorama wagon lurched along behind to great cheers. Its three-by-six-foot panels were explosions of unblended reds, yellows, and greens. "As an outburst in art," wrote one critic, "it is as awful as it is unique. Browne has to explain it, or one wouldn't know whether it referred to national banks or the Orkney Islands." The Chinese appeared fascinated by it, possibly since they were unfamiliar with either American art or American finance. It was magnificent in its mysteriousness.

The policemen and soldiers standing guard outside the Treasury Building looked less welcoming. Once beyond it, the head of the march turned onto Pennsylvania Avenue and saw their goal close at hand: the columns and dome of the Capitol, bracketed by an estimated twenty thousand spectators. An additional three or four hundred policemen in front of the building did nothing to deter Coxey and Browne. Tim, standing with a group of journalists, muttered in disbelief that there was nearly one policeman for every marcher.

"That ought to be enough to make sure they don't overrun the place, armed to the teeth as they are with dangerous rhetoric," he whispered to a fellow demon.

"Attention, Commonweal, halt!" Browne's voice boomed the column into a standstill. He escorted Mamie Coxey to the shade of a maple tree by the curb, then made his way to Coxey's buggy. Coxey kissed his wife and climbed down. While the crowd cheered such marital affection, Browne handed Mrs. Coxey his sombrero to hold.

A mounted policeman immediately confronted Coxey and Browne, who froze into immobility for only a moment on the walkway. And then, as Tim watched in disbelief, all hell broke loose.

Brown and Coxey leaped the low stone wall around the Capitol and vanished into the crowd, pursued by infuriated policemen. The policemen's horses flattened small trees, bushes, and flower beds while Browne, an unmistakable target in his Buffalo Bill outfit, emerged from the crowd every now and again to egg them on. Coxey, less conspicuous, simply climbed the Capitol steps and was halfway up before anyone spotted him.

The police finally caught up with Browne. A dozen law officers tackled him and attempted to stuff him into a patrol wagon. The crowd would have none of that, however. They caught at the bridles of the officers' horses and spilled several policemen onto the ground. The authorities lost all semblance of self-control and charged the crowd on foot and on horseback.

Tim, trying to keep sight of Coxey, found himself inadvertently caught up in the melee around Browne. A horse thundered nearly over him and scattered a family of children. Outraged, Tim snatched up a small girl and screamed a cautionary warning at the mounted policeman. But no one could hear anyone else in the din. Panicked spectators were running in all directions. Some of the more irate ones charged the police, while the others fled from them. A frantic woman surfaced through the chaos, screaming "Bessie!"

"Are you Bessie?" Tim asked the child in his arms.

The little girl nodded.

"Over here!" He waved an arm at the woman, who ran over to Tim, and he deposited the girl in her care. He pushed his way at a run back toward the Capitol steps. It was rough going. The police had lost their tempers and so had the crowd. Carl Browne was at the window of the paddy wagon, invoking the wrath of God on the government in Washington, and the police were trying to drag the disheveled spectators from the Capitol grounds.

One ruddy-faced officer grasped Tim's arm. "You come with me!"

Tim jerked his arm away. "I'm a journalist!"

"I don't care if you're Moses. We're gonna clear these steps."

The beefy policeman lunged at him again, but Tim ducked, dodging beneath the upraised arm of a citizen who was using a barrel stave as a club. The stave caught the policeman hard in the jaw, and with a howl of fury he swung his truncheon into the mob and apparently forgot about Tim, who wriggled on up the steps in pursuit of Coxey.

With a full-scale riot going on below, Coxey continued his climb. A shout went up when he was recognized, and two officers hastened to bar his way. Tim pushed his way to the eye of the storm around Coxey.

"What do you want here?" one officer demanded.

"I wish to make an address," Coxey responded politely.

"But you can't do that." The policeman sounded as if he was attempting to be patient, but his eyes nervously followed the chaos below. The riot was spreading.

"Then can I read a protest?" Coxey drew a typewritten manuscript from his pocket. The officers took him by the shoulders and pushed him back down the stairs by way of answer. Coxey spotted Tim and tossed the manuscript to him. "That is for the press, young man!"

Tim caught it and ducked back through the crowd. A policeman showed signs of coming after him, so Tim took to his heels, shoving the typescript into his shirt. The officer gave up in disgust. As the authorities escorted the squelched leader to his carriage, the crowd surged around Coxey, chanting his name. Voices cried, "Speech! Speech!" but no one could have been heard over the tumult. Mounted police charged the loyal followers.

Coxey waved a hand to his drummer, and the procession moved on again in an orderly fashion. The whole stop at the Capitol Building had taken no more than fifteen minutes. Behind it the District of Columbia Police were still battling with the citizens it was sworn to protect.

Coxey and Browne were officially charged with the only crimes that the government thought it could make stick: injuring the shrubs and turf and carrying banners, which was against regulations on Capitol grounds. Two

Washington ladies put up the money to bail the men out of jail, but the Commonweal's enthusiasm was gone.

The army did the best they could to make the new camp habitable and decided to stay in Washington for three more months. Westerners from other armies joined them, but the biggest splash had been made. The force of the movement was spent, according to the press, which had generated so much of that momentum. Ray Stannard Baker of the *Chicago Record* received a telegram from his employers that read, "Drop Coxey tonight. Report in Chicago Monday noon." Most of the other demons were issued similar orders.

Coxey's message, a Populist appeal for better treatment for "the poor and oppressed," appeared in Tim's *Clarion* and numerous other papers, and in the *Congressional Record*. But if anyone in the government felt any further interest in it, Tim couldn't find him. He stayed on a little longer than most of the other journalists, to cover Coxey's trial. He and Browne got twenty days apiece, and Tim found he had more to say. He sat down and wrote an impassioned editorial:

> Every detail of the proceedings was stamped with the prosecutor's efforts to make a mountain out of a molehill. The crimes: Carrying banners on Capitol grounds! Trespassing on the grass! Great Caesar. If the fools managing the anti-Coxey crusade at the national capital were instead in the employ of Coxey himself, they could not do him better service than they are doing him today.

"Sarcastic little squirt." President Cleveland harrumphed and frowned to cover the fact that he was amused.

"I can't say it was our shining hour, sir," Toby Holt remarked.

"No, indeed," Cleveland agreed. "But our citizens get worried by mobs, as well they might."

"So the police turned their own citizens into a mob." Toby made a rude noise in his throat. "Coxey's people were perfectly quiet. It was Washington citizens the police were beating up."

"Don't lay the police at my door, Senator. Congress controls the city government. And Coxey and Browne don't seem any the worse for wear. I hear the ladies have been sending food. At last count the army had three hundred pies."

Toby chuckled. "So Tim tells me. He's been hanging around the jailhouse with the local press. He says he's moving on, though. I'm afraid the labor strikes are only beginning, sir. My son believes that the Pullman workers are almost certain to go out this week."

Cleveland sighed. "We can't have that," he said somberly. "If the American Railway Union joins them, it will have gone too far. This country cannot be brought to a halt by strikes."

"Let's hope it doesn't come to that," Toby said. "If the government decides to support the railroad owners, Tim warns of a very real threat of violence."

Cleveland gave him a long look, extremely serious now. "That won't be permitted," he said. "The labor unions do not run this country."

Pullman, Illinois

Like something out of a toy shop. That was Tim's first impression of Pullman, the company town of George Pullman's Palace Car Company. For his workers Pullman had created a model village with all the amenities, including a library. The women of the Pennsylvania coal camps would have thought themselves very lucky indeed to have lived in Pullman's bandbox little houses.

And it all, explained Eugene Debs, the man escorting Tim, made money for Mr. Pullman. Workers even had to pay for their library cards and for the utilities that Pullman bought from the city of Chicago and resold at an exorbitant profit.

Debs surveyed the dollhouses along Main Street. "It's not nearly such a cute little town as it looks," he confided. "Pullman fired a third of his workers last year and cut the wages of the rest by thirty percent. He did not, however, cut prices in the company store, and he did not lower their rent. These people pay double the going rent of the neighboring town."

Eugene Debs was not yet forty, and he spoke with the passion of a reformer. He had tow-colored hair receding at the temples and a bright blue stare that made Tim think of a parrot. As the organizer of the new American Railway Union, Debs had succeeded in merging all the smaller craft unions into one force that could not be divided against itself. The Pullman workers were part of the ARU, and the town of Pullman was to Debs an infuriating example of company abuse.

"George Pullman might as well be a medieval baron," Debs said disgustedly. "The company owns every square foot of ground here, every house, every church. He keeps their morals clean for them, too, mind you. Saloons and trade unions are forbidden, and the eight-hour day won't be instituted because 'idleness promotes mischief.' I've got a man I want you to meet."

He turned abruptly down a side street, and Tim followed. Out of the corner of his eye, he saw a policeman. Company police reported to company headquarters on all activity in Pullman. If the authorities spotted Debs, they would order him out of town. Tim picked up his pace. They would probably toss him, too, and the visit was just getting interesting.

Debs brought Tim to an adorable little house. They were welcomed by Lake Ewert, a welder, and his wife, who worked in the Pullman shop's laundry. Neither one of them was working now, but it was not the strike that had put them out of jobs. Their bosses had simply not called them in. Neither of them had enough days' work since winter even to pay the rent on their house. They owed the Pullman Car Company sixty-five dollars.

"We're gonna protest," Lake said as he and his wife led Debs and Tim into the small parlor. "Tom Heathcote's written a statement. We know we ain't gonna get anywhere, Debs, but we got to try something. We got no pride left." He handed a typewritten page to Debs, who beckoned Tim over to read it:

We do not expect the company to concede to our demands. We do not know what the outcome will be, and in fact we do not care much. We do know that we are working for less wages than will maintain ourselves and families in the necessities of life, and on that proposition we absolutely refuse to work any longer.

"You know what you're risking?" Debs asked. "Thousands of businesses have gone bankrupt in the last year. God knows Pullman isn't among them, but he won't find any shortage of replacements for you."

"He will if the American Railway Union backs us," Lake pointed out.

"The ARU hasn't authorized this strike."

"Well, we can't wait for you," Lake said. "The last time I worked, it was for ten hours a day for twelve days, and I got a paycheck for seven cents. The bastards took nine dollars out for my rent. In advance."

"Patsy Bent that works in the laundry with me," Mrs. Ewert said, "her dad died owing the company. She got a notice that she can't work no more if she don't pay off his debt. She's hardly making enough to feed her kids as it is."

"Do you have children, Mr. Ewert?" Tim asked.

"We got two," Lake answered. "When I got that check for seven cents, I thought about them, and I made up my mind. When a man's sober and steady and has a saving wife, and he works five years for a company and finds himself in debt for a common living, then something is wrong."

Tim quoted Lake Ewert verbatim in the story he filed. It seemed to sum up everything unjust in these people's existence.

At noon two days later three thousand workers left their jobs in the Pullman shops. The company's first act was to lay off the remaining three hundred. The walkout was calm, with no hint of violence, and the strikers even posted guards to make certain that no company property would be damaged by vandals. The company, not impressed by its employees' scruples, complained loudly about anarchists and ungrateful riffraff.

Debs came back to interview more laborers and make

his decision as to whether or not the American Railway Union should strike, also, in support of the Pullman workers. Debs knew the odds of winning were not good. These people had been driven by desperation to the end of their tether and had snapped it. They had no strength except from their own desperation. Martyrs might be made of them, though, and maybe that was enough. A gesture, no matter how futile, was better than subservience.

Tim filed a profile of Debs, which was unique in that it was reasonably flattering. Most of the other reporters were laboring under the restrictions of antiunion newspaper management. The notion of the workers being able to halt the passenger trains that Americans took for granted smacked of anarchy to a lot of people. But the prevailing theory of hard work as a surefire means of getting ahead did not apply in many cases. In companies where hard work was not enough, management relied on the fact that in a depression year there was always some poor, desperate man who would work for seven cents if the first fellow wouldn't. Tim said as much in his last story and got a wire back from Waldo Howard: "You sound like a blasted socialist, and we're getting nasty letters from our readers and advertisers. You're the boss, though, and personally I agree with you."

The Pullman Palace Car Company felt differently. Tim discovered that he was persona non grata in Pullman when two police officers, their nightsticks drawn, pulled him off the sidewalk and into an alley.

"This is a clean town," one of them warned, advancing on him. "We don't allow degenerates here."

Tim eyed the nightsticks. He had a pistol in his pocket, but he didn't want to start a shooting war if he could help it. The alley was a cul-de-sac, with the solid back of a grocery store at the end.

"No degenerates," the other policeman growled. "We're gonna teach you a lesson."

"Degenerates?" Tim said indignantly. "Is that your definition of people who report the news?"

They kept coming. Tim risked a quick look over his shoulder. He saw a door and a big loading bay at the back of the grocery, but both were closed, and he doubted anyone would come through them to offer aid. The policemen were herding him away from the smaller door, trying to back him into the tangle of about seventy wooden crates outside the loading dock.

In one swift movement Tim bent down, grabbed a crate, and smashed it hard against the brick wall. The crate shattered, and he tore away a jagged board. It was not as heavy as a nightstick, but it was the best he had. It might prove nearly as effective as a broken bottle in a fight. He crouched, ready for his assailants.

They rushed him and battered at him with the nightsticks, trying to beat him senseless before he could close with the jagged wooden weapon in his hand. Tim felt the heavy thud against his upper arm and staggered. He dropped and rolled, frantically scrabbling among the crates, as another blow came down. He could barely breathe, and as numbness ceased, a horrible pain replaced it. He managed to get to his feet again, but another blow fell. He dodged most of the force of this one, although what did land turned his other shoulder numb and then fiery. Tim's right hand shot out with the jagged wood and laid one of the policemen's cheeks open.

The man howled and clutched at his face. Blood ran between the fingers of his free hand. "Kill him, Mort!" he bellowed. "Kill the bastard!"

Mort looked wide-eyed at his partner. "We ain't supposed to kill him," he responded. "Just hurt him."

"He didn't cut you!" the other man said, furious. "I'm gonna kill him!" He shook the blood from his hand and charged at Tim, the nightstick at the ready.

"Fine," Mort said. "But remember, Seaborn, you done it." He loped along behind to help.

Tim dodged and lashed out with the board, but he was beginning to be afraid. If they really wanted to, they could kill him, unless he could get away—or shoot them. If the one called Seaborn was riled enough, he would probably be glad to shoot Tim and take a chance on somebody hearing the shot and investigating. Even if a witness recognized them, the partners would probably get off scot-free in this town. But if Tim shot a Pullman policeman, he knew he'd be hanged from a lamppost by next Monday.

He couldn't get past the men. His only chance for escape was through the grocery's back door. He prayed it wasn't locked, then began to back up, angling toward his goal. His assailants kept coming.

The grocery door was only a few feet away to his right. Tim backed up another step. The policemen were nearly on him.

"Come on, you bastard," Seaborn taunted. "We got you now."

Tim snatched up a crate and hurled it at them, and then another and another. He had a pretty good throwing arm, even injured, and the attackers staggered under the onslaught.

Tim got around them to the door and tried it, but it was locked. He frantically rattled the handle. No one came—no one in his right mind would come—but the door shook. It didn't have much of a lock. *I might have a chance,* he thought, ducking away and turning to face his attackers as a nightstick came down past his head.

He heaved another crate at his opponent and kicked hard into the man's crotch. It was Seaborn. Tim allowed himself a small smile as the policeman howled and doubled over, allowing Tim time to turn and kick the rusty door, ramming his boot into the knob. It went flying, and the door sagged open. Tim hurled through it, with Seaborn hobbling on his heels and Mort trying to get past his partner to Tim.

"Lemme by!" The policemen bumped together in the narrow doorway like bulls in a chute.

Tim looked around. He was in a storeroom. He sprinted for the door at the far end and burst through it to find himself in the middle of the grocery store. A stout woman in a brown gingham dress stared at him in surprise and dropped her cabbage. The Pullman policemen charged through the door on his heels. Seaborn was still hunched over from the kick to his groin, but there was determination in their stride.

Tim scooted farther into the store and scooped up the fat woman's cabbage. He was out of breath and slightly disheveled. "A thousand pardons, madam." He presented it to her, and she placed it warily in her shopping basket.

Tim glanced around and was relieved to see three or four other customers—probably foremen's wives. With the strike on, not many people were shopping in the company store. But there were enough to rein in the policemen's violence.

Tim sidled into the women's midst, tipping the hat he had somehow managed not to lose. Casually he picked up a salami and a bread knife, which would make a fine weapon, from a display by the vegetable bins.

"I don't have scrip," he said genially to the startled clerk. "Will you accept cash?"

"Uh, sure," the clerk said.

"Just scrip!" the injured policeman insisted angrily.

The clerk shook his head. "Oh, no, sir. Scrip ain't good elsewhere, but there's no regulation says cash ain't good here. That'll be seventy-five cents, sir."

"Don't you sell him that knife!" Mort bellowed, and lunged at Tim.

The customers shrieked and scattered. A pyramid of tomatoes came down with a solid splatter on the wooden floor.

"Now look what you done!" the clerk shouted.

Seaborn slid in the tomatoes, upended himself, and came to rest against a thin woman's birdlike legs, nearly knocking her down. She screamed and smacked him with her net shopping bag, which had canned beans in it.

"Defend yourselves, ladies," Tim urged. "They're sex maniacs." Two younger women had taken refuge behind the pickle barrel. Tim ducked behind them, and as Mort came over to him, the women indignantly shoved the barrel in his path. It tipped over and flooded the floor in brine.

"My husband's a foreman! You can't treat me this way! I'll have you thugs hauled up before Mr. Pullman!"

"I don't want you, damn it, lady. I want him!" Seaborn yelled. He continued to come at the women because Tim was still behind them.

"Get away! Look at that face, Belle. Dumb brute, bursting in here and frightening women to death. They've had too many privileges since this strike started. Get away from me, or I'll write down your badge number and report you!" She threw a pickle out of the wreckage of the barrel at him. Mort, meanwhile, stepped on another one and sat down suddenly in the brine.

Tim put seventy-five cents on the clerk's counter and, peeling his salami with the bread knife, strolled toward the front door.

The two policemen pulled themselves from the wreckage of the grocery, eyed the length of the bread knife, and decided not to go after him.

As he pushed through the door, the fat woman with the shopping bag was inspecting the injured policeman's cut cheek and advising him to put a bandage on it.

Tim strolled nonchalantly until he was out of sight of the grocery. Then he ran. Mort and his pal were not the most intelligent examples of their profession, but when they had collected themselves, it would occur to them to telephone for assistance.

Outside Pullman's city limits, Tim hailed a streetcar and rode it painfully, unable to find a comfortable position into Chicago, where he filed an account of his adventure that was guaranteed to make George Pullman froth at the mouth.

"You got a wire waiting, Mr. Holt," the telegrapher said.

Tim took it gingerly. Whenever anyone sent *him* a telegram, it usually pertained to something he didn't want to know about.

"Oh, hell," he said after a moment.

"They expect the boss to go to Portland to cover a flood?" the telegrapher inquired. "Must be mighty short-handed."

"That's my hometown," Tim told him. "Any way to get a wire through to Portland?"

"Not if it's underwater."

"Give me that." Tim reached for the telegrapher's pad.

"All right, all right. I'll try." The telegrapher snatched it back again. "I know you newspaper people. You think you know the code, but you'll get it so gummed up, no one will be able to read it. Just hold your horses and write out what you want to say."

"Eulalia Blake, Madrona Ranch, Portland," Tim dictated. "Just say I'm coming home."

XII

Tim changed trains in Kansas City and was only mildly surprised to see the tall, muscular figure in a frock coat who climbed on board ahead of him. He tapped the man on the shoulder and smiled when Toby turned around.

"Rallying around the constituents, I see," Tim said.

"Making sure everything I own doesn't float out to sea," Toby corrected. He spoke lightly, but he looked worried.

The floodwaters had come up swiftly, far more swiftly than anyone could have envisioned. The Willamette and the Columbia had both been over flood stage when Tim and Toby had learned of it. By the time father and son arrived in Portland, whatever had been going to happen would have happened, and all they would be able to do was help dig out. Both men felt powerless, sitting high and dry in a Pullman car leaving Kansas City.

"I wired Gran," Tim said.

"So did I," Toby muttered. "The operator wasn't sure he could get it to her, so I didn't wait for an answer. Damn." He looked impatient.

"We're lucky to get a train, I suppose," Tim said. "A Pullman, anyway. A couple more weeks, and it could have been a boxcar. Hoboes' accommodations."

Toby grunted and took a notebook from his carpetbag. His face was creased with worry. "Your grandmother is frail, too frail for this."

Toby began to write, and Tim knew Toby was giving himself something to do, to stave off his fear for his mother.

As a senator, Toby had more responsibilities than the Madrona; the whole city was his concern now. There would be damage to assess, the bereaved to be comforted and aided, cleanup to be organized, and disaster relief to be gotten from Washington if possible.

Toby looked up again, irritated. "Is just me, or is this train overcrowded and moving far too slowly?"

Tim offered his father a look of understanding and sympathy.

"How long is this strike going to go on?"

"Until Pullman starts to treat his people decently, I expect," Tim answered. "Or until hell freezes over. Or until the Pullman workers starve. That might come first if they don't get some support."

"If it interferes with the railways too much, some action's going to be taken," Toby remarked. "Don't quote me," he added hastily.

"All in the family," Tim assured him. His eyes took on an interested gleam. "What kind of action?"

"A back-to-work order, possibly," Toby said. "The President's got the railroad interests on his back. Washington's even thicker with lobbyists than usual; they're like a plague of rats—pretty sleek rats."

"A back-to-work order has to be enforced," Tim commented. "Is he planning to send in troops?"

"I hope not. And you just remember this is all off-the-record."

"You hope not, but you think he is?"

"Yes."

"What's your opinion?"

"I think it would be a mistake," Toby replied, "and I've told him so. The unions have a legitimate beef. There'll be more armies like Coxey's, more strikes, more trouble, if Washington doesn't start to do a better job of looking out for the working man."

"Well, well," Tim murmured. "Senator Holt and Eugene Debs are brothers under the skin."

"I can't afford to be seen or linked in any way with Eugene Debs," Toby said irritably.

"I'll keep your secret," Tim said, chuckling.

"You'd better. I'll do what I can, but I can't do anything

if I don't get reelected. Sometimes I wish I'd never gone into politics."

Tim laughed. "I bet there are other people who feel that way."

Toby smiled reluctantly. "And some of them have been quite pointed about it. Right now I plan just to worry about Portland and your grandmother. At least she's got Dieter Schumann's boy with her. I'll just have to trust to him and White Elk to take care of her."

Portland, Oregon
June 7, 1894

Eulalia stood on the front porch and looked out through the rain at the rising sea of brown water. The Madrona's fields had vanished under the muddy lake. Although the house was on a small rise, water was already lapping at the porch steps. It had been raining steadily for ten days, but no one had had any real warning that a flood was imminent. The earth had simply, suddenly become waterlogged and ceased to absorb the rain, and the water had begun to pool. The rivers rose, overflowed, and began to rush swiftly. The current had foamed into a torrent, and within hours Portland was underwater.

Inside, Amy, Abby, and a ranch hand were wrestling the furniture up the stairs to the second floor. Eulalia had tried to help, but Amy and Abby had shooed her away. She wasn't strong enough, they said.

Eulalia rested a comforting hand on the top of Tommy White Elk's head as the child clung to her skirts and whimpered. White Elk, Mai, Paul Kirchner, and Dan Schumann had all gone to Portland that morning and were trapped there. Mai's infant was in a cradle in Eulalia's bedroom.

Eulalia watched Howie Janks drive the brood mares and their foals through belly-deep water onto a small hill that was now an island. The panicked geldings, which were to have been taken to auction the next week, were floundering in their own pasture. There weren't enough hired men to herd them all.

A frightened neighing came from the barn. Eulalia, startled, turned her head in that direction. The barn should have been empty. Then she remembered that White Elk had put the dun stallion in there—it had broken a fence and picked a fight with the Madrona's other stud two days before and come away with a bite that needed treating.

Eulalia looked over her shoulder. *Well, I haven't been of much help today,* she thought, dejected. She took Tommy by the hand and pointed him into the house. "Go and sit with the baby, darling. That's how you can help me until your mama comes home."

Tommy nodded, but he didn't let go of Eulalia's skirts.

"Into the house," Eulalia said firmly. "And don't you go near that water. You hear me?"

She gave him such a steely glance that Tommy scooted abruptly inside. Feeling guilty, Eulalia picked up her skirts and went down the steps and into the downpour. If Amy and Abby saw her . . .

The water was dank and heavy with mud. At its deepest, it was almost to her waist, and she stumbled and nearly fell into it as her heavy skirts dragged her down. Above her in the madrona trees, a flock of chickens huddled, clucking miserably. The water felt scummy and cold. Odd things floated in it, items from some disjointed dream—a ball of knitting yarn with the needles still in it, an apple crate, a Panama hat. She pushed through the flow, shivering with the horrific memory of having been caught in a silt-filled pothole in Alaska, with the tide coming in, years before. That vivid recollection nearly sent her back to the porch and safety, but the stallion in the barn neighed again, this time in shrieking panic.

The water pressed against the barn doors and rushed through the cracks. Eulalia let the bar down but found she couldn't pull the doors open against the weight of the water. She beat on them furiously while the brown floodwater swirled around her and sucked her against them. She got her fingers between the doors and pulled one open just an inch. The water swirled through faster. Eulalia felt her teeth chattering, and she couldn't stop them. She inched the door open some more, but it slammed shut again. The water rose around her, and she wondered if she was going to drown here, flattened against the barn.

The hinges creaked behind her, and then the doors gave way under the weight of the flood. They buckled inward the wrong way and tore loose from their hinges. With a rush the water swirled over Eulalia's head, and she tumbled head over heels, inhaling a lungful of foul water. She flailed her arms, caught the wooden upright of a stall, and pulled herself up, choking and spitting water that was foul with straw and manure. She gagged, and more water came up as blackness threatened to sweep over her.

I will not faint. She clung to that thought with a tenacity that was all too uncommon in her recently. Slowly her light-headedness receded, and her eyes focused in the dim, water-filled barn. The dun stallion was rearing and splashing in its flooded stall. She half staggered, half swam toward it and managed to get the stall door ajar. The stallion snorted and rolled its eyes. It tried to rear again, and Eulalia shot out a hand and grabbed its halter. A lead line hung on the wall, mercifully out of reach of the water. She snapped it to the halter ring.

"You behave yourself," she said through chattering teeth to the stallion. "I'm the only one who can get you out of here, and I think you're the only one who can help me."

The stallion snorted again but seemed calmed by the sound of an authoritative human voice.

"You behave," she said again. "I've ridden worse beasts than you."

It was strange how, through her fear, Eulalia's memories of the wild horses she had helped Whip to tame came back, unbidden, clear across so many years. Those horses had been the beginning of the Madrona, and she had been young and strong then. The reminiscences calmed her, fortified her for the waiting test of courage.

Eulalia gripped the stallion's halter and let the waist-high water lift her as high as it could against her dragging skirts. The dun stallion wasn't very tall—not as big as Alexandra's thoroughbreds, who were mercifully in their own barn at the top of a gentle hill. They were no doubt wet and terrified but safe. Eulalia jumped, letting the water buoy her, and got one heel over the dun's bare back. He snorted again but let her wriggle up.

"That's a fine boy," Eulalia crooned at him. "A fine fellow. We're going to find out how well you swim." The land between the barn and the house dipped down, and she thought the water might be over her head by now. "Come on then."

She urged him out the loose box door and through the contaminated water. Beyond the barn the flood rolled like a sea, carrying everything on its tide. She had lost her shoes, and a dead fish brushed past her bare foot. Its white belly turned upward to the air for a moment before it disappeared again. The stallion slogged toward the house, and the water rose to its shoulders. Snorting with fright, it began to swim. Eulalia, skirts billowing around her, wet hair plastered to her face, clung to the horse's back. Her hands on the halter rope were blue with cold, and her legs and feet felt numb.

She was nearly fainting again by the time the stallion stumbled onto higher ground and began to wade toward the house. By now the water was up over the front porch and running under the front door, and she noticed Abby's horrified face at the upstairs window. The face vanished abruptly, and seconds later Abby, Amy, and a hired man, Coot Simmons, were dragging on the stallion's halter rope and urging him up the steps.

Eulalia slid into Coot's arms, while Abby looked dubiously at the stallion. It stamped its foot and sent a new spray of muddy water over them, then bent its head and took a bite of the bedraggled ferns that sat in pots on the porch rail.

Coot lifted Eulalia through the front door, and she saw that the whole first floor was under several inches of water.

"What do you want me to do with the horse?" Abby wailed behind her.

"Put him in the kitchen," Eulalia said wearily. The kitchen was up two steps from the parlor. It would still be dry. "He'll get thrush if he stands in water."

Then she laid her head against Coot's shoulder and fainted.

*   *   *

At first the floodwaters rose swiftly in Portland, the brown froth spreading through the streets. The initial rush had done the damage. And then the current slowed, compounding the destruction. Paul Kirchner climbed halfway up a lamppost, clung there, and watched the Madrona Ranch's buckboard float away down the street. He had managed to cut the mules loose in time, to save their lives, but he had no idea where they were. He assumed they could swim and hoped they had found someplace to swim to.

White Elk and Mai had come to town with him. Mai had wanted to shop in Chinatown, and White Elk had escorted her, a gently menacing presence at her side, for many of Portland's Chinese thought her a wanton and disgraced woman for having left her family to marry an Indian. She had sadly told Paul that she did not feel quite safe there, among her own people, anymore.

Dan Schumann had ridden into Portland that morning, too, on his own, unknown errands, but, to be truthful, Paul had no inclination to worry about Dan.

White Elk could take care of Mai, Paul hoped—there was no way for him to locate them in the chaos. But another fear was pressing at him. From his vantage point, Paul could see the salmon cannery on the banks of the Columbia River. The factory building was half-underwater, and men leaned frantically from the top windows. Through the pouring rain the building looked to Paul as if it were about to buckle under the pressure of the water. If it did, it was going to take everyone inside with it. Two men in boats were trying to throw ropes up to the windows, but because the boats wobbled and ducked in the swirling currents, their efforts were in vain.

Paul looked down from his lamppost at the floodwaters— plenty deep enough to drown in and as swift as the devil, hurtling logs from the sawmill through the debris. He was scared to death of that water, but inside the cannery were men with whom he had worked side by side, with whom he had spent his pay and lived for months in the waterfront flophouses. Some were rough-and-tumble hoboes; others were family men trying to eke out a living. All were friends.

A long wooden packing crate tumbled by, spinning in the water. Paul said a silent prayer and let go of his lamppost. He caught the crate and wriggled himself over the top so that he was spread-eagled across it. The crate kept him just above the water, and praying it wouldn't sink, he began to kick, aiming himself and the crate toward the boats below the cannery.

Mother of God, I'm going to die in this muck. The thought went through his mind as filthy water slapped him in the face and made him gag. He kicked harder. A log spun by him, smacking into the crate and splintering it. The impact drove Paul under the water, and he kicked to the surface again. The water pulled at him like hands, trying to pull him down. Choking, he gave up on the crate and began to swim. Another log, smaller this time, rolled by, and he caught it and draped himself over it. This time he lay gasping along it and paddled with his hands and kicked his feet.

The cannery was nearer now. He could hear the cries of the trapped men and the frustrated curses of the men in the boats below. The boats bucked and slapped up and down, rocking dangerously in the water. They were small fishing dinghies, not sturdy enough for one man to tramp about in the prow with no counterweight in the stern.

Paul slid off his log and kicked it away into the floodwater before it could collide with the nearest boat. He caught the stern and pulled himself up. The dinghy steadied, and the man in the prow managed to sail his rope through the cannery window. He turned to Paul, and his eyes widened in recognition.

"I don't know where you came from, Kirchner, but thank God for you. We've got ten men up there, and someone's hurt."

"There's not much time, Blacky," Paul said. "The whole damn cannery's going to come down."

Blacky nodded grimly and stretched the rope taut as men began to climb out the cannery window. One by one they twined themselves around the rope and slid slowly and precariously down. The other dinghy man gave up trying to throw his own rope and instead maneuvered his boat alongside Blacky's to take on the rescued men.

The boats rocked and settled perilously low in the water. Rain was still coming down, and it cascaded off Paul's head, sheeting into his eyes, making it difficult for him to see. He was cold to the bone.

"Is that the lot?" he asked, gasping, when no more men appeared at the window. He thought he heard a faint shout from above.

"McCarty's up there," the last man down the rope said, panting. He staggered a little and collapsed in the bottom of the boat. "He busted his leg when the conveyer belt got knocked loose. Rain punched a piece of the roof in."

McCarty. As Paul looked grimly at the rope still stretched to the top-floor window, he knew he could not abandon his friend. He pulled a pair of sodden gloves from his back pocket, amazed and thankful that they were still there. He gripped the rope and tested it.

"I'm going up."

Blacky nodded and looked uneasily at the foaming water. "I hope we're still here when you get down," he muttered.

As Paul pulled himself up the rope he weighed the risk of falling and drowning. It was a possibility, but still he dragged himself up, hand over hand, and looked at the window, eyes squinted against the pelting rain. His arms ached, and the cold had stolen all feeling from his fingers. *Grip tighter. Hold on. Don't look down. Another six inches . . . another . . .*

He wriggled upward, clinging with his knees around the rope, driven by desperation. The cannery looked lopsided, gray, waterlogged, and ready to buckle. It seemed to shimmer in front of his eyes, but maybe that was due only to the rain. He inched up another foot, and slowly the window drew nearer. When he could touch the sill, he gave one last wriggle and caught the weathered wood, hoping it wouldn't come away in his hand. He got his other hand over the sill, then his elbows, and heaved himself through.

Paul, breathing hard, sat for a moment in a sodden heap on the floor. Then he shook the water from his head like a dog and struggled to stand. McCarty lay a few feet away, his mouth twisted into a grimace of pain. One leg was stretched in front of him, his ankle at a strange, unnatural angle. He blinked at Paul.

"Where the hell did you come from?"

"Off the wharf with the water rats," Paul said, staggering over to his friend. "What are you doing here? I thought you quit to romance the policeman's daughter." He peeled off his jacket and slid it under McCarty.

The young man winced and gritted his teeth as Paul moved the broken leg. "Moonlighting. I'm gonna get married. Got me a good job with the coppers—her old man put in a word for me. But she wants a honeymoon."

"Women are like that."

"Copper's pay won't run to it. I'm gonna do this right, turn over a new leaf. So I went back to the cannery in my off time. More fool I." He looked dismally at the rain sheeting down outside the broken window and began to cry. "Reckon I'll drown here now. I never wanted to die with all these damn fish."

"You aren't going to die." Paul grasped McCarty's upstretched hands and hoisted him up on his one good leg. "Fancy you a copper, you old barroom brawler. Can't let you die now."

He put his arm around McCarty's waist, and the man slung his arm around Paul's shoulders. Together they made it to the window and eased onto the sill. The boat was still below. The men in it peered up, shielding their eyes with their hands. Paul maneuvered himself and McCarty over the sill so that they hung feet first above the water.

"Hold tight now. Hang on to my neck but try not to choke me." Paul grasped the rope; he could hear McCarty praying in his ear. "You're a little late to get religion," he joked. "I'm not sure it's retroactive, but hang on."

He pushed off the sill and, with McCarty as dead-weight on his back, began to slide down the rope. It dug into his hands through the heavy gloves, but he held tightly. If he let them slide too fast, they would capsize the dinghy. They inched downward with McCarty muttering Hail Marys through clenched teeth.

Hands reached out, steadied them, and pulled them into the boat. They fell into the bottom, McCarty still clutching Paul from behind.

"Holy Mary, Mother of God, pray for us sinners now and at the hour of our death—*ow, damn it!*" McCarty howled as his broken ankle bent under him.

Paul sat up, feeling sick to his stomach. He had never been so terrified in his life. He looked at McCarty.

The young Irishman's face was white, and he was shaking with pain, but he managed to speak. "You're a square fellow, Kirchner. You're one hell of a square fellow." His eyes rolled back in his head, and he passed out. His hair floated in the brown water that sloshed in the bottom of the boat.

"Mai! Mai!" White Elk shouted again, but no one answered from the shuttered windows of the Chinese drugstore where Mai had once lived.

The bottom floor was underwater, and the fireman in the boat with White Elk shook his head dubiously. The rain poured off his oilskin coat and hat. "They must have run away when they saw the water coming."

"She wouldn't have gone anywhere without me," White Elk said desperately. "Oh, God, why did I leave her?"

He had been gone only long enough to see if he could order a load of feed before everyone else got in ahead of him and depleted the supply. This rain was going to ruin the pastureland, and every stock farmer in Portland was going to be wanting feed. Mai had promised him that she would be all right. The Wongs, who had bought her parents' store when they left for China, had a daughter who was Mai's girlhood friend. Surely they would offer her no insult or threat. She had promised to wait there for him.

But then the water had come, and before he could get back from the feed store, Chinatown was flooded past the first floor, and the streets were full of frantic Chinese in boats and rafts—anything they could cobble together. Some buildings were only one story high, and the others were dim rabbit warrens with narrow stairwells and cramped passageways. Those who had made it to the second floor hung over the balconies crying out in Chinese, which sounded to White Elk like the shrill calls of birds. The upper floor of the drugstore was shuttered, and merchandise that White Elk recognized floated in the filthy water outside—wooden boxes of ginseng and powdered horn, and dried sea turtles that now looked as if they were alive and swimming.

"I can't stay," the fireman said. "If she's on the second floor, she's safe. . . ." White Elk was aware of what the fireman had left unsaid: *If she's not . . .* "There's other folks to be gotten out of here." He moved the oars in the water, and White Elk knew that the man had stretched the rules as far as he could just to let White Elk into the boat, to look for someone in particular instead of rescuing the people screaming from their balconies.

"*Mai!*" White Elk shouted again, and this time he thought he heard a faint cry, which was half-drowned in the pouring rain and the dozens of other voices calling out.

"I'm getting out!" he said to the fireman. He couldn't leave her, even if it meant that he would drown, also. She was his love, his wife. He would never be whole again without her.

"Where the hell do you think you're going to go?" the fireman demanded. "You invited yourself along, so you stay and help me with these folks."

"I can't." White Elk went overboard with a splash and clung to the wooden shutters of the second floor. They were rotten and came away in his hand.

"Get back in this boat, you damn fool!"

White Elk didn't answer. He punched through the inner shutter with his fist and hooked his elbows over the sill. The fireman snatched at him, but when the current carried the boat away, the man gave up. After White Elk hauled himself through the window and stood up, he saw the fireman paddling his boat toward a family clinging to a sagging balcony across the street.

White Elk looked around at the Wongs' sleeping quarters. There were beds on the floor, curtained into alcoves with embroidered hangings. The carpets between the beds were splashed with the water that had come through the second-floor windows. As he watched, more trickled over the sill. The flood was still worsening.

The room was deserted, and he rushed frantically into the other two rooms, a tiny kitchen and a little sitting area.

In the sitting room, a niche held a little stone Buddha with an incense burner. The faint smoky smell of incense still clung to the damp room. There was no one there, either.

"Mai!" he bellowed at the top of his voice, and again he heard that faint cry in response. It seemed to come from below him. Where were the stairs? he wondered. He found a narrow, rickety flight descending into black water. He had only been in the drugstore once, years before, but he remembered Mai's father's office—a room with a low door at the foot of the stairs, with a higher ceiling than the shop in front. A tiny pocket of air might have been caught there. If no air pocket existed, he would die in that room.

White Elk looked at the water again and prayed as he had never prayed in his life, to the Christian God he had been brought up with, to the spirits of his Shoshone ancestors, to the little Buddha in the corner. *Please let me find her.*

He stripped off his boots, shirt, and trousers—anything that might catch on something, weigh him down, or otherwise encumber him. He took a deep breath and, eyes clenched shut, dived into freezing blackness. There was nothing to be seen anyway in the muddy water, no guideposts but his faint remembrance of the interiors.

White Elk kicked himself down, feeling his way with a hand on the stair rail.

At the bottom of the stairs, he found the doorway and drew himself through it, praying he was turning in the correct direction. If he lost himself in the shop, he would never get out. He bumped past the doorway as drifting debris brushed past his hands. His lungs burned. He kicked upward again. If he was wrong, he would die and Mai, also.

White Elk felt as if his lungs would explode, that he must open his mouth and gasp for breath and drown. And then his hand felt the cold outline of a foot floating in the water. He rose swiftly and surfaced into blackness above the water, smacking his head into the ceiling of the room. He drew in deep, rasping breaths. There were only a few inches between the water and the ceiling, and he could see nothing.

"White Elk?" Her voice was weak, thready.

"Mai?" His hands frantically searched and touched flesh. He tried to find her face. The skin he touched was cold and clammy. "Mai!"

She clasped his hand. "There's a beam just above us; you can hold on to it."

He reached up, treading water, and found it. It ran just below the ceiling so that he could get his hand over it. He steadied himself. He felt again and found two bodies in the blackness.

"I have Lin. I'm holding her up, but I think she's . . ." Her voice trembled into a whimper. "We've got to get her out."

White Elk felt the other woman's face, which Mai was holding just above the water. There was no response from her.

"I don't think she cares anymore," he whispered.

"I can't leave her! Not here!"

She might be alive, he thought. It was possible. But if she was unconscious . . . "She may drown, just getting out," he said gently.

"I can't leave her!"

"All right, darling." It was Mai he cared about. He would do whatever he had to to get Mai out. "We can't stay here. It may be days before the water goes down. There isn't enough air, and we can't keep afloat that long."

"I know," Mai whimpered. "My hands are numb already. And I've been holding Lin."

"Give her to me." White Elk got his arm around Lin's rib cage, then held her face above the water. "We have to swim. Dive down through the doorway and up the stairs. Are you wearing a sash or something? Give it to me."

There was a stirring in the water, and Mai pushed two pieces of cloth at him. "My stockings," she said.

"They'll do. While I knot them together so they'll be long enough, edge over here. We'll tie them around my waist. I want you to hold on to one end and not let go, you hear?" He felt her grip the end of the stocking. "Wrap it around your wrist. Take a deep breath." There wasn't anything to do about Lin. If she wasn't already dead and he could bring her up the stairs fast enough, she might live. "All right, dive. Don't let go of me."

Several times they filled their lungs, then exhaled deeply in preparation. Then, with one final deep breath, they sank into the water again, Mai kicking frantically to follow him. She wasn't a strong swimmer and had never swum at all until White Elk had taught her. He swam well and strongly, and she had learned a little, simply to please him.

By the time they reached the doorway, White Elk felt as if they would be trapped forever. He was moving up slowly, too slowly, because of Lin's limp weight under his arm. Stars were exploding behind his eyes when he came out into the air of the stairwell.

As Mai came up and took a choking breath, White Elk was already hauling Lin onto the floor. He turned her over on her stomach and tried to press the water from her lungs. Mai crawled out and huddled beside him. Lin never moved.

After a long while, White Elk gave up. "I'm sorry, darling. I think she was already dead down there."

Mai burst into great choking sobs. White Elk pulled her to him, trying to warm her with his own cold body. After a moment he untied the stockings from his waist and Mai's wrists, then stripped her clothes off, cutting her sodden, knotted corset strings with the knife from his abandoned belt. He pulled the cover off one of the beds in the sleeping area and came back to wrap them both in it.

"I'm sorry. It's all right. I'm sorry," he whispered over and over in her ear.

"The water," Mai wept. "It came so fast. I don't know where the Wongs have gone. We were having tea. We were talking. It was so nice with the stove burning and the rain outside."

"I know, darling. I know."

"And then it just . . . happened." Mai hiccuped. "It was like someone pouring water into the room from a glass. All the lights went out, and the room filled up before we could get out, and—" She burst into sobs again. "And I couldn't find Lin. I called and called, and then I found her, just floating. I was so scared. I tried to tread water, and then I found the beam, and—and I tried to hold her up. But she kept slipping, and I couldn't see. I tried to hold her up!"

"Oh, baby, poor baby. It's not your fault. You were so brave." Cradling her, White Elk crooned into her ear. "I thought I'd lost you."

"And I was more afraid for you than Lin!" Mai wailed.

"Of course you were. That's the way it's supposed to be. And you have me. I'm here. You did everything you could for Lin. She knows that."

"Are you sure?"

"Of course I am," he lied, and also repeatedly assured her that their children would be safe with Mrs. Blake at the ranch.

Mai let her head fall to his shoulder, and he felt the warm tears running down it. Slowly the weeping ceased.

He stood and wrapped the quilt around Mai. Next he picked up Lin's body and carried it into the sleeping room and laid it on one of the mattresses, then pulled the quilt over it.

The water still lapped outside the window but had risen no higher. White Elk rocked his feet back and forth on the floor, testing it. It felt solid, and the building itself was sturdy—Mr. Wong kept it in good repair. White Elk hung another quilt out the window for a flag, then went back for Mai. She was still shivering, but some of the color had returned to her face. Her long black hair, tangled with floodwater and debris, hung over her shoulders. White Elk touched the little Buddha as he passed him. *Thank you*, he said silently to all the dieties who might have aided them—Christian and heathen alike. *Please keep our little ones safe*. To ensure Mai's and the children's well-being, he would have endured any test. He picked her up, carried her to the sleeping area, and pulled blankets around them both.

"I'm here, darling. I'll always be here. I'll always find you, because *I* would die without you. And if I die, I'll still be with you." He pulled her close, and they wrapped their arms around each other, waiting for someone to come and find them.

Dan Schumann searched through the first-floor office of Maisie Mennen's brothel with the tenacity of a badger digging into a burrow. It was just sheer good luck he had been there, to do a little talking with Maisie about his investment, when the flood hit.

All around him were the frightened wails of Maisie's girls and Maisie's voice urging them to drag the valuables upstairs. Dan didn't care whether they all drowned so long as Maisie didn't think to look in her office. The water was still coming up, and if Dan did not find the evidence of his investment before the room was underwater, that paperwork was far too likely to float to the surface later.

Maisie wouldn't care; everyone already knew she ran a whorehouse. But the solid citizens who had a financial interest in prostitution and the police Maisie had paid off to leave her alone wouldn't want her record books floating around.

Dan riffled through the desk, throwing papers on the floor while his shoes filled with water. He had broken the desk lock by smashing it with a brass candlestick. He looked into one cubbyhole after another, heaving the contents into the muddy water that swirled around his feet. In the hallway Maisie shouted at the girls to get her Persian rugs up.

Where the hell is her investment book? Dan fumed. *She has to have one.*

If the newspapers got hold of it, if someone found it when the digging out and cleaning up began and realized what it was . . . if Eulalia Blake heard about it . . . The scenario was all too clear in Dan's mind. He had the old woman just about eating out of his hand, and if he didn't gain control of her money soon, he wouldn't be able to pay back Louis Wessell for the money he had fronted for Dan's investment. And Louie Weasel's boys would be around to see him again. On their so-called courtesy call, the thugs had warned that Louie was getting impatient.

Dan had picked up enough rumors on the shadier side of Portland by now to know that when Louie got impatient, the debtor ended up with broken bones. Louie had had one man killed that Dan knew of and probably many more that he didn't. Dan pulled out another book, flipped it open, and tossed it away, gritting his teeth in fury. Grocery expenditures! The old bat kept track of every pea and chicken leg that was eaten, but where were her important

ledgers? The water was up to his knees, and he was ready
to scream with fury.

The water got higher suddenly, rushing in like a tidal
wave and buffeting Dan backward against the wall. The
desk tilted and toppled into the water. Dan scrabbled for a
handhold and caught a curtain rod. He pulled himself
toward the door and got through it just as foaming brown
water filled the room. Maisie and the girls were halfway up
the stairs, and he swam toward them, howling as a dining
room chair, carried on the rising tide, smacked into his ribs.
He stumbled up the stairs through a crowd of wet whores
in sodden negligees. Pursued by the rising water, they
lurched together up to the second floor as they dragged
along lamps and mirrors and Maisie's silver coffee service.

In the upstairs corridor the women huddled together,
wailing and clutching at Dan as if he could save them. He
brushed them away and ran to the window. With the record
books gone, his only thought now was to get out, so as not
to be rescued from a whorehouse by someone who would
blab it around until old Mrs. Blake found out.

Dan put a leg over the sill and hesitated at the
swift-flowing water. It was turbulent and dangerous, but he
was driven by panic. The terraced slopes of the respectable
Council Crest neighborhood were just around the corner. If
he could just get to the Crest, he could get away.

As if guided by some providential hand, a canoe slid
past the window and tangled itself in the debris caught by
the shade trees that surrounded Maisie's house. Amazed at
his good fortune, Dan slid back inside, picked up a hall
chair, and smashed it against the wall until it broke. The flat
back would serve as a paddle. He slid over the sill again and
let go, allowing the water to carry him into the rat's nest
that was collecting in Maisie's trees. The water was freezing
and the current swifter than he had estimated. It tumbled
him into branches, which lashed his face. The canoe was
just beyond reach, rocking and bobbing precariously. In
another moment it would work free.

Dan pulled a broken tree limb loose from the debris,
hooked the edge of the canoe with it, and dragged it toward
him until he could grip the side. He braced it against the
mess in the trees and then thought better of it. More wood

and other strange odds and ends were hurtling along on the water. If the canoe was smashed between that and the trees, he would be a goner. Dan pushed the canoe out toward the moving water and, his makeshift paddle in one hand, pulled himself over the edge. He righted himself with some difficulty as the canoe began to move, then realized he had company. A small boy lay prone in the canoe, his face buried in his hands. Dan could barely hear the child's terrified whimpering over the noise of the rain and the roaring water.

The kid was in the way, and Dan had a momentary impulse to toss him out, but fearful that somebody might be watching, Dan merely shoved the little boy to one side and began to paddle furiously. The water swept the canoe along like a leaf, but Dan made headway toward the slopes of Council Crest. The child wrapped his wet arms around Dan's leg.

It took all Dan's strength, but he managed to ram the canoe against the terraced slopes of the Crest, and he flung himself upward at a rock wall as the canoe shattered against it. Only then did he realize that a crowd of people had gathered on the top of the wall and seen everything. He looked up, dazed, as hands reached to help him up and to raise the boy.

"Daddy!" the child wailed.

A woman bent and picked the boy up in her arms. "Is that your daddy?"

"No!" the boy sobbed. "Daddy went in the water. We was fishing."

"Oh, poor little mite." The woman cuddled him.

A portly man pumped Dan's hand. "Bravest thing I ever saw, saving the little fellow like that."

They clustered around him, exclaiming. A man in a dripping felt hat and an oilcloth overcoat was trying to write in a soaking notebook. "Gilcrest of the *Oregonian*," he said by the way of introduction. "Amazing feat of courage. What's your name, sir?"

XIII

Daring Feat of Strength!
Courageous Man Saves Child From Floodwater!
Schumann the Hero of the Hour!

Toby looked at the *Oregonian* with pride and knew that Dieter Schumann would be prouder yet. The story had been the next day's lead, running three full columns across the front page, with an artist's illustration of Dan pulling the child from the raging water.

Toby clapped the young man on the back. "You're a credit to your father, Dan. I'm glad my mother had you here to watch over her."

Dan smiled modestly. "Someone had to save the poor tyke. That boat was going to break up in another minute." He had scanned the story and satisfied himself that there was no mention that he had begun his "daring leap into danger" from Maisie's brothel. Maybe no one had noticed, or maybe Gilcrest hadn't wanted to spoil his story with that particular information about the selfless hero. It didn't matter, although Dan thought nervously about the clean-up process that would begin soon. There was still the matter of Maisie's record books.

"I wouldn't have gone into town of course, had I known Mrs. Blake would be in danger," he said. "But since she's resting now, I thought I'd go back into Portland today to see if I can help."

"Certainly," Toby agreed. "Commendable of you. Matters are fairly well in hand here."

198

"Well, I felt it my duty to stay, sir, until you arrived. And Tim, of course. White Elk and his wife and Kirchner were brought back this morning, but . . ." The words trailed off in a tone that implied that Dan would not criticize them, but they had been at fault to have saved only themselves. Dan flicked a finger at the newspaper. "Don't make too much of it, will you, sir?" he asked with a shy smile.

"Rats," Tim said when Dan had left. "He loves it."

"He's entitled to," Toby pointed out. "If he's even trying to be modest, it's to his credit."

"Mmmm," Tim said. "I want to see Gran."

They went up the stairs, leaving their bags on a floor still wet with mud. The house was in chaos, with furniture from downstairs rooms still piled in the upstairs hallway. In Eulalia's room Dr. Bright was bending over the bed. He had gone without sleep since the flood and looked bone weary, but he shook the senator's hand.

Toby looked down at his mother. Eulalia's eyes were closed, but her cheeks were flushed, and she moved her head restlessly on the pillow. She looked very old. "How is she, doctor?"

"She has a high fever," Bright answered. "I've given her a sedative to keep her from trying to get up. I'm glad you're here. The place is a madhouse, and those Givens women are dithering like hens. There was a horse in the kitchen yesterday," he added.

"The horse has been removed," Toby told him.

Bright sighed. "The entire city is at sixes and sevens. I don't suppose a horse could make things more unsanitary than they are already. You'll have to scrub the whole house with carbolic soap. Floodwater is liquid pestilence. We'll be lucky if half the population doesn't get tetanus. I've given your mother some antitoxin, but there isn't nearly enough to go around."

Tim sat down and took Eulalia's hand.

Dr. Bright quirked an eyebrow. "And how is Janessa?" He had known Toby's elder daughter for years. But Janessa and he had rarely seen eye to eye on any matters, medical or otherwise. Janessa thought he was a stuffed shirt, and

Bright considered her to be unwomanly and too much inclined to argue with male doctors. Toby was well aware of both sentiments.

"We had a telegram from her this morning," Toby said. "She's fit to be tied because she can't get leave to come home. She and her husband are in the middle of an assignment in Mississippi—yellow fever again; they're becoming recognized as experts on it—and they can't be spared."

"We may need more doctors here," Bright said, looking worried. "Tetanus isn't the only risk. There's a good chance of a typhoid epidemic, too, if the water supply isn't cleaned up fast."

Toby nodded. "I've asked for help. Or at least I've told Washington I'm going to. When I've assessed the damage, I'll make a full report."

"Request double what you want," Bright advised cynically. "The budget conscious generally feel obligated to do some trimming."

"The thought had occurred to me," Toby said. He grimaced. Politics was a game with rules, unspoken but universally known. He intensely disliked playing that game, but he would to get Portland what it needed. "I'll hitch my horse to your buggy and ride back into town with you," he offered. "On the way you can give me your assessment of what's needed." If he wanted to know what really needed doing, Toby had discovered, it was more useful to ask a doctor than the mayor. Doctors did not have to set their priorities with an eye toward reelection.

"Then start with the slums and the riverfront," Bright said, proving this theory. "Council Crest residents have the money and the clout to look out for themselves."

Council Crest had indeed begun to dig itself out, and so had the downtown business district. Erickson's Saloon was still dispensing drinks from a scow chartered by its enterprising proprietor when the waters had begun to rise. Erickson had anchored it at Second and Burnside and proceeded to do business as usual. The scow was now sitting on the ground but was still in operation, while Erickson mopped out his saloon's interior. The downtown crews took regular respites from their labors at Erickson's scow.

The Chinese also were looking after their own, and the funeral of Lin Wong and others drowned in the flood had united the population of Chinatown. The Wongs, who had been across the street, had survived to mourn their daughter, and Mr. Wong, his braided queue fairly quivering with fury, informed his disapproving neighbors that anyone who wished to prevent Mai Li and her Shoshone husband from attending Lin's funeral would have to answer to him.

Since Mr. Wong was reputed to have tong connections, no one argued, and Mai and White Elk went unmolested. Mai stood close against her husband's side, in air thick with the smell of incense and mud, and let the tears slide down her face. She knew that she was saying good-bye not just to Lin but to an old life. She might return to Chinatown, but she would never have the feeling of coming home to the old neighborhood. She had chosen her path, and it was with White Elk. He would have died for her, and she for him. It suddenly made everything very simple.

In Portland's red-light district, cleanup had also begun, and wherever a dry spot could be found, business continued. Portland liked to pretend that it did not have a red-light district—vice raids looked bad in the newspapers, and it was much more comfortable to ignore the situation. Worse, Portland's police were far too often willing to do the same. But, in truth, it was a flourishing district and an excellent investment for a number of solid citizens, who could manage to keep money matters secret from their wives.

Dan Schumann, making his way through the lower levels of sin toward Maisie Mennen's posh whorehouse, noted the number of pious, churchgoing citizens selflessly helping the shadier sections of Portland to dig out from the disaster. *I know what you're after,* he thought, smirking. *Looking for evidence on one another and hoping nobody finds any on you.* He chuckled, appreciating his knowledge of the way the world worked. It was the same everywhere, and fools who didn't look out for themselves finished last.

He was less good-humored by the time he left Maisie's, however. He found her establishment full of mud and police—sent by an uneasy police chief who didn't want any uncomfortable evidence tarnishing his own badge, either—and Maisie with a shovel in the wreckage of her office. She kept her investors private from one another, and she wouldn't let him in.

"Not you nor nobody else." She looked disgustedly at the police. "Them I got to put up with. You I don't. Out."

Stymied, Dan walked to Erickson's scow, had a drink, and thought about his predicament. Probably nothing would surface, he comforted himself. On the off chance that something did, he could bribe someone to keep mum—if he had enough money. That was running short, and for a while Maisie would be in no position to pay profits to investors. He had to work fast on the old lady, but now Toby Holt was in town getting in the way, damn him. Not to mention his son, who ran a newspaper and like all newspapermen probably stuck his nose into everything. Tim Holt hadn't seemed nearly as impressed with Dan as the reporter from the *Oregonian* had been. Dan had another drink and thought about how he could keep the old lady sick but not dead until Tim and Toby Holt both got out of town.

Eulalia turned her head in the big bed where she seemed to have lain for days now, weary, feverish, never getting worse but never getting better. Lying in bed was like sinking into quicksand. Sometimes she thought that she was drowning in it. Again she remembered how she had nearly drowned in Sitka, Alaska, when she was there with Lee. She remembered the way the soft, sucking mud had caressed her, drawn her down. Then the tide had come in to cover her face. She had prepared to die, but she hadn't. Lee had gotten her out. Maybe it was time now, to reunite with Lee. And with Whip . . . Eulalia moved her head restlessly on the feather pillow.

In heaven there was no marriage nor giving in marriage. What did one do in heaven with two husbands? Assuming that she got to heaven, of course. Eulalia couldn't honestly guess where she might be bound in her afterlife. She drifted in the feather bed while fragments of her

life unaccountably floated up around her: Lee asking her to
marry him, a year after Whip and Lee's wife, Cathy, had
been killed in a landslide. . . . Old companions, they had
walked up to the point above the fort and stood arm in arm,
looking at the river below. Lee had kissed her when she
said she would have him, and then laughed because some
junior officer and his girl might come and catch them. They
were middle-aged and, in the eyes of youth, beyond
amorous adventure. But the passions Lee had wakened in
her after a year without Whip had had nothing to do with
middle age.

She envisioned herself and Lee now, moving in a
stately dance against a night sky. Lee had been solid,
comforting, loving . . . but Whip had been the love of her
youth. Whip had made her heart stop and start again just by
looking at him. He was wild and risky and a self-made man,
who had roamed the Rockies on his own since he was very
young—the opposite of all the well-dressed, well-bred,
well-mannered beaus who had danced attention on her in
South Carolina. How had she come to love an unruly man
like Whip?

Memory slid into nightmare and fever dream, and
Eulalia watched herself as if she stood on some formless
promontory above her life. She had been a beautiful young
belle, petulant, resentful, outraged at being expected to
work. She dawdled her way through the woods toward the
river, water buckets in her hand. If Whip Holt, wagon
master, expected her to fetch water like a field hand, he
wouldn't see her hurrying to obey him, that was certain! He
had even warned her to stay out of the woods and take the
long way around to the stream. He just liked to make her
work harder, she had thought, pouting.

The Cheyenne raiders had come from out of nowhere,
from out of the trees, riding on a wave of such stark terror
that Eulalia cried out now in her nightmare as the younger
version of herself was thrown down across a buffalo-robe
saddle, facedown, while clouds of dust rolled around her.

For months she had slaved among the Cheyenne, in
conditions that not even the black field workers in her lost
world of South Carolina had had to endure. The fever and
the drifting patches of darkness that befuddled Eulalia's

mind let the vision of the land of the Cheyenne in clearly. She crawled on hands and knees in a dusty field, hungry and thirsty, filthy and bitten by insects, pulling the weeds from the rows of Cheyenne corn. An Indian woman with a whip stood over her, and the welts on her back came anew every time she paused in her work. At night she was fed only if the Cheyenne braves who had come to her tent for sex that night decided that she was worth feeding. By the time Whip Holt had found and rescued her, Eulalia Woodling had become someone else altogether.

The people on the wagon train feared that she had gone mad; white women captured by the Cheyenne often did. But she had found within herself a stubborn determination to survive. She had been tried by fire, and located an inner reserve of strength that no one, herself included, had expected. Different things had become important to her. Happiness was not idleness but freedom, and with a new clarity she had seen that same instinct in Whip and learned to love him for it.

How she had loved him! The visions of the Cheyenne faded, and Eulalia ceased to whimper in her sleep. She saw herself with Whip, riding through the box canyon where he and the ranch's first foreman, Stalking Horse, had trapped their wild horses, where she had once saved Whip's life in return. . . . She envisioned herself and Whip riding endlessly, the wind blowing like sparks around their faces, soaring through the canyon on wings while a hawk wheeled wide above them. They flew without the horses now, and Whip, smelling of dust and sweat, with the sparks about his head, pulled her into his arms. They were young, and the land was very new. They would settle here, raise children, build the ranch, and become a proud part of the new Oregon Territory. He slid the shirtwaist from her shoulders in the July sun, and they rolled together in the long grass. Then slowly the sky darkened again, and she could not hold the vision.

She slept fitfully, the fingers of her right hand turning and turning the wedding band on her left.

While Eulalia lay ill, the work of cleaning up the Madrona went on without her. Everyone on the place worked from sunup to sunset, shoveling, scrubbing, salvaging. There were miles of fence to be rebuilt; the waters had toppled the pasture fence and strewn it like toothpicks, tangled in trees and drowned hedges. Thirty horses were missing, and White Elk sent Paul Kirchner and a crew of hands to scour the countryside for them. They found most, as well as a pig, three goats, and a goose belonging to Amy and Abby's father, old Horace Givens. Five horses were drowned, lying bloated in the water, and the unsavory task of burying them had to be done immediately. The ranch hands, tying their bandannas around their noses against the stench, dug graves where they found the corpses and toppled the bodies in. They washed in carbolic soap, per Dr. Bright's orders, until their skin peeled.

Abby scrubbed the kitchen first thing and spent the day in it cooking for the whole ranch because the bunkhouse kitchen was full of mud. Mai cleaned the bunkhouse and her own cottage, attacking them with carbolic soap, turpentine, and lye until her fingernails split down to the quick.

Toby spent most of his time in Portland, assessing the city's damage and reporting its needs and recovery status to Washington. Tim, meanwhile, stayed at the Madrona, working with the hands, shoveling mud, and doctoring his stepmother's thoroughbreds. Alexandra's show beasts were of a more delicate constitution than the cavalry remounts the Madrona raised, and they all promptly developed the sniffles and inflamed joints. He slept in the barn to monitor them more closely. One more whiff of an oatmeal poultice, Tim was heard to remark, and he would go to his grave smelling it. As it was, he would never eat oatmeal for breakfast again.

He communicated by wire with San Francisco and made a pest of himself at the *Oregonian* offices, monitoring their AP wire until the editor threatened half seriously to charge him for a separate franchise. But he invited Tim to dinner, and they talked shop amicably, particularly since Tim had arrived with a bottle of good whiskey for the editor and a dozen roses for the editor's wife. Tim was a Portland boy and knew that he was trading on that as much as on professional courtesy.

The editor's wife was a pretty blond who reminded Tim of Rosebay . . . but so had mixing another oatmeal poultice or pouring tonic down an ungrateful horse's throat. Tim thought wistfully of making a quick trip to San Francisco and decided he must be going crazy from too much work. Even when he was dog tired, the faint, shimmering image of Rosebay Ware danced in the haze before his eyes as he went to sleep—and was with him when he rose in the morning.

Toby looked at him at dinner and said, "You look like you're fifty. Sleep in a bed tonight."

"The blasted beasts are just about well," Tim said. "If I lose one now, Mama'll shoot me sure."

"She's in Washington," Toby said. "She can't get at you."

Tim yawned. "I'll see." He got up stiffly. "How's Gran?"

"No worse," Toby answered. "A little better maybe. She drank some of Abby's soup this afternoon." He rubbed his eyes with the heels of his palms. "She's just old, Son. It takes her longer to bounce back than she used to. Bright says she's doing as well as can be expected."

Tim went upstairs to find Eulalia awake, with Dan Schumann sitting in the chair by her bed. A pair of empty glasses sat on the bedside table.

"We've been having some lemonade," Dan said as he rose. "I'll give you my place here. I know your grandmother wants to see you. But don't stay too long. We don't want to tire her."

"I'll keep it in mind," Tim said dryly. He looked after Dan's departing back. "You take a lot on yourself, buddy," he muttered.

"He's been very good to me, dear," Eulalia murmured. "I'm grateful to him." Her voice was slurred and sleepy.

"Sorry, Gran." Tim took her hand penitently and sat with her while she drifted into sleep.

In the darkness behind the house, Paul Kirchner, heading wearily from the brood-mares' barn to the bunkhouse, saw Tim at Eulalia's lighted window and nodded with satisfaction. As long as Tim and his father were here,

Paul could relax about Mrs. Blake's well-being. Dan Schumann could do nothing untoward during their stay. He doubted that either Tim or Toby would listen to the vague, unproven suspicions of an aimless drifter devoid of the ambition that drove the Holts. But now, with them staying in the house, he didn't have to voice his suspicions and possibly get fired for criticizing the local hero. Toby Holt would be here all summer. By fall Dan might move on to greener pastures and easier pickings.

Paul turned into the bunkhouse and fell on his bed without even undressing. He was exhausted. It was a relief just to slog through his work and not worry about trying to protect a woman who didn't even like him.

The Holts were all as dead set as bulls, Paul thought as he tried to relax into sleep. They radiated a charged energy and focus that he could not match. He didn't fit in here, any more than he had filled the niche his mother had planned for him. Did he belong anywhere? Paul wasn't sure. He thought wistfully of Teddy Montague. She hadn't fit, either, but she had managed to make her own place.

Tim might have been a more receptive listener than Paul supposed, since Tim, too, had conceived a dislike of Dan Schumann, whom he found far too self-important. But Tim was too moody to appear approachable to Paul, and when he wasn't doctoring his stepmother's horses, he was in Portland, keeping tabs on the railway strike. And then he was gone, with a hastily packed bag and an equally hasty explanation for his father:

"Debs has called out the Railway Union. They're all going on strike. There's going to be hell to pay."

"Oh, damn!" Toby said, and reached for his hat.

The senator nearly beat his son into Portland. He wired several hundred well-chosen words to President Cleveland and gnashed his teeth because he couldn't deliver them in person.

When he got home, Ephraim Bender and Donald McCallum were waiting for him in the parlor, brandishing fresh copies of the *Oregonian*.

"We want to know what ye're doing about this labor-union outrage, Holt," McCallum demanded.

Toby groaned. "No, you don't. What are you two doing in my house? I have an office downtown and a secretary who makes appointments for people who want to annoy me."

"You weren't in your office."

"Well, I'm not here, either. I'm a figment of your imagination. Will you two go home? My mother's sick."

McCallum thumped the paper. "Debs ought to be jailed. He'll ruin this country. We elected you to look after our interests. Now you tell me what you've done about that."

"I've pried more disaster relief out of Washington than even I thought I could, that's what."

"About this strike!" McCallum exploded. "Don't pussyfoot with me, Holt. Ye're a damn union lover. But Debs isn't going to get away with it. The Railway Managers' Association is taking steps."

Toby raised his eyebrows. "Then you don't need me. Have a drink, McCallum, and simmer down. Your engine's boiling over."

"We've authorized the hiring of thirty-six hundred deputy marshals," McCallum said with satisfaction. "That'll put a stop to the union's nonsense."

"With what? Shotguns and clubs?" Toby handed McCallum a glass and poured a drink for Bender. "You'll start a war."

"This is war already," McCallum said. "The unions will bring this country to a standstill if they're not stopped. We've petitioned the President for an injunction against this strike. Now are ye on our side, or are ye not?"

"You're getting Scots again," Toby said. "I notice it comes on you when you're riled."

"Damn and blast ye for a stinkin' socialist!" McCallum leaped up and smacked his glass down on the coffee table so that its contents splashed onto the mahogany. "Ye'll get no support from me this election, Holt! That's a fair warnin'."

"Tsk. That'll leave a stain," Bender said when McCallum had taken his abrupt departure. He was mopping up the spilled whiskey with his handkerchief. "You could have been a little more conciliatory, Holt," he remarked. "This town needs the railroad."

"The railroad isn't going away," Toby pointed out. "McCallum knows what side his bread's buttered on."

"Well, you've buttered your bread, so now you'll have to lie on it," Bender said with a fine disregard for metaphor. "Don't say I didn't warn you."

"You warned me," Toby said. "And I warned you. It's a draw. Now will you please go home? Here's a word in your ear, Bender: Just now I would delightedly and voluntarily retire from politics and wish joy to whoever gets elected in my stead. You may, however, be trading me in for the evil you know not of."

Toby ran his hands distractedly through his hair after Bender left. He knew he could have been more conciliatory, but he was too worried about his mother and the flood losses on the Madrona—not to mention the last letter he had received from Alexandra about Mike's behavior—to be willing to dance a political waltz with either McCallum or Bender. Ephraim Bender stayed just this side of the law, but he was not a bedfellow, in the political sense, who appealed at all to Toby. Still, Toby had taken on a responsibility and he would see it through, no matter who didn't like it. He sighed and sat down to compose a lengthier letter to the President than he could send by wire. He would put it on the next train—supposing that any of them were still running tomorrow.

In the morning Toby picked up the newspaper—the letter to the President in hand—on his way into Portland and chuckled in spite of himself. It seemed that Congress, with its usual flair for too little too late, had declared Labor Day a holiday in the District of Columbia. It was already a holiday in many states but not a declared national holiday.

"Well, that ought to just set the unions right up," Toby said to his horse as he swung into the saddle. "You figure Debs is going to be so grateful that he'll send all his brakemen back to work?"

Tim, Runyon, and another reporter-colleague were sitting in an empty boxcar, eating lunch and watching the parade of placard-carrying railroad workers who were getting their point across in the stalled rail yard in Chicago. It was as hot as the devil's firebox.

Tim shook his head, feeling a jaded cynicism for the workings of government, local and national, that many newspapermen eventually felt. "The President shouldn't have listened to Olney. My Lord, if ever there was a man with 'ulterior motive' written across his brow—"

Richard Olney, the United States attorney general, had persuaded President Cleveland to issue an injunction against the strikers on the grounds of interference with interstate commerce and the U.S. Postal Service. Olney was a former railroad director and member of the Railroad Managers' Association. He still served as the attorney for several railroads.

"Pullman cars don't carry mail," Runyon remarked. He had been reassigned by the AP to Chicago to the rail strike, which was becoming far more interesting than the coal miners' travails. He propped his back against the other side of the boxcar door, spread a linen napkin across his lap, and unpacked his own lunch of roasted beef and blueberry trifle from one of Chicago's best restaurants. Runyon took his creature comforts where he could find them.

"Mail cars do," Tim's companion pointed out. "They're stopped, too."

"That's a lousy excuse," Tim scoffed. "I happen to know my dad recommended an alternative order to resume mail service and passenger-car service while the Pullman strike's negotiated, but Cleveland wouldn't listen."

"He listened to Olney," Runyon said, cutting the beef with the serviceable blade of a pocket knife. His crinkly hair was wet with sweat. The shade of the boxcar was only marginally cooler than the yard outside. He looked at his compatriots. "My God, how can you eat that salami? You'll poison yourselves. Holt, if I owned a newspaper, I'd go home and eat oysters in Frisco and assign some poor dumb bastard like me to cover this strike."

"I like to keep my hand in," Tim muttered. Rosebay was in San Francisco. Tim wasn't going to make a poor dumb bastard out of Hugo Ware if he could help it.

"At least you can write what you want to," the third

man said glumly, munching his salami. He was from the *Chicago Tribune*, which was firmly antiunion.

Over the next week, the striking railroad men played havoc with the rail lines, but on Debs's insistence there was little violence—although there was always some hothead getting out of hand.

Governor Altgeld of Illinois called in the state militia to maintain order, and although the militia and the strikers regarded each other warily, no open fighting broke out. Altgeld was accounted a fair man, and the strikers had no wish to lose his goodwill. Those still working cut Pullman cars from any train they handled and thereby infuriated a great many people, but peace held.

The Railway Managers' Association met in a closed session in the Rookery Building in Chicago while the outraged press howled outside the door. Tim and the others learned later that the managers had agreed not to rehire any man who struck. The economic depression would make it easy for them to find replacements.

Railroad management began to disrupt their own schedules, hopeful of fanning public opinion against the strikers. Pullman cars were attached to trains that did not ordinarily carry them—freights, suburbans, and mail trains to incite the strikers to interfere with the mail and cut their own throats. The *Chicago Tribune* wrote:

> Westward from Chicago, Mr. Debs's imperious hand stretched. Kansas was numb, and trade stood still. . . . The U.S. mail for six hundred miles had to catch local trains from town to town. . . . The mysterious Mr. Debs, like the Black Death, was spreading over the continent, and there was no escape from him. . . . Mr. Debs leans too decidedly to the side of revolution, and there is a suspicion that he may be a Caesar in his ambition.

"Hooey," Tim jeered. "This country was founded on a revolution against high-handedness."

"Revolution in the past is sacred," Runyon said. "Present-day revolution has a less appealing look."

In the union hall, Eugene Debs and his aides sent detailed instructions to hundreds of railroad towns to bolster up the weak spots. The hall was packed with restless, excited men, shouting questions, yelling, and singing. The executive board appeared periodically before the crowd, spoke briefly, then staggered back to the board room. They hammered out press releases while Debs, in a tweed suit and hard white collar, incongruous among the burly railroad men, answered all the questions that were put to him, made decisions, smiled, and went without sleep.

There had never been such a strike in the United States. More than a hundred thousand men had walked off the job. Between Chicago and the Golden Gate only one railroad, the Great Northern, kept even a semblance of its regular schedule.

The country was divided by the strike. A few newspapers sided with the union, Tim's *Clarion* among them. In a speech quoted by Tim, Debs had said:

> "The struggle with the Pullman Company has developed into a contest between the producing classes and the money power of the country. The fight was between the American Railway Union and the Pullman Company. Then the railway corporations, through the General Managers Association, came to the rescue and, in a series of whereases, declared to the world that they would go into partnership with Pullman, so to speak, and stand by him in his devilish work of starving his employees to death."

The American Railway Union was young, and Debs had been afraid that they weren't ready to handle successfully a strike of this magnitude.

"I was wrong," he said jubilantly, clapping Tim on the back and shaking Runyon's hand. "I was wrong, Holt, and you can quote me on it. We'll defy their damned injunction, and we'll make such a change in the way this country is run that the workingman will be able to stand tall from here on out!"

Debs's eyes gleamed with excitement, although Tim thought that he looked brittle from lack of sleep. The bright eyes had dark hollows beneath them.

"There will be plenty of time to sleep when we've won," Debs said in answer to Tim's concern.

Runyon sighed, watching Debs's departing back. "He doesn't know Olney," he said. "I've met him, and he's a formidable adversary. President Cleveland's so busy fighting Congress over the Wilson Tariff Bill, he's going to let Olney run this show."

Tim looked interested in this bit of domestic gossip—the AP man seemed to know everything—but he was too caught up in the euphoria of the strikers to pay heed to Runyon's assessment of Cleveland's interest. "No, by God, I think they're going to do it," he said.

"Remember Homestead and Coeur d'Alene," Runyon said gloomily. "Ill-fated strikes both. Federal troops came in, locked the strikers up behind barbed wire, and nearly starved them to death. When management broke the strike, the workers were blacklisted. Not a man there has worked since."

"It has to stop," Tim said. "Someone has to do it."

"You're a newspaperman," Runyon reminded him. "Report the news and take a side if you want to, but don't break your heart."

"You're a cynic," Tim said happily. "Don't you believe in anything?"

"Human nature at its worst," Runyon answered. "It hasn't disappointed me yet."

"Human nature has been known to find its way to altruism despite itself," Tim retorted. "I've caught myself in the act occasionally."

He grinned, feeling drunk on the excitement of the moment and the shouting and cheers that still pulsed in the union hall. As long as there was excitement, as long as he was caught up in it, he could keep Rosebay Ware in the back of his mind and allow his altruism to function as it ought . . . except at night, of course. Rosebay troubled his dreams almost unfailingly. He dreamed of her silvery hair tangled in his hands and her pale legs twined with his. Tim had tried to shake his obsession with her and had even taken a few railroaders' pretty daughters out dancing, but Rosebay didn't shake.

"Come on," he said suddenly to Runyon. "I'll buy you a drink to lubricate all that cynicism. Tomorrow's the Fourth of July. We'll get a headstart on celebrating the American Revolution."

"Wait a minute," Runyon said. He was listening to the shouting in the hall, which had taken on a more ominous sound.

"Troops!" someone shouted in outrage. "The government is threatening to send federal troops from Fort Sheridan!"

Attorney General Olney angrily paced the halls of the Capitol. In his hand was a telegram fired off by Senator Holt and another from Illinois Governor John Peter Altgeld, protesting that neither he nor the state legislature had requested military assistance. The attorney general was determined to provide it anyway, and Grover Cleveland had listened to him. After all, hadn't Altgeld pardoned the survivors of the Haymarket Riots? Hadn't Mayor Hopkins of Chicago contributed openly to the Pullman strike relief fund? Dangerous men both, not to be trusted, warned Olney, truculent and stubborn in stern pursuit of duty.

Olney's conception of duty was honest by his own lights, but rigid and narrow by most other men's. His daughter, for example, had been barred from his house for the last two years simply for marrying, and to a man of whom Olney approved.

Any notion of a drink abandoned, Tim and Runyon followed Debs back to his digs in the Leland Hotel and camped outside his door all night with a crowd of similarly minded reporters. Behind the door Debs managed to sleep briefly.

In the governor's mansion in Springfield, John Peter Altgeld weighed his options against his conscience and decided to continue his protests against military interference.

*   *   *

Not long after dawn, the harsh sounds of bugles and marching feet awakened Debs and the reporters now sleeping on the floor in the hall. Debs stumbled sleepily to the window and looked down at Jackson Street and Lake Michigan. Hundreds of federal soldiers were encamped on the lakefront. Then he went to the door and beckoned Tim and Runyon inside.

Tim, incredulous, stared out the window.

"Remember Coeur d'Alene," said Runyon.

XIV

With the coming of the federal soldiers, the first violence of the strike occurred in Chicago. The federal army, Debs said angrily, was simply a signal for civil war. On 5 July, unemployed Chicagoans—by no means all of them railroaders—blocked the tracks against the orders of Eugene Debs, stalled a freight train, and set fire to the signal house. The soldiers made a bayonet charge against the mob, and several people were injured.

Tim watched grimly from a vantage point atop a water tank, which, he hoped fervently, the rioters wouldn't topple. He reported in a lengthy telegram to the *Clarion* that Mayor Hopkins, swearing furiously—Tim had heard him—had issued a proclamation against riotous assemblies and at the suggestion of Governor Altgeld was requesting state troops to assist him.

Worse yet were the hundreds of special federal deputy marshals who had been hired. No man with a regular job wanted this temporary assignment, particularly since it offered an excellent chance of getting shot. As a result, Federal Marshal J. W. Arnold of Chicago deputized whoever came to apply: professional strikebreakers, labor spies, petty hoodlums, and every layabout with good muscles in the city. Governor Waite of Colorado, a state that had its own labor troubles, called them "desperadoes," and he wasn't far from the truth.

The next day, incensed by what it considered to have been an invasion, a furious mob near Pullman began overturning freight cars. Tim, with a reporter's notebook in his hand and a pistol in his pocket just in case, watched the great cars pushed over onto their sides with a shrieking of torn metal and a clangor that rose above the shouts of the mob.

"Heave!"

"Turn 'em over!"

"Burn 'em!"

Only a handful of the mob wore the white ribbon badges of the striking ARU, but that didn't matter; all violence was now being attributed to strikers, despite evidence to the contrary. Tim had even seen federal deputy marshals deliberately cutting fire hoses as the engine crews struggled to put out burning boxcars. He had reported as much and now wondered uneasily if the marshals were going to turn their rifles on him if they spotted him. The railroad management kept track of who supported its side and who did not.

Another boxcar, this one loaded, was levered over, spilling baled cotton into the chaos of the yard. A man in an oil-stained jacket flung a flaming torch into the cotton, and the cotton bales went up in a cloud of fire, which spread rapidly to the overturned wooden car.

The deputy marshals raised their rifles at the mob around the cars, and Tim eased away toward a knot of spectators a hundred yards distant. Any commotion attracted onlookers, Tim knew, but if he were these folks, he would find tamer entertainment. Shots rang out, and Tim spun around and then back in horror as the spectator beside him dropped with a startled grunt to the cinder-strewn ground. The man, by the look of him not a railroader but an innocent curiosity seeker, tried to rise, his hand gripping the iron track on which he had fallen. Before Tim could kneel beside him, the deputy who had fired the shot saw what he had done. Dumbstruck, Tim saw the deputy take a few steps forward and deliberately fire again. The wounded man fell back.

The witnesses scattered, and the deputy vanished into the crowd, leaving Tim beside a bloody corpse. In anguish, Tim wondered who the man was—some out-of-town shopkeeper on an ill-fated holiday? He had neither a white ribbon nor the callused hands of a railway worker. His bowler hat lay upturned in the cinders while blood seeped down slowly to pool in the soot of the tracks. Tim raised his head with tears streaming down his face and wondered what his beloved country was coming to.

A huge wall of flame shot up around them suddenly, as if the earth were trying to burn away its own festering spores. Tim pulled the dead man as far away from the flames as he could, then ran. Pandemonium surrounded him. The screaming of the wounded and the angry shouting of both the mob and the deputy marshals blended with the howling of fire engines and the hideous noise of exploding boxcars. There seemed to be blood everywhere, but maybe it was only the light of the flames, Tim thought.

He stumbled over a man lying facedown across the tracks. He rolled the figure over and saw that this one was still breathing. His stomach lurched when he saw too that it was a boy of no more than sixteen. Tim cradled him in his arms, then lifted him. "Hang on, buddy."

"They shot me," the boy said in disbelief. His dirty face was nearly white beneath the smudges of soot.

Tim realized that his arms were soaked with the boy's blood. He put the fellow down beside the track and pulled off his cravat. An ugly hole gaped in the boy's corduroy trousers, and his whole thigh was soaked with blood. Probably his first pair of long pants, Tim thought, sickened, as he tied his cravat around the boy's leg, pulled on it with his teeth to knot it as tightly as he could, and hoped the bullet hadn't hit an artery.

Damn the marshals, damn the army, and damn Eugene Debs, too, while he was at it. And where the hell was a doctor? Tim picked the boy up again, staggering a little under his weight over the uneven rail beds that crisscrossed the yard. The rioters had managed to lever some of the track up with crowbars.

"Bloody deputies," the boy whispered. Hatred seemed to be all he had to hang on to. "Stinking bloody deputies."

The yard was still a roaring, howling mass of flame and battling men. Tim looked around desperately and saw a Red Cross wagon draw up on the outskirts. The firemen were loading one of their own men, burned and writhing, into it. Tim began to run.

There was a middle-aged nurse in the back of the wagon, her white apron already stained with blood and soot. Tim pushed past the firemen and laid the boy in the wagon bed.

"He's been shot."

The nurse looked angrily at Tim. "The blame's on you, then. He's no more than a boy."

"I don't even know him," Tim protested.

"And which are you, then? A hoodlum striker or a hoodlum marshal?" the nurse demanded, slitting open the boy's trousers and pushing a pad of bandage against the wound. "I see no difference between any two men with guns."

"I'm a newspaperman," Tim said, but he didn't feel very virtuous. If the country couldn't settle differences between its own people without this, the blame rested with everyone.

"I was at Gettysburg," the nurse said. "I thought we were done with civil war."

But it was only the beginning. Despite Governor Altgeld's protests, neither Cleveland nor Olney would relent on the use of the army. The President was determined that the mail would not be stopped, and the attorney general was committed to breaking the strikers. The government would not give in, despite dissension within its own ranks from men like Toby Holt, who was still in Oregon.

The railroad managers, enjoying the upper hand, announced loftily that they would not confer with municipal authorities or any other party to resolve the dispute. The union claimed that the railroads were burning their own cars to collect insurance on obsolete equipment and discredit the strikers.

In Chicago alone, the cost to the United States Treasury for deputy marshals was $125,000,000 despite the fact that the maximum pay for a deputy was $2.50 a day plus $1.50 expense money, and much of that was paid by the railroads, which were willing to pay what they had to, to break the union. They would recoup it later in starvation wages.

The riots, the arson, and the bloodshed continued

until even some of the army had had enough. Several army officers decided that the strikers had a reasonable cause and that the military was being used solely to break the strike. They met to issue a statement to that effect and were held for court martial. Cleveland squelched the court martial, but the highest ranking man among them, a colonel, was retired from active service.

As the setting for much of the strife, Chicago itself was divided by the issue. Several newspapers came out for the strikers, and others trumpeted the cause of the railroads. The *Tribune* fired the reporter who had shared Tim's salami when he wouldn't authenticate for a grand jury the printed version of his interview with Eugene Debs. It had gone enough against his conscience, he said, to write a pack of lies; he wouldn't put his hand on a bible and swear to them.

The out-of-town press were similarly divided, but Tim noted that one contingent was united almost to a man. The Chicago newsboys, many of whom had strikers in their families, wore white ribbons on their jackets and dropped into the sewers those papers that opposed the union.

Despite their sentiments, all the journalists thronged outside the meeting rooms of the union and the railway managers, buttonholing any man who stuck his head out. They followed the sounds of riot and the smell of smoke like hounds on the trail until Tim began to wonder if they did more harm than good by printing news of violence. Certainly the articles that made it sound as if the entire city was in flames were not helping. Tim wired the *Clarion* as carefully a balanced report as he could. The reality was bad enough.

On 10 July he found himself in the thick of it again, with a somewhat more personal story than he'd had in mind. It was sheer accident—there were always plenty of riots to choose from because the army had kited itself and the mobs both up to the pitch where something was bound to happen.

Rioters in Spring Valley built a bonfire on the tracks, and when they halted a freight train with a Pullman car attached, they decided to burn it, too. The train's crew hastily departed in a shower of rocks. Soldiers arrived just as the mob was systematically torching the cars, starting with the hated Pullman.

"Fire!" No one knew quite who had given the order, or even if it was one, but the soldiers leveled their rifles, and two men went down in the smoke and flames.

Tim dived under a boxcar at the front of the train and then decided that that wasn't the best place to take refuge. Gunfire blazed all around him, but the flames were rolling ominously nearer, and there was no telling what was inside the car. Rumor had it that the railroads were intentionally stuffing their boxcars with flammable cargo.

Tim rolled out from under the car, and a shot zinged over his head. He had a notebook in his hand and a press card in his hat, but no one noticed—or maybe they did. There was a growing blacklist of undesirable reporters, and Tim Holt's name was very near the top.

He sprinted for a shack beside the rail bed and discovered that it was a coal shed. Crouching in a coal bin seemed preferable to getting shot, so he stayed, curled into a ball well away from the window.

Finally, when no shots followed him, he uncurled, sidled over to the window, and peeked out. The scene was a hellish roil of smoke and flame billowing from the boxcars, rising to sear and blacken the sky. Tim would not have been surprised to see the devil himself striding through it. The nearly unbearable heat scorched his lungs when he breathed. A coal shed was no place to be. It would burn like the Connellsville mine. *Out of the frying pan into the firing line,* he thought. He edged toward the door and inched it open.

"There's one of the bastards!"

A shot thudded into the door frame, and Tim retreated inside, only to see that the shed's roof was burning. Sparks were dropping from it into the coal. Tim stayed by the door, waiting for the coal to flare up. It would, and then nothing would put it out. A soldier with a rifle was waiting just outside to shoot him.

A piece of burning board fell from the roof. Tim knew that the whole ceiling would collapse in a minute. He had been trapped by fire before Connellsville, and each experience only increased his terror of it. He pulled his pistol from his pocket, slammed the door open, and hurled himself at the soldier before the man could take aim. They rolled together, coughing and choking and clawing at each other, in the cinders, with the smoke billowing above them. It was impossible for Tim to see anything through his stinging eyes but the man under him.

The soldier lashed out with his fist and caught Tim in the eye. Desperate, Tim raised his pistol, butt end first, and brought it down hard on the soldier's head. The man went limp, and Tim dragged him away from the flames, threw his rifle back into the fire, and stripped off the man's jacket. He shrugged it on and dived for the army hat that had been lost in the struggle. He pulled it down over his eyes and ran. Behind him in the coal shed, his favorite field hat, with the press card still in the band, was going up in flames.

He ran past the embattled soldiers, shouting, "Pull back! The captain says to pull back!"

That ploy might work, or it might not—Tim didn't stop to see. When he was clear of the riot, he stripped off the army jacket before someone realized it didn't match his trousers and sailed it and the hat into a ditch.

Limping, he set off down the tracks toward the town of Spring Valley proper. A fire engine drawn by galloping horses passed him going in the other direction. In half a mile, he found Runyon of the AP sitting with his notebook on his knees under an apple tree.

"You look like hell," Runyon commented.

"It's hell back there," Tim said. "This madness has got to be stopped. How did it get so far out of hand?"

"Pigheadedness," Runyon responded. "Greed."

They watched the black column of smoke rising in the sky. "Union's dead," Runyon said. "That's its funeral pyre."

Runyon's statement proved prophetic. When Tim had gone back to Chicago in a hired wagon and filed furious and lengthy copy at the telegraph office—he had to wait in line behind a contingent of out-of-town press—he headed for the Revere Hotel on North Clark Street. Debs had taken up residence there soon after the army had camped under his window at the Leland. At the hotel Tim learned that the federal grand jury had indicted Eugene Debs for conspiracy to interfere with interstate commerce.

That Debs had urged his union to avoid violence and that they had done so—most of the mobs at Spring Valley and elsewhere were not union men—made no difference. Federal marshals arrested Debs at once and seized his books, papers, and private unopened correspondence. A judge ordered the items returned the following day, but no one was sure exactly how much of it found its way back. Debs and four alleged co-conspirators were released on ten thousand dollars bail each.

Only a miracle would save the strike now. The strikers were hungry, nearly penniless, and incapable of fighting the United States Army. Trains began to move, and the railroad managers announced that there would be no negotiation with the union. Eugene Debs was rearrested on a charge of contempt of court and this time jailed without bail. The railroads sent agents to each town to inform the workers that the men in the next town had returned to their jobs. The union locals wired Debs for confirmation or denial, but he was in jail and could not answer. Desperate, hungry men began to go back to work.

On 20 July, the U.S. troops were withdrawn from Chicago. Since their arrival, fire alone had caused three million dollars' worth of damage. Prior to the military's arrival, strike damage in the city had totaled less than six thousand.

"I want a good lawyer," Tim said.

"You look like you need one," the man across the desk from him drawled. "That's a nice shiner."

"No, not for me," Tim said. "I've been told that you're good, that you're hungry, and that you've never worked for the railroads."

"Sort of makes me an oddity, doesn't it?" Clarence Darrow grinned at him, and Tim looked back dubiously. Darrow was thirty-seven, already stoop shouldered and slouchy, and his clothes looked as if he slept in them. Noting the worn leather couch and its tangled afghan, Tim suspected that he did.

"I'm hungry if you mean I'd like a nice splashy case,"

Darrow said. "Other than that I don't take much feeding. Good thing, too, if you want me to represent Eugene Debs." His voice still drawled, but his eyes shot interested sparks at Tim.

"I can't hire you," Tim said hastily. "The ARU has to hire you. I just want to make sure they get someone competent. You were highly recommended."

"I don't think I'll ask which of my erstwhile clients sang my praises," Darrow said. "I'm a criminal lawyer. Not all my clients are as natty as Mr. Debs."

"He's not so natty now," Tim said. "He's in the Cook County Jail."

"Disgraceful place," Darrow sympathized.

· "The mattresses are infested, and the cells are full of rats the size of terrier dogs," Tim said indignantly. "I'm not allowed to see him. He's not permitted to give interviews."

"But you met the rats," Darrow murmured.

"I sneaked in," Tim explained. "I didn't get as far as Mr. Debs's cell, though." He shuddered, thinking of Cook County Jail. It was a bleak granite structure with narrow barred windows so begrimed with cobwebs and dirt that they did not afford a view. The corridor floors were slippery with slime and tobacco spit, and the bunks in the cells stood three-high against the filthy walls. The cells were lightless, and the inmates were locked into them for twenty hours a day. For the other four, they were permitted to roam the damp corridors.

The women's cell block was just within earshot of the men's block. Tim had heard the dreadful wailing and moaning of the women prisoners. The thought of the dapper Eugene Debs in this loathsome place had driven Tim to abandon all pretense of impartiality and go hunting for the best lawyer available. Local scuttlebutt had recommended Clarence Darrow. He was young; he was getting a reputation; and he was accounted to be a labor man.

"I wouldn't care to be in there myself," Darrow admitted. "Are you certain *you* don't need me? I hear you impersonated an officer."

"I impersonated a private," Tim said. "And how the hell did you know that?"

"I have my sources," Darrow said complacently, "same

as you. If the union wants me, I'll take the case. I warn you, I don't have much hope. I can probably get him out of jail, though. Edwin Walker's been ill—troubled conscience manifesting itself in his gut, no doubt." Edwin Walker had been appointed by Attorney General Olney as special federal attorney, despite the fact that he was the Illinois attorney for the Chicago, Milwaukee & St. Paul Railroad and a member of the Managers Association. "If we're lucky, he'll fall down dead," Darrow said, beaming, "and we can get the case postponed."

Edwin Walker wasn't so obliging as to fall down dead, but he did get sick enough for the judge to postpone the hearings until September. Darrow got the prisoners released on bond again. Eugene Debs, looking like a frail shadow of the man who had begun the ARU strike, went home to Terre Haute, Indiana, where he fell ill himself and spent two weeks in bed, with his indignant wife, Kate, to nurse him. She gave several pithy interviews to the press and blamed the government for her husband's illness. Kate Debs was an elegant woman, both informed and intelligent about politics, and the press took a liking to her.

The Cook County Jail was enough to kill anyone, Tim thought, reading Mrs. Debs's interview appreciatively. She had described its horrors in outraged tones, and he hoped Cook County was ashamed of itself, but he doubted it.

Tim stayed on in Chicago because the strike had not officially ended—Debs had yet to call it off formally—and he wanted to see the story through. Besides, every time he thought about going home, the image of Rosebay floated before his eyes, provoking such longing that he could hardly bear it. The more he wanted to go home, the more he knew he had better not.

He took a brakeman's daughter dancing and to a vaudeville show and tried to fall in love with her but only succeeded in drinking too much in the effort and waking with a hangover the next day.

A letter from Waldo Howard arrived, and when Tim's head cleared enough to read it, he learned that Mr. Barlow, the business manager handpicked by Peter Blake, had died after an apparently lengthy illness.

Tim leaned against the Cook County Post Office wall, swearing steadily under his breath until a passing woman gave him such an indignant look that he bit his lip and stalked out. Why the hell hadn't Waldo told him when the man had gotten sick? What was happening to his newspaper?

"You're a baboon, Waldo," he informed the empty air. "I've got to go home."

No, he didn't; he couldn't. Tim walked through the streets of Chicago, dodging wagons and foot traffic, his hat pulled down over his eyes and his coat collar turned up against the wind. The strike wasn't over yet, but it was as good as dead. He could pick up the AP wire. He could send Hugo.

A wagon driver with a load of beer barrels shouted at Tim as he walked in front of the plodding horses. He leaped back to the sidewalk. If he went home, he might break down and send Hugo. Tim crumpled Waldo's letter into a ball and stared at the sky. No flames rose there anymore. Only dark clouds scudded across it. What in the name of God was he going to do?

XV

Grevenburg, Germany, June 1894

"Germany is very lovely in the autumn," Herr Grumman, the chief of Peter Blake's trustees, said hopefully. "There is the Oktoberfest and magnificent colors on the trees. Many beautiful girls." He looked at Peter and sighed. Young Blake wasn't even listening. He was looking out the window of Grevenhof into the sweeping carriage drive, where a motorcar that sounded like sewing machines being pedaled at full speed and that belched black smoke had pulled up. "You will set fire to the castle," he informed Peter.

"Mmm," said Peter. "The De Dion's here. Will you excuse me?"

"No, I will not excuse you!" Herr Grumman snapped. "You are an incorrigible young man, and you will not spend a penny of your mother's money on such nonsense!" He stalked to the window and peered down. Somehow every lunatic inventor with a motorcar to demonstrate had discovered that the boy had money to invest. The baron von Kirchberg, eating a roasted turkey leg and watching the row, was perched astride one of the stone lions that flanked the front stairs of Grenvenhof. Really, Grumman thought, young Blake was a most unfortunate influence.

"We've been all over this," Peter said. "If my father can't dissuade me, you certainly can't. I'll be twenty-one in eight months. Come along, and I'll take you for a ride."

"Never." Herr Grumman regarded the vehicles in the carriage drive with loathing. Young Blake had been in Germany since April, surrounded by all the loveliest girls of

Grevenburg and the adjacent countryside, as well as their most determined mamas, and he had not so much as given a second glance to one of them.

Instead, young Blake had written letters, without notifying Herr Grumman, to every oil-stained tinkerer in France and Germany, inviting them to Grevenhof. When confronted, he had said that the baron had given his permission. Did Herr Grumman own Grevenhof, he inquired blandly, or did the baron? Henry Blake, meanwhile, had laughed and gone back to the library to read some more. If Herr Grumman could have arranged it, he would cheerfully have strung up the American colonel by his thumbs in Grevenhof's unused dungeon.

"How do you know you don't like something if you've never tried it?" Peter inquired in the same reasoned tones that his stepmother had used to get him to eat spinach. It had much the same effect on Herr Grumman.

"I do not need to have my bones rattled loose from their cartilage to be assured that I should not like it," he informed Peter. But he sighed again and followed Peter's disappearing back. He descended the ornate brass-railed stairs, expostulating to empty air. Peter had hurried ahead of him and was already in the carriage drive when Herr Grumman caught up, puffing. Before Grumman could speak, Peter disappeared beneath the undercarriage of the De Dion, which was steaming gently at both ends.

"Amazing, isn't it?" the baron asked happily. "I haven't had so much fun in years. We're all going for a ride." He indicated a wicker picnic hamper, which sat by the lion's front paws.

"Get down from there. You are inelegant."

"I find it refreshing," the baron said thoughtfully. "I don't get many chances."

Herr Grumman snarled and descended the marble stairs to the drive. A man in an oil-stained duster had his head under the hood of another motorcar. "Give me the wrench, if you please." He held out his hand without looking up. Herr Grumman passed the tool to him without thinking and then stalked away, his dignity affronted.

Peter emerged from under the De Dion. "Amazing machine," he said. "It runs on coal."

"Obviously," Herr Grumman remarked. Peter's coat and trousers were streaked with black.

"I'm convinced that the internal-combustion engine is the better system, however," Peter continued. "A steam engine requires too much water, too many stops."

The driver of the De Dion expostulated urgently in French. "But no, she carries enough fuel to go thirty-five miles without more coal!"

"And has to stop every twenty miles for forty-five gallons of water," Peter retorted in the same language. "She's a beauty, though."

Herr Grumman saw nothing beautiful about her. Like the German Benz and Daimler cars parked beside her, the De Dion smelled like a factory and looked like an obscenity: a small carriage with unnatural additions and a clattering, sputtering engine where the horse ought to be.

"Come and see the Benz," Peter invited. "She's the pick of the lot," he whispered under his breath so as not to offend the drivers of the other machines. "The Daimler's all very wonderful, but she's old-fashioned. Benz has made remarkable improvements. I wish I could have gotten a Panhard for you to look at, but Krebs wouldn't ship it across the Channel unless I wanted to buy it."

"And you do not?" Herr Grumman asked, relieved.

"Certainly not. I'm going to build my own. I'm just studying the competition."

Grumman rolled his eyes.

To a connoisseur of motorcars, however, the Benz was impressive. It was elegantly fitted with leather upholstery and brass trim and possessed a silver horn with a rubber bulb at the end and a silver vase containing a single rose. Its headlamps gleamed, and the spokes of its chain-driven wheels were of wood lacquered a bright Chinese red. Except for the steering tiller and the hellish noise beneath its hood, it still looked very much like a phaeton from a good carriage maker.

Grumman was not deceived. "The smoke will aggravate my lungs," he said. "It will frighten the baron's horses. It will break down, and we will have to walk."

"Undoubtedly," an amused voice said behind him. Grumman turned to find Henry Blake, wearing a duster like the drivers' and helping one of the baron's footmen to stow the picnic hamper into the Daimler. "But the adventure will build character. You fellows always like that." The American colonel's eyes seemed to be laughing at him.

Upstart American cowboy, thought Herr Grumman.

"Let's go!" called Peter, and the baron climbed off his lion.

Grumbling, Grumman found himself in the Benz with Peter, while Henry and the baron rode in the Daimler, and the footman followed in the De Dion. They set out down the winding drive at a steady pace of three miles an hour, and a horse in a nearby pasture neighed in terror and raced for the hills.

"There. You see?" asked Grumman.

"Nonsense," Peter told him. "Horses can get used to anything. They got used to railway trains."

"Railway trains stay on the railway, where they belong. They do not invade city streets, running down women and children."

The motorcade was passing through Grevenburg now. Its citizens stopped to stare openmouthed while the baron waved regally at them from the Daimler.

"You ought to be proud that Germany has taken the lead in developing the motorcar," Peter remarked.

"It is an aberration," Grumman said. "A-a sport, an undesirable mutation that will die for lack of strength. Hmmph!"

"That's what the English thought," Peter told him. "I had assumed Germany would be more farseeing." The German emperor was a grandson of Queen Victoria's, and she disapproved of him mightily. The Germans thought the English weak-willed.

"Tell me about the English," Herr Grumman said, rising to the bait of national rivalry.

"Well, they let their railway companies and carriage makers pressure Parliament into passing the Red Flag Act," Peter explained chattily as the Benz chuffed and clattered through Grevenburg. "It requires that every self-propelled road locomotive be preceded at sixty yards by a man with a red flag. That makes motoring completely ridiculous, of course. So except for Krebs's Panhard, there hasn't been much development in England. Public opinion will probably force the law to be repealed eventually, but in the meantime the French and the Germans have made all the advances."

"Is that so?" Grumman began to look interested in spite of himself. If the English did not approve of the motorcar, perhaps there was something good in it after all. Certainly the ride in the Benz had been less bumpy than he had expected, he thought grudgingly. Although it was devilishly noisy. There wouldn't be a bird for miles. . . .

Past Grevenburg the countryside was in full summer foliage. The dirt road was shaded by towering oak and beech, and the air felt pleasantly cool. A small girl, out berry picking with a basket on her arm, stared at them wide-eyed as they approached. When they neared, she suddenly took flight into the woods, screaming "Mutter!"

There! You see? thought Grumman. The motorcars seemed to him an alien and diabolic invasion into his peaceful country. Still, if young Blake thought there was money to be made . . .

After months of argument with Peter, his trustees had been forced to admit that the boy did understand finance. If he would only agree to marry a German girl and keep the baroness's money where it ought to be, perhaps some arrangement could be made. . . .

A sudden bang and grinding of gears startled Herr Grumman from his thoughts. The Benz came to an abrupt halt, and the trustee bumped his nose on the back of the driver's seat. He looked around, outraged, rubbing his nose and becoming aware of a strong smell of gasoline.

The other two cars halted, and their drivers stepped out to survey the Benz's trouble.

"*Merde,*" the French driver said wonderingly. "There is a hole in your fuel tank."

"I have noticed." The Benz's driver glared at him. "The chain snapped."

Everyone else climbed down to look. The chain had flown off with such force that it had cut a gash in the tank, and gasoline dripped steadily into the road. Grumman sighed and took a cigar from his waistcoat pocket.

Peter leaped at him. "Don't light that!"

"Hmmph!" Grumman stuck the cigar back in his waistcoat.

"Here it is." Henry, with the broken chain dangling from his hand, came up the road. He presented the piece to Peter with a bow. "I think it's going to rain," he observed.

Everyone looked at the sky.

"*Merde*," said the French driver again. He extracted an umbrella from his vehicle and opened it. The baron's footman produced another, which he held over his employer.

"Fetch the hamper, Gottfried," the baron requested. He appeared unruffled. "Herr Grumman, allow me to give you a sandwich. Goose liver paste on pumpernickel, quite good. And a glass of wine."

Peter shot the baron a grin over his shoulder. He thought the man was enjoying himself. He imagined that Gisela von Kirchberg's trustees must be as great a trial to the baron as they were to him. He joined the drivers, who were staring glumly at the broken chain.

"We will return to town and bring back a wagon to tow your machine," the De Dion's driver offered with just a touch of satisfaction.

"Wait," Peter said. "Find me a piece of wire, someone. Or a nail."

There was a general searching of pockets and automobiles, and the Daimler's driver produced a wire of sufficient thickness from his tool kit. With his father's assistance, Peter wrestled the chain back around the wheel and secured it with the wire. The Benz's driver watched glumly, obviously wondering what the young American thought he was going to do about the leaking fuel tank.

A few drops of rain spattered on Herr Grumman's hat. "We will go home," he announced.

"Oh, we can't," the baron said. "This is fascinating."

"I will catch pneumonia," Herr Grumman protested as the heavens opened.

"Did you bring any coffee?" Peter shouted at them.

The baron waved a flask.

"That will not help," said Grumman mournfully.

Henry turned his face to hide a chuckle as Peter took the tin flask and emptied its contents in the road.

"It would have helped some," Grumman yelped too late.

Peter filled the flask with fuel from the Daimler's tank, using a length of tubing from the tool kit for a siphon. The Daimler's driver started to protest and then subsided. National rivalry outweighed individual competition. Perhaps the French De Dion's coal would get wet, and it would have to be towed instead.

After Peter had filled the flask, he punched a hole in its cap with his pocket knife, inserted the tubing into the hole, and screwed on the cap.

"Aha!" The Benz's driver got the idea and snatched the flask from Peter. He climbed into the seat and pulled some string from his pocket.

"They will feed the tubing into the carburetor," the Daimler's driver informed the others while Peter and the Benz driver experimented with the proper angle for the flask. "A most ingenious young man."

Herr Grumman sneezed. The baron motioned to his footman to hold the umbrella over the old man. Henry Blake produced another flask from his own pocket, this one full of brandy. They huddled together over cold goose-liver-paste sandwiches while the rain poured around them in a torrent. Herr Grumman appeared too wet even to complain, but his expression was wrathful and boded no good for later, when he got home and dried off.

He was wetter yet by the time the motorcar cavalcade limped back to Grevenhof, with Peter sitting beside the driver in the Benz and holding the length of tubing in the carburetor's intake.

The baron would not hear of Herr Grumman driving back to Grevenburg in his own carriage in such a downpour. He solicitously put the man to bed in the castle with a hot toddy and had a maid take the chill from the sheets with a brass warming pan.

When Peter looked in on him, Herr Grumman sniffled balefully and declared he was as good as done for.

"The baron is sending up some excellent soup," Peter consoled, "and a bottle of port."

Herr Grumman brightened momentarily, then said, "I shan't even be able to taste it. Fearful cold."

"The doctor says you'll live to be ninety." Peter grinned. "Long enough to vex me for years. And me you, I suppose."

"Most surely." Herr Grumman coughed and spat into his handkerchief. "What are those?" He looked with suspicion at the sheaf of papers that Peter laid on the quilt beside him.

"Financial figures on my proposed motorcar company," Peter replied.

"Take them away. I'm dying."

Peter put his hands on his hips and looked down at the stubborn old devil in the four-poster bed. "Let me repeat that in eight months I will be twenty-one. If you don't give me the money, I will take you to court."

"You're a whippersnapper. Would you really do it?"

"I would."

"Then the funds will be available to you on your birthday and not a half second before. It is to be hoped"—Herr Grumman looked as if he didn't have much hope left—"that you will have come to your senses by that time."

"You can pray for it," Peter invited.

"I shall pray that the baroness your sainted mother is not waiting for me with a pitchfork when I meet her next, being dead of this miserable ailment you have inflicted on me," the old man said. "Now go away and send me that port."

He picked up the papers Peter had left and regarded them with the irritable air of a man who expects to read bad news.

Chicago, July, 1894

"They gave in!" Peter said jubilantly to Tim Holt. "And I have enough money to start the company right now with a loan on my expectations."

"What does Uncle Henry think about it?" Tim asked him.

"He claims to have given up thinking about it," Peter replied. He had left Henry in Washington, where he was somewhat overdue at the offices of the army general command—quite overdue, in fact. Peter had been left to go to San Francisco and lose his shirt in the motorcar business if he so desired. "He says if I come home broke, I'll have to join the army," Peter continued. "Now there's an incentive. Aunt Alexandra told me you were here, so I came this way. The trains are a mess."

Tim nodded gloomily. "At least they're running again, I'm sorry to say. How's the family?"

"Mother's fine. She has a new artist under her wing, a man who looks like a hobo and paints amazing pictures. I'm not quite sure what they're of, though. Frank's in school. Midge is full of airs and graces. She was a junior bridesmaid in some senator's daughter's wedding, and now she thinks she's Mrs. Astor. Your sister Sally and Alice Roosevelt were confined to quarters for three days for sneaking out to the Coxey camp to look at the sideshow. Washington's still full of Coxeyites who won't go home, and no one knows what to do with them. Aunt Alex was in a terrible state over the girls till they came home. Mike's not looking too good."

Tim's laughter at this account of the family doings faded. "Is his heart worse?"

"Only in the metaphorical sense," Peter answered. "Pining for Eden Brentwood. I hope I never fall in love."

"Keep hoping," Tim said grimly.

"He's got a flighty look about him. Aunt Alex says he's going to Georgetown University in the fall, but Mike wasn't making any plans that I could see. He's got something under his hat."

"Brains, I hope," Tim said. "As for your ambitions, I think you're on the right track. Nobody appreciates a pioneer, but the internal-combustion engine is going to revolutionize this country. Rufus Gooch said so ten years ago."

Peter chuckled. "I met him once. The old inventor with the beard and the suit coat held together with string?"

"That's he."

"Aunt Alex says he's crazy."

"He probably is, but that doesn't mean he doesn't know what he's talking about. All visionaries are a little crazy."

"Like Mother's artists," Peter mused. He filed that

thought away for reference. Financial organization and an eye for spotting what was going to make money were his strong points. Perhaps design required a different outlook. He'd have to master that.

Tim pulled a crumpled letter from his pocket and handed it to Peter. "That's from Waldo. The business manager you hired died. I'd be grateful if you'd get to the *Clarion* as soon as you arrive in San Francisco and see what he's let happen to my paper."

"He's got a nerve, dying on me," Peter said indignantly as he scanned the letter. "He wasn't sick when I hired him."

"I don't expect he did it on purpose," Tim remarked. "But Waldo and Hugo haven't got enough money sense between them to balance a checkbook, much less a business."

"Why didn't Waldo tell you sooner?"

"Because he *thinks* he's capable," Tim said. "That's what makes him so dangerous. Just straighten out whatever mess he's made and find me another business manager."

"I thought I was off the hook at the *Clarion*. I need to devote all my attention to getting my new company rolling."

"If you don't help me," Tim threatened, "I'll write Uncle Henry and tell him you're wasting your inheritance on dance-hall floozies."

"He might be relieved," Peter said, laughing. "At least he'd understand that." He held up a hand at Tim's cajoling look. "All right, all right, I'll look in on things. But why don't you do it yourself?"

"I can't," Tim said. Peter raised his eyebrows questioningly, and Tim said hastily, "The whole country's in an upheaval over the labor movement. If you hadn't been lollygagging around in the Black Forest with foreign aristocracy, you'd have some idea. I've spent too much time on it to send in a new man now. I know the sources, and the unions trust me."

"Uh-huh," Peter said. If the unions trusted Tim, they'd trust any *Clarion* reporter now. He didn't press the issue, but he thought Mike wasn't the only Holt with a flighty look in his eyes.

*   *   *

When Peter got to San Francisco, he paid a quick visit to the *Clarion*. Everything seemed to be in order. The city room had a new coat of paint, and there were no lunatic editors in the halls. Hugo was out on a story, but Waldo Howard took Peter to lunch at the Press Club.

"How are things?" Peter asked, trying not to let his eyes stray to the real-estate listings he had been carrying around all morning. An empty warehouse near the wharf was practically going for a song. . . .

"Everything's fine," Waldo assured him. "All under control. I'm interviewing business managers."

"Good." Peter approved. "Very good. I'll come by in a few days and take a look at the books, get things ready for him."

"No hurry," Waldo said. "It's all under control."

"Good," Peter said again, absently.

That afternoon, Peter went to see the warehouse.

"Of course it needs a little fixing," the real-estate agent remarked in vast understatement.

"I'll say," Peter retorted. The glass in most of the windows was broken, and the rafters were full of pigeons. As Peter craned his neck upward a feather drifted down and brushed his nose. Worse things could be said about what was on the floor.

"But at this price you can afford to do some sprucing up. It's a flat-out steal, Mr. Blake."

"For somebody," Peter muttered. He scraped a clean place on the floor with the side of his shoe and inspected it. The floor was concrete and appeared to be solid. The brick walls were solid, too. Everything else was a shambles: Window frames leaned from their apertures like bums on a three-day drunk, the antique gas lighting fixtures were rusted into a state that promised to blow up the building if they were lit; the wooden staircase to the second-floor loft was rotted, and there were indications that someone had been using pieces of it to build a fire on the floor.

"You won't find a sounder place of construction," the real-estate agent protested. "A few nails here and there—"

Peter put his foot on the first step, and it gave way under his shoe. "You go up first," he suggested.

"Perhaps a few more minor repairs here and there . . ." The real-estate agent looked as if he wouldn't go up the staircase if the hounds of hell were on his heels. He thumped the banister instead to indicate its soundness, and the whole flight wobbled ominously. The pigeons in the rafters flew up squawking, and something splatted onto the agent's bowler hat. He inspected it in vexation, then put it back on his head in a hurry to prevent further accidents to his brilliantined hair.

"You'll have to come down on the rent," Peter said firmly.

"This is already rock-bottom."

"There are rats, too," Peter pointed to the evidence of that and kicked a toe at the snarl of old newspapers and empty cans in a corner. "Large and small."

"Well, perhaps ten dollars off."

"Fifteen," Peter countered, and he held his breath in delight when the agent agreed. When he was through with the renovations, the area would be perfect.

The deal done, Peter set about evicting all trespassers, rodent, bird, and human. That last proved a problem. Peter put new locks on the doors and boarded up the windows until they could be reglazed, but whoever had taken up residence in the lower floor came back anyway. Workmen were there in the daylight, building new stairs and repairing the loft; they left at dusk, only to find fresh evidence of a fire on the floor and another empty can of beans in the morning.

Finally Peter went down to the warehouse at night, carrying a pistol and a lantern and feeling determined to throw the bum out once and for all. When he put his key in the lock, he found it already unbolted. Dying embers gleamed from the far end of the cavernous room, and a huddled heap snored beside them. Peter stepped around the ever-present can of beans and put his pistol to the man's temple.

"You have exactly three seconds to get out of my building and stay out, or I'll have you arrested—if I don't shoot you first."

The figure under the blanket convulsed into an upright position and stared at him.

Peter found himself looking into the eyes of a black man who might have been anywhere between fifty and two hundred years old. A fringe of white hair clung to the edges of his wrinkled scalp, and bloodshot, watery eyes blinked under a forehead that sagged like a bulldog's.

"I don't do no harm," he said. "Just sleep here. Eat my beans."

"Well, you can't sleep here anymore." Peter put his pistol away. He felt a little silly holding it now.

"Ain't got nowhere else." The man shifted his filthy blanket, and Peter saw that his clothes were almost in ribbons.

"How did you get in?" Peter asked.

"I pick the lock." The man threw up his hands. "I ain't no burglar! Just cold, got me no sleepin' place."

Oh, Lord, Peter thought. *Now how do I throw him out?* "How long have you been here?"

"Since last year mebbe. Since the boss die, young boss he don't want me no more, I get too old. Had me a nice place up on Nob Hill, horses to drive," he said wistfully. "But I ain't a savin' man, didn't have me much to live on when they threw me out. It ain't so good in here," he added, "but it better'n the street. Police don't trouble me, and the rain don't come in much. My bones ache somethin' fierce when it rain."

Peter rocked back on his heels. *Oh, fine. I come to throw out a shiftless layabout and find a poor old coachman with rheumatism.* "Young boss," whoever he was, ought to be ashamed of his actions, but it had been Peter's experience that people like that generally were not.

"Well, you can't go on sleeping here," he said gently. "This is going to be a factory. You can't make fires on the floor."

"What kind factory?" the old man asked him.

"Automobiles," Peter said. "Motorcars." This lantern-lit conversation was beginning to depress him. So much for progress: build motorcars for the nobs and leave old granddad here on the street. Oh, hell.

"I'd like fine to see one of them," the old man said.

Peter looked at him helplessly. *What am I going to do with you?*

The old man seemed to divine his thoughts. "You gonna need a watchman. Keep the bums out." He cackled, showing a nearly toothless mouth. "You let me stay, I make sure don't no one else get in."

"You trying to sell me protection?" Peter inquired.

"That's right. Like the mob." He seemed taken with the notion. "Only I honest."

"You know how to pick a lock," Peter pointed out.

"Well, now, I learn that trick sometime back, you see. I don't use it no more, not since I got right with the Lord. Been respectable thirty years." He regarded his shirt and trousers sadly. "Don't look like it now, I reckon, but you ought of seen me in my drivin' clothes."

"What's your name?" Peter asked him, and wished he hadn't. Once he knew the man's name he felt that he would be stuck with him.

"Hobart."

"Well, Mr. Hobart—"

"Naw, Hobart's my Christian name. They calls me Hobie." He blinked at Peter. "You gonna call me Mister?"

"Well, I don't see why not," Peter said. "I expect you to call me Mr. Blake. That is, if I hire you," he added hastily, with the uncomfortable suspicion that he had already done so.

"Well, I be damned. That bein' the case, you can call me Mr. Ellison." He tried the sound of that. "Nobody ever done called me Mister."

Peter sighed. "Mr. Ellison, if I give you a job, you'll have to stick with it. And you'll have to clean up around here, too, not just watch things. And no more picking locks."

"No, sir! I forgot how to do that right away."

Peter fished in his pocket and handed the old man a five-dollar bill. "Get yourself some clothes," he said, resigned to his fate. "And a bath." Mr. Ellison was no nosegay, but who would be, living like this? "Do it tomorrow and come see me here in the afternoon."

Mr. Ellison grinned broadly.

And later we'll see about getting you some teeth, Peter

thought. "I'll pay you fifty cents a day, but you'll have to be a janitor *and* a watchman for that."

"Yes, sir! You build me a little place up on that loft, I keep the place spic-an'-span for you. I always wanted to see one of them motorcars close up."

Peter started to lay down a few more rules, but Mr. Ellison was lost in his plans. "I scrub this place down good, take a broom to them pigeons. Maybe I get me a little cat, keep them rats down. . . ."

Well, I've hired my first employee, Peter thought. *God help me.* Somehow this wasn't going exactly as he'd planned.

Peter let the "few days" he had promised to Waldo Howard slide into a few weeks. Now that he was ready to launch the Blake, the excitement of the venture was electrifying. He had no thought for the *Clarion*, its new business manager, or his obligation to Tim. He took a room in a boardinghouse but rarely went there except to sleep.

If, by chance, he saw the *Clarion* being sold on the street corner, he assured himself that the newspaper was in good hands and that Tim had nothing to worry about.

XVI

Portland, July, 1894

Toby had intended to stay at the Madrona until fall, but near the end of July he left as hastily as Tim had. His departure was precipitated by a frantic telegram from Alexandra.

"I've got to go to Washington, Mother." Toby took Eulalia's hand. It felt limp, and she still looked frail. Her fever was gone, but she seemed to have no energy and still spent most of the day in bed. "It's Mike," he said, torn between his worries for each of them.

"He's not ill?" Eulalia struggled to sit up.

"He will be when I find him," Toby said. "He's run away."

"Oh, no! Toby, you must find him. Leave today. Where could he have gone?"

Toby ran a hand through his hair. "Not to Hawaii, at any rate. He left a note saying that he hadn't and that we weren't to blame Eden."

"She would know where, though," Eulalia guessed. "I don't think we've paid enough credence to this romance with Eden."

"I've given plenty of weight to it," Toby said. "That may be the problem. I've written to Eden and the Brentwoods, but it'll take a couple of weeks or more to get an answer. I can't wait. I have a suspicion that Tim may know. I cabled him and got a very unsatisfactory answer. I'll go through Chicago on the way to Washington and throttle it out of him personally." Toby's blue eyes blazed wrathfully.

"Try to keep your temper, dear," Eulalia advised.

"Keep my—" Toby glowered. "Was I this incorrigible when I was young?"

"Worse," Eulalia answered with a faint smile. "Much worse. You still are. Of course, you didn't have a bad heart. Poor Mike, life is so unfair. Please cable us as soon as you know that he's all right. Now go and pack, dear, and let me rest. I am so tired. . . ."

In Chicago Toby controlled his temper enough so that he didn't literally attempt to throttle Tim, but he was angry enough to convince Tim that he had better spill the beans. When Toby took the train from Chicago to Washington, he was armed with the name of Thomas Edison and a capsule description of Mike's foolish plans.

"Toby, how could he?" Alexandra flung herself into her husband's arms as he came through the door of the big house on Connecticut Avenue.

"Hush, darling." Toby stroked her hair. "I think I know where he's gone. The little devil's gone to New Jersey to wheedle a job out of Thomas Edison."

"Edison!" Alexandra wailed. "But Mike was going to college. He's enrolled at Georgetown and never said a word about not wanting to go."

"Yes, he did," Sally said, appearing at her mother's side. "Daddy, you haven't hugged *me*."

"But I didn't think he meant it!" Alexandra moaned. "He—he didn't refuse."

"He was biding his time until he was eighteen," Sally said. "I wish *I* could go to New Jersey."

"Sally, will you stay out of this?" Alexandra snapped. "You went quite far enough with Alice Roosevelt."

"I didn't run away from home!" Sally was furious. She looked at her father, who was still holding Alexandra to him. "Maybe I will, since nobody's interested in *me*!" She ran from the room.

"Oh, damn," Toby groaned. He went up the stairs after Sally and pursued her into her bedroom. "Pumpkin, I'm sorry. I do want to hug you."

"Well, I couldn't tell," Sally sniffed. "Everybody's so worried about Mike."

Toby sat on the ruffled bedspread and pulled her into

his lap. "You're getting hard to cuddle, you're getting so big. I didn't mean to ignore you. It's just that your mother's worried to death."

"I know," Sally said. "I might as well be an orphan for all the mind anyone pays to me."

Toby looked around the elaborately furnished pink and white bedroom and chuckled. "Yes, we dress you in rags and feed you on crusts, don't we?"

"Mama locked me in my room for three days."

Toby put his hand under her chin. "Sarah Holt, look me in the eyes and tell me that again."

"Well, she shut me in the house," Sally admitted grudgingly. "Alice and I just wanted to see the Coxey men. Anyway, when I ask her anything she's always too 'distracted' to talk to me."

Toby kissed her. "It's not fair, is it? You go on a jaunt across town and get punished. Mike runs off to New Jersey, and everyone has fits and yells at you. Adults are like that when they're worried. Now come downstairs and hug Mama and make up while I try to think what to do."

"Maybe." Sally swung one foot, clad in a white kid boot, and studied her toe. "All right." She got off his lap, and they went down the stairs together.

Alexandra was coming up to meet them. She sighed. "I'm sorry I snapped at you, darling. I'm at my wits' end."

"I know." Sally sniffled. "But I'm lonesome." Her eyes overflowed suddenly with tears. "I wish Mike would come home."

"Oh, dear heart." Alexandra put her arms around her. "I know you do."

"I'm afraid he'll die," Sally whispered through a constricted throat.

"Nonsense," Toby said as Alexandra's face paled. "A train ride to New Jersey won't hurt him. Let's go in my study and look up the timetables. Sally, you come, too."

In the study Alexandra paced nervously and wrung her hands. "What kind of place could he be living in up there?"

"Maybe he's sleeping on a pallet in an unheated garret," suggested Sally, who read novels. "It would have rats and a cruel landlord."

"He's sleeping in a bed in a boardinghouse," Toby guessed.

Sally looked disappointed. She was genuinely worried about her brother, but a garret would have been more romantic.

"What if he was robbed on the way?" Alexandra asked, still pacing. "The doctor said he mustn't undergo *any* stress."

"There's a train first thing in the morning," Toby said, folding the timetable. "I'll be on it, and I'll find him. Alex, you've got to try to unwind."

"We had a birthday party for him!" Alexandra dabbed at her eyes with a handkerchief. "With red, white, and blue streamers because of his having been born on the Fourth. And a huge cake. And all his friends from school came. He seemed perfectly happy!"

Possibly because he had just turned eighteen, Toby thought, but he didn't say it. *But why eighteen? Mike won't reach legal majority till he's twenty-one.*

"They played games and were silly the way boys are, and he looked so young, not as if he was eighteen at all. It never occurred to me he would do something like this. He's not old enough!"

"I'm afraid that's our problem, Alex," Toby said gently. "He considers himself to be old enough. I'm afraid we may be the only people who didn't see it."

"It's that Eden Brentwood! I should have known that any sister of Sam's—"

"Now Alex, that's not fair," Toby said. "Eden's seven months younger than Mike. She's hardly a femme fatale."

"Well, the Brentwoods should have stopped it."

Sally looked up from her chair. "I think Mike would have run away without Eden," she said.

Toby cocked his head at her. Mike and Sally were close despite their quarrels. "Just straining at the leash, you think, honey?"

Miserable, Sally nodded.

Alexandra burst into tears. "Oh, my baby!"

Toby sighed. "It's natural to pull at the leash. Tim always did. But Tim was never sick a day in his life. I'll find Mike, and he'll have to come home. He just can't risk it."

*   *   *

Eulalia sipped the cup of camomile tea that Dan had brought her. "Is there any word yet from Toby?" she asked.

Dan shook his head. "None. I would have told you."

"I rang and rang for Amy," Eulalia said. She felt light-headed and pressed her hand against her eyes. "Where is she?"

Dan blinked. "She's gone to her brother's. He was up all night with a sick cow, and now he has lumbago. She's gone to iron his back or something." He hesitated, then said quietly, "I told you that this morning. Don't you remember?"

"No," Eulalia whispered. "Oh, Dan, I don't remember." She looked frightened.

"Well, you've been under a strain." He patted her hand reassuringly. "Now you rest, and drink your tea. It will help you to sleep."

"I sleep all the time," Eulalia said plaintively. "I don't know why I'm not getting better."

"You will," Dan soothed. "I can call Dr. Bright again, if you think you can stand it."

"No, I can't bear to be prodded and poked anymore. All he'll say is I'm getting old."

"Well, you are," Dan said with a smile, "but it happens to all of us. It's no disgrace."

"Very well, dear. I'll try to rest." Her words were slightly slurred now.

Dan bent, kissed her forehead, then went downstairs, smiling in relief. He didn't want Dr. Bright around. There might be ways to tell that someone had been drugged with laudanum.

In the morning Eulalia woke with a headache and a feeling that something was closing in around her—something threatening, built of jagged shards like dark glass. She had an image in her mind's eyes of a shattered mirror, with herself unclear behind it.

Eulalia sat up shaking, and the room spun slowly. She put her hands to her face, and goblin faces out of the mist jeered at her. Was this called senility, this horrible sinking into incompetence and fear? It must be. She couldn't even remember what day it was. After a struggle she could bring forth only that it was July. Or was it August already?

She shivered in the faint morning chill and pulled the quilt around her. Where was Whip? She was frightened and wanted Whip. No, not Whip, of course—Lee. Lee . . . Eulalia began to cry because Lee was dead, too. And Toby? Where was Toby? Surely not— No, he had gone to look for Mike. Was Mike dead, too? Was she alone with her failing mind?

Eulalia crept from the bed and splashed her face with cold water from the basin. The mists receded a little, and she tried to push them farther, to clutch at reality before it faded. The room steadied and drew into focus, and she hurried to her writing desk, afraid to wait.

She couldn't tell Toby. He would rush home, and then what would become of Mike? She uncapped her fountain pen and began to write carefully, making sure that the letters were what she bade them to be. She must do this before sanity vanished again, before the mist crept back in.

When she finished she rang the bell, not knowing who might answer it. She was relieved when Dan came in.

"Sit down," she whispered. "I'm glad it's you. I don't want—I can't bear—"

"Mrs. Blake, what is it?" He hurried to her side. "You'll catch your death." He put her dressing gown around her shoulders.

"Dan." Eulalia was relieved to find that her words came clearly now. She spoke quickly, afraid that the ability to speak would leave her, blown away like leaves. "Dan, this is a power of attorney. I want you to get someone up here to witness it. Amy, Abby, someone. Hurry."

Dan read the fine copperplate script that covered the page. He turned to the window for better light, and his eyes lit in triumph. "Me?" He turned back, his face carefully surprised. "Mrs. Blake, are you sure you want to do this?"

Eulalia clenched her hands tightly. "Dan, I am not right in my mind. You have been very kind to me, but I think you realize it, too. Someone must be empowered to act for me. I cannot trouble my son while he is in the midst of his own crisis."

"But—"

"I know it's a great deal to ask of you. But you have been such a comfort to me. Will you do this as a favor until Toby comes home? Please?" She began to twist her hands together in agitation.

"Of course." Dan patted her shoulder. "You know I'd do anything for you."

"Then please call someone. Quickly."

"Amy's back. I'll get her and her sister." Dan hurried down the stairs.

It was done in a matter of minutes. Amy and Abby looked almost relieved. And it didn't take Dan long to inform the ranch hands that he was now in charge.

White Elk stared at Dan and demanded to see the paper; but after he had read it, he handed it back without a word. He had been preoccupied with the almost endless labor of rebuilding and repairing after the flood, and maybe he hadn't paid as much attention to Mrs. Blake as he ought to, he thought, feeling guilty. He didn't applaud her choice, but if she thought it had to be done, he had to respect it. Anyway, it was only in effect until Toby came home.

The other ranch hands were less enthusiastic.

"Dapper Dan," Coot Simmons said in disgust. "Reckon he'd just love the chance to lord it over us."

"It shoulda been you," Howie Janks told White Elk.

"Well, it's not," White Elk said. "And you'll abide by it and take orders, or you'll answer to me. Mrs. Blake is troubled enough without your questioning her decisions. You let be, and give her some peace of mind."

Paul Kirchner was horrified. He took White Elk to one side and voiced his suspicions about Dan.

"Paul, you haven't got a thing to go on," White Elk said. "Except that you don't like him."

"I've seen him do things and then tell her that she did them but just forgot."

"Can you prove that?" White Elk's expression was suddenly very interested.

"No," Paul said reluctantly.

"Well, when you can," White Elk said grimly, "you come to me." He wondered if Paul was right and tried to tell himself that his willingness to believe the worst was based on the fact that he didn't care much for Dan, either. But he remained uneasy. He didn't like the look of things, and that was a fact. He was relieved when Paul began to dog Dan's footsteps as much as he could.

Dan took note of it, too, and he didn't like it. He cornered Paul in the house in the evening, his eyes blazing. "You don't have the run of the place anymore. Get out of here and stay in the bunkhouse."

"I have an invitation from Mrs. Blake to sleep in the house any time I so desire," Paul said between his teeth. "I so desire."

"The invitation has been withdrawn," Dan shot back.

"I'd like Mrs. Blake to tell me that."

"Mrs. Blake cannot be disturbed. If you don't get out, I'll throw you out."

Paul eyed him speculatively. "You could try."

"Consider it done," Dan said. "You're fired."

Paul's hands clenched into fists at his sides. He knew he had pushed Dan too far. "I won't start a fistfight in Mrs. Blake's parlor," he said evenly. "But if I were you, I wouldn't get the impression you're invincible. Things have a way of catching up with people."

Furious with himself, Paul took his grievance to White Elk, but the foreman only confirmed what Paul already knew.

"You shouldn't have gotten into it with him," White Elk said. "If he's fired you, I can't rehire you, you blasted hothead."

Unhappily, Paul packed his bag in the bunkhouse while Howie Janks and Coot Simmons looked on sympathetically.

"You should have slugged the son of a bitch," Coot grumbled.

Paul shrugged. What good would it have done? It would only have served to get him barred from the Madrona completely. As it was, he might still have visiting privileges based on family acquaintance.

"You're too easygoing, Kirchner," Howie said. "Don't you like to fight?"

"Not as recreation," Paul said. He stuffed his only good shirt into the satchel.

"You ever get in a fight?" Howie asked curiously.

"On occasion."

"You win?"

"Yes," Paul said shortly. "But I can't say it solved anything." He lifted a hand in farewell, then went to tell Mai good-bye and to hug a tearful Tommy.

"I've got to go, Short Stuff."

"Don't want you to." Tommy clung to his leg.

"He'll come back and see us," Mai said. She had the baby cradled in one arm, and she put the other around Paul's neck and kissed him on the cheek. "Practice your Chinese. You were just getting somewhere with it."

Paul slung his satchel over his shoulder and went to saddle one of the Madrona horses. He could send it back with a messenger boy from Portland. Maybe he could get work in the cannery again, he thought. It was in operation once more, shored up and repaired after the flood.

The idea of being up to his elbows in dead fish was almost more depressing than the thought of going back to his mother's brewery. But at least the cannery wasn't run by his mother, and no one wanted him to taste fish or dedicate his life to them. *Am I going to drift all my life?* he wondered morosely as he mounted the horse. Was there something lacking in him, intrinsic in his soul, that made him incapable of having the ambition that drove other people, of tolerating the lives they led? What was wrong with him?

White Elk, meanwhile, had gone to confront Dan Schumann.

"The next time you fire one of my hands, I'd appreciate your letting me know about it," White Elk said. His voice was level, but he was furious, and Dan Schumann could see the menace in his eyes. "I'm still the foreman here, and hiring and firing is my job."

Dan shifted uncomfortably behind the desk in Toby's study, which he had appropriated as his own. "He got out of hand," Dan said. "Mrs. Blake holds the ultimate authority here, and she's given it to me. You'll have to live with that."

"I'll live with it so long as you don't interfere with my job again. I decide when someone's gotten out of hand. And it won't be just because you don't like him." White Elk leaned over the desk, his dark face very close to Dan's, his black eyes narrowed in suspicion. "Why were you so eager to get rid of Kirchner?"

"That's my business," Dan said. *And maybe it's time I got rid of you.* He didn't like the way this talk was going, and he didn't need a damned Indian stirring up trouble just when he was ready to implement his plans. "Now go back to work. Those layabouts don't do a lick unless someone's watching them. You can hire a replacement for Kirchner," he added. "If he seems promising, I'll approve it."

"I'll hire whomever I please," White Elk said angrily. "And Senator Holt will approve it." He jammed his hat back on his head and stalked out. Even his disappearing back looked dangerous.

Dan stared after him thoughtfully and then went up to see Eulalia. With any luck she would be a little groggy by now from the carefully administered dose of laudanum in her evening tea.

"I'm afraid we're going to have to do something about White Elk," Dan said when she had greeted him with a confused smile and patted the chair beside her bed.

"What do you mean, dear?"

"Well, I'm afraid I had to let Paul Kirchner go. You've really been very patient with him, but he was hopeless. I'm not sure he's ever going to grow up."

"Oh, dear," Eulalia said. "No, poor boy, I'm afraid he's not. I had hoped, because of his mother—"

Dan smiled. "One can stretch things only so far for a family friend. After all, the Madrona is not a charitable institution, as I am sure Senator Holt would be the first to agree."

Eulalai sighed. "No, indeed. Well, I'm sure you did right." Her eyes looked glazed, as if she were already losing the thread of the discussion. "But what was it you said about White Elk? I don't understand."

"I'm afraid we're going to have to let him go, too," Dan

said. "He was insubordinate just now about Paul Kirchner, and the flood repairs aren't going as they should. He doesn't have the men under his control and—"

"Oh, no!" Eulalia's hands fluttered up from the blanket in agitation. "Oh, no, Dan, we can't! White Elk has been here since he was a child. That's impossible!"

"Suppose you let me worry about that," Dan suggested. "You're overwrought, and you mustn't strain yourself. I'll see that he gets a good reference."

"No!" Eulalia twisted her head on the pillow. She didn't seem to have the strength to sit up, but she clung to the subject tenaciously. "He's been like a son to Toby. I couldn't."

"You don't have to, Mrs. Blake," Dan said quietly. "You rest, and let me worry about it. That's what I'm here for, to take the burden from you."

"Dan, no! Toby would never forgive me." She clutched at Dan's hands. "You mustn't. Toby . . ." Her anguished voice trailed off into an incomprehensible murmur, and then she seemed to fight her way back to consciousness again. "I must wire Toby and let him talk with White Elk if there are problems." She slumped back on the pillow.

Dan thought she had passed out, and he rose to leave.

Eulalia's eyes fluttered open again. "Toby will know what to do."

Damn, Toby will come home, Dan thought. He wouldn't put it past the old lady to get a wire sent to Holt somehow. She was almost hysterical. He weighed his choices. "All right, we'll leave things as they are," he said finally. "Since it distresses you."

Eulalia's head moved uneasily on the pillow. "You don't know White Elk well . . . enough. He's a good . . . man. You can . . . work together. It's only . . . until Toby comes home."

Which had better not be too soon, Dan thought. "Mrs. Blake, I will do as you wish, of course," he said with as much geniality as he could muster. "I'm sure you're right. I'll get to know him better."

"I knew I could count on you." Eulalia's whisper died into silence, and she closed her eyes.

I'll get to know him better, Dan vowed as he went back

downstairs. *I'll know where that Indian bastard is every minute.*

In Toby's study Dan slammed his fist down on the desk, but he knew he was stymied. He would have to work around White Elk. If the old lady had second thoughts and tried to see a lawyer . . . Dan picked up a ledger and threw it across the room in a fury.

The next morning's mail brought a note from Louis Wessell couched in such threatening terms that Dan knew he had to hurry. He ordered Howie Janks to saddle a horse for him. Irritated, Howie gave him the worst horse in the stable, but Dan didn't take the time to argue. He rode into Portland to see Ephraim Bender.

"I hope you've made some progress, Schumann," Bender said. "I understand some folks are getting impatient with you."

Dan sat down in Bender's expensive leather visitor's chair and crossed his feet on Bender's desk. Grinning, he tossed him the power of attorney.

"Well, well," Bender said, smiling. "Good till Toby Holt comes home. And how long is that?"

Dan shrugged. "Holt's chasing his kid. The boy ran off from his mom. I call it obliging of him."

"Let's hope he's gone a long way. I've got the deeds ready, but you've cut the time pretty fine."

Dan took the stack of typewritten papers and began to read through them. "I moved as fast as I could. I never thought the old lady was such a tough nut. She's still giving me trouble. Stay away from that foreman of hers. I don't like his looks."

"Neither do I," Bender agreed. "You can't trust an Indian an inch. He didn't know where you were going today, did he?"

"I don't make it my business to be stupid," Dan retorted.

"See that you don't. I've got enough to contend with. And you better watch your back, too." He made an exasperated face. "Portland's finest are beginning another of their celebrated vice investigations."

"Those never amount to much, do they?" Dan grinned. "Or did somebody forget the payoff?"

"Naw, public opinion's just got all riled up again—a delegation of ladies shocked and horrified at immoral goings-on. Every so often they want all the whores run out of town."

"Has Portland's police force got enough manpower?" Dan laughed.

"Women!" Bender said, shaking his head. "When they get tired of trying to close all the saloons, they start in on the whores. Mostly everyone just ignores them, but this time they've really got the bit in their teeth. One of them's a councilman's mother, and another's married to the district attorney. They've raised so much fuss with letters to the editor that the *Oregonian* had to come out in favor of an investigation. Now the chief of police is afraid he'll get voted out of office if he doesn't oblige."

"No skin off my nose," Dan said. "I don't plan to stay. You better look out for yourself, Ephraim. You're the one with the Sunday school reputation to protect."

"Why do you think I'm being so careful with this?" Bender growled. He flicked a finger at the sheaf of papers in Dan's hand. "Just sign those, for Pete's sake, and let me get on with it."

"Not till I've read through everything," Dan said. "Because of your Sunday school reputation and all." Bender had managed so far to stay on the right side of the law and general public opinion, but he was well-known in certain circles, and suspected in others, to be on the shady side of ethics.

Dan perused the papers thoroughly with the air of one shark sharing a flounder with another. It was an elaborate scheme, but highly profitable in its potential: A large tract of Holt pastureland that Bender had been coveting was to be sold to him by Dan, using Eulalia's power of attorney. With the proceeds Dan was to buy a piece of relatively valueless property, and the papers would be fudged to look as if the entire sum had gone into the transaction. The difference would be pocketed by Dan, and the worthless land then split into building lots and sold at inflated prices to Easterners who wouldn't know until they got to Oregon

that there was no water on it—except for the parts that were
nearly swamplands. The profit from the sale of those lots
would be divided between Bender and Dan, with Dan's
share ostensibly going to Eulalia's account.

By the time Toby Holt came home and discovered
what had been done and that there was no money in
Eulalia's account, Dan would be long gone. And if Toby
wanted to protest, he would have to admit that this fast
dealing had been done in his mother's name and apparently
with her approval. A fine mess for a senator who wanted to
be reelected, Dan thought, pleased with himself.

For his defense Ephraim Bender could claim that he
had seen the power of attorney and had had no reason to
distrust a young man of whom Eulalia Blake thought so
highly. Any charges of fraud against Bender would have to
be brought by the luckless souls who had purchased the
lots, and Bender was used to dealing with those situations.
And he would still have the piece of Holt land he had
wanted, and Toby would have no way to get it back. As a
bonus to Bender, Alexandra would be fit to be tied; it was
common knowledge that Alexandra didn't like him.

It all appeared foolproof, as long as they could put it
together before the senator came home. Bender got out
glasses and a bottle of whiskey, and Dan and he toasted
young Mike Holt, with the devout hope that the young man
had gotten himself in a passel of trouble.

Toby stood seething on the steps of Edison's laboratory
in Orange, New Jersey, as he waited for someone to bother
to answer the bell. He could hear voices inside, but no one
seemed to be paying much attention to the pealing of the
bell. He pounded with his fist and twisted the bellpull
again, and eventually a young man in a canvas apron
appeared. He had a glass-blower's rod in his hand and a
strong German accent.

"*Ja?*"

"I'm looking for Michael Holt."

"He went home. Dinnertime," the glassblower explained.

"Then he *is* here."

"*Nein, nein,* he went home."

"That's not what I meant." Toby made a flying grab at his temper. "I want to speak to Mr. Edison."

The German boy nodded and disappeared into the laboratory. From the door Toby could see four or five men, most of them young, working. They were doing things with oddments of machinery and glass bulbs and tubing, the uses of which Toby had not the faintest idea. The whole place had the air of a wizard's den.

"I'm Edison." A clean-shaven man in his late forties appeared at the door. He had a shock of graying hair and thick eyebrows. The tightness of his mouth indicated that his concentration had been interrupted and he wasn't grateful for it. His trousers and collarless shirt both bore stains and small holes, as if a chemical of some sort had eaten through the fabric.

"I'm Toby Holt. Michael's father. Do I understand that you have given him a job?"

"I've given him a tryout," Edison clarified. "I can't promise you I'll keep him on."

"I don't want you to keep him on. I've come to take him home. He's frightened his mother to death. Mr. Edison, do you make it a habit to hire runaway adolescents?"

Edison's gray eyes began to look faintly irriated. "I hire young men who appear promising."

"Do you know where he is now?"

"He's gone back to his boardinghouse," Edison answered. "He was in very early this morning, and I finally let him go home. I believe he would have fallen asleep here otherwise."

"I want his address."

Edison appeared to consider that. He folded his arms across his disreputable shirt.

Toby knew he had gotten off on the wrong foot. "He has a bad heart, Mr. Edison. He isn't strong enough for such an escapade."

"The work is not particularly stressful," Edison commented. "Except mentally, of course."

There was a loud bang and the sound of breaking glass from the laboratory. A voice said, "Aw, hell, she's blown up again."

"He has been advised to lead a sedentary life," Toby stated.

"I assure you, I have never blown up an assistant." Again the wide mouth quirked into the hint of annoyance. "Have you and your wife considered letting him lead his *own* life, Senator?"

So Mike had given him some family history. Toby suspected that Mike had also told Edison that his father would almost certainly come looking for him. "Michael is enrolled in Georgetown University for the fall."

"That's not the right school for what he wants to do," Edison said. "He should go to the Stevens Institute at Hoboken if he must go somewhere. But he'll do better to work with me. Half the professors at Hoboken are nearly fossilized."

"Just give me his address," Toby said grimly.

"Oh, very well." Edison seemed bored. In the corner of the laboratory, a flare of white light blazed up, and Edison turned his head toward it. "He's at 364-D Spring Street," he said, and disappeared in the direction of the light. The door swung closed in Toby's face.

Toby ground his teeth and went back to the hack that was waiting in the street. He gave the address and watched his surroundings deteriorate ominously as the hack made its way through an industrial slum and a dispirited cluster of shanties to Spring Street.

If spring ever got to Spring Street, Toby thought, it must be unrecognizable by the time it arrived. The single tree that grew on the one-block avenue was thin leaved and looked as if it might be overcome at any moment by the sheer squalor of its surroundings. Disreputable-looking men drifted fitfully down the unpaved street and sat on the stoops of a row of paint-peeled houses. Toby told the hack driver to wait. Mike's living space was on the top floor of a structure that looked more like a tenement than a boardinghouse. He ascended the steps under the basilisk stare of a woman who was bent over a laundry tub on the first floor.

Since the upper door wasn't locked—the lock appeared to be broken—Toby opened it gingerly and looked in. The room contained a rusted white-iron bedstead, a desk made of a board and two packing crates, a chair, a gas

ring and sink, and Mike's trunk. The bundle of blankets on
the bed was presumably Mike. Toby prodded him in the
back.

Mike sat up suddenly, staring. "Oh, Lord," he
groaned. His red hair stood up on end, and he had been
sleeping in his long johns.

"If you robbed a bank and got sent to prison, you'd
have a better room," Toby remarked.

Mike grinned sheepishly. "It's a dump, isn't it? But it's
cheap. I get a raise next month if Mr. Edison keeps me on,
and I'll move to something better then. I'm trying to save
all I can."

"Your mother would faint if she saw this place," Toby
said. "I devoutly hope you won't describe it to her. Now
pack your trunk. I have a hack waiting outside."

Mike took a deep breath. "No, sir."

"I beg your pardon?"

Sensing himself at a disadvantage, being sprawled in
bed in his underwear while his father, in frock coat and top
hat, tapped one polished toe on the floor, Mike pulled his
trousers off the back of the single chair and drew them on.

"I'm not going back, Dad. How did you find me? Tim
ratted on me, didn't he?"

"Under duress," Toby admitted. "How could you go off
like that without a word to your mother? She's made herself
ill worrying about you."

"I was going to write in a couple of weeks, when I have
a better place—I can't say I want Mama to see this
one—and tell you where I was. If I'd told her I was going,
I never would have gotten away."

"I am very angry, Mike. You have made enormous
trouble and endangered your health. Now pack your
trunk."

Mike shrugged his shirt on and buttoned it. "No, sir.
Now don't poker up at me. I don't want to fight with you
about it."

Toby sat down on the unmade bed. "Mike, you aren't
strong enough. That's a fact of life that you're going to have
to face. Both your mother and I would gladly give our own
lives to change that if we could, but we can't."

Mike tucked his shirt in his trousers and sat down on

the chair. "It's no life for me, living the way I have been, with everyone cosseting me and saying I look pale and wanting to take my pulse. I missed everything that other children got to enjoy—" His voice rose angrily. "I don't want to wait until my twenty-first birthday. I'm going to live the rest of my life, however long it is, starting now. I'm going to have what other men have. Otherwise, I might as well give up and die today."

Toby folded his hands, uncertain what to say. Mike's gray-green eyes challenged him, fiercely protective of his new-won freedom. Except for their color, they were the eyes of Whip Holt, Mike's grandfather. Whip's given name, which no one but Eulalia had ever called him, had been Michael, and there was more of Whip's spirit in his namesake than anyone had reckoned on, Toby thought. When, in middle age, arthritis had begun to confine Whip's freedom, he had nearly gone mad. How would he have borne Mike's malady? Whip's eyes continued to stare at him out of Mike's face, and Toby thought that it wasn't fair to have Holt blood and a bad heart.

"Tell me about Mr. Edison," Toby said slowly.

The gray-green eyes gleamed, as incandescent as the lights of Edison's invention. "I'm working with the motion-picture camera. I showed him the film I took in Hawaii, and when he saw what I'd done, he said my camera was just a prototype, and he showed me his new one! It's light years beyond mine. Mr. Edison doesn't think there will be any public interest in screen projection unless a phonograph can be linked to it, but I don't agree.

"Anyway, he's letting me work on it, although he doesn't seem interested in the phonograph right now. He says he's finished with the project now that it's available to the general public. He's working on a magnetic method of concentrating iron ore. Mr. Edison says that as long as only a trained man can use an invention, it's only a guess in the dark that you have brought into the light. You have to bring new products down to the level of the lunkhead."

"Well, that's a reassuringly practical statement," Toby said when Mike paused for breath. "He struck me as being cantankerous and as if he had bought his clothes from the rag-and-bone man."

"Well, he forgets to wear an apron," Mike explained. "He drives his wife crazy. When he gets a new notion for something, he doesn't surface for hours."

"Mike, couldn't you come home and work on this?" Toby asked. "I'll buy you this new camera if that's what you want."

"It's experimental," Mike said. "There isn't but one. We tinker with it all the time. No, sir, I couldn't come home. I don't know enough."

They faced each other at a standoff. "I can't tie you up and take you home and lock you in your room," Toby said.

"No, you can't," Mike said. "I'm banking on that."

"You know that you're risking your health, maybe your life."

"I don't think frustration is good for my heart, either." Mike said flatly. "Sometimes this last year, I've felt like I was going to bust."

There might be some truth in that, Toby reflected. He had never felt so helpless. "And what about Eden Brentwood? Are you planning to support a wife in this palatial establishment? I'll tell you right now that if you pursue this course, you'll have to live on what you earn."

"I know," Mike said somberly. "But Eden's only seventeen. I'll be making more money next year."

"By that do I take you to mean that Sam Brentwood has forbidden Eden to marry you and she has to wait till she's eighteen?" Toby inquired.

"Something like that," Mike admitted.

"Sam has more sense than I thought," Toby muttered. He watched his son's eyes light up again at the mere sound of Eden's name. "You're children."

"We belong together," Mike said flatly. "That's not negotiable, either."

Toby stood up heavily. There was nothing more he could do. He felt defeated and helpless, much as he had many years before, when he had sat by Mike's bedside all through the long bout with rheumatic fever that had come so close to killing him. He put his arms around Mike, held him close for a moment, then went back downstairs to the hack, leaving Mike alone in the world he had chosen.

XVII

San Francisco, August 1894

"You can't come in, Alfred," Peter Blake said firmly to the plump young man who was peering over his shoulder into the refurbished warehouse. Alfred Wellington, perhaps five years Peter's senior, had an apple-cheeked farmboy's face, a sunny smile, and the inquisitive eyes of a ferret.

"Just like to see what the competition's up to," Alfred said.

"Precisely," Peter said. "Go away." He had met Alfred dining with his stout and pessimistic-looking mother at the Palm Court. The Wellingtons were on a sight-seeing trip to San Francisco. Alfred and Peter had discovered by chance conversation that each was working on a motorcar and that Alfred hoped to arrange financial backing in San Francisco. Mrs. Wellington, pursing her lips, had said that she did not approve but that Alfred had always been stubborn.

Alfred had ignored his mama in a manner that suggested he had had long practice at it. "The Wellington's just about ready for a public trial. I'm calling it the Wellington. My name, you know, but I fancy the other connotation—serviceable in all weather, don't you know, just like the overshoes. What sort of engine are you using?"

"Gasoline," Peter had said.

Ever since then Alfred had been ubiquitous, prattling innocently of the coming revolution in transportation and trying to get Peter to show him the prototype of the Blake.

"Goodness, is that it?" he said now, peering over Peter's shoulder again. "My, my, you do have trouble."

"What do you mean by that?" Peter demanded indignantly.

"Carriage design, my boy, carriage design. The ladies like a turnout with elegance, if you know what I mean. Don't want something that looks like an ice wagon. Let me have a look, and I'll give you some pointers to smarten her up."

"I don't want her smartened up," Peter responded. "Yours probably looks like the swan boat on a carousel. A reliable engine is what will sell."

"My boy," Alfred said sadly, "I believe that your Blake doesn't run at all. Otherwise, why would you be so reluctant to show her to me?"

"My Blake can beat your swan boat any time," Peter said, stung.

"Oh, come, come," Alfred said. "Large talk. You'll have to back that up."

Peter crossed his arms against his chest. "Any time."

"I have a capital idea, then. Let's have a race! I need to take Mother home to Milwaukee next week, but I'm planning a visit again at Christmastime. I'll have the Wellington shipped by rail, and we'll be the wonder of the holiday season."

"Well . . ."

"What a smashing plan! We'll have a wager on it just to make it interesting. Say five thousand dollars? That ought to bring the press out."

"Hold on!" Peter managed to get a word in edgewise. "I haven't even said I'll race."

"Of course if you don't think the Blake's up to it. . . . I'll bring the Wellington with me anyway, to drum up some business. It's a wide-open market here in San Francisco."

"Of course the Blake's up to it," Peter said, cornered. "I'll run your overshoes into the ground, friend."

"Capital!" Alfred said. "Nothing like a little friendly competition. My backers will be delighted." He nodded cheerily and strolled off, whistling.

"Your backers better bring a towrope!" Peter shouted after him.

A certain amount of enthusiasm died away as Alfred turned the corner. Peter slumped against the warehouse door. *I've been had,* he thought. If a San Francisco-manufactured motorcar lost to an interloper from Milwaukee, Peter would be a laughingstock. And if he lost five thousand dollars to Alfred Wellington, *he,* instead of Alfred, would need backers. He looked at the ornate wooden sign over his head: Blake Motorcar Company. Suitably adorned with gilded curlicues, it implied a prosperous company.

A string of invectives from within interrupted his thoughts. Peter sighed and went inside. Ezra Tolliver, his head mechanic, was nursing his hand and cursing the Blake. Its engine sputtered fitfully, almost malevolently. It seemed to Peter to be cursing back. Hobart Ellison stood off to one side, watching. The other mechanics had gone home.

"This engine's no damn good," Tolliver complained, "and I ain't working on it no more. I'm lucky I still got all my fingers. It musta been designed by baboons."

"It was made to my specifications," Peter said, "and it ought to work. You know better than to stick your hand in there without shutting it off."

Tolliver sucked his knuckles. "Shut it off? When it takes half an hour to get it started in the first place? I'm telling you, you might as well scrap it."

"Can't you redesign it?"

"I work on 'em," Tolliver said. "I don't build 'em. Mr. Blake, I'm outta my depth here, and there's no point in going on trying to tread water."

"Sure looks pretty," Mr. Ellison said. "Till you try to start her, of course."

"You're a janitor," Peter said. "I don't need another critic."

"Yes, sir." Ellison bent lovingly to polish the Blake's brass trim. He had improved with a bath and new clothes and a set of false teeth—when he could be persuaded to wear them—and he adored the Blake. He groomed it as he used to groom his carriage horses, and the little car gleamed from its wire wheel spokes to the little silver Diana that served as its hood ornament. "You're just a crotchety thing, ain't you," he crooned. The Blake, unmollified, sputtered and coughed at him and died suddenly.

The engine had been designed by a man who built

stationary hoisting engines for mining, and he had claimed that it would power a motorcar just fine . . . what was the difference? But it made the Blake too heavy, and the two-cycle motor had proved wildly unreliable. What was it that Tim had said about inventors and all visionaries being a little crazy? They had been talking about old Rufus Gooch in Portland.

Peter took his apron off and picked up his hat from the shop desk in the corner of the warehouse. "Don't tinker with it anymore," he told Tolliver. "Just pull the engine out of the carriage."

"You got something better in mind?"

"I hope I do," Peter replied gloomily. "I'm going to Portland. I'll be back in a few days." He turned in the door to fire a parting shot. "Just to give you boys something to worry about, I bet Alfred Wellington five thousand dollars this machine could beat his by Christmas."

"You can't just build an engine and then jam it into any old contraption," Rufus Gooch, an eccentric inventor, said to Peter in the workroom of his Portland shack. "An engine has to be designed specifically for the machine it's going to power. Calvin Rogers and I had better come to San Francisco with you. I will require a separate hotel room for Mr. Rogers, and you must hire a cook who understands my needs."

Peter, glancing at the affable-looking Rogers, had mental visions of vanishing cash and wondered what Gooch's needs might be. Judging from the half-eaten concoctions on the dirty plates that littered his work area, they looked peculiar, to say the least. Any hotel cook would have a fit.

Peter shrugged mentally. As strange as Rufus was, he could probably be kept somewhat in line by Calvin, who had worked for the Holts for many years as a handyman. He had taught Tim about engine mechanics when Tim was only a boy.

"Can you make my motor carriage run by Christmas, Mr. Gooch?" Peter asked desperately.

"Certainly," Gooch replied. "I can make anything run. Now observe this." He turned the crank on a contraption that looked like a cross between a baby carriage and a small harrow. When its motor coughed into life, it scuttled across the rug, then became entangled with the fringe. Bits of thread flew out behind it. It rolled over a plate on the floor, scattering what appeared to be cold grits. Calvin Rogers lunged at it and shut it off as it made for a pile of laundry in a shallow basket.

"A gasoline-powered lawn mower," Gooch announced proudly. "Of course a few safety features still need to be implemented."

"Possibly a warning not to run it indoors," Rogers murmured.

Peter thought that given the state of the interior of Gooch's house, the effects of a mowing machine on it would probably go unnoticed, although Gooch looked as if he had trimmed his beard with one.

It was impossible to tell how old Rufus Gooch was. His flying beard gave him a faintly biblical air, and his suit coat was fastened that morning not with string but with wooden clothespins. Calvin Rogers appeared more normal, but he was getting on in years, and his checkered career included employment as a hot-air balloonist—his limp was the result of a crash landing—and as design chief in a shop that produced steam engines. Now, having retired from his work with the Holts, he seemed to be Gooch's aide-de-camp.

But Tim Holt had said that old Rufus was mad only north-northwest, and he was extremely fond of Calvin. Anyway, Tim knew far more about mechanics than Peter did. Gooch didn't pay much attention to money, Tim had said. He spent what he had until his checks began to bounce at the bank, and then he didn't spend any more until he had put some in—usually when Calvin Rogers had gone out and collected an overdue bill from some farmer whose machinery they had repaired. Peter suspected that Rogers was the ballast of common sense that kept Gooch out of jail or the madhouse and reasonably within his neighbors' good graces.

Gooch was shuffling between the oddments in his parlor: buckets of nuts and bolts and electrical fittings, a drafting table covered with drawings, a grinding wheel, and waist-high stacks of magazines weighted down with bicycle wheels.

"Here it is!" he said triumphantly. He dove at a stack of newspapers and pulled from the middle a clipboard with an incomprehensible design sketched on it. "I knew I'd get a chance at a motorcar. I never had the money myself for the carriage. But someone always comes along, I find. I have ninety-seven patents registered," he added proudly.

Once the deal was set, Calvin Rogers unearthed a few clean shirts and packed them for Rufus, who seemed uninterested in any luggage save his clipboard. They took a train to San Francisco, and during the trip Rufus made further drawings.

Peter settled the men at a hotel whose cook, he thought, could put up with Gooch, and then brought them to the shop of the Blake Motorcar Company.

Gooch inspected the sign with mild derision. "Fancy is as fancy does," he said, and plunged his head into the inner workings of the Blake.

"That's your designer?" Tolliver asked, incredulous.

"Fancy is as fancy does," Peter said. "Give him his head."

Gooch straightened up. "A complete redesign," he decided. "Are you set up to machine parts to my specifications? See that you are. Rogers will supervise."

Calvin had taken his turn to inspect the Blake and was making notes of his own. "Clutch," he said cryptically. "Leather lined."

"Just so," Gooch agreed. "First of all, Mr. Blake, we'll produce and install a four-cycle motor. Two-cycle motors are useless in moving vehicles, as you have no doubt discovered. It will be electrically ignited and water-cooled. We'll mount it in the rear. Just because you put a horse in the front of a cart does not mean you have to put your motorcar engine there. Of course you will have to rebuild the carriage entirely. You may be able to salvage the wheels. And this little lady here." He touched the top of Diana's silver head. "I rather like her. We'll mount her in front, atop an electric headlamp."

"Uh, how much do you estimate this is going to cost?" Peter asked.

"Oh, I haven't any idea," Gooch said airily. "That's your department. Our expertise is in internal-combustion engines. Yours is money, or so I hear."

"Up until now," Peter said uneasily.

"Well, go and take care of it and let us work." Gooch made shooing motions at the shop doors. He handed his clipboard and his overcoat to Mr. Ellison, who was listening in fascination. "Stand by," Gooch said, and picked up a wrench.

Evicted by his designers, Peter decided to go and do what he should have done weeks before—check up on Waldo Howard. It would keep him from wondering what Herr Grumman would say if he were there. Thank God he wasn't.

Two hours later, he had plenty of other things to worry about. Waldo's idea of "under control" seemed to mean that no one had actually sued them yet. The *Clarion's* books were an impenetrable snarl of red ink. Waldo had labored valiantly to balance the accounts, but his efforts wandered, perplexed and elliptical, from page to page and leaped blindly from one ledger to the next, where they reduplicated themselves into cosmic disaster.

"Why the hell didn't you get another business manager in?" Peter demanded.

Waldo coursed back and forth through the ledgers like a hound that had lost its quarry hours ago and was trying to put a good face on it. "Well, I thought I'd try to straighten it up first, so he'd know where we stood."

So he wouldn't tell Tim, Peter thought.

"Hugo helped me some," Waldo added.

"Oh, very good." Peter put his head in his hands.

"I didn't volunteer for the job," Hugo called from the doorway. "Waldo, I told you we'd make a muddle of it." He brightened. "Rosebay's here," he told Peter, offering distraction. "She wants to say hello."

Peter rose to greet her while the other two beat a retreat.

"How are you, dear?" Rosebay kissed his cheek. She

looked as fetching as ever, in a walking suit of plain blue linen. Her slight figure was ideal to carry off the extravagance of its huge puffed sleeves.

"I'm fit to be tied," Peter fumed, "that's how I am. If those two morons had set out to cook these books into a stew, they couldn't have done a better job. The whole thing's hopeless, and Tim had better get home fast."

Rosebay sighed. "I don't think he will," she said quietly.

Peter didn't appear to hear. "I feel responsible. I'm going to kill them. I was supposed to come and look things over last month. Waldo said it was all under control."

"Waldo always says that." Rosebay looked over Peter's shoulder at the ledgers on the desk behind him. "Goodness, what chicken scratching. What is—? Oh, I see what he's done. Now why on earth? . . ." She bent to take a closer look, flipping pages and marking them with her fingers. "Didn't Tim say not to buy paper from Fortney because they always short the rolls? I know he did. And then Waldo's tried to correct the balance, but it doesn't make any difference whether the roll was short or not; it's what you paid that counts. My goodness, you do have your work cut out for you."

"Rosebay," Peter said, "do you understand what's going on in these?"

"Well, I would if these books weren't such a tangle. I have to keep books at home, you know, because of the boarders. And I do know how a newspaper is run, from listening to you and Tim and poor Waldo."

"Waldo doesn't know how a newspaper is run," Peter growled.

"He knows how to run a newsroom," Rosebay said, defending him as well as her husband. "That's what they're supposed to be doing. I wouldn't have any idea how to do that."

"But you understand these?" Peter asked in awe.

"I don't think even God could understand some of this," Rosebay said, giggling. "But I do have a head for figures. And, of course, Hugo talks to me about his work, and some of the reporters board with me."

"Sit down," Peter ordered. "You've been around the

last few months, and I haven't. Maybe you can tell me what
'*Ell. eels*' means."

"I don't have any idea," Rosebay said, peering at
Waldo's scrawl. "But they paid ninety-seven dollars for it."
She unpinned her hat, set it on the filing cabinet, and gave
the ledger further study. "These are the advertising accounts," she said. "Oh, mercy, I don't think anyone's
collected the overdue ones. You have to send someone
around to some of these places, you know, or they simply
won't pay. Goodness, no wonder they have a cash problem."

"Rosebay," Peter said. "I have a headache from talking
to Waldo, and I expect you had other plans for your
afternoon. But please come back tomorrow, and between
the two of us maybe we can undo this mess."

Rosebay looked startled. "Do you really think I can
help? I mean I never thought of—I mean in a *business*."

"You run a business," Peter pointed out. "What do you
think your boardinghouse is?"

"Oh, that's just me cooking," Rosebay said with a
smile. "I haven't had any schooling, you know."

"Rosebay, I don't care if you didn't get past third
grade—"

"Well, I didn't. Pa didn't hold with it, and there was
always plenty to do at home."

"I was speaking figuratively," Peter said. "You're a
self-taught woman, Rosebay Ware, and you seem to have
been a pretty good teacher, so don't denigrate yourself."

Rosebay looked embarrassed. "Well, I won't, then. I
just get sort of embarrassed about it sometimes. I feel like
everyone here knows I'm just a mountain girl."

"Rosebay, if I don't get this mess in line, this paper's
going to go under. I need all the help I can get."

"Well, sure," she said. "But don't tell Hugo. It might
make him feel funny."

"I've got other things to tell Hugo," Peter said grimly.

He told most of them to Waldo—the situation wasn't
really Hugo's fault, and the blind had been leading the
blind—and Rosebay did come back the next morning,
wearing a plain dress and an apron, and settled in with

Peter to try to translate. When desperate, they called on Waldo. *"Ell. eels"* turned out not to be "elliptical eels," as Hugo had first suggested when he stared bemused at the notation, but "eleven wheels" for the rolling carts that were used in the pressroom.

"You've got handwriting like a jumping bean," Peter growled.

At lunchtime he sent Rosebay home to fix lunch for her boarders and sent Tim a telegram, advising him that his investment was sinking in a slough of financial ineptness, and a return at his earliest convenience would be advisable.

Tim wired back that he couldn't come home just yet and was counting on Peter. Peter swore and irritably shredded the telegram into flakes, thinking that Tim wasn't like himself at all and what in the world was the matter with everyone? Peter was used to an orderly world, but just now, and on all fronts, he seemed to be galloping riderless toward disaster.

Rufus Gooch and Calvin Rogers had pulled the engine out of the Blake and dismantled it until the shop looked like Gooch's parlor. Now they were working on the carriage, which Peter himself had designed and which he was convinced would be rebuilt to look like Rufus's lawn mower.

They had installed a new system of gearing with a clutch so that the car had three forward speeds and one in reverse and could, so Gooch claimed, do eighteen miles per hour—or it would when it was finished.

"Ought to be just about ready to test by the end of the year," Gooch said from beneath the Blake. Only his toes showed.

"By Christmas, damn it," Peter said.

"Huh? Oh, yes. Well, I suppose."

Peter turned to Calvin Rogers. "By Christmas," he repeated. "Make a note of it. We're running a race at Christmas, and if we forfeit it, it is extremely doubtful that I'll be able to afford so much as your return tickets to Portland."

"Don't worry about that," Gooch called. "I'm beginning to like it here."

"By Christmas," Calvin confirmed as Peter himself showed signs of combusting. "The tests today have been excellent."

"The radiator boils over in the reverse gear," Tolliver said.

"Goodness, you're a breath of fresh air," Calvin remarked sarcastically. "It takes experimentation to build a prototype. Two failures for every success, we've learned. And in any case, Mr. Blake isn't going to race backward."

"I should like to drive backward without disaster, however," Peter said. "Since I intend to market this machine."

"Well, we think we've solved the problem," Calvin assured him. "Of course, it sometimes gets stuck in reverse."

"I'm going back to the *Clarion*," Peter said. He didn't think he could stand much more of this. He looked at the calendar and shuddered.

Rosebay was waiting for him. "You don't look so pert," she said. "I bet you haven't had a square meal in weeks. You come to dinner tonight."

"Bend your maternal instinct to these books," Peter muttered.

Rosebay unpinned her hat and set it carefully on the filing cabinet. A woman's hat—a contraption of ribbon and feathers and straw on a steel frame, constructed to sit jauntily atop high-piled hair and secured with a twelve-inch hatpin—could never be hung on a hat rack. She sat down and adopted a pair of the paper cuffs that the men in the newsroom wore to keep their shirt-sleeves clean.

"Rafe Murray tells me that Waldo is despondent," she informed Peter. "That was Rafe's word, *despondent*. He's afraid you're going to tell Tim what he's done and get him fired."

"I'll only have him barred from these books," Peter said. "Waldo hasn't got bat brains. Tell Rafe to let Waldo know he can quit being despondent." He laid down his pen, an idea having dawned on him. "And that he'd better hire you, so he won't have any more troubles. You've got a knack for this like I've never seen."

Rosebay, aghast, stared at him. "Me? Now, Peter, nobody hires a female business manager. Bookkeeper, yes, or secretary, but nobody puts a woman in charge."

"Tim would."

Rosebay flushed. "Maybe Tim wouldn't."

"Tim would do anything that would keep this paper afloat. I don't know why I didn't think of it sooner. You'd be perfect. You won't come in drunk or rob him blind, and you're healthy enough not to die on him."

Rosebay laughed in spite of herself. "I don't know when I've heard such a flattering description. But I still have a boardinghouse to run, in case you've forgotten. I've served hash three days running as it is, and the boys are getting right tired of it."

"You could hire a housekeeper for less than the job here would pay," Peter pointed out. "I'll make Waldo offer you what he'd give a man."

"Peter, I have to think about it. Tim . . . well, I just don't think Tim will like it," she finished helplessly.

"Then Tim can fire you when he gets home," Peter decided. "I've got to get out of here and see what those lunatics have done with my motorcar. And Waldo isn't paying *me* anything," he added. He pushed his chair back and stood up. "You wait here."

"Peter—!"

But Peter was gone down the hall, stalking Waldo. He found him in the newsroom, talking to Hugo, Rafe, and Stu Abrams. "I've chosen Rosebay as your new financial director," he informed Waldo. "And if you want to stay in the black and keep Tim from killing you when he gets home, you'll make my choice official, for the last man's salary," he added. "You've cost me valuable time, and if it hadn't been for Rosebay, I never would have unsnarled it. That woman's got a knack." He looked at Hugo. "God knows she didn't learn arithmetic from you." He bent his eyes on the other two. "And if either of you clowns so much as looks at her sideways, I'll tell Tim that none of you is fit to run a high-school yearbook."

Well, that takes care of that, he thought as he went back to his office. Behind him he could hear Rafe Murray hooting with laughter.

Rosebay looked up as he came in, and Peter stopped short at her expression. She looked as if she had been tied to the railroad tracks.

"Now, Rosebay, don't look at me like that. I'm going to teach you everything you need to know before I turn the books over to you. Besides, I just pinned back Waldo's ears. He won't give you any trouble. And you know Hugo just wants you to be happy."

"Hugo . . ." Rosebay moaned. "It's not Hugo. Well, I guess it is Hugo, but—" She burst into tears. "What am I going to do when Tim comes home? I can't be here all day!"

"Don't cry!" Peter tried to hand her a handkerchief. "What about Tim? Now don't tell me you're still— I thought you were over that," he finished helplessly.

Rosebay looked up and mopped her eyes. "Over what?" she demanded.

Peter gulped. "Over Tim, I guess. I couldn't help but notice how you felt about him back in Guthrie. Before you married Hugo, I mean. But I figured— You see him all the time."

"I *used* to see him all the time," Rosebay corrected sadly. She rubbed at eyes that were already red rimmed. Then she pointed a finger at him, outraged. "Peter Blake, you never went and told Tim, did you?"

"Of course not," Peter protested. "What kind of tack-head do you think I am? And as far as I could tell, he was too thickheaded to have a clue. You don't need to worry about that."

"He has a clue now," Rosebay murmured. "Why do you think he lit out? You know he was goin' to send Hugo." In her agitation the accent of the southern mountains suddenly came back in strength, so that she sounded like the girl Peter had first met in the boomtown days of Guthrie.

"Did *you* tell him?"

"Of course not." Rosebay sniffled. "Peter Blake, I don't think you know a *thing* about women."

"Probably not," Peter conceded. "And you aren't helping any. If nobody told him, then how did he find out? Why would that make him take off, anyway?"

"Because he's a gentleman," Rosebay said, rubbing her

eyes again. "He just . . . found out. Well, he kissed me," she muttered.

"Why?" Peter asked, floundering in deep romantic waters. "What would he do that for?"

A flash of Rosebay's old spirit came back. "I hope you get more tactful before you start courtin'," she said acidly. "He kissed me because he wanted to, I reckon."

Peter raised his eyebrows. "I see. His being such a gentleman and all."

"The gentleman part came later," Rosebay explained. "That's why he left. Now he doesn't trust himself to be around me. The big dumb galoot, he's gone and fallen in love with *me*, when it's purely too late, and I'm so miserable I can't hardly stand it!" She burst into tears again.

Peter looked uneasily at the door. This would be a fine tableau to explain to Hugo. *Hugo will probably think it's all my fault*, Peter thought. He picked up the abandoned handkerchief and handed it to her again. Rosebay took it and pressed it against her mouth, stifling her sobs.

"I'm not ever going to fall in love," Peter vowed. "I never saw anything that could make so much trouble."

Rosebay wiped her eyes and looked at him balefully. "It isn't something you go asking to do, you dope. And if you think you're immune, you just wait and see, that's all. Now give me them books. I'll work on 'em till Tim comes home."

"Those books," Peter said automatically, and then regretted it.

"Don't you go tryin' to fix my grammar. I've had about all the fixin' up I can stand, and just look where it got me." She bent her head over the ledger and stared at it stubbornly, daring him to pursue the subject.

XVIII

Terre Haute, Indiana, August 1894

Eugene Debs still looked frail, Tim thought. A paisley shawl, solicitously spread around Debs's shoulders by his wife, gave him a faintly gypsyish look. The steely determination in his eyes hadn't changed, but his hands were thin. Kate Debs, in a gray taffeta skirt and a dotted silk shirtwaist, looked elegant and unruffled, but she watched her husband closely for signs of fatigue.

"It was kind of you to invite me," Tim said, knowing that he mustn't stay too long or Kate would, in the most tactful way possible, shoo him out the door.

Debs smiled. "You've taken your lumps for us, Holt. We appreciate it."

"Not so many as you've taken," Tim said. "Or the strikers."

He felt weary and bitter. Debs had officially called off the ARU strike on 4 August and on 15 August had returned to Chicago to answer questions posed by the U.S. commissioner of labor in hearings investigating the strike. Rumor had it that the commission's findings, when released, would be critical of the Pullman Company and of the railroads. That was small consolation, however, to the railroaders who had returned to work under conditions that went unchanged by the walkout. Debs still had to stand trial in September on contempt charges, but he professed to feel a certain moral justification from the commission's findings.

Tim, who had come to interview Debs but been asked to stay to dinner, felt that he ought to make a stab at what he had come for. "Is there any chance you'll change your mind about releasing the union's books, sir?"

"None whatsoever," Debs responded.

"They will only be used to blacklist those poor men," Kate Debs said. "The workers are toiling for starvation wages now, and they won't have anything if the railroads have our membership lists. And don't try to tell me that management wouldn't get its hands on them," she added.

"I wouldn't tell you any such thing, ma'am." One railroad official had admitted as much to Tim outright. Troublemakers, he had called the strikers as he sat smugly behind his massive stomach and even more massive desk.

Debs sighed and glanced around the parlor of his Terre Haute house, Kate's refuge from the turmoil of her husband's work. It was a three-story frame residence with a wide, breezy porch, built with money that Kate had saved for years. "We, at least, have food on the table," he said, "and a salary to depend on."

"He never takes it," Kate confided to Tim. "We rely on income from his writing."

Debs smiled. "The union doesn't have funds to pay me, so it is an academic question, my dear."

"In terms of improved labor conditions, what have you accomplished with this strike?" Tim asked.

"Greater public sympathy and understanding, I believe," Debs answered.

"And what is that worth in terms of food on the table for some worker's children?" Tim was angry—angry over the futility of the strike, angry over the things he had seen, angry with himself that he had led such a privileged childhood. He had never stopped to think about thin, ragged youngsters painting Pullman cars in a cinder-strewn yard. Nor had he thought about breaker boys picking over coal in an airless room at an age when he had been running free on the Madrona, with a pony to ride and no work to do except get into devilment and go reluctantly to school. The children of the coal miners had no time for school. The children of the Pullman workers went to Pullman schools where Pullman teachers taught them only enough to prepare them for the drudgery their parents endured. "What have the kids got," he asked, furious, "besides good reason to distrust their government? What kind of new day will dawn for them because of the strike?"

"The walkout will make the new generation into committed union members," Debs said. He paused, then: "You've seen things you didn't know about, haven't you, Holt? Having your eyes opened is always painful."

"The railway officials isolate themselves very carefully from that possibility," Kate Debs said resentfully. "Otherwise they wouldn't be able to function. How such men can go to church on Sundays and claim to be Christian is beyond me. I have no patience with such hypocrisy."

"Perhaps hypocrisy is not so much a sin as a shield," Debs murmured, "against the knowledge of one's own sins. Mr. Holt, I am afraid that we have *not* accomplished much—most certainly not what we set out to do. But one must gladly take what progress one can."

"And what about you, sir? What if you are sent to jail?"

"I shall have to accept that, too," Debs said. "I fear I am practically bound to be sent to jail. Truth and justice will have very little to do with my trial, although perhaps this clever lawyer you found for me can cut the sentence down a bit."

"Where will they send you? Not back to Cook County, I hope."

"Oh, no!" Kate blanched. "Oh, anywhere but that fearful place. Eugene, it will kill you."

"I'll go where I go," Debs said, but he reached out and took her hand with more reassurance than Tim suspected he really felt. "I am very hard to kill, my dear. Much like the unions."

Tim was finally headed home to San Francisco. He had made the decision shortly after his conversation with Debs, for reasons that he couldn't quite put his finger on but that had something to do with just getting on with his life.

I've spent half my time around trains lately, he thought as he listened to the mournful shriek of the engine up ahead. *Either riding in the blasted things or trying to get out of the ones that people have set on fire*. He felt a great desire to get home, saddle up Trout, and let the horse work its long idleness off in Golden Gate Park, trying to throw him.

The train was pulling into some midwestern prairie

town—Tim had lost track of where he was—yet another village with fields of nearly ripe corn flowing out from it, studded with red barns and white farmhouses, the tall towers of the silos rising above them. The town was just another busy settlement around a bend in the tracks, as flat as the prairie except for the depot's water tank and the white steeple of a church beyond it.

As Tim's train slowed, another passed going in the opposite direction—a freight train hauling boxcars. In one of them Tim caught sight of a rider, a railroad bum, sitting feet splayed out in the open doorway, watching the paying passengers opposite sway past behind the curtained windows of their Pullmans.

Tim had a fleeting urge to be that bum, with no destination, no ticket, no job, just a boxcar full of straw and the clatter of the wheels. But it would be winter soon, and then a boxcar would be no paradise.

A song he had heard once from an old Shaker woman ran through his mind to the rhythm of the rails: "'Tis a gift to be simple, 'tis a gift to be free. . . ." Easier said than done, Tim thought. Too many entanglements. Unless, of course, one wanted to join the Shakers and be celibate. Maybe that wasn't such a bad idea—except he knew he couldn't stand it. He leaned his head back against the horse-hair upholstery and sang the rest of the song under his breath:

"When true simplicity is gained,
To bow and to bend we shan't be ashamed.
To turn, turn will be our delight,
Till by turning and turning we come round right."

Tim found the idea of the circular nature of life very appealing, but he didn't feel that his own existence was coming round right. He felt one step out of synchronization to the music of the world.

Tim's introspective moods never lasted long—they weren't in his nature—but he was still feeling vaguely pessimistic and dissatisfied when the train pulled into San

Francisco. He hadn't notified anyone that he was coming back, although judging from Peter's first telegram, the *Clarion* staff must have expected him to show up soon, breathing fire. Peter had sent another telegram, short and cryptic, a week ago, saying only that he had retained a business manager.

Tim hired a hack, dumped his bags in the foyer of his house, and went straight to the *Clarion* to see if he was going to strangle Waldo. Doing so, he decided, might make him feel better. On the way to Waldo's office, he first ducked in, curious, to look into Peter's old office and see who was in there. He stopped short in the doorway, choking on the introductory remarks he had had on the tip of his tongue.

Rosebay was bent over a ledger, making aggravated *tut-tutting* noises at it. She wore a severe white shirtwaist that should have made her look like an old schoolteacher but did not. Her corn-silk hair was topped with a green celluloid eyeshade against the glare of the overhead electric light. She finished whatever calculation she had been working on before she looked up. When her eyes met Tim's she looked nearly as startled as he did.

Rosebay took a deep breath, fixed a businesslike expression on her employer, and pointed her pencil at him. "Tim Holt, you are in a passel of trouble."

Tim swallowed. "Yeah, I know."

Rosebay gave him a long look. "Well, some things have to be ignored, but these books aren't among them. You might have said you were coming home."

"I wasn't really sure I was till I was on the train," Tim said. "What the devil are you doing in here?"

"I'm your new business manager." Rosebay looked embarrassed. "At least I am till you fire me. Peter talked me into it. He says I have a knack."

She looked a little proud of that, and the expression in her cornflower eyes was so pleading that Tim did not have the heart to tell her he didn't think he could bear it if she was there, only two offices away from his, all the blessed day.

He put his hand across his eyes. Her beauty burned a little too brightly for him to look at without being singed, he thought. *"Oh, she doth teach the torches to burn bright,"* *like Juliet.* That was what Hugo always said of her. *Hugo . . .* Tim groaned.

"I'll go," Rosebay whispered. "I knew it wasn't a good idea."

"No, don't! We just have to find a way to deal with it. Your leaving won't make the situation better," he said helplessly.

Rosebay laid her fingertips on a some typewritten papers that were weighted down with the telephone and took a deep breath. "These are overdue notices," she said. "I phrased them pretty strong. If we can call these in, we'll do all right. I've made Waldo give me an accounting of everything that's ordered for the *Clarion* instead of just hauling off and sending for it when the spirit moves him. I'm beginning to get it in hand."

"You really know what you're doing?" Tim marveled.

"Yes, I do. I know it's not the conventional thing, but like Peter said, I've got a knack." She gave him a grin, faintly mischievous under her obvious yearning for him. "But if you ever let Waldo Howard get his hands on anything but a copy pencil ever again, I'll get a gun and shoot him."

"And save me the trouble," Tim muttered. He still looked as if his world had been rocked even more off balance, but he gathered himself together enough to say with creditable detachment, "Well, I've got no objections to having a woman in the office. It may tone the fellows down some—keep them from cussing and coming in drunk."

Rosebay chuckled. "Don't bet on it. Peter read them such a lecture on treating me like a real accountant that they're all acting like I was a man."

"Nobody could act as if you were a man," Tim said flatly.

"Peter made Waldo give me a man's salary," Rosebay informed him. "Just in case you were thinking you were saving any money."

"All right, you've got the job." Tim backed toward the door, afraid to come in any farther. Maybe he could learn to think of her as just an accountant, too. And maybe pigs had wings. Oh, hell . . .

Tim beat a hasty retreat, not even stopping to see Waldo. He would find Peter and go have a drink at the Press Club. Maybe not in that order, though.

By November Tim was thinking that if anyone had told him back in Guthrie that little Rosebay Basham could take charge of a business office the way she had done, he would have thought they'd gone crazy. Although she had made her rustic restaurant profitable in Guthrie, it was mostly because half the bachelors in town were in love with her and would have eaten rocks if she had served them. He had assumed that her San Francisco boardinghouse was prosperous for the same reason. Obviously he had been wrong. What had made her ventures such a success were her common sense and her talent at bookkeeping, two traits Waldo didn't have.

Thanks to Rosebay, the *Clarion* was no longer going broke. She had the newspaper nearly in the black, and some wag had even suggested that she be invited to join the Market Street Club, an association of professional accountants. He had just been making a joke, but she had nearly been voted in. When Tim heard about that, he had reacted with unreasoning anger. She *ought* to have been voted in; it was unfair and unethical to keep her out just because she was a woman. He had said it so often and with such indignation that Rosebay finally told him to hush. She didn't want to be a pioneer and hadn't asked to join their silly club.

Unfortunately this newfound competence neither repelled Tim nor made Rosebay seem less desirable in his eyes; it just gave him something else about her to love. This was a new side to Rosebay, and he was fiercely proud. Tim had grown up in a family of intelligent and capable women, and except for the year when he had been in the throes of first love with Isabella Ormond, he had never been attracted to stupid females. Here was a woman who could be partner as well as lover, who would never say with a pretty air of incompetence, "Oh, well, I leave all that to my husband." Here was a woman who would give him the sort of marriage that his father enjoyed with Alexandra, or his sister Janessa provided for her doctor husband. Except, of course, that he couldn't have Rosebay.

Would Hugo like the way that Rosebay was turning out? Tim wondered. Then he pointed out to himself that that wasn't his business. His inner voice declared unbidden that Hugo had better be appreciative, or Tim would knock his teeth in. Hugo had better remember how lucky he was, the voice continued. Tim found himself talking to himself a great deal, and occasionally answering, and he wondered if he was going to be as crazy as a loon pretty soon.

He forced himself to stay out of Rosebay's office and, now that he didn't have to wonder if they were going to stay solvent, concentrate on the paper's editorial side.

Financial stability must be refreshing, Peter had said gloomily. Peter's Blake had gotten stuck in high gear and nearly run into the bay the previous afternoon, to the joy of the wharfside loungers. As Thanksgiving approached, San Franciscans were in a holiday mood, ready for any spectacle. The nobs of Nob Hill gave glittering parties, and Tim, as an up-and-coming citizen and prospective matrimonial catch, received numerous invitations. The denizens of the Barbary Coast, meanwhile, knifed one another with even greater regularity in a kind of seasonal exuberance. And a waiter at the Poodle Dog strangled his laundress girlfriend for accepting a pair of diamond earrings from a mutual customer. San Francisco avidly read about all of it in the *Clarion.*

Mr. Woolwine, from whom Tim had purchased the *Clarion,* was found wandering in Golden Gate Park with a nest of cotton batting on his head. He believed that without this protection the electric light standards in the park were telegraphing his thoughts to foreign spies. Tim printed this theory with a certain amount of glee, thus forestalling the rival *Chronicle,* which had prepared a humorous exposé of the former management of the *Clarion.* But he sent Mr. Woolwine's sister a Thanksgiving ham and the name of a trained nurse who, so Rafe Murray assured him, outweighed Mr. Woolwine and would prevent further unauthorized outings.

Nothing, however, eased his longing for Rosebay Ware or his growing tendency to drink himself into oblivion because of it. The latter brought Tim up sharp one day, glass in hand, midway through an afternoon's excursion along the Cocktail Route. It was five o'clock, and his only plan for the evening was to get drunk enough to sleep that night without dreaming of Rosebay. With a shudder he set the glass down and stared at it. His eyes lifted to the mirror above the mahogany bar, and the face that stared back at him was marked by new lines and haunted eyes. It wasn't a face he knew.

Tim took his overcoat from the rack and walked out into a fine rain. He turned his collar up against it and whatever else might be pursuing him. A hack slowed beside him, but he wanted to walk. The genial notes of a piano beckoned temptingly from the next saloon, and he crossed Market Street to avoid it, turning his head away from the golden glow enticing cold pedestrians in from the rain and from whatever their troubles might be. *I won't turn into a drunk*, he thought doggedly.

It was nearly dark already, and Market Street had a festival shimmer. Light standards created gold clouds in the mist, and the stores' display windows were hung with Thanksgiving decorations and artistic arrays of merchandise calculated to interest the Christmas shopper. Tim passed the *Clarion* building again without turning in and saw that two newsboys had climbed the façade and were tying a wreath around the head of the *Clarion*'s gargoyle.

"Get down from there!" Tim bellowed up at them.

"Push off, copper!" one of them called back, feeling safe from pursuit.

"It ain't no copper. It's Mr. Holt," the other said, peering down.

"Get down before you fall off, or I'll come up after you!" Tim yelled.

They gave the wreath a last tweak and scrambled downward. He was waiting for them, but they dodged him and ran, howling with laughter, into the darkness. Tim cocked his head at the gargoyle. It looked festive. He decided to leave the wreath alone.

His mood lightened, and he went on walking, determined to clear his mind of the alcohol he had consumed. He bent his steps toward the wharf and Peter's shop. Away from the business district, the holiday splendor dimmed. The frequenters of San Francisco's wharf side had no money for decorations or the inclination to hang them. They celebrated in their own way, the seamen mostly by getting roaring drunk. Thus, the crimps increased their business, which was cause for their celebrating.

Peter's shop wasn't on the worst section of the wharf, but all the same, Tim remained alert for trouble. Rolling the swells who ventured off their own turf was a wharf-side pastime. As he approached the Blake shop, a figure in the mist caught his eye, and Tim stiffened, intently watching the shadow as it slipped along. As the man walked away, he hugged the lee of the looming brick warehouse row and looked bent on no honest errand. When he slipped into the narrow alley that ran between the Blake shop and the next warehouse, Tim followed.

There was no sign of the man at the alley's mouth. Tim peered into the darkness between the buildings. Although no movement could be seen, he heard a faint scratching, just audible above the hiss of the rain. Peter's shop had a back door, Tim remembered, which opened to a storage room behind the main shop, under the overhang of Mr. Ellison's loft. What might a man be wanting in it? Tim wondered grimly.

The unlit alley was slick with rain. If Tim had not had so much to drink, he would not have ventured into it unarmed. But he hadn't quite walked off the effect of those cocktails, and curiosity got the better of him. He slipped into the alley, moving as quietly as he could on the wet cobbles.

At the end of the Blake building, he flattened himself against the brick wall to peer cautiously around the corner. Light spilled from the rear door, so at first Tim thought it was open. Then he realized that the intruder had unshuttered a lantern. The rain soaked up much of its light, but it was bright enough for Tim to see that the man, a stocky figure in corduroy trousers and a tweed cap, was removing the windowpane from the back door.

"Who the hell are you?" Tim bellowed.

The man, whose nerves must have been stretched taut

anyway, spun to stare into the darkness. He held a glazing knife.

Tim yelled again. "Get away from that door!"

The man didn't move. Tim realized that the alley was a dead end, and the stranger could escape only by going past him.

"Drop the knife, and I won't hurt you," Tim growled, hoping he sounded like a man with a pistol. "We'll just have a little talk."

Panic-stricken, the burglar dived at Tim to fight his way free. The glazing knife flashed in the wet light, and Tim felt it rip down his overcoat sleeve. He snatched at the man's arm and swung at him with his other hand. The intruder, fighting back violently, wrenched his arm from Tim's grasp. The glazing knife slid past Tim's cheek and nicked his ear. The scent of blood in his nostrils goaded him into enraged action. The intruder, in a seaman's sweater, was more agile than Tim, who was hampered by a heavy overcoat. Tim swung at him again in blind fury but slipped on the cobbles. The man tried to leap past, and Tim made a flying grab at his leg so that they fell together on the wet stones.

The man raised the knife again, and Tim grabbed the man's hand and squeezed. The fingers didn't uncurl, so Tim sank his teeth into the back of the knife hand. The man writhed like a wet eel on top of him. There was a howl, and the knife clattered across the cobbles. Tim rolled—he was heavier than his opponent—and pinned the burglar to the stone.

"Be still, damn it!"

The man heaved under him. Tim pulled his fist back and slugged him in the jaw as hard as he could. The man sagged. Before the burglar could recover, Tim had him up on his feet with one arm twisted behind his back and a rigid forefinger in the man's spine.

"If you don't want me to blow a hole through you," Tim threatened, "you'll come along quietly."

The would-be thief didn't say anything, and when Tim shoved him down the alley toward the street, he did not fight. At the front of the shop, Tim kicked on the door until Calvin Rogers opened it. The older man blinked with surprise as Tim shoved the burglar inside. "Give me a rope."

Calvin produced one while Peter, Mr. Tolliver, Mr. Ellison, and the mechanics gathered around them. Rufus Gooch was oblivious to what was happening. He was under the Blake, muttering unintelligibly to the motor. Tim tied the man's hands together and sat him on a crate.

The intruder glared at Tim in the bright light. "You aren't a copper," he said accusingly.

"That's right," Tim said. "What's more, I haven't got a gun."

"You're bleeding," Peter said.

"He was taking out your back window with a glazing knife," Tim responded.

"Fool," Peter said disgustedly. "There's nothing in here worth stealing."

"Wasn't going to steal anything," the man muttered grumpily. He was about forty-five and looked like a tough, but he was at a disadvantage now.

The design team stood over him, arms folded, while Tim asked, "What were you doing then? I'd advise you to tell us everything. Since I'm not a cop, there's nothing to stop us from taking turns punching you until you do." He was going to be black and blue from the cobblestones, and his ear still dripped blood.

"I was hired," the prisoner confessed sulkily.

"Hired to what? And by whom?"

"How the hell do I know by who? Man give me some money, said he wanted that contraption wrecked." He jerked his thumb at the motorcar.

"Why that swindling, weaseling, little— Alfred Wellington!" Peter exploded.

"Do I hear the name of the opposition?" Gooch slid out from under the Blake.

"This man was hired to wreck your machine," Tim said. He touched his ear gingerly. "And I'm going to look like a pirate. What should we do with him?"

"Turn him over to the police," Rogers said.

"Hang him up by his thumbs," Gooch suggested. He fixed bright and furious eyes on the prisoner. "If you touch that machine, I will cut out your liver."

"Tell him we won't kill him if he blows up Wellington's car instead," Tolliver proposed.

"Beat the tar out of him," Peter decided, rolling up his sleeves.

"Hold on," Tim said. "I appreciate your ideas, but I caught him so he's mine. Have you got a telephone? He goes to the police."

"I go call," Mr. Ellison said. He returned minutes later with a cotton swab and a piece of sticking plaster. "They coming. Mr. Holt, you let me look at that cut. You don't fix it, you goin' have a cauliflower ear." Tim kept twisting his neck trying to see his own ear. "Hold still now!"

"You could put a ring in it," Peter suggested.

"I'm glad you're so grateful to me," Tim muttered. "Ow!"

"I'm going to have that bastard in court," Peter seethed. "I'm going to see that Wellington goes to jail until he's ninety-five. I'm going to ruin his reputation so that not even his own mother will so much as bake him a pie." Peter, his attention returned to the prisoner waiting glumly in his chair, began to froth again.

"I don't think you can, you know," Tim said, calmer now that Ellison had let his ear alone. He turned to the intruder. "You know the name of the man who hired you?"

"I told you I didn't."

"You might get off easier if you did."

The prisoner looked interested. "What did you say the name was? Wellesley?"

"Oh, no, you don't," Tim said. He put a hand to Peter's mouth as Peter started to speak. "Either you know it, or you don't. And you, use your head," he added to Peter. "If you prime him, you know it won't stand up in court. Your, uh, competition could sue *you*."

"Not if I get my hands on him first," Peter muttered.

The authorities arrived before Peter could get his hands on their prisoner, and the fellow was stuffed in a police wagon.

"Attempted breaking and entering," a bored policeman said. "You can't charge him with what he just *said* he was gonna do. Assault maybe, if you want to, Mr. Holt." He looked at Tim's ear and, with a faint smile, at the glazing knife, which had been found in the alley. It wasn't long enough to be considered potentially lethal.

"Never mind," Tim said. He was going to be the joke of the Press Club, as it was.

Peter had stayed in a fury for days after the sabotage attempt and nearly drove Rufus and Calvin crazy, haunting the shop, tinkering with the Blake, demanding to know when it would be ready for the next trial. By Thanksgiving they were ready to tie Peter to a chair.

Rosebay had invited Tim, Peter, Rufus, and Calvin to Thanksgiving dinner and with characteristic motherliness had sent a covered tray down to the shop for Ellison and Tolliver, who were standing guard. It had been unanimously decided that there should always be at least two of them on the premises.

Tim's ear had nearly healed, but there was a noticeable nick in it that was going to be permanent. Tim's reporters, Hugo informed him joyfully, were now referring to him as Blackbeard. Hugo had been restrained by Rosebay from presenting him with a pirate's eye patch to go with it.

"Lord make us thankful for what we are about to receive." Hugo bowed his head over the Thanksgiving turkey. "And for what we have." He smiled gently at Rosebay, who smiled back, startled, and hoped she didn't look as guilty as she felt.

Lord, make me grateful for what I've got, she prayed silently as the boarders and guests tore into the meal. They were always as ravenous as hounds, but she had found a good cook to take her place, and it was a relief not to have to peel potatoes anymore. Sometimes she had thought her whole life would be spent feeding people who would be hungry again in a few hours.

She looked at her plate of turkey and stuffing swimming in gravy and felt a little queasy. Guilty conscience probably; whenever she thought she'd been bad, she got sick. When she first married Hugo, she had gotten so sick she thought she was pregnant. Then she had been scared to death because the baby might have been Tim's. But, fortunately, she hadn't been pregnant—just guilty, she

reckoned, for having married Hugo when she was in love
with Tim.

Lately she had quit even wondering about becoming
pregnant; she had been married three years, and there
hadn't been a baby yet. Maybe something was wrong with
her. Maybe it was the price of sin. That was what Pa would
have said, she knew.

Rosebay looked down the table at Tim. He was a
handsome man—she had thought so from the first time she
saw him. He had dressed for the occasion in a cutaway, and
his stiffly starched shirtfront was fastened with pearl studs.
But his good looks had long since ceased to be the thing that
stood out about him. Now when she thought of Tim, the
way his sandy hair curled around his ears came to her mind.
And the mule-headed look he got when something pro-
voked him, and the shape of his hands, and the set of his
back. She could have picked him out in a crowd just from
his back. How could he decide to love her *now*?

Rosebay raised up her fork and made herself eat her
stuffing and gravy, the green beans she had picked out
herself at the market yesterday, and then the mince pie and
the ice cream that she and Rafe Murray had churned out on
the porch that morning. When she was finished, she wished
she hadn't eaten at all.

After dinner was over, everyone went into the parlor
and sat, feeling stuffed. Hugo asked Rosebay to play her
guitar.

"I've been working all day, and I'm just plumb too
tired," she said. "Let's listen to the phonograph instead."

"I'd rather hear you sing," Hugo said wistfully.

"You hear me sing all the time." Rosebay got up and
opened the phonograph's wooden case. It was new, and she
was proud of it. Everyone was beginning to buy them. She
lifted the apparatus out of its case, fitted it into a slot on the
lid, and folded up the megaphone-shaped horn that ampli-
fied the sound. A second case held cylindrical wax records.
A dozen had come with the phonograph: waltzes, polkas,
and novelty songs, and for the patriotically minded, the
United States Marine Band playing the "Washington Post
March" and Maurice Barrymore reading the Gettysburg

Address. Rosebay passed over Barrymore and put on Strauss's "Gypsy Baron Waltz."

Rufus Gooch immediately bent double inspecting the mechanism of the phonograph.

"It's a plain miracle, isn't it?" Rosebay said, her eyes shining. "There's records you can talk into and make your own, too. I sang 'Home Sweet Home' for it, but I was so awful we scraped it off."

"It just doesn't do justice to your voice, my girl," Rafe Murray said. "It didn't do poor old Barrymore any good, either."

"The music's nice, though, isn't it?" Rosebay swayed in time to the waltz. "One of you boys come on and dance with me."

Rafe got up and bowed, and he and Rosebay whirled around the parlor. Hugo folded his arms and watched. From his expression, Rosebay knew he still preferred to hear her sing. She knew all the old mountain songs and stories, and her voice did justice to them. She felt another stab of guilt because in spite of her excuse of being too tired to sing, she obviously had the energy to dance. The minute she had started to dance, she stopped feeling ill. She loved to dance.

Hugo suddenly stood up and tapped Rafe on the shoulder. "You'll have to share. There isn't enough of her to go round."

Rafe let him cut in without complaint. "You need some lady boarders, m'dear," he said.

Rosebay's cook, Mrs. Bismarck, came in with a tray of champagne glasses, and Rafe took the tray out of her hands, set it on the parlor table, and swooped the woman into the waltz.

The cook was stout, with iron-gray curls and a stiffly starched calico work dress. She looked startled as Rafe encircled her with his arm. "Mr. Murray!"

"It's Thanksgiving, Mrs. B. Put on your dancing shoes."

Mrs. Bismarck laughed and let him swing her around the room, her white apron flying. Tim and Calvin Rogers pulled the parlor furniture out of the way. Even Peter seemed to have mellowed and was tapping his foot to the music. When the record ran down, Rafe cranked the machine up again and put another on. He presented Mrs. Bismark to Rufus.

"Now, Mr. Murray, I'm all out of breath!"

Gooch bowed with a flourish. "An excellent dinner," he informed her. "Quite within my standards." He grasped her firmly by the waist and strode solemnly into the music.

"Did you ever?" Peter whispered to Tim. "I would have guessed the old fellow to have two left feet."

"He does," Tim whispered back, watching them. "But he's got grit. Mrs. B's no ballerina."

Peter picked up a glass of champagne. "To success," he said with a grin. "Confusion to the enemy."

Tim reached for a glass and then drew his hand back. "By all means," he agreed. "Pretend that I've drunk to it."

He got up and ambled over to the phonograph, which was running down again. It had to be wound up for every record. He lifted the wax cylinders one by one, looking at the labels. He put on "Trilby," a schottische that was the current craze, and took Rosebay away from Calvin, who, in spite of his limp, had cut in on Hugo.

"My turn." He felt reckless, almost as if he had drunk that champagne, which further confirmed his feelings that he had better not. But he didn't see how he could get in any trouble in a room full of people, and he probably wouldn't get to dance with her for long, anyway.

Rosebay slid into his arms, fitting as if she belonged there. The schottische was very like a polka, only in slower tempo, more suitable for a parlor containing too many furnishings to bump into. They circled in stately and proper fashion, holding each other at arm's length. Rosebay's eyes glowed.

"You look mighty good tonight," Tim said.

"You look pretty good, too," Rosebay whispered.

"I moved up my Saturday-night bath," Tim said, grinning. He couldn't help it; it made him joyous just to dance with her. They circled the parlor, and he dodged Peter, who looked like a man about to cut in.

Peter, with a knowing shake of his head conveying plainly that he thought his cousin was a fool, appropriated Mrs. Bismarck from Calvin Rogers instead. Hugo was sitting down again, sipping champagne. Rufus, having done his duty dance, was sitting cross-legged on the floor in front of the phonograph, where he was vastly in the way, and making notes with a mechanical pencil on the back of a *Scribner's Magazine.*

"Improving on the phonograph's design?" Peter asked. "Make it so that it could be powered by the dancers, operating a treadmill."

When the schottische ran down, Rosebay put her hand to her side. "I've got a stitch," she said. "I've got to stop. That's no dance for after dinner." Her face was flushed, and her eyes gleamed brightly at Tim. She cast a quick glance at Hugo, who was still drinking champagne, then looked back at Tim. "I'm reluctant to take Mrs. Bismarck away when she's at such a premium," she whispered. "Come help me open another bottle."

Tim followed her into the kitchen.

"You shouldn't be in here with me," Rosebay said. "Don't think I don't know it. But I just wanted to thank you for coming. I was afraid you wouldn't."

"I know." Tim began to ease the cork from the champagne bottle. "I wanted to tell you I'm going to try to do what you suggested and just make the best of things." He looked into her eyes. "As far as I can," he whispered. The cork came out with a pop, and the champagne foam cascaded down the sides of the bottle. Tim hurried it over to the sink.

"Hugo's sent his manuscript to a publisher in New York," she said. "I think they're going to buy it. That's why we're celebrating."

As long as Rosebay and Tim had known Hugo, he had been working sporadically on a volume entitled *Sketches of America*. He had shown no particular interest in having it published.

"I've been after him to send it out," Rosebay admitted. "I think it's real good myself."

Tim took a swig of champagne straight from the bottle. "Damn Hugo," he said distinctly. Then he put his hand on the back of Rosebay's neck, kissed her hard on the mouth, and walked out of the kitchen.

XIX

Portland, December, 1894

Portland was in the throes of its Christmas shopping, but Paul Kirchner didn't have anyone to shop for. He had money in his pocket—he had just been paid. Maybe he would buy his landlady's daughter a doll, he thought, before the money slipped through his fingers. He strolled along the streets, looking at the elaborate displays in the department-store windows, watching Christmas shoppers, bundled in furs against the cold, scurry by. The women's arms were full of boxes, and children lagged behind to press their noses against toy-store windows. He watched a small girl breathing steam onto the glass, rapt in the vision of a blond bisque doll in a blue velvet dress.

"Lulie, *will* you come along?" Her mother took her by the arm and dragged her down the street.

Paul walked on. He couldn't afford any of those dolls. He had seen some in a drugstore on the cheap side of town that were more in his price range. His landlady's little girl would be happy with any sort of toy—her house was on the cheap side of town, too. He hunched his shoulders against the wind and headed that way for want of anywhere else to go. Holidays made him restless, as if there was something missing in them or in him, which he ought to be able to find.

When he got to the drugstore, he found the bin of dolls and considered them. They were pink bisque babies with jointed arms, ten cents undressed, fifty cents dressed. He decided to splurge and buy a dressed one. He doubted his landlady had any time or inclination to sew doll clothes.

He turned to the counter with the doll in his hand and stopped, staring through the crowd around the cash register. Dan Schumann was in line, three customers from the counter. What was he doing in this place? Paul wondered. The Madrona bought its supplies at Callahan's Emporium on the nice side of town. What was more, Dan was dressed in work clothes, as if disguised to blend in. Paul pulled his battered hat a little lower over his eyes and edged through the crowd of customers, clutching the doll and trying to get a better look.

Dan glanced around with a hint of furtiveness, scanning the other customers, so Paul backed away. Dan was at the druggist's counter now. A great many people were crowded into the store. Because of the housewives chatting and children complaining that they were tired, Paul couldn't hear what Dan asked for; but he saw the druggist hand Dan a pair of paper-wrapped bottles from the shelf behind him. After Dan paid, the druggist wrapped the bottles together in brown paper tied with string. Dan put them in his coat pocket. Paul turned his back swiftly and waited until Dan had edged his way out of the store. Then he made for the counter.

"Say, what did that fellow buy just now?" Paul asked the druggist while he wrapped the doll.

"What fellow?"

"The one in the plaid shirt and the sheepskin coat," Paul said. "Big fellow, about my age."

"I don't look at 'em," the druggist said. "I just make up their orders. And I got no time for remembering what they buy, either. You know how many people been in here today?"

"Then what's that stuff on the high shelf?" Paul asked him. "In the brown paper with the black label?"

The druggist looked behind him. "Where?"

"There." Paul pointed.

"Laudanum," the druggist answered. "Tincture of opium. Who's next?"

"You can't prove it, Paul," McCarty said. He pulled off his policeman's boots and massaged his feet. His broken ankle was healed, and he was back on the beat. Christmas was the police department's busy season: Every pickpocket and smash-and-grab man in the city was out doing his own Christmas shopping.

"He bought two bottles of laudanum," Paul said stubbornly, "in a store where he wouldn't be recognized. You tell *me* what he wanted it for. Mrs. Blake should have been better by now, and now I know why she's not."

"I follow your reasoning, Paul," McCarty said. "All I said was you couldn't prove it. Tell the foreman, this White Elk fellow, and let him handle it."

"I intend to," Paul replied. "He can put a stop to it. But I want Schumann off that place, and that'll take proof. He weaseled a power of attorney out of Mrs. Blake."

McCarty's new wife came in and put a plate of ham sandwiches down in front of them. "Tsk. Poor old woman. You eat, Joe, and I'll make you a footbath."

McCarty sighed with pleasure. "You ought to get married, Paul. Get out of that cannery." Having financed his honeymoon, McCarty had bid salmon farewell again.

"Who'd marry me?" Paul asked. "Will you kindly pay attention?"

McCarty heaved a sigh. "I am," he said. "But you got to have proof. You might drop a word in Dr. Bright's ear."

Paul thought about that. "That might get Schumann off the place if the doctor convinced Mrs. Blake. I suppose Dr. Bright could manage that easily enough. But Schumann will just take off. He's doing something with Mrs. Blake's money, and I want to know what. If we scare him, he may get clean away with it before we can stop him."

McCarty looked uncomfortable. "Couldn't you just settle for getting rid of him?"

"No. I am feeling unreasonably vindictive. I don't see why he should get off scot-free. I don't want Mrs. Blake's reputation damaged, either. She was good to me. Why are you so willing to let him go, anyway?"

"Oh, damn it all." McCarty glanced over his shoulder for his wife, but she was still in the kitchen drawing his footbath.

"McCarty," Paul said suspiciously, "what do you know?"

"More than I want to. It's as much as my job is worth."

Paul folded his arms across his chest. "Your job, or the hand you've got in someone's till?"

"You don't understand how it's done, my friend. Some things are expected, and a new man doesn't rock the boat."

"And a little payoff on the side sure beats canning salmon on the side." Paul nodded, not particularly surprised. Any big-city police department had its well-oiled machinery of graft—unmarked envelopes of cash, which appeared in desk drawers, from anonymous donors who expected in return an occasional blind eye from the authorities.

"I need the money," McCarty muttered. "We don't get paid enough to keep a family alive."

"I know." Paul waited.

"And, well, I married into it, like. I can't—"

Paul ate a ham sandwich and thought while McCarty's bride bustled back in with a pan of hot water. McCarty stuck his feet in it gratefully. The police were not paid enough for what they did, and it wasn't Paul's business to try to reform them, either. The system was far too complicated.

"I hate to be crude," Paul said finally when McCarty's wife had gone out again. "But I saved your life. Now, I think Mrs. Blake's in danger, and I'd like a bit of reciprocity. I don't want to know *how* you know, and I'll forget who told me as soon as I'm out your door, but I've got to have enough information to nail Dan Schumann's butt."

McCarty looked guilty. "All right, all right. He's got money in one of Maisie Mennen's whorehouses, for one thing. It may be Mrs. Blake's money, for all I know. And he owes money to Louie Weasel. That's just scuttlebutt, but I'd bet my gold teeth on its being true. I heard Louie was getting impatient, and Schumann fobbed him off with Ephraim Bender's name."

Paul chewed his thumbnail. "Bender. He's the land developer. Crony of Toby Holt's."

"Definitely not a crony. He supported Holt's campaign, but word is he's not supporting the senator now, and Holt doesn't have much time for Bender, either. Bender's the fellow behind this." McCarty rummaged in a drawer and produced a flyer headed, in extravagant Old English type: VALUABLE BUILDING LOTS ON THE BEAUTI-FUL WILLAMETTE RIVER. "I took it off an eastern dude who bit on it, poor chucklehead."

Paul frowned. "I don't get it. Why would Bender let Schumann in on his scam? What's in it for Bender?"

"Must be something good," McCarty said. "Otherwise Bender wouldn't waste his time."

"That's all you know?"

"I swear to God. And I don't want to know more."

Paul stood up. "All right. Take care of your feet then."

"Give my love to the fish," McCarty said.

The next morning, Paul rode out to the Madrona and lurked under the trees, feeling a little foolish but determined, until he saw Dan Schumann leave the house and go into the barn. When Dan was out of sight, Paul sprinted for the foreman's cottage. He left an hour later with a reasonable assurance that there would be no more laudanum administered to Mrs. Blake without her knowledge, and a promise from White Elk not to rend Dan Schumann limb from limb or to tell Mrs. Blake until Paul could learn what Dan was up to.

"I'll send Dr. Bright out," Paul said, "but you'll have to get him past Schumann. Laudanum's nasty stuff, and she's going to feel mighty sick when she stops taking it. Poor woman's old and fragile. She won't be able to handle Schumann."

"I'll handle Schumann," White Elk vowed grimly.

"Not yet. There's no telling what a tangle he's made of her affairs. His mess will need to be unraveled carefully. If it appears that whatever he's done was accomplished with her connivance, the scandal would cost the senator his reelection."

"Toby wouldn't blame Mrs. Blake for that," White Elk said.

"No, but she'd blame herself," Paul said, "and he'd still be out of office for no good reason."

"I suppose so." White Elk looked at him curiously. "You're taking a lot on yourself for someone who hasn't been treated fairly. Mrs. Blake thinks you're a lightweight, you know."

"Maybe I am a lightweight," Paul replied. "I wonder about that myself sometimes."

"Well, you've got a good heart," White Elk said. "I've sent Mai to sit with Mrs. Blake. But you let me know when you learn something. I don't like this. Schumann's too slick—too plausible. My people would have called him a bad spirit."

"Did your people say what to do about bad spirits?" Paul asked, curious. He was as prepared to believe in a Shoshone remedy for evil as in anything else.

"Nothing a white man's court wouldn't string me up for," White Elk informed him.

Paul knew he had better do something before White Elk acted upon it anyway. The Shoshone foreman regarded Mrs. Blake as a foster grandmother, and if he got fed up enough, there was no telling how he might come to her aid. Paul was beginning to get the uneasy, skin-prickling sensation that someone was likely to get killed over this. There was more to it than Dan Schumann running some scam. Paul wasn't certain what it was, but when he had thought of Dan Schumann as evil, it was not an idle metaphor. Something was twisted inside Dan. Paul rode slowly, thinking.

He returned his rented horse, which left him nearly without funds until payday. The next time he went out to the ranch, he realized, he would have to hop one of the freights that ran up the river past the Madrona's outskirts. The idea did not trouble him; he had done it before and become adept at dodging the railroad police. Still thinking, he walked back to his seedy lodgings near the cannery and found an unlikely ally waiting for him.

"Well," Lady Teddy Montague said as Paul opened his door to find her brewing tea on his gas ring, "I understand your name is mud at the Madrona. Not with White Elk, of course. He told me where to find you. Said you had a tale to tell that I ought to hear."

"So I do," Paul confirmed. "Where did you spring from? I'm sorry this is such a dreary place to entertain a lady friend."

Teddy looked around, appraising the dingy room with its faint odor of fish. "Heavens, I've lived in worse. I remember a place in Cairo. . . . Well, never mind that. Drink your tea and tell me what devilment you've been up to."

Paul took the steaming tin cup of tea. Teddy had apparently produced the leaves from the leather-banded satchel on the floor. "It's not *my* devilment," he said, and told her all of it.

"Well, it just shows you were right to stay on," Teddy said. "One should always trust one's instincts. Although I would have liked to have had you with me. The expedition was quite exciting and enjoyable." She stuck out a sturdy ankle and rolled down her brown cotton stocking, exhibiting the healed scar of what Paul was fairly sure was a bullet hole. He had never met another woman with Teddy's notions of what was enjoyable.

"Perhaps fate was attempting to stay your wandering foot?" he suggested.

"If my wandering foot had stayed *there* any longer," Teddy said, "so would would the rest of me—on my back, six feet under. But never mind that. What are we to do about this Schumann fellow?"

"I don't want you involved in this," Paul said. "I think it's going to get dangerous."

Teddy gave him a faint hoot of laughter. "And you aren't talking to the secretary of the Garden Club. I was not, however, planning to go out and horsewhip the lout. There are better ways to deal the likes of Mr. Daniel Schumann."

"Good. I hope you know of one."

"Land-office records," Teddy said. "That's where to start. Of course, if we end up with horsewhips, I won't object."

It took them awhile to nose out the information they wanted, but Teddy proved to have the instincts of a ferret. She plowed through a trail of papers, from deed to corporate buyer to yet another file, where the identities of the corporation's members were buried in a cloud of legalese and "parties henceforth referred to as the buyer." Paul, lost in the maze, stumbled along behind her while a bored clerk tapped his fingernails on the table and looked repeatedly at his pocket watch.

"How on earth do you know what to look for?" Paul whispered.

"My dear man, I once deciphered a marriage contract in Swahili and translated it into German. It involved a herd of white goats and a crocodile-tooth necklace that was the groom's family heirloom. Having done that, American real estate holds no terrors for me." She bent a stern eye on the clerk. "Someone's going to be in trouble over this. You have been shockingly lax."

"It's all in order," the clerk protested. "It wouldn't be recorded if it wasn't."

"Hmmph," said Teddy. "I shall require a fair copy of these five papers, together with your notation that the copy is correct."

"We're closing," the clerk said. "It's five o'clock."

"Young man, I am not going anywhere until I get those copies. You may just as well resign yourself to it. If you should care to help me write them out, it will speed matters along."

The clerk, who probably would have argued with Paul, wasn't up to battling Teddy. "There's a fee for that," he said sulkily. "Two dollars."

Teddy turned out her pocketbook and produced a pile of coins. "I have one dollar and ninety-eight cents," she said. "I have no intention of removing my money belt in the presence of gentlemen."

The clerk gave up and started to copy the records.

"What it boils down to," Teddy said when they had departed in triumph with their notarized copies, "is that he's sold this Bender fellow a piece of Madrona land and bought this swamp to sell to luckless souls who're foolish enough to buy a pig in a poke. But the deal hasn't closed yet, so we have a chance to upset his applecart if we can prove fraud and malice. Dosing a highly respected elderly woman with laudanum ought to take care of that. And now we have a logical motive for him to have done so."

"How do we prove Mrs. Blake wasn't in on it? Make it clear to public opinion, I mean?"

"My dear boy, I can tell that your checkered career has never included a stint at treading the boards."

"Have you been in the theater?" Paul asked, astounded.

"No," Teddy admitted wistfully. "But I've always wanted to be an actress. Here, I'm famished. Let's stop and have dinner, and I'll tell you what's to be done." She steered him toward the opulent doors of the Esmond Hotel.

"I thought you didn't have any money."

"Just wait." Teddy pushed Paul through the hotel doors and left him in the green plush lobby while she vanished into the ladies' coatroom. She returned in a few minutes, stowing a handful of gold coins into her pocketbook.

Paul looked impressed. "It must have been a profitable expedition."

"It was," Teddy responded. "The fellow who did this"—she lifted her brown tweed skirts and wriggled her ankle—"I sold him to a native chief who liked his blond curls. Come along." She took Paul's arm and led him to the dining room. "Dinner for two," she told the maître d'. "A quiet table, please."

Paul was laughing so hard he could barely sit down. "If I were older," he informed her, "I'd marry you."

"You'd hate it," Teddy said. "But you can come along on my next trip. Now then. I don't suppose you want fish."

"I do not," Paul said firmly.

"Steak," Teddy told the waiter. "And a bottle of Bordeaux."

When the bottle was presented, Paul went through the ritual of tasting the wine and giving it his approval. He would have approved anything short of vinegar as long as it wasn't beer, but he didn't think the waiter was up to being told to let the lady taste it. He didn't think Teddy was much of a wine connoisseur, either, apart from her preference for something hearty.

"Now see here," Teddy said. "It's all in the approach, all in the role you play. It's got me out of many a scrape, and it will get Eulalia Blake out of this one. She's originally a southerner anyway, isn't she? They have an admirable flair for drama. All she needs to do is let the entire city of Portland know—with suitable wailing and indignation—what that scoundrel has done to her. Just a touch of embarrassment at being so taken in by a good-looking blackguard wouldn't hurt. Put that news on the ladies' grapevine, and Eulalia will have instant sympathy. The women will be so morally outraged, no man in Portland will dare think that Mrs. Blake had a hand in it, much less would he say so, for fear of his mother and his sister and his wife."

"Wouldn't it be better just to try to keep it quiet? I don't know what Mrs. Blake will think about this scenario."

"Keeping things quiet makes one seem so guilty," Teddy remarked. "And nothing ever stays buried anyway. It pops to the surface later with the inevitability of a frost heave, and then everyone wonders why you kept it so secret. No, the best thing is to make as big a noise as possible right now and fix the proper guilty party firmly in the mind of public opinion. Public opinion always latches on to the first villain it's given and is rarely interested in changing its mind. Frankly, I think that's what Schumann is counting on. I think he wants to discredit Mrs. Blake, although I can't imagine why."

"He must have a reason," Paul mused. "Otherwise he would have just cleaned out her bank account and run."

"Of course he has a reason. People aren't wicked for the fun of it—it's too much trouble. But right now we need to plan how to hoist him with his own petard."

"And how to convince Mrs. Blake to go along with your methods," Paul said. "I doubt she's going to care for looking so foolish."

"She's *been* foolish," Teddy retorted. "She'll have to live with it. Now eat your steak while I tell you how we are going to arrange everything."

Obediently, Paul picked up his knife and fork. He felt as if he had been blown down by a high wind. Teddy was as managing as his mother. Why didn't he resent that? he wondered.

The Englishwoman seemed to divine his thoughts. "I've always wanted children," she explained. "It's just that I never found a chap I thought I could stand to marry.

You're a blessing to me, young man. I know you've been on the road for quite a while, and I imagine it has taught you a great deal. I wouldn't be surprised if you knew far more than I in a number of ways. That's why you won't mind letting me run the show this time? . . ."

Paul smiled and cut into his steak. There was his answer. "Go ahead, Captain," he said with a chuckle. "I'm at your command."

They needed two days to lay their plans. Teddy and Paul spoke earnestly with a judge and a district attorney, then Teddy paid a visit to Ephraim Bender, which would have earned her the leading role in any drama. Her plain round countenance took on an expression of guileless trust—a rabbity English spinster with no sense, who oughtn't to be out without a keeper.

She claimed to be interested in investing in American land and spoke casually of her brother the earl. She seemed a little scatterbrained and dropped her pocketbook several times. She said she could always tell when a man had an honest face, but she acted exactly like a woman who couldn't—the perfect mark. Bender bit.

She was staying at the Madrona, she said airily. So kind of them to put her up when Senator Holt was away and Mrs. Blake was still so ill. Mr. Bender would have to come there to clinch the deal.

Mr. Bender, learning that the coast was clear, agreed with alacrity. Tuesday at four? That would be delightful.

Teddy settled in at the Madrona. Dan did not try to discourage her presence; he probably saw no reason to, and he was preoccupied with the fact that White Elk's wife had taken up residence in Mrs. Blake's room. Mai was reading aloud to her, which Eulalia seemed to enjoy, and fixing the woman's meals herself. Mai saw to it that Amy or Abby Givens was in Mrs. Blake's room every second that Mai was not, foiling Dan's attempts to be alone with his hostess.

To Dan's chagrin, Eulalia was growing ever more alert, and Dr. Bright had been to see her twice. She was, however, suffering very restless nights and showing symptoms that Mai, who would have seen them before among the hapless opium addicts of Chinatown, might very well recognize as opium withdrawal. Dan was becoming nervous.

On Sunday a telegram from Toby Holt arrived, announcing that the senator was returning to Portland for the holiday season, to kiss babies and court the state legislature. Before it reached Dan's hands, the missive was intercepted by Mai, who gave it to White Elk. They read it, looked at each other with mutual decision, and destroyed it in the stove. Thereafter, they watched Dan Schumann with the secretive stares of cats until the interloper grew edgier still.

Toby, with Sally and Alexandra, arrived on Tuesday, expected by no one but White Elk, Mai, and Teddy Montague. Dan, caught off guard, flew into a momentary panic, then managed somehow to keep up a pleased expression while everyone exchanged greetings, wondered where the telegram had gone astray, and made exasperated remarks about Western Union.

As soon as he could, Dan slipped upstairs to his bedroom, put a pistol in his pocket, and packed a suitcase. Then he sat down to work out a plan that would, he thought with satisfaction, blow up in Toby Holt's face. He started with a letter to the Oregon legislature, outlining the fraudulent business dealings conducted by the senator's mother with the senator's obvious connivance. When that trap had been laid, Dan thought, he would get his cash out of Bender and be gone. The letter would make its way to where it would do the most harm before the senator knew it had been mailed. And then, Dan thought viciously, just let his old man try to tell him again what a saint Toby Holt was.

Toby, Alexandra, and Sally had all come up to see Eulalia, and Dan could hear their voices down the hallway. No doubt the old lady was telling them what a comfort he had been to her. She would change her tune soon enough, the silly old bitch. Dan was just sorry he wouldn't be around to see it. The hours he had wasted, fetching and carrying for her and listening to her drivel about the past.

The stubborn old besom had held out on him far longer than she ought to have done. Maybe she would have a heart attack and die when she got the news, he thought. It would serve her right.

Eulalia looked so ill to Toby that he felt frightened for her, but she assured him that she was, at last, getting better. "For some reason I haven't been able to keep food down lately, but I'm not nearly so tired today as I have been. Dr. Bright says I'll be all right now. He won't tell me why he thinks I've been so sick. I believe he just doesn't know and is too stiff-necked to admit it."

"I wouldn't admit it to you, either, if I didn't know," Alexandra said, smiling. "You're a terror, darling. But we're so glad you're better."

Sally was cuddled on the bed beside Eulalia, and Eulalia put an arm around her granddaughter. "So good to have you home. I don't want to talk about me anymore. I want to know about Mike. Where is he? I thought he would be with you."

"Mike's in New Jersey," Sally answered. "He won't come home. *I* think it's romantic," she added.

"Oh, no!" Eulalia said. "Toby—"

"We're at an impasse," Toby admitted.

"That boy won't even listen to reason," Alexandra said unhappily.

"He listened," Toby corrected. "He just didn't agree. I can't force him to go to college. He has Tim in his corner, too. Tim went so far as to write me a long letter about it."

"Toby intends to drag Tim up here for Christmas," Alexandra said. "The letter was devoid of any news about his own goings-on. If something's wrong we'll pry it out of him then."

"What does Janessa say?" Eulalia asked. Janessa was the family letter writer. Seldom in one place for any length of time, she kept abreast of everyone's doings by mail and generally had an opinion about them.

"About Tim or Mike?" Toby asked. "She says what Tim said—that Mike has to take his own risks now; we can't take them or deny them for him. And she thinks Tim's up to something, too. Or up against something."

"Janessa has always had excellent sense," Eulalia commented. She looked at Toby with a certain amount of wry sympathy. "Although I don't imagine you're finding it pleasant to be advised by your children."

"I'm finding it extremely disagreeable," Toby confessed.

"Yes, I always did, too." Eulalia smiled at him with so much of her old spirit that Toby's irritation washed away in a tide of relief. He had lost his father and stepfather. Now, in middle age, he found himself clinging more tightly to his mother, aware of her fragility. He couldn't bear to lose her, too, not now. He wasn't ready. Were you ever? he wondered.

A rattle of carriage wheels in the gravel outside distracted him. Alexandra went to the window. "Goodness," she said. "It's Ephraim Bender! What on earth do you suppose *he* wants?"

XX

Teddy Montague was lying in wait in the foyer, as much to keep Dan from going out as to usher Bender in before he found out that Toby was home. She felt like a spider.

"Do come in." She showed Bender solicitously to a parlor chair and listened with satisfaction to the tread of feet, feminine as well as masculine, coming down the stairs. "So nice. Senator and Mrs. Holt just returned to Portland."

Bender blanched, but it was too late for him to excuse himself. Furthermore, two riders were coming up the carriage drive.

Bless the boy, Teddy thought. *He can be on time when he has to.* She leaned out the parlor doorway and seized Alexandra by the wrist as she came down the stairs, then hissed in her ear, "Whatever you do, don't let Bender leave."

Alexandra looked at Teddy, nonplussed. "I wish he *would* leave," she whispered as Teddy pulled her toward the parlor. "I can't abide him. How do you do, Ephraim? What a nice surprise," she added, holding out her hand as Teddy gave her a little shove toward the visitor.

Bender looked to Teddy as if he was not doing well at all. He had made his way to the parlor doorway but no farther. He was not reassured by the knock on the door that produced Paul Kirchner and Elliott Loman, the district attorney for Portland. But there was no escape. As instructed, Alexandra had him firmly cornered and was asking him for a donation for Christmas baskets for the needy.

"You can afford to be charitable, Ephraim, I'm certain of it. I'll put you down for one hundred dollars."

Bender started to protest and then to his horror saw Dan Schumann at the top of the stairs. Toby Holt had come down behind Alexandra, and Dan was stranded at the landing.

Paul Kirchner and Teddy Montague headed for Toby and explained the situation in urgent undertones. The senator's eyes began to glow with an unwholesome fury. The district attorney stood beside them.

Glancing at the door, Bender dug into his pocket. "I'll write you a check," he agreed desperately.

"That will be very generous of you," Alexandra said sweetly. "So charming of you to drop in." She moved forward a little so that Bender couldn't get out the front door without stepping over her. "Tell me, how is your sister? I do hope her sciatica is better. And your aunt in Philadelphia? Why don't we go back inside and sit down?"

Teddy cast a quick look at Bender, squirming in his starched collar, and decided he would keep. Alexandra looked prepared to inquire after all his relatives down to his fourth cousins.

"That's about the gist of it," Teddy said briskly to Toby. "Mr. Loman's prepared to press any charges you see fit. It's very fortunate, your coming home. We were afraid your mother might not quite be up to the denouement, but I feel sure she'll rally now that you're here."

Toby's blue eyes snapped like an electric arc. He spun and bolted up the stairs three at a time to the landing. He grabbed Dan Schumann by the throat. "You son of a bitch! You gave my mother laudanum! Do you know what I'm going to do to you?"

Dan, struggling furiously, looked as if he might have a very good idea. Bender paled and tried to edge past Alexandra.

Elliott Loman moved toward the parlor and laid a firm hand on Bender's shoulder. "Stick around a few minutes, Ephraim. It's just getting interesting."

Toby dragged Dan downstairs to the foyer and had his hands around the young man's throat.

"Toby! What are you doing?" Alexandra cried.

As Toby turned toward his wife, Dan lashed out, and they toppled off balance to the floor. They thrashed on the carpet and sent a small drop-leaf table flying. A crystal vase filled with holly shattered on the floor. Elliott Loman looked on calmly as the men flailed at each other on the polished floor. The shards of the crystal vase sliced into their clothes and left streaks of blood on the wood. Dan heaved himself forward, laying his knee open with the glass.

"*Toby!*"

They all looked up again as Eulalia came slowly down the stairs, a cane in her hand, and leaning heavily on Sally's arm.

"Don't come down, Mother!" Toby shouted.

"Of course I'll come down." Eulalia proceeded.

"Look out, Mother! Someone get her out of here." Toby was breathing hard, and his fingers tightened on Dan's neck. Dan lashed out with a booted foot at Toby's shins, and Toby lifted Dan's head and smacked it down against the hardwood floor. Now Elliott Loman appeared to be trying to decide whether Toby was really going to kill the fellow and thus force Loman to interfere, or whether he was just going to pound the young fellow senseless, which a senator could do with a district attorney's blessing.

"Tobias Holt, you listen to me!" Eulalia smacked her cane on the floor. She had fire in her eyes, and she looked like one of the Furies. "I will deal with this man, Toby, do you hear me? This is my affair. *I* have been made to look the fool, not you."

"You don't know what he's done," Toby growled, climbing to his feet and lifting Dan with him.

"I know I gave him a power of attorney," Eulalia said. "However he's abused it is for me to correct." She raised her eyebrows at the group across the parlor. "Mr. Loman, how fortuitous to find you here."

With a howl of desperation, Dan redoubled his effort to get free. Toby found it difficult to argue with his mother and hold Dan simultaneously. Toby had pure rage on this side, but Dan was younger. Dan pried one of Toby's hands off his neck and sank his teeth into it. Toby drew it back with a yelp, ready to slug Dan, but Dan twisted away.

Eulalia stepped forward, too angry to think, and Dan pushed her away from him. Fear made his face look like a stranger's to her. The urbane charm, the gently flirtatious smile, the air of command and certainty, all were gone, and the face that was laid bare without them was not pleasant to behold.

She fell backward against her son, and Toby caught her with both arms. As Dan lurched toward the door, Eulalia tried to straighten herself in her son's grasp. "You let me deal with him."

"Don't be ridiculous."

"Eulalia dear—" Alexandra, Teddy, and Sally clustered around her, enclosing her, encasing her fury. Dan looked capable of anything.

Ephraim Bender moved slowly toward the door, but again Elliott Loman put a hand on the developer's shoulder and stopped him. Dan was scrabbling at the front door, which Teddy had thought to lock behind Paul and Loman. Toby lunged toward him. Before he could reach Dan, Paul Kirchner had his nemesis by the shoulders and had drawn back his fist with purpose.

"Relax and take a deep breath, Senator," Teddy invited. "That boy's got a debt to pay. Give Paul his chance."

"If you're all going to take turns beating Dan Schumann up," Elliott murmured, "I'll really have to put a stop to it."

Ephraim Bender looked nearly green, as if he thought they might start on him next. The Holts were notorious for their tempers.

With a bang Dan crashed against the front door. It slammed open, tearing the lock and hinges out of the wood, and Paul and Dan lurched out onto the porch. Something caught the sunlight, a quick flash like fire.

"Daddy! A gun!" Sally screamed.

Toby pulled his own pistol from his pocket, but it was impossible to aim at the two thrashing men. Paul had Dan's wrist in his hands, the gun pointing upward. There was an explosion as it discharged. Dan struggled to bring his arm down, to level the barrel at Paul. Paul forced the hand away and then leaped sideways as Dan kneed him in the chest. Slowly the gun came down again with deadly point-blank aim. Paul flung himself away from Dan, down the steps, and rolled, rising as he did so. Dan followed, the gun trained on Paul. Toby shouted, "Drop it!"

Dan made no move to do so. There was another crack of gunfire, and the pistol spun from Dan's hand. Paul raised his eyes to see Toby Holt standing on the porch, his gun still smoking.

Paul looked as if something had snapped in him. He launched himself at Dan Schumann in blind, unreasoning fury. He ran at his nemesis, and Dan sidestepped contemptuously.

He smirked. "Kirchner, you're no threat. I've been intimidating you for a year."

Paul smiled darkly. "But when I get mad enough, Schumann, a tether gives way in my brain. That's why I don't like to fight—I lose control and could kill somebody. I'm mad now, Schumann. Come on, you bastard. Show me what you've got."

Dan gathered himself for one good swing, then reeled under Paul's weight as Paul unaccountably swerved and tackled him like a football player. Dan fell on his back in the grass. The breath gusted from his mouth, and his chest tightened in pain. Paul sat on his enemy's chest, and his fist smashed down into Dan's face. Dan heaved under him, but Paul didn't budge. He hit Dan again.

Dan lashed out with his own fists, managed to knock Paul loose, then wriggled out of Paul's grasp and staggered toward the driveway, but Paul came after him.

A fallen madrona-tree branch lay across the gravel. The end was sharp and jagged. Dan bent and hefted it, then whirled, lashing out at Paul. It grazed Paul's face, leaving a line of blood down his cheek.

Dan's hands, cut on the broken vase in the parlor, were slippery with his own blood. He gripped the branch again with both hands and swung it. Paul dodged and came at him under the arc of the branch. His fists battered Dan's face and chest, and when Dan swung the branch again, Paul seized it and twisted it from his grasp.

Paul's breath was coming in heaving gasps now, and the light in his eyes was as brilliant as an explosion. He could see that Dan was beginning to be afraid of him. That knowledge gave him strength to hit Dan again and again, driving him back against one of the madrona trees. Dan held his hands out in front of him, a reflex gesture of protection. But he couldn't get away—Paul had him pinned against the tree, and Paul's fist slammed into his belly.

Dan bent double, vomiting, and a voice from somewhere said, "Take it easy, son. You'll kill him."

Someone drew Paul away, and Toby turned Dan's arms behind his back, none too gently, and tied them with a cravat.

"He tried to kill me!" Dan gasped. "I can explain, Senator. It was Kirchner who—"

"If you don't shut your mouth," Toby warned evenly, "I'll put your own boots in it. I had the story from Teddy and my mother, and you can consider yourself lucky I didn't let Kirchner have you—or kill you myself."

Paul bent, his hands on his knees, and breathed deeply until the fog cleared from his head and the murderous rage died down.

"Steady," Teddy Montague advised, putting a supporting hand under his elbow. "Where the devil did you learn to fight like that?"

"Natural talent," Paul said with a crooked grin.

Nearly everyone on the Madrona was in the driveway now. White Elk had appeared and was deep in consultation with Toby. Eulalia had tottered down the steps in her dressing gown, and Mai had brought a white wool shawl to put over her shoulders. Sally was excitedly telling Amy and Abby Givens and Howie Janks and Coot Simmons and the other workers what had happened. She glanced periodically and with considerable interest at Paul Kirchner.

Ephraim Bender stood morosely beside Elliott Loman. There wasn't anything Bender could do now but let it all come out.

Toby was briskly searching Schumann's pockets, in case Dan had another pistol. He found the letter addressed to the Oregon legislature and drew it out of the envelope with interest. "Busy, aren't you?" he inquired of Schumann.

"You have no business reading my private correspondence," Dan protested.

Toby put on his spectacles and began to read. After a

few lines he looked as if he might very well try to throttle
Schumann again. He handed the letter to Loman. "Is this
libel?"

"Could be," Loman said after a minute. "Probably is.
Ephraim here could probably sue him, too." A faint grin
creased the district attorney's lips. "Of course, Ephraim's
got to prove it's not true."

"Let me see that!" Bender snatched at the letter.
Loman let him look over his shoulder but wouldn't turn
loose of it. "Why, you little—" Bender glared at Dan. "You
weaseling turncoat!"

Eulalia came over and laid a hand on Paul's shoulder.
Her lips tightened for a moment. "This is not an easy
speech for me to make," she said finally. "I am a very
stubborn old woman and given to snap judgments based on
characteristics that it appears I do not understand. I hope
you can forgive me."

Paul looked angry and defensive for a moment. He
glanced over at Teddy, who smiled with gentle encourage-
ment toward forgiveness. Mrs. Blake's apology wasn't lip
service; she was wrestling with the discovery that she was
capable of being just as wrong and silly as anyone else. That
must be a very painful epiphany to experience in one's
seventies.

"Everyone makes snap judgments," Paul said finally.
"We go by the familiar signs. If we stopped and questioned
everything, we wouldn't have time to get by."

Eulalia snorted. "Fine words from a young man who
appears to question everything. If you hadn't questioned
Dan Schumann, I might very well be dead. I won't permit
you to let me off so easily."

Paul bent his head to hers. "I'll tell you a secret. I was
suspicious of Dan Schumann because I took an instanta-
neous dislike to him, based largely on the fact that his hair
was too well combed. I am as capable of illogic as the next
fellow. So I won't permit you to give me credit so easily,
either."

"Come in the house, Paul," Eulalia invited. "We can
argue later. In the meantime, I am going to put iodine on
that cut. You, too, Toby," she added imperiously. "Just look
at the state of your hands."

Alexandra made a motion to go with them to help, but Teddy pulled her back. "Let Eulalia take charge," Teddy murmured. "She's embarrassed. Give her something to do."

Elliot Loman looked at Bender. "You might as well go on home before Holt gets back out here. Whether he decides to prosecute you for fraud is his decision, but if I were you I'd cancel the sale on that Madrona land you bought from Schumann. And don't squawk about it. You might be safer."

"Where's my money then?" Bender demanded. "I'll have to get my money back."

"I'm sure you can," Loman soothed, "if you can get it out of Schumann. Of course he'll have to repay Mrs. Blake first. If there's any left, I expect the court will let you have a stab at it."

"This is outrageous! I'll sue."

Loman chuckled. "You better hope the Holts don't sue you for fraud and conspiracy to defraud."

"It was his idea!" Dan Schumann said suddenly. "He talked me into it. It was all Bender's idea."

"Why you little—" Bender returned his attention to Dan.

"You can sue Schumann," Loman suggested genially. "Once he gets out of jail."

Upstairs in Toby and Alexandra's bedroom, Alexandra voiced her concerns to Toby. "Dan is your dear friend's son," she said, biting her lip. "Toby, what are we to do?"

Toby flexed his fingers, grimacing at the sticking plaster his mother had stuck across his palms. She was applying the same treatment to Paul's face in the next room. "I don't know," he said unhappily. "Dan deserves everything he gets, but Dieter— How do I press charges against Dieter and Abigail's son and keep the friendship? Punishing Dan won't do *me* any good."

"But it might do Dan some good," Alexandra observed.

Toby sighed. "I'll sleep on it," he decided. "I'll wire Dieter tomorrow. I have to tell him before I do anything."

Dieter Schumann, whose red-hot temper had not become civilized along with his business practices, balled up Toby's telegram, threw it across the room, and hurled an onyx paperweight after it. He put his head in his hands. What was Abigail going to say? It would break her heart. Toby had offered not to press charges. Dieter knew Abigail would accept the offer and make restitution—anything to keep Dan from prison.

Dieter closed his eyes. When his wife found out what he was about to do, he hoped she would forgive him. He opened his eyes and picked up the telephone on his desk.

"Get me Western Union."

The telegram that was tapped across the wires back to Portland was short and allowed no leeway in its instructions.

LET DAN STAND TRIAL STOP I SEE NO HOPE FOR HIM OTHERWISE STOP DIETER

It was a depressing Christmas season. Toby brooded about the house, worrying about Dieter. He had hired Dan Schumann a good lawyer, as the only gesture he could make to Dieter, and was now morosely courting the state legislature with an eye to the spring elections. He was about as cheerful as an undertaker.

Finally Alexandra and Eulalia decided that something had to be done. Now that Eulalia was relieved of the fear that she was growing senile, she had rallied with amazing strength and showed signs of deciding to straighten out everyone else's life, too.

"This can't go on," Eulalia decided. "Toby can't take Dan's shortcomings on his own shoulders just because Dieter is his close friend."

"What are we to do?" Alexandra would have been happy to have had Eulalia straighten out Toby, if possible.

"I've done it," Eulalia said. "I've telegraphed Tim and Janessa and that devil Mike and told them all that they're to come home for Christmas with no excuses."

"You didn't!" Alexandra eyed her mother-in-law with considerable respect. "What did they say?"

Eulalia smiled and set a few more stitches into the eyeglass case she was embroidering for Toby. "Mike said he'd have to be wired the train fare because Mr. Edison doesn't pay very much. Janessa sent a wire saying she couldn't possibly get away from the Hospital Service, but Charley sent another afterward that just said 'Yes, ma'am.' Tim said of course, but he wants us all to meet in San Francisco first and watch young Peter's motorcar race someone else's."

"Good heavens," Alexandra said faintly. "Are we going to do it?" She felt quite certain they would if Eulalia wanted them to.

"Certainly," Eulalia replied. "I've told Tim so. He said to bring anyone else we could think of, so I've included Teddy and Paul. I believe that Tim wants Peter to have as large a cheering section as possible. Of course I thought I'd leave it to you to tell Toby the plans."

Alexandra got up and kissed Eulalia's forehead. "You cowardly darling. Very well, I'll go and tackle him. You can provide reinforcements if he balks."

When Alexandra found Toby in his study, he looked not so much balky as vaguely preoccupied. His spectacles were on the end of his nose, and he was peering over them at the stuffed head of an elk that hung above his desk, as if it might have something crucial to tell him.

"Toby."

"Hmmm?" He patted the elk's nose absently and prowled across to the other side of the room to stare into a bull's-eye mirror that hung over the mantel. His reflection stared back at him, pear-shaped and distorted. The elk loomed behind him in the glass.

"Toby, what on earth are you doing?"

"Just looking at things," Toby answered. "Looking at the way they change, depending on your point of view. Dan Schumann *looked* all right," he tried to explain.

"Are you still brooding over pressing charges?" Alexandra's eyes sparked. "He gave your mother laudanum and tried to cheat all of us. He deserves anything he gets. And so does Ephraim Bender, who is going to get off scot-free because he's 'only' unethical instead of legally guilty."

"Ephraim Bender's father isn't one of my best friends," Toby said wearily. "Alex, I tried to strangle Dan with my bare hands. Now that I've calmed down, all I can think is that if I could have seen Dan for what he truly was, I might have been able to help him—or at least to stop him from doing something that would hurt Dieter and Abigail so terribly."

"You are not responsible for the behavior of everyone else in the world," Alexandra said flatly. "Or even for the happiness of your friends. Now then, I've been talking to your mother, and I have some wonderful news. Mike's coming home for Christmas!"

Her green eyes glowed with so much relief that Toby stopped his pacing and put his arms around her. "I'm sorry I've been preoccupied," he said. "It's just that—"

"I know. You want to fix the whole world for everybody, and it breaks your heart when you can't." She stroked his hair.

He kissed her and stood back, feeling a little foolish. He must be behaving like a child to bring out this much maternal instinct in his wife. "Tell me about Christmas," he said. "I haven't even started to shop."

"You never do till the last minute." Alex was unperturbed by that. "It makes your presents interesting, since they are bought on the whim of the moment and are always beautiful and impractical. That's exactly the sort I like. Anyway, you'll have plenty of chances to shop," she informed him. "We're going to San Francisco."

"Where are they?"

"Are they coming?"

"Don't tell me they've broken down before they even got to the starting line."

The Holts waited impatiently in Golden Gate Park for the first sign of their wayward cousin's new automobile. There was quite a crowd of them, and they were noisy and in constant motion, as this clan usually was when it was all together.

Janessa Lawrence was discussing tropical diseases with Teddy Montague while they waited. She listened to Teddy's description of a particularly loathsome set of symptoms with the enthralled expression of a collector, while her husband, Charley, helped Eulalia settle herself in a folding chair near the starting line.

"I'm glad you were able to bring Janessa," Eulalia told him.

"I detached her from the hospital in the manner of prying a barnacle off a rock," Charley confessed cheerfully. "But now she's glad she's come. She wants to talk to Tim. I—She's convinced he's harboring some dark secret that she ought to know about."

Janessa overheard him and sidled closer. "I certainly do. Just look at him."

They all swung their heads around to stare at Tim. He looked very dapper and citified in a frock coat and a tall silk hat. Having been dissuaded from riding Trout on the outing, he was reasonably unrumpled. But his face looked "as if he had slept in it," as Janessa remarked. There were lines around his eyes that hadn't been there before, and his eyes seemed to be set a little deeper under his brows. His mouth, even when he smiled, looked hungry somehow, as if there were some lack that was always with him these days.

"You're right. He doesn't look well," Eulalia said. "Is he sick with something, do you think?"

"Not with anything physical," Janessa said.

"It's mental," Charley suggested. "An overdose of busybodies."

Janessa made a face at him. "He's my brother. I'm concerned about him."

"Nesting instinct," Charley said solemnly. "She's practicing."

Eulalia's eyebrows rose with interest. "Does that mean what I think it does?"

"It means you're going to be a great-grandmother, darling," Janessa said.

Eulalia's eyes gleamed happily as she squeezed Janessa's hand. "And your father is going to be a grandfather. Break it to him gently. He's been feeling his age lately. I'm sure it will send him right over the brink."

"We already told him," Charley said. "He managed to rally."

"I'm going to be an aunt," Sally was informing Paul Kirchner. She had been highly impressed by his performance in thrashing Dan Schumann and had attached herself to him. Of course it would have been more exciting if they had been fighting over *her* instead of some boring old money, but she was only eleven and not old enough for that yet. Being an aunt seemed reasonably important, however. "Janessa says I may hold the baby when it's baptized. I hope it's a girl. So does Janessa."

"I hope so, too, then," Paul said. "You Holt women strike me as being extremely strong-minded. If Janessa wants a girl, she could probably produce one by sheer willpower."

Tim watched his little sister practicing on Paul Kirchner. Sally was going to be a heartbreaker in just a few more years, he thought. Janessa had never been willing to acquire any feminine airs and graces, but Sally had them by instinct.

"Look at the little devil," Tim said to Mike as they watched Paul lift her into the fork of an oak tree, where she could see better, and stand beside her to steady her there.

"She's going to be a corker," Mike agreed. "Knows it, too."

"You don't look so bad yourself," Tim remarked. "Rebellion seems to suit you. How's Mama holding up?"

"She's all right," Mike replied.

A little guiltily, Tim thought. Alexandra was holding up because she didn't have any other choice. Her worried eyes followed Mike everywhere. "Have you heard from Eden?" Tim asked in a low voice.

"Once a week, bless her," Mike said. "Sometimes she just says everything is boring, and she has nothing to say, but she writes anyway."

"Watch your step," Tim muttered. "If that child runs away and joins you, Sam Brentwood will shoot you dead."

"You let me worry about Sam Brentwood," Mike said equably.

"You haven't got bat brains. You're too young to get married."

"Just because you aren't married," Mike teased. "If you'd quit helling around with reporters and act like the boss, you might meet somebody eligible."

Tim winced, and Mike looked at him curiously. What was the matter with Tim? *Who* was the matter with Tim?

"I've met enough debutantes," Tim muttered, "to make me want to hell around with reporters as an antidote."

"What do you hear of your friend Debs?" Mike asked, deciding that a change of subject might be in order.

"They convicted him," Tim answered sourly. "The judge dismissed the jury and just convicted him out of hand. It was a blatant miscarriage of justice. He got six months. Not in Cook County, thank God."

"Here they come!"

Tim and Mike swung around as a shout went up. The noise of gasoline engines sputtered and clattered across the green lawns of the park, and in a moment they could see the motorcars, one behind the other, chuffing down the carriageway.

Alfred Wellington's vehicle contained Alfred, his mechanic, and Alfred's mother, who looked like an osprey perched on a rock. She appeared to be exceedingly uncomfortable and held her hat down with one hand. The Wellington was a sleek black machine, with a front-mounted engine, one seat for the driver, and one bench seat for passengers. It was nearly as ornate as the swan boat of Peter's imagining, with brass clasps and hasps everywhere, the word *Wellington* spelled out in ornate script across the front grill, and silver flower vases on either side of the rear seat. An enormous sunburst adorned the radiator cap.

The Blake, behind it, was more sedate. The little silver Diana still leaped joyously from the central headlamp, but the rest of the car was almost austere. The engine was rear mounted, as Rufus Gooch had decreed, and the gears in the clutch were leather lined so that it shifted from speed to speed with a minimum of racket. Calvin Rogers was driving, with Peter and Rufus in the back. Tolliver and Ellison and the mechanics followed in the wagon in which the Blake had been transported to the park. To drive it through the sacred precincts of San Francisco's business district, scaring every cab horse for miles, would have caused a riot. In a buggy were Waldo Howard, Rafe Murray, and Rosebay and Hugo Ware.

The motorcars drew abreast of each other at the starting line, and Mrs. Wellington gratefully stepped down. Alfred stepped down, too, reluctantly, leaving the mechanic to drive. Alfred had not admitted to having had a hand in the sabotage attempt that Tim had foiled.

"You watch him," Peter warned Calvin, who was driving the Blake. "He looks like a farmboy, but he's got the instincts of a rattlesnake."

"He won't be driving," Calvin said. "*You* watch him. I got enough to watch."

"Are the gears going to gum up again?" Peter demanded.

"Certainly not," Gooch said. "I have the entire problem solved. You will win handily." He laughed confidently. "You could win in reverse. The Wellington machine is a toy."

"Pretty fast toy," Calvin murmured. He pulled down his goggles and set his cap on his head. He wore a linen duster over his suit and looked more like the mad baron von Frankenstein than a mechanical engineer. He climbed into the Blake, which was chugging on the starting line, and had a last-minute conference with Gooch.

"Are you ready, gentlemen?" Waldo was the official starter. He raised his pistol skyward. Rafe and Hugo and a reporter from the rival *Chronicle* had been inspecting the underpinnings of both machines. At Waldo's question the men scooted backward. Rosebay clung to Peter's hand excitedly as Calvin and the Wellington's driver lifted their hands in signal to Waldo.

There was a bang from the starting pistol, and both machines lurched forward, jerkily at first, and then more smoothly as they made their way up through the gears. The Wellington also had three forward speeds, although no reverse gear.

"Tsk, that's a mistake," Peter said, mostly to annoy Alfred. "Slapdash engineering."

"Most people don't want to go backward," Alfred defended, shading his eyes to watch the motorcars, in a common cloud of dust, round the first bend in the oval carriage drive that was their designated racetrack. "Perhaps you haven't grasped the purpose of the machine."

"And how are you planning to turn it around?" Peter inquired sarcastically. "Pick it up?" He wanted to sound calm, assured of himself, not panic-stricken with the notion that the blasted machine was going to blow up at mid-course, showering the spectators with minute shards of metal and all of Peter's future financial prospects. He had invested money he didn't even have yet. The San Francisco banks had been most obliging.

"Get your checkbook ready," Alfred said gleefully. One dust cloud was beginning to pull ahead of the other, and he watched it smugly.

Dimly through the dust they could see the distinctive nose of the Blake edging ahead, and Alfred's expression darkened.

Rosebay's fingers gripped Peter's arm. "Oh, come *on*," she breathed. Then she gave a little hop. "Oh, Peter, look, it's not the other one! It's yours!"

A large crowd had gathered in the park to watch the well-publicized race. To the spectators the two cars looked like dust devils, indistinguishable in form and full of thunderous noise. A large sheepdog, panting at the end of a loosely held lead, found them sinister, something from which he should protect his young mistress at all costs. He lunged into the carriage drive, barking furiously, while the girl tried to call him back.

Inside the dust cloud, Calvin Rogers grinned as the Blake sailed along. It had run through the gears without the slightest hitch—old Rufus was right; the whole problem was solved. And it was traveling fast enough to be picking up a longer lead on the Wellington every minute. Eighteen miles per hour, and steady as a rock. Think of it, Calvin reflected, a whole new form of transportation that didn't need iron rails to run on and could go at undreamed-of speeds all day.

Calvin suddenly caught sight of a dog in the car's path. Cursing, he jammed his foot down on the brake pedal before he hit the stupid animal.

A girl in a velvet cloak ran up and snatched the sheepdog's lead.

"I'm so sorry," she said, panting through the dust.

"Come *along*, you bad thing." She dragged the dog back to the edge of the track.

The Blake hadn't quite stopped, but it had slowed too much to run in the highest gear. Calvin depressed the clutch before the engine could stall and tried to shift into low gear. There was a furious grinding noise and the sound of vital parts ejecting from the transmission.

"Damn you, Rufus, it won't shift *down*!" Calvin howled, more out of fury than anything else. Rufus wouldn't hear him over the distance and the roar of the engines. The sound of the Wellington was growing nearer behind him. The Blake had rolled to a stop by this time, while Calvin frantically tried to get it in gear. The finish line wasn't more than a hundred yards away. Low gear produced only a horrible sound, and it couldn't be started up in the higher gears. It wouldn't go into them anyway, Calvin discovered. He tried all the positions and finally the Blake slipped into gear. When Calvin let his foot off the clutch, the motorcar shot backward.

The Wellington was coming up on him fast. Calvin swung the tiller around and turned the Blake in the track. Then he gave it as much power as it would take and shot backward down the carriage drive, head turned in an owllike fashion over his shoulder. He could hear the Wellington coming up closer. Unfortunately the Blake couldn't go any faster in reverse than it could in low gear. The Wellington was level with the Blake's front wheels, then with Calvin's seat. But the finish line was just ahead.

Calvin jammed his foot down on the gasoline pedal as hard as he could, prayed he wouldn't blow up the engine, and shot across the line a foot ahead of the Wellington's nose. The little silver Diana, traveling backward, seemed to be waving at the crowd behind her as she passed.

A howl of furious outrage rose from Alfred Wellington. "It was going *backward*!"

"Nothing in the rules says it can't go sideways," Peter informed him. Out of pure delight he danced a little jig in the grass, then held out his palm. "Pay up, Alfred, and maybe I'll let you have a ride in her."

"You'll never sell any," Alfred snarled. "Not when the gears jam like that. *My* car ran trouble-free."

"Sure," Peter allowed. "It just didn't win. I'm sure that with the money I won from you, old boy, my mechanics can fix the transmission problem."

Calvin was backing the Blake in circles, to the admiration of the spectators. He scooted in reverse past Peter and doffed his cap in salute. Rosebay produced a circlet of artificial flowers from her purse and now tossed it around the silver Diana.

Someone popped a champagne cork, and Tim shouted, "To the Blake!" He handed each family member and friend a glass and touched his to Rosebay's. "Merry Christmas." He looked into his glass and then slowly poured the contents on the grass. "It's the thought that counts."

"Tim . . ."

"I'm going home for Christmas," he told her. "When I get back, I'm going to find a girl to court. I've got to."

"Yes," she agreed fervently. "I think you do."

Tim nodded. Someone opened another bottle, and the celebratory mood gathered the family and friends together. The next night was Christmas Eve, and Alexandra began to sing "God Rest Ye Merry Gentlemen," and the rest chimed in. It was cold, and they linked arms, and the old familiar feeling of belonging flowed through Tim.

> ". . . to save us all from Satan's power
> When we were gone astray,
> Oh, tidings of comfort and joy . . ."

Tim threw back his head and laughed. Comfort and joy were here, all around him, and he thought Satan would be sorry if he messed with the Holts.